LARRY DARTER

Come What May

A Malone Mystery Novel (Book 1)

Fedora
PRESS

First published by Fedora Press 2022

Copyright © 2022 by Larry Darter

All rights reserved. No part of this publication may be reproduced, stored or transmitted in any form or by any means, electronic, mechanical, photocopying, recording, scanning, or otherwise without written permission from the publisher. It is illegal to copy this book, post it to a website, or distribute it by any other means without permission.

This novel is entirely a work of fiction. The names, characters and incidents portrayed in it are the work of the author's imagination. Any resemblance to actual persons, living or dead, events or localities is entirely coincidental.

Larry Darter asserts the moral right to be identified as the author of this work.

Larry Darter has no responsibility for the persistence or accuracy of URLs for external or third-party Internet Websites referred to in this publication and does not guarantee that any content on such Websites is, or will remain, accurate or appropriate.

Designations used by companies to distinguish their products are often claimed as trademarks. All brand names and product names used in this book and on its cover are trade names, service marks, trademarks and registered trademarks of their respective owners. The publishers and the book are not associated with any product or vendor mentioned in this book. None of the companies referenced within the book have endorsed the book.

To receive notification of new books in this series when they become available, please visit the author's website to sign up for email notifications.

ver_1_e_2

Second edition

This book was professionally typeset on Reedsy.
Find out more at reedsy.com

For Suzanne, in acknowledgment of your faithful support and endless inspiration.

"Come what come may, time and the hour
run through the roughest day."

— WILLIAM SHAKESPEARE, MACBETH

Contents

1

Home Invasion

It was an unseasonably warm late-January morning, even by Los Angeles standards. Seated in the front passenger seat of the nondescript gray Ford sedan parked at the curb a block west of the exit from the Vista del Lago Townhomes, the watcher's flat cold eyes peered impatiently out from beneath the dark hoodie. Then, finally, the red 1992 BMW sedan rolled through the gates and turned west towards Sherman Way. The distance and glare from the early morning sun made it impossible to identify the driver of the brand-new BMW. No matter. The watcher knew who owned the car.

Twenty minutes after seven, almost an hour later than expected. The bitch was usually out of the house and on her way to work by six-thirty. The stalker glanced at the driver of the Ford, nodded without speaking, and then got out. After the passenger stepped onto the sidewalk and had closed the car door, the driver started the car, pulled away from the curb, and sped away.

The intruder pushed on the wrought-iron gate after hurrying to the pedestrian entrance. It yielded easily with the lock disabled the night before. After entering the grounds, the interloper walked quickly to the west side of the targeted townhouse to the garage side door. They had expected and planned on finding the door locked. A screwdriver penetrated the gap between the latch plate and striker plate, providing leverage to complement a forcible shoulder bump against the lock side of the closed door. The door popped open easily and almost soundlessly. Then the intruder entered the garage and then closed the door quietly. The focused beam from a small flashlight illuminated a black Audi 5000 parked inside and then swept to the door that opened from the garage into the townhouse. That door proved to be unlocked, saving the need for the screwdriver to make entry.

The trespasser placed an ear to the door and, after listening intently and hearing nothing beyond it, opened the door and stepped inside a utility room that opened onto the dining room and kitchen. To the left was the living room. Across from the front door, the stairway leading to the second floor was at the far end of the living room. After treading quietly up the stairs, the predator crept toward the open master bedroom door at the end of the hallway.

Mary Beth Anderson was lying on her right side on the king-size bed, facing the doorway. She had planned to sleep in, but it hadn't worked out. She was a habitual early riser, usually at work at her orthodontic practice this time of morning every weekday. But Mary Beth had a stomach bug and had stayed home for the day. Her husband had awakened her before leaving for work, and she couldn't go back asleep. Mary Beth had asked him to drive her car, so he could drop it off for the scheduled oil change appointment she had booked the previous week. She debated getting up and calling her dental assistant to have her call and cancel the day's appointments before the first patient arrived. She had asked her husband to do it, but sometimes he forgot such things. Just as she decided and swung her legs off the bed to get up, a figure wearing a black hoodie over dark pants appeared in the open bedroom doorway.

Recognition was instantaneous for both. It would have been

difficult to say which was more surprised to see the other under the circumstances. The predator hastily revised the original plan, pulled a snub nose Model 36 Smith & Wesson revolver, and fired two hastily aimed shots at Mary Beth.

The hypothalamus portion of Mary Beth's brain immediately kicked into overdrive, activating the sympathetic nervous system and the adrenal-cortical system, producing the classic fight-or-flight response. Instinctively knowing there was nowhere to run when she saw the gun, Mary Beth was already in motion, springing off the bed and charging at the intruder.

Both bullets missed their intended target. Instead, they struck the bedroom window beyond the bed, blowing out the glass, which then fell and crashed in jagged shards to the driveway below.

Mary Beth reached the doorway before the gun discharged a third time. She slapped the gun aside, simultaneously aiming a shoulder at the predator's chest with her momentum propelling her forward. Surprised by the suddenness and ferocity of Mary Beth's counter-attack, the attacker fell backward against the wall, and the revolver thudded to the floor. Having never been in a fight in her life and seeing the gun on the floor, Mary Beth immediately pivoted from fight to flight and raced down the hallway toward the stairs. The predator paused only long enough to scoop up the dropped pistol and then gave chase.

Mary Beth stumbled down the stairs and headed straight for the front door. She frantically turned the lock and tried to release the deadbolt. She almost made it.

Arriving at the bottom of the stairs only steps behind her, the predator spied a silver vase on a wooden stand positioned beside the landing, grabbed it up on the way to the door, and slammed the heavy metal vase against the back of Mary Beth's head. The blow stunned the woman, but she didn't go down. Instead, she turned to face her assailant and lifted her hands to ward off further blows. But the vase was already coming down again. It collided with the left side of her face, causing a laceration above the eye. Faint now and dizzy, Mary Beth did the only thing that came to mind. She wrapped both arms around her attacker's neck, twisted, and used her weight to pull them both to the floor of the tiled entryway. Again, the assailant lost hold of the gun, and the vase skittered away across the tile.

Fueled by pure terror and adrenaline, Mary Beth maintained a death grip with her arms wrapped tightly around her attacker's neck as they rolled and struggled on the floor for several minutes. Finally, the predator viciously bit Mary Beth's exposed upper left upper arm in desperation. Feeling the victim's grip weaken, the intruder drove an elbow upward beneath Mary Beth's chin, breaking her grip completely and the woman's jaw.

The assailant rolled away and crawled quickly to the dropped pistol. After grabbing the weapon, the predator spun and aimed just as Mary Beth got shakily to her feet. Time seemed to move in slow motion. Just as Mary Beth turned to run towards the dining room, the attacker fired. The bullet struck Mary Beth in the chest, just above her left breast. She wasn't completely aware she had just sustained a gunshot wound, but her legs lost feeling and her knees buckled. The room spun and then went dark. She thudded onto the floor on her left side. The bullet had punched through the skin and underlying subcutaneous tissue before entering the chest cavity. It then passed catastrophically through the descending thoracic aorta before lodging in Mary Beth's spine. Her last conscious thoughts were feelings of regret that she hadn't gone to work that morning as usual.

The killer approached Mary Beth warily, ready to fire again. Mary Beth's eyes were open, and her bruised and bloody face frozen in a look of surprise. Despite the lack of movement, the predator wanted to be sure and fired two more bullets into Mary Beth's chest from point-blank range. But Mary Beth Anderson felt nothing now. Her heart had already stopped. She was already dead.

The killer couldn't believe how fast things had spun out of control. Mary Beth's quick reaction and decision to fight back upstairs had been completely unexpected. Neighbors might have heard the gunshots. The police might already be responding. But the assailant fought the nearly irresistible urge to flee the house immediately. The circumstances required some damage control first. The scene had to be staged to camouflage what had happened.

After glancing around the room, a plan quickly formed. The predator dashed to the entertainment center against the far wall. After ripping out the electrical cords, the VCR and DVD player were swept off the shelves, stacked, and placed beside the door to the garage. On the way, a set of car keys hanging from one of the wall hooks beside the door was noticed and grabbed. A new getaway plan came together easily.

After stepping out the door into the garage, the predator punched the button on the wall beside the door. While the garage door was going up, hustling into the Audi, the killer put the key in the ignition and started the engine. There was no need to take the electronics. Leaving them stacked beside an exit door would accomplish the intended purpose.

Nothing had gone according to plan that morning, but the end result had satisfied the predator. There certainly were no feelings of remorse. The bitch had got what she deserved. After reversing the Audi out of the garage and down the driveway, the predator spun the wheel, shifted the gear selector, and drove away.

For several reasons, long years would pass before anyone came even remotely close to solving the murder of Mary Beth Anderson.

2

Cold Case Homicide

Twenty-three years later

The eight-mile drive from Malone's apartment on Hollywood Boulevard to LAPD headquarters in downtown Los Angeles took over fifty minutes with the morning rush hour traffic conditions.

The Robbery-Homicide Division (RHD), moved in January 2013 to the fifth floor of the new Police Administration Building (PAB) on West First Street, occupied a modern, large, open floor plan. It provided the cubicle-dwelling LAPD detectives access to natural light from the unevenly spaced windows. Offices, interview rooms, and a conference room lined the floor's perimeter.

The office of Lieutenant James Turner, currently Malone's immediate supervisor, was at the far end of the floor. The office door was closed, which was not unusual given the noise level in the open detective workspace. But the blinds on the windows facing out on the floor were also closed, which was unusual. Malone smiled. Someone else must have moved up on the old man's shit list. Maybe the boss wouldn't notice he was twenty-five minutes late to work, mostly because of the snarled morning traffic. But, of course, the mother of all hangovers he was nursing was why he had got a late start in the first place that caused his encounter with the snarled traffic. He hadn't even had time for the coffee shop drive-thru on his way to work, which required making do this morning with the less than spectacular break room blend. After a detour to the break room to fill a white Styrofoam cup from the coffeemaker, he headed to his workstation.

While regarded as an exceptional homicide investigator with an exemplary case clearance record, Malone's assignment wasn't to the prestigious Homicide Special Section distinguished by the many high-profile crimes the section's detectives had investigated over the years. Homicide Special had investigated such notable cases as the Tate-LaBianca murders, the Hillside Strangler murders, and the Nicole Brown-Simpson and Ron Goldman murders. Instead of assignment to the section immortalized in countless movies, novels, and television shows, Malone found himself temporarily assigned to the Cold Case Homicide Special Section, one of the peripheral sections of RHD.

The temporary assignment was just the most recent example of why 2015 had not been exactly a banner year for Detective Ben Malone. Another example was his failed two-year marriage that had ended in March with a final divorce decree. Not that he was unhappy about the divorce. Relieved would be a much better characterization of his feelings on that subject. However, his bitch of an ex-wife was slowly bleeding him to death, financially speaking, with the monthly alimony payments.

The temporary, involuntary duty assignment resulted from Malone's three separate fatal officer-involved shootings during the preceding eleven months during his assignment as a detective on the murder table at the Hollywood Division.

All three shootings had been righteous. In each OIS incident, he had fatally shot an armed suspect. All three had been hardcore felons. All three had made the same fatal error, attempting to take down a cop whose weapon was already out of the holster. None of them had been equal to the task.

The Force Investigation Division, the DA, and the civilian Board of Police Commissioners had exonerated Malone in all three incidents. But the common-law wife of the last dead suspect had filed a wrongful death suit, which was slowly making its way through the civil court system. His supervisors at Hollywood, not to mention the chief of police, had already felt more than a little uncomfortable over the three shooting incidents before the plaintiff's attorney filed the civil lawsuit. Given the politically correct climate of the post-Rodney King and Rampart Scandal racked LAPD, the lawsuit was the proverbial straw that broke the camel's back.

The complete absence of any demonstrated wrongdoing aside, the brass decided a change of scenery would be good for Detective Malone and, more importantly, good for the LAPD. Since there were no grounds to pull him off of street duty, the cold case homicide unit assignment seemed the next best thing. Moreover, it seemed to the brass that Malone would find it far more challenging to find suspects he deemed in need of a double-tap while working homicide cases that had gone unsolved for years if not decades.

Unlike recent homicides, where most suspects and witnesses typically still lived in Los Angeles, with cold cases, it was common for those same people to have moved far away from the city. A good many of them statistically might even be deceased themselves.

Malone understood the theory of working cold homicide cases. Supposedly, over nine thousand unsolved murders committed since 1960 were in the LAPD cold case files when the department formed the special unit in 2002. And with relatively few cases cleared and more added every year, those numbers Malone assumed were likely not much different over a dozen years later.

While the annual number of homicides committed in Los Angeles had declined dramatically since the early nineties, the LAPD homicide clearance rate of around ninety-five percent from back in the sixties had also declined to somewhere around seventy percent. The clearance rate for cold case homicides was far lower. Working with those odds didn't interest Malone. He felt his talents were better and more productively used for working on active cases. Consequently, he was not at all pleased with his current duty assignment. In fact, he was more than a little annoyed with it. In his view, the brass was punishing him when he had done nothing wrong. Personal feelings aside, Malone had a superior work ethic and would give his best efforts at working the cold cases. He really couldn't do any less. That was just the sort of cop he was.

Malone threaded his way through people and cubicles until he arrived at his assigned workspace. It, too, was temporary. There had been no available cubicles when he arrived for duty at the unit two weeks ago. So instead of a desk, they gave him space at one end of the long table in the RHD conference room. His temporary partner, Detective Jaime Reyes, occupied the other end of the table. Malone and Reyes were often summarily evicted when someone needed the conference room for its intended purpose: conferences. At least they had an office with a door instead of cubicles whenever they were lucky enough to have use of it.

Reyes was a couple of inches short of six feet and muscular. Not like a bodybuilder, but more in an athletic sort of way, like a football linebacker or a boxer. He styled his jet black hair in a fade cut with lots of hair products. He had large dark brown eyes, which seemed to be perpetually smiling. Malone figured Reyes was about his age, early thirties. Reyes had a quick and infectious laugh. He didn't seem to take life in general too seriously. He was a likable enough guy and seemed a competent detective. As far as his partner was concerned, albeit a new one, Malone had no complaints about Reyes.

Reyes was also on temporary assignment to the cold case unit. Malone assumed he, too, was doing penance for some real or imagined sin against the LAPD gods. He had asked Reyes about it. Sort of like one con in San Quentin asking another, "What are you in for?" But Reyes had not been particularly forthcoming. He brushed aside the question by saying his assignment to the unit was just a bureaucratic screw-up that the brass would clear up soon, and his happy ass would be back at Van Nuys before the end of the week. He had said the same thing the week before, but he still wasn't back at Van Nuys. Reyes was already at the table when Malone walked into the conference room. He looked up when Malone walked through the door.

"Malone," he said. "Nice you could join us, bro."

"Give it a rest, Reyes," Malone said. "Traffic sucked, and I woke up a little late."

"Dude, you look like shit," Reyes said. "I don't like your chances if Turner sees you and gives you a PBT."

"I'm not drunk, Reyes," Malone said. "Just a little hungover, nothing serious."

Reyes winked and laughed, closed a file he had been reading, and shoved it down the polished tabletop towards Malone. "Check this one out," he said. "It's an interesting read, but it won't be a keeper. We can check that one off the list and ship it back to the records division."

Malone glanced at the full cardboard file box in the center of the table. "Yes, well, there are still plenty more where that one came from, amigo. But how did you eliminate this one from contention so fast? You always have two donuts and three cups of coffee before you start work. You couldn't have had more than a twenty-minute head start on me."

"There isn't any DNA evidence to be analyzed for one thing," he said. "And look at the date. The murder happened in 1992. Dude, we were both probably like ten years old back then. That case is so cold it's blue, bro. What are the chances we'd find any fresh evidence or witnesses? And the original witnesses are probably scattered to hell and back. Some of them may have already died of old age."

"If you're so sure, let's just mark it off the list, and I'll start the next one," Malone said.

"No," Reyes said. "Read it, bro. While I don't think it's worth re-opening, when I read it, I got the impression that the original investigating detective had the theory of what happened all wrong. Probably the big reason they never cleared the case, and it went cold. I'm curious to see if you see it the same way. Besides, it's Friday, and they have a meeting scheduled for the conference room this morning. So we will not get any actual work done today, anyway."

Malone nodded and dropped his six-foot, two-inch frame into his chair and pulled the file over in front of him. He ran a hand through his reddish-brown hair, trying to take his mind off his splitting headache so that he could concentrate. That reminded him he was past due for a haircut. He had meant to get his hair cut days ago, but had forgotten about it. But he had let himself go recently, in more ways than one. He hadn't been running or going to the gym, had put on a few pounds, and drank a little too much. Malone silently resolved to do something about all that, starting with a haircut. He looked at the faded label on the folder: Mary Beth Anderson. He opened the file, also known in cop-speak as the murder book.

The first item Malone saw was an 8 X 10 photo inside a transparent document protector. The photo was of a young woman with light-brown hair, a broad face with high cheekbones, and wide-set blue eyes under dark, arching eyebrows. She had a Scandinavian look. The "big hair" hairstyle was a dead giveaway as to the age of the photo, but the woman's attractive features were timeless. The photo looked like those taken for college yearbooks. Next, he found the report written by a patrol officer first-responder.

The first police officer to arrive at any homicide crime scene is a uniformed patrol officer in almost all instances. They usually arrived in response to a radio dispatch based on an emergency call made by some citizen who had witnessed the crime or had stumbled upon a dead body. On arrival, the patrol officer confirmed whether the victim was alive or dead and then took the necessary actions based on the circumstances. A patrol officer secured the scene after detaining potential suspects and witnesses. The first responding officer summoned a patrol supervisor to the scene. The supervisor called for detectives when circumstances were inconclusive or suggested the deceased was the victim of a homicide.

Later, the first responding patrol officer wrote an offense report that detailed the circumstances of their arrival at the scene and all the basic pertinent facts learned by the officer after arrival. Offense reports were simply a recitation of facts not in dispute. There are no opinions expressed, and no theories expounded. That wasn't the job of a patrol officer. It was the job of the detectives who worked the scene.

Malone skimmed the report to acquaint himself with the basic facts of the case. He learned that the victim had been twenty-eight years old when she died in January 1992. Her husband found her deceased inside the townhome they shared. He had last seen the victim alive early that morning when he left for work. According to the husband, it had been a workday for the victim too, but she had taken a sick day because of a stomach bug. The husband discovered the deceased on the living room floor in their home a little past six that evening when he returned from work. He had gone to a neighbor's house to call the police. He and the male neighbor had then returned to the scene to wait for the police to arrive.

Malone noted that the reporting officer had observed a stack of disconnected electronic equipment removed from the living room, near the door leading to an attached garage. According to the victim's husband, the equipment had been on an entertainment center shelf and connected to the television when he left for work that morning. The circumstances suggested that a burglary might have gone sideways and culminated with the murder.

Malone turned the page and looked at a series of full-color crime scene photos, the same type of photos he had seen many times during his career. But, unfortunately, these were a little faded and washed out. Back in 1992, digital cameras weren't in common use. Instead, crime scene techs were still shooting and developing film photos.

The first photo was of the exterior of the townhouse, probably taken from the street. It showed the house numbers beside the front door to establish the address of the scene. The garage door was up, and no vehicles were inside the garage. In the next shot, Malone saw broken glass fragments on the driveway and then a close-up of the second-floor windows above the garage with missing glass. The fourth photo was of a garage side door followed by a close-up of the door's striker plate with apparent tool marks, possibly evidence of forcible entry.

Malone continued flipping through the photos. Finally, he arrived at one that depicted a female lying on the floor on her left side near a couch. Her back was to the camera lens. Another photo snapped from the opposite angle showed her from the front. She had a substantial laceration above her left eye, like the cuts boxers sometimes got from taking a hard punch to the eye. There were also some contusions, other minor lacerations, and noticeable scratches on her broad face. Her eyes were open, lifeless, but clearly blue. The victim had medium-length light brown hair that looked like the hair of someone who had recently gotten out of bed. She was wearing only a white tee shirt and panties. She had a fair amount of dried blood on her face, but clearly, she was the same woman in the 8 X 10 portrait at the front of the file.

After several more photos of the deceased from different angles,

Malone looked at a photo of a couch upholstered in tan fabric. There was a purse resting on the right-hand cushion next to the arm of the sofa. The next photo showed the purse contents dumped and arrayed on one of the couch cushions. There was a pocketbook, a significant amount of cash, coins, several credit cards, and the usual mirror, hairbrush, and cosmetics.

There were several photos of the living room that suggested a violent struggle. Two large tower-type stereo speakers were lying on the floor. There was a silver metal vase lying on the tiled entryway floor. Marks on the carpet showed the sofa had moved. Malone sensed from the photos that Anderson had not gone quietly. Instead, she had put up a protracted fight.

The last photo showed a VCR with a DVD player stacked on top beside a doorway. The DVD player had what appeared to be a blood smear on its surface. If it was blood, that could be some telling evidence. Malone was so intent on the contents of the file and the questions occurring to him in rapid-fire fashion while he worked through it, he hadn't even noticed when he had taken a memo book and pen from his shirt pocket and jotted some notes.

Finished with the photos, Malone flipped through several witness statements and the autopsy report straight to the case summary prepared by the original primary investigator, a detective out of the Van Nuys station, who had drawn the case. Malone copied down the detective's name: Kenneth Myers. He then read the summary.

The theory Myers developed about how the murder went down was clear. He saw it as a burglary that went sideways. The victim was at home, sick on a weekday. Normally, she would have been at work. But she was asleep or resting on a bed upstairs and possibly awakened to a noise downstairs. She investigated and surprised unknown suspects in the middle of a burglary. Myers, without explanation, assumed there were two suspects. Perhaps the victim confronted the suspects, or she resisted, and they just decided to shut her up. They beat her with a metal vase, according to the summary, and then shot her multiple times. She died at the scene of her wounds. The suspects had then fled the scene in the victim's husband's car, which was inside the garage.

Malone found it curious that the suspects had removed no property from the victim's house. According to the summary, the suspects had taken only the black 1991 Audi 5000 that belonged to the victim's husband from the garage. Myers related in the summary that the husband had left his car at home and had driven his wife's car to work that day so that he could have it serviced for her.

After completing the original case summary, Malone turned the page to a supplement prepared by Myers two days after the murder. It detailed the recovery of the husband's stolen Audi 5000 on the date of the supplement. Uniformed Van Nuys patrol officers had located the vehicle. They found the car abandoned in a strip mall parking lot located a few miles from the murder scene. The keys had still been in the ignition. According to the supplement report, a crime scene team had processed the vehicle for evidence, but discovered nothing relevant and collected no evidence or classifiable latent prints. The police had later returned to Audi to the registered owner.

Another supplement, dated two weeks after the first and also prepared by Detective Myers, detailed the occurrence of a similar burglary that occurred in the victim's neighborhood a few blocks away. Myers had summarized that burglary.

According to the female victim, noise downstairs woke her, and she went to investigate. She had discovered two Hispanic males disconnecting her stereo, who physically restrained her. According to the victim, they bound her wrists and ankles with electrical cords, told her to keep quiet if she didn't want to get hurt, and left her lying on the living room floor. The suspects took the stereo, television, jewelry, and a few hundred dollars in cash from her purse. After the burglary, the suspects left the residence with the property through the front door. The victim eventually freed herself and called the police.

Myers used the burglary to support his Anderson murder theory. He assumed the same suspects had burglarized Anderson's townhouse and subsequently shot her to death. He had transported the other burglary victim to the Van Nuys station and had her describe the two Hispanic male suspects to a police artist who drew composite sketches of them. They had distributed the sketches and physical descriptions of the two suspects to patrol officers and selected businesses in Van Nuys and neighboring LAPD divisions. Local media also published the sketches and descriptions in the LA newspaper and news broadcasts. Initially, a few tips came in, but none panned out. The police never apprehended or even identified the suspects. The leads quickly dried up. No one reported any similar burglaries in the vicinity. When the detectives developed no new leads, the Anderson case went cold.

Malone wanted to look at the autopsy report and evidence log before forming any conclusions. But a few things were already clear to him.

Someone had shot Anderson to death, but not the other burglary victim. The suspects hadn't even displayed a gun. They hadn't physically assaulted the second woman beyond manhandling and tying her up. After they had bound and neutralized her, the suspects continued with the burglary until they finished the job. Then they actually removed property. To Malone, it also seemed important that they didn't just stop at some nominal street value electronics. They also took jewelry from a bedroom and cash from the victim's purse. They hadn't taken the victim's vehicle parked in her driveway. That suggested the suspects had their own transportation nearby. Certainly, they wouldn't likely have wanted to risk being seen by neighbors carrying a stereo and television down the street. The modus operandi had been completely different in that burglary, yet Myers used the case almost exclusively to buttress his burglary gone sideways theory for the Anderson murder. Malone saw some serious holes in his theory.

Malone flipped back to the crime scene photos and found the close-ups of Anderson's gunshot entry wounds. There were three chest wounds. It was reasonable to assume any of the three could have been fatal without immediate medical intervention, which obviously hadn't occurred. There was an obvious difference in the wounds, which showed up clearly in the photos.

The two lower chest wounds revealed stippling or "tattooing." When a bullet leaves the barrel of a firearm, super-heated gasses follow it with burning gunpowder, and some amount of unburned gunpowder. Therefore, the presence or absence of gunpowder residue on a victim's clothing or the margins of an entry wound showed whether a gunshot wound was a contact, close, intermediate, or distant wound.

While it varied depending on the type of firearm and ammunition used, Malone knew that typically when stippling was present, the shooter fired the bullet at close range, within thirty-six inches. No stippling showed they fired the bullet from a distance, at least over thirty-six inches away. The wound above the victim's left breast was a distance wound. Thus there was no stippling.

The other two wounds weren't contact wounds, but the killer fired those bullets from very close range, hence the stippling. Given how close the killer had been to the victim when firing those two shots, it seemed like those were the coup de grâce. Those two last bullets made certain that Anderson was dead. That just didn't fit with an interrupted burglary turned violent. Why would the suspects have done that? It made no sense.

Malone knew residential burglars were non-confrontational criminals who relied on stealth and actively tried to avoid confrontations with homeowners. Few of them he had ever encountered even carried a gun. Confrontational criminals like armed robbers, bangers, and carjackers used guns, not residential burglars.

While Malone could imagine a burglary suspect bringing along a gun as a safety measure and even using a gun as a last resort if confronted by a homeowner, it didn't follow a burglar would shoot someone three times, intentionally committing a murder. Why would they? If a suspect got popped for burglary, they were looking at maybe two to six years in prison if a court convicted them. But in 1992, someone popped for intentionally murdering a homeowner during a burglary would have been looking at getting the needle. In Malone's opinion, the murder of Mary Beth Anderson hadn't resulted from a burglary gone sideways. It had been an execution.

Malone was flipping back to the autopsy report when a woman walked into the room and said, "Sorry guys, but I will need the conference room in a few."

Malone looked up and saw an attractive, petite Latina standing in the doorway who could have been near fifty but could certainly pass for forty. Dressed in a stylish and tailored black pantsuit, she was very attractive, even though middle age had obviously taken its toll as the fine lines at the corners of her eyes and mouth showed. Her stylishly cut, straight black hair was shoulder length, and her bangs fell at an angle to either side of her forehead. She was smiling, but just for an instant, Malone had the impression that there was something dark and menacing just beneath the surface of her almond-shaped, dark brown, almost black eyes.

Whatever Malone thought he had seen beneath the surface of her demeanor evaporated as quickly as a Los Angeles summer rain shower. She certainly had that look—the hard, world-weary expression that meant only one thing. She was definitely a cop. Even without the LAPD identification card suspended from the lanyard around her neck and the conspicuously large, gold LAPD shield clipped at the waist of her black slacks, he would have made her for a cop.

"Hi," she said. "We haven't met. I'm Vanessa Bachmann, Special

Assault Section supervisor. You guys must be the new temps assigned to cold case homicide."

3

An Attractive Lieutenant

Reyes spoke first. "Yes, ma'am. That's us. I'm Jaime Reyes, and this is my partner, Ben Malone. Guess the cold case unit needed some experienced help, so they sent for the A-team. I'm from Van Nuys, and Hollywood loaned Malone to the unit."

"That's great," Bachmann said. "The unit often pulls in extra help because the cold case section is dreadfully understaffed given their caseload. Usually, they only get rookie detectives. So it's terrific that they got a couple of seasoned investigators for a change."

Bachmann turned her attention to Malone. "I've heard your name before. I'm guessing you are *that* Malone, since you're from Hollywood."

Malone winced and nodded. "If you mean the Malone that has been involved in three separate OIS incidents in less than a year, then yes, I am that Malone."

"Yes," Bachmann said. "Obviously, I have heard about that. Seriously, who in the department hasn't, right? But I didn't mean just that. I've heard other things about you as well. So, you should know you have a very favorable reputation beyond just Hollywood. In Special Assault Section, we keep up with what is going on out in the other bureaus.

We're always looking for trends where we might offer support or get help with cases we're working here. So, we hear things, and I've heard from several sources that you have an excellent clearance record on the cases you've worked over at Hollywood Division, and I know you guys carry a big caseload."

"Nice to hear I'm known for something besides just shooting people," Malone said. "It's not like I go looking for human targets. Those things happened because the suspects pushed it. Nothing else I could do except let them shoot me, and that would not happen."

"You don't need to justify anything to me, detective," Bachmann said. "I know the department exonerated you in all three incidents. And that's good enough for me. How long have you been with the LAPD?"

"Six years," Malone said. "Three years in patrol and I just finished my third year as a detective."

"What did you do before you were a cop?" Bachmann asked.

"I was in the army," Malone said.

"Oh, really," Bachmann said. "Were you military police?"

"No, infantry," Malone said. "I was with the Rangers."

"Oh, I see," Bachmann said. "My brother was in the Marines, so I know all about the infantry."

Malone glanced at Reyes and noticed that he seemed a little crestfallen that Malone was getting all the attention from the attractive lady lieutenant, so he threw his partner a bone.

"Oh yeah, the Marines," he said. "Yes, I know whatever the MOS, all Marines are infantrymen first. Reyes could probably tell you all about that. He was a Marine."

Bachmann turned her attention back to Reyes and smiled again. "Oh, really. Well, Semper Fi detective."

"Ooh-Rah, ma'am," Reyes said with a laugh, clearly happy to be included once again in the conversation.

Bachmann looked at her watch and then said, "Well, it was great meeting you guys, but I've got to shoo you out the door now. We're hosting the quarterly meeting with detectives from stations throughout the city to discuss crime trends, suspect information, and investigative techniques. The meetings help to ensure we're all on the same page across all the geographic boundaries. Sorry to have to kick you guys out of your office, as it were. The meeting will go until two o'clock this afternoon with a break for lunch. Hopefully, you guys have something to do away from the PAB until then."

"Oh sure," Reyes said. "We've been looking at an old homicide case this morning that we may be reopening. No time like the present to get out and knock on some doors and maybe do a few interviews."

"Really?" Bachmann said. "An old one, huh? How old is the case?"

Malone wondered why Reyes had brought up the case they had been reading. Hadn't he already said that there was no way it met the criteria to be reopened? Malone assumed he was just showing off for the benefit of the attractive lieutenant.

"It's ancient," Reyes said. "It's a 1992 Van Nuys murder. I was just saying to Malone that we were probably 10-years-olds when it happened."

"Well, hopefully, you don't think of me as ancient, detective," Bachmann said. "But I was a second-year patrol officer in 1992. I remember that year very well. There was a lot of gang violence, a lot of drugs, civil unrest, and a lot of guns on the street. There were a lot of homicides, too. In fact, if I recall, correctly, I think the number of 1992 homicides set a record in LA."

"Yes, homicides in 1992 did set a record," Malone said, deciding to show off a little himself. "According to the coroner's office, there were 2,589 homicides in Los Angeles County in 1992, an eight percent increase over 1991."

"Damn!" Reyes said. "It must have been like a war zone back then."

"I know you guys have specific criteria for what justifies re-opening a cold case homicide," Bachmann said. "So, I'm just curious here. What's the deal with this one? DNA evidence collected that they couldn't process back in 1992 but that we have the technology to analyze now? I really can't imagine anything else that would meet the criteria for reopening a case over twenty years old."

"No," Reyes said. "Nothing like that. Malone and I haven't asked Lieutenant Turner for authorization to reopen it just yet. We need to review it a little more first. We've just been discussing it because it's clear that the original investigator came up with a very weak theory and never really pursued anything else. Last week, we cleared a 10-year-old homicide that didn't have any DNA evidence to process or any new leads to speak of at all. DNA evidence is great, but it's no substitute for good old-fashioned police work."

"So, how did you solve that case?" Bachmann said.

Reyes said, "We hit the street and beat the bushes and did some good old-fashioned police work. We interviewed several convicted felons who had moved in the same circles ten years ago when the murder happened. One of them gave us the name of a con doing life in San Quentin. We went up and interviewed him. He gave us another name, the name of a viable suspect. We just kept following the breadcrumbs. Finally, we found a couple of witnesses who corroborated the con's statements, and we had our man. We ran him through the computers and learned that he was doing twenty to life in Arizona on another homicide."

"What happened then?" Bachmann asked.

"We contacted the Arizona Department of Corrections to arrange an interview," Reyes said. "Unfortunately, they told us the guy had died of natural causes while in custody last year. But hey, at least we cleared the case."

"I don't know," Bachmann said. "I'm just not sure clearing an old case like that is worth the cost and resources it requires. Knowing how I must fight the budget wars every year to get even close to the minimum my unit needs to operate effectively, I think we could better devote the money and resources to working on active cases. Considering how your 10-year-old case turned out, I really can't imagine there is any real benefit to working a case over 20 years old, even if you guys could actually clear it."

"Funny you should say that, lieutenant," Malone said. "Less than two hours ago, I was thinking the same thing and would have totally agreed with everything you just said. Truthfully, I was feeling more than a little sorry for myself being stuck here looking at all these cold cases when what I wanted was to be back at Hollywood doing something productive, like working on an active murder investigation. But now I'm not so sure that what this unit does isn't just as important."

"How so?" Bachmann asked.

"Well, just think about the victim's families represented by all these unsolved cases," Malone said. "Don't they deserve closure just as much as the husband, wife, child, brother, or parent of someone murdered yesterday? Can you really put a dollar figure on that? It would be hard enough to deal with losing a family member to a senseless act of violence alone. I can't even imagine how much worse it must be to go year after year, never seeing your loved one even get any justice."

"That's certainly an idealistic view, detective," Bachmann said. "I'm not saying we shouldn't give every effort to clearing cold cases where there is a reasonable chance of identifying, arresting, and prosecuting the killer. But at the same time, we must face reality. We have limited resources and a duty to the citizens of Los Angeles to use those resources wisely and effectively. Re-opening a homicide case that's nearly a quarter-century old is not, in my opinion, the way we do that. This whole discussion is moot, anyway. I think I know Jim Turner well enough to say he isn't about to approve of reopening a 23-year-old homicide case unless there is a very compelling reason to do so. And I know I sure wouldn't approve reopening an old case like that if I were in his shoes. I'd never be able to justify it to the captain."

The meeting attendees filtered into the room, so Malone picked up the Anderson file and replaced it in the file box, which he then moved off the table and placed on the floor in a corner. He and Reyes said their goodbyes to Lieutenant Bachmann and headed out the door.

4

Missing Evidence

Malone and Reyes took the elevator down to the ground floor and walked out of the PAB.

"So what do you want to do to kill time until two o'clock?" Reyes asked.

"I didn't get any decent coffee this morning," Malone said. "First, let's walk over to The Daily Grind on West Second and get some. We can discuss the Anderson case since you already told Bachmann we were going to re-open it."

Reyes agreed, and two minutes later, they walked into the coffee shop. Malone ordered two large house brews. They found a table near the back wall.

"Seriously, bro, I don't see that old case fitting the criteria they gave us for re-opening it," Reyes said. "I was just trying to make conversation with the lieutenant. Was she hot or what?"

"Yeah, she was okay," Malone said.

"Just okay, bro?" Reyes asked. "You blind or what? She was smoking hot. Yes, she is a little older, but I've been thinking about dating older women. They are more settled than the girls our age. They know what they want and are more confident about exploring their sexuality.

Plus, they have experience. I bet Vanessa Bachmann could show you a few things in bed that would blow your mind, bro. Things you've never even imagined, much less experienced."

"I think she is attractive," Malone said. "But she just isn't my type. Besides, Bachmann isn't a Latin name, so it's obviously her married name."

Reyes said, "Damn Malone, are you nuts, bro? I wish she had been paying half the attention to me she paid to you. I think you could get in her pants without even trying. Like a lot of cops, I bet she's probably divorced."

"Yeah, well, Reyes, I'm not interested," Malone said. "First, I just got a divorce, and I'm not looking to get into another relationship right now. Second, with all the shit going on in my life right now, the last thing I need is getting involved with a superior officer."

"Okay, Malone," Reyes said. "Have it your way, but you're passing up a golden opportunity, bro. Waste not, want not, I always say. The way she was looking at you and hanging on your every word made it clear. That was as close to a sure thing as you're likely to see, dude. Hell, if I hadn't been there, she might have closed that door and been in *your* pants before you knew what happened."

Malone laughed.

"Reyes, you're full of shit, you know that?" Malone said. "Now, let's forget your cougar dream girl and women in general, for that matter, for just a few minutes. Let's talk about the case."

"Okay, bro," Reyes said. "What did you think about Meyers' burglary gone sideways theory?"

"I think it was full of holes, lots of holes," Malone said. "I think that murder was personal. It was an execution. It sure as hell wasn't some tweaked out burglar losing it and popping a homeowner. I just don't see it going down that way, no way, no how."

"Exactly," Reyes said. "When I get back to Van Nuys, I'm going to ask some of the old-timers about Meyers. He was way before my time. I've never heard his name mentioned. But there are a couple of guys over there in patrol who were there back in 1992. Probably even before who might have known him. Just from reading the file, I feel like he wasn't the sharpest tack in the LAPD detective box."

"I hope that was the explanation," Malone said. "I hope he was just incompetent. Otherwise, you could make the case that his investigation was borderline criminally negligent. He latched onto that burglary theory like a pit bull and never even looked in any other direction."

"I hear you, bro," Reyes said. "I wish we could re-open it. There are a few strings we could pull on, and the whole thing might unravel. But I see nothing there that would convince Turner to let us re-open it. But we're both on the same page. Meyers screwed the pooch big time. Still, Turner told us two weeks ago what the criteria for reopening cases are. We're expected to read the case files and bring to his attention any cases where there is potential DNA evidence or other physical evidence it wasn't possible to process at the time of the crime. Evidence that we now have the technology to analyze. And we've got nothing like that with this case."

"Yeah, I know," Malone said. "But that's what bothers me the most. Clearly, there was blood at the scene. Did you see the blood smear on the DVD player? There was blood spatter on the tiled entryway, on the front door, and the walls around the door. It looked to me like the victim put up a hell of a fight. SID must have collected blood samples at the scene. Did you check the evidence log?"

"No, dude," Reyes said. "I read the narratives. I didn't find any evidence log in the file. It's an old case. Things can go missing from physical paper files. The department wasn't as computerized back then as it is now. The only thing I found about evidence is what I picked out of the narratives and the autopsy report."

"All I know is I'm not ready to give up on it yet," Malone said. "We don't have to ask Turner right away to re-open the case. We can spend time on it while we're working on the other files. Maybe we'll shake something loose. We could go down to the archives and find out what evidence SID collected and booked."

"Okay with me, bro," Reyes said. "What Turner doesn't know won't hurt him. Better yet, what he doesn't know won't get us in the biz bag with him. We will just keep it on the down-low unless we find something. Then, if we find something significant, we'll take it to him then. If not, no harm, no foul."

"That's a plan," Malone said.

They finished their coffee, left the shop, and made the short walk to the Los Angeles Police Department's Evidence and Property Management Division on North Los Angeles Street.

* * *

Malone led the way through the double glass doors at the front entrance, and Reyes followed him to a chest-high wooden counter. Wire-reinforced glass ran from the countertop to the ceiling the length of the long counter. There was a uniformed property clerk seated on a stool behind the counter. He looked up as they approached. Malone pressed his badge to the glass.

"Hello, I'm Detective Malone from robbery-homicide, and this is my partner, Detective Reyes. We would like to see the evidence from a 1992 homicide case."

"Sure, detectives," the clerk said. "Got a case number?"

Malone fished out his memo book and flipped to the page where he had recorded notes from the case file.

"Yes," Malone said. "92-014387."

"Just a moment," the man said.

He turned to the computer on the counter and started typing on the keyboard.

"Victim name Anderson?" he asked.

"Yes, that's the one," Malone said.

"Wait one," the clerk said.

He got off the stool and walked to the bank of file cabinets behind the counter. Then he searched the labels until he found the drawer he was looking for and pulled it open. Next, he flicked through the folders inside and then extracted a light green, legal-sized folder and pushed the drawer closed. He returned to the counter and opened the folder. He flipped through the first several pages, secured to the folder backer with a two-pronged silver metal clip. Finding the page he wanted, he used an index finger to trace down a column of numbers on the left side of a pre-printed column with handwritten entries until he found case number 92-014387. Then his finger followed the line across to the right-hand side of the form.

Looking up, he said, "A Van Nuys detective named Sandoval signed the box out for forensic testing in March 1999. But no one ever signed the evidence back into the property division."

"Isn't that unusual?" Malone asked.

"Yes," the clerk admitted. "It's an old case, but since there isn't a statute of limitations on murder, it's still considered an open case. Once forensics did their thing, they should have returned the evidence here and signed it back in. Although it's not the policy, I guess it's possible the evidence is still at SID."

"Can you give us a copy of the evidence log?" Malone asked. "It's missing from the murder book."

"Sure, no problem," the clerk said. "It was an actual paper document back then, but we've scanned all the physical documents and uploaded them to the computer system since then. I can print you a copy."

The property clerk returned to the computer, typed on the keyboard for a moment, and then the laser printer next to the computer spit out a printed document. He passed it to Malone through the rectangular opening at the bottom of the glass barrier. Malone glanced at it and then folded the letter-sized sheet of paper and put it in his inside jacket pocket.

"Thanks," Malone said. "We'll check with SID."

* * *

In 2007, the LAPD and Los Angeles County Sheriff's Department crime lab combined at a single location on the campus of Cal State University Los Angeles with the construction of the Hertzberg-Davis Forensic Science Center. The center, located about five miles east of the downtown Los Angles CBD off the San Bernardino Freeway, wasn't within reasonable walking distance. It was almost one o'clock, so Malone and Reyes grabbed lunch at a sub sandwich shop on the way back to the PAB.

After arriving at the sandwich shop on North Los Angeles Street, Malone ordered a classic Italian sub and Reyes a ham and Swiss Ciabatta toasty. After getting their food and a couple of soft drinks, they found a table near the window looking out on the street.

"We will need a pool car to get out to SID," Malone said.

Reyes, who had already taken a large bite from his sandwich, finished chewing and swallowed before speaking.

"We should probably hold off on that until Monday," Reyes said. "Don't you think, bro? We haven't reviewed more than a half dozen cases this week, and we've already lost the entire morning today. I think the lieutenant is going to be expecting a little more production from us at the weekly progress meeting Monday morning."

"Yeah," Malone said. "You're probably right. We can spend the rest of the afternoon on case reviews. Maybe we will get lucky and find one that gives us an excuse for driving out to SID."

They finished lunch and walked back to headquarters. They arrived back at the empty conference room just after two o'clock. Reyes hoisted the file box back onto the table and grabbed a case file. Malone lifted the Anderson case file from the front of the box where he had left it.

"I just want to look at the autopsy report first, and then I'll shelve this one until Monday," he said.

Reyes nodded, already turning pages in the file he had selected. Malone opened the Anderson murder book and flipped to the autopsy report. It wasn't an original, but a faded, dog-eared photocopy. It began with the narrative prepared by the coroner's investigator that detailed the crime scene, the decedent's location and condition at the time of the investigator's arrival, and the traumatic injuries he had observed. After describing the injuries, the investigator had noted the location of each visible injury by annotating them onto a genderless outline diagram of the human body.

Among the many lacerations, abrasions, contusions, and the gunshot wounds, the investigator had also noted a bite wound on the victim's left upper arm. Malone had known of both men and women using their teeth during a physical fight.

An extreme but infamous example was that where professional boxer Mike Tyson bit off a portion of Evander Holyfield's right ear during a 1997 bout billed originally as "The Sound and the Fury" but afterward referred to mockingly as "The Bite Fight." Not only had Tyson bitten off a portion of Holyfield's ear and spit it on the canvas early in the third round of the fight. Later in the round, after having the referee had warned him after the first biting incident, the fight official disqualified him after he attempted to take a bite out of Holyfield's other ear. While some might assume that women were more given to biting during a physical fight than men, the Tyson example showed that Anderson's bite wound didn't reveal the sex of Anderson's killer.

Malone continued reading the actual medical examiner's autopsy report, which provided more detail on the various traumatic injuries. The medical examiner who made the cut had described the entry, exit, path, and trajectory of each of the gunshot wounds, along with the details of the internal trauma caused by each bullet. The report contained a disclaimer, explaining they had arbitrarily labeled the gunshot wounds and that such labeling did not infer the actual sequence of the wounds. Nevertheless, it was clear to Malone, based on his experience, that the wound labeled "Gunshot Wound #2" was the kill shot, the one that he was certain the killer had fired from further away than the other two. That bullet had lacerated Anderson's descending thoracic aorta before lodging in her spine. The mechanism of death had been determined by exsanguination. She had bled to death internally. Probably quickly, and probably even before her assailant fired the other two bullets into her chest from nearly point-blank range.

Malone closed the file and put it aside, more convinced than ever that Mary Beth Anderson had not died at the hands of a stranger during a botched burglary attempt. Someone she knew had killed her. That assumption would significantly limit the suspect pool.

Malone and Reyes spent the last two hours of the day reviewing files and got through another ten by four o'clock. In one of those reviewed by Reyes, he had found potential DNA evidence existed that SID hadn't analyzed. That case provided a plausible reason for the two detectives to pay a visit to the forensic science center on Monday.

The pair tidied up their workspace, returned the box of files to the floor in the room's corner, and then left the PAB for the weekend.

5

Surfing Invitation

Malone knew he had been drinking too much of late. On the drive home from work Friday afternoon, he had resolved to cut back. But remembering he had polished off the last of the bourbon on Thursday, he stopped off at a liquor store on the way home and bought a fresh bottle of Jack Daniels. He might want a couple of drinks over the weekend just to relax. No harm in that. Bourbon was his favorite. He had developed a taste and appreciation for it during his army days. He was enough of a connoisseur to know that while they marketed Jack Daniels as Tennessee whiskey, it was bourbon, even though the word "bourbon" did not appear anywhere on a bottle of Jack.

Once Malone had arrived home Friday afternoon, his resolve to cut back on his drinking evaporated as soon as he checked his phone messages. There were two. The first was a particularly nasty message from his bitch of an ex-wife informing him she planned to go back to court to get her alimony payments increased, adding that she had quit her job and was returning to school to work on a master's degree. He deleted that message only to find a second that was almost as annoying. It was a reminder from Dr. Sara Bernstein's office about his appointment for the following Tuesday afternoon.

Bernstein was the department shrink they had assigned him to after the last on-duty shooting incident. By policy, it was mandatory that LAPD officers involved in on-duty fatal shooting incidents see a department provided mental health professional. The party line was that they aimed such an intervention at reducing stress and providing counsel and support. But Malone was quite certain that the actual goal of the policy was a cover their ass move by the department by which the brass hoped to diagnose and identify officers with anti-social tendencies that might make them too quick to solve problems with deadly force. The proof of that, in Malone's opinion, was the fact that the LAPD did not release officers involved in fatal shootings from administrative leave and allow them to return to street duty without the shrink's approval.

With the first two shooting incidents, it had been straightforward. Malone had been required to visit a department psychiatrist within days of the incidents. Afterward, he got his gun and badge back and was immediately returned to duty. Things became more complicated for Malone after the third shooting incident.

Bernstein believed Malone displayed symptoms of PTSD, which he found a ridiculous notion. Ultimately, she had given her approval for him to return to duty, but recommended that he continue seeing her twice a month for counseling. His supervisor made it mandatory that he did so. Malone felt certain Bernstein's recommendation was also a big part of the department's decision to assign him to the cold case homicide unit instead of allowing him to go back to work in Hollywood.

Not that Malone disliked Bernstein as a person. She was quite an attractive woman close to his age, tall and lean, but not model-like skinny. And she had an athletic build, but still all the curves in all the right places. She had an angular face with large, intelligent brown eyes, a small nose, and full lips. A healthy tan accented her luminous, unblemished complexion. She had shoulder-length, shiny brown hair with hints of red, which she parted on the left in such a way that often required her to brush it away from covering her left eye. Under other circumstances, he might have asked her out to dinner, or at least for a drink. But seeing her in her professional capacity was more than a bit of a mood killer, especially considering the PTSD label she was trying to slap on him. Besides, it was a moot point. Since he was seeing her in her professional capacity, he assumed it would be some kind of ethical violation for her to see him in a social capacity at the same time. Even though he didn't get the married vibe from her, she was probably already in a relationship with someone.

Malone had a couple of drinks just to relax. He sat down in his favorite chair and turned on the Dodger game. During the game, he poured a couple of more just to take the edge off. After the fourth drink, or was it the fifth, he lost count. The next thing he knew, he woke up in the chair with an infomercial blaring on the television. Malone rubbed his eyes and looked at his watch, finding it was after three o'clock on Saturday morning. So he picked up the remote and clicked the television off. Then he got up and stumbled to the bedroom, falling onto the bed. He immediately went back to sleep, still wearing his work clothes, minus only the sports coat and tie.

At seven, he stirred. Some loud and annoying noise had awakened him. Without opening his eyes, he slapped at the alarm clock on the table beside the bed, thinking the alarm was going off. But to no avail. The racket continued. Finally, he surfaced to the necessary level of consciousness to realize it was the phone, not the alarm clock. He grabbed the receiver and placed it to his ear and mouth, still without opening his eyes.

"Hello," he croaked.

"Well, hello, and good morning," a cheery female voice said. "I didn't think you were going to answer."

The voice sounded familiar, but half asleep and suffering from a serious hangover. He couldn't place it. He also didn't ask who it was because he didn't, at that moment, really care.

"This is Vanessa," she said. "Vanessa Bachmann. We met yesterday."

Like molasses, his brain slowly processed the information and made the connection between the voice, the name, and the female lieutenant he and Reyes had talked with the day before.

"Oh, yeah," he said. "What can I do for you, lieutenant?"

"You can start by dropping the lieutenant and calling me Vanessa," she said.

"Yeah, okay, sure," he said sleepily. "Is this about work? Because it's Saturday, at least I think it is Saturday."

"No," she said. "I called to ask if you would like to go surfing with me."

"Surfing?" he asked. "Like now?"

"Yes," she said. "Like now, or in an hour or so."

"Not really," he said. "I mean, it has nothing to do with you. It's just that I don't surf. Haven't even ever tried it."

"What!" she said. "A Southern California guy, and you've never tried surfing?"

"Yeah, unbelievable, isn't it?" he said.

"Why not? Don't you like the ocean?" she asked.

"Yes," he said. "I like the ocean just fine. I just never had a reason to try surfing. That's all."

"Oh, I get it," she said. "You're afraid of the water."

"Hell, no," he said. "I'm not afraid of the water. I just never had an interest in surfing, that's all."

He had been less than candid. He was terrified of the water. Well, deep water, at least. He'd almost drowned as a child and had never been crazy about the beach since. In fact, if he exhibited PTSD symptoms as Dr. Bernstein maintained, it was likely because his mother forced him to take swimming lessons the summer after he almost drowned. Or maybe it was the Florida phase at the Army Ranger School. As difficult as the entire 61-day course was, the seventeen days at Camp James E. Rudder, Eglin Air Force Base, in the swamps of the Florida Everglades, were hell on earth as far as Malone was concerned. Part of it involved small boat operations and expedient stream crossing training, which involved deep water, deep water chock full of various reptiles, many of which were deadly venomous snakes. Malone didn't particularly like snakes either, but at Eglin, poisonous snakes were nothing but an afterthought compared to being in rushing water that was invariably always over his head in depth. At least to himself, he admitted to his water phobia back then, but he could control the fear and remain operationally effective. Still, the day his class left Eglin and moved on to Utah for the Desert phase was one of the best damn days of his life.

"Are you still there?" Bachmann asked.

"Huh?" he said. "Oh, yeah, yeah, I'm still here."

"So, no surfing?" she asked.

"No," he said. "Maybe another time. I was up late and learning to surf is just not something I feel up to this morning. But thanks for the invitation."

"Okay," she said. "Hey, how about this? Just come watch from the beach. Then afterward, we can talk, grab an early lunch. Mostly, I just thought maybe we could get better acquainted."

"Shit," Malone thought. *"She just will not give it up."*

"Yeah, okay, I guess," he said. "I can do that."

"Jeez, don't sound so eager," she said. "If you aren't up for it, just say so."

There it was again, that edge in her voice that had noticed yesterday. The fleeting impression of that menacing look lurking just beneath the surface came quickly back to his mind. She might be a cop, but she was still a woman and obviously one who wasn't happy when made to feel she wasn't getting the same level of interest she was giving.

"No, no," he said. "Not that I'm not up for it. I was up late, um, out late, and I didn't get much sleep. But I'm good. It's a great idea. I'll come watch, and we can grab lunch after."

"Great," she said, sounding cherry again and pleased.

"So where?" he asked.

"I could pick you up," she said.

"Oh no," he said. "I just woke up. I need to shower and get a cup of coffee. Just name the place, and I'll meet you."

"Okay," she said. "Well, I was thinking Leo Carrillo Beach Park. I expected you surfed but, of course, did not know on what level. It consistently has a great break, but it's good for surfers of all levels."

"Yeah, okay," Malone said. "I know it. It's like an hour from my apartment, so with a shower and coffee, let's say we meet at around nine."

"Awesome," she said. "See you then."

Bachmann clicked off and left Malone with his thoughts.

First, he thought, *"What the hell was that all about?"* And then, *"Maybe Reyes was right. Maybe she wants to get in my pants."* And then, *"Why didn't I say no? I have stuff to do today, damn it."*

Wearily, he forced himself to get out of bed and realized he was still wearing his work clothes from the day before.

"Shit, I have to stop drinking so much," he said aloud.

Malone stripped off his clothes and tossed them on the floor of the bedroom closet. Then he padded down the hall to the bathroom, stepped in the shower, and turned on the faucet. After standing beneath the showerhead for about fifteen minutes, letting the water run off his head and down his body, he felt almost human again. He turned off the water, stepped out on the mat, and dried himself with a towel.

After shaving and brushing his teeth, he walked back to the bedroom and dressed in a pair of board shorts and a tank top. He put on some sneakers without socks and tied the shoelaces. On the way out, he grabbed his Dodger's ball cap off a small table beside the door and put it on. He walked down the flight of stairs to the ground floor, to the parking lot and into the sunshine. He got into his three-year-old Toyota Camry. It wasn't flashy, but after the alimony payments, it was all his budget would allow. At least it was dependable transportation. He retrieved his Ray-Bans from the dash, turned the key, and drove out of the parking lot.

Malone pulled into the drive-thru lane of a coffee shop with the familiar white and green color scheme a few blocks from his apartment. After grabbing a Venti Americano with an extra shot, he drove another couple of blocks on Hollywood Boulevard before making a left and hitting the on-ramp to the 101. Then he started the 60-minute drive to Leo Carrillo State Park. He sipped the strong coffee as a drove along, wondering what Bachmann had in mind for the day.

6

Getting Acquainted

It was nearly nine o'clock when Malone turned off the Pacific Coast Highway onto the Leo Carrillo Beach Park access road. He found a parking spot, locked up the car, and set out for the beach. He knew little about surfing. But based on the number of surfboards on the water, he assumed it must be a good place.

He didn't know if Bachmann had arrived before him. If she wanted to get some surfing in, he guessed she was probably already out on the water. It simply made sense that if the actual goal behind the invitation had been to get better acquainted, she would likely have arrived early to surf before he got there. He staked out a spot on the beach and settled in to wait. He expected she would find him when she was ready. After all, it was her meet up.

Malone thought about the Anderson murder while he waited. He mentally started building a suspect list. It significantly stunted the process that he knew little to nothing about Anderson's social and familial connections. He needed to learn a great deal more before he could develop a viable suspect list. Malone knew the statistics behind female homicide victims.

He knew, for instance, that strangers killed only about ten percent.

That was another knock against the botched burglary theory, followed by the original investigator. While the scenario was possible, compared to other theories, it was statistically improbable. Women were most usually murdered by people they knew. A family member or intimate partner killed around sixty-four percent of female homicide victims. Of that percentage, about twenty-four percent died at the hands of a spouse or ex-spouse. A boyfriend or girlfriend or former intimate partner, accounted for nineteen percent of the murders of woman. And another family member killed about twenty-one percent of the victims. Of the remaining twenty-six percent of female homicide cases, others the women had known, such as employers, co-workers, friends, or neighbors, committed the murders.

The statistics always drove Malone's focus in a murder investigation. Mentally, he put the victim in the center of a circle. Within the circle, he placed the people the victim had known with the most intimate acquaintances closest to the victim and the least intimate acquaintances furthest away. Conceptually, he viewed it as a tiny solar system where the victim represented the sun with the victim's social and familial acquaintances and associates orbiting around him or her. The more intimate the connection, the closer the orbit. The less intimate, the more distant the orbit. He then started at the center of the circle and worked outward. Everyone the victim knew was a person of interest until eliminated from consideration as a suspect. He eliminated an individual only when he determined one or more of the three aspects of a crime that represented the summation of American criminal law didn't apply to them—means, motive, and opportunity.

Means referred to a person's practical ability to commit a crime, things like physical strength or demonstrative access to the type of weapon used. Motive referred to whether a person might have felt the desire to kill another. What benefit would a person gain from killing the victim? In training, Malone had seen lists of a dozen or more murder motives, but he knew that all of them fit one of four major categories—sex/jealousy, revenge/hate, money/greed, or the urge to safeguard a secret. All of those reasons were the fruits of emotion, which further supported the facts borne out by the statistics. Someone had murdered Mary Beth Anderson for one of those reasons, someone who knew her.

The sound of approaching footsteps crunching on the sand interrupted Malone's train of thought. He looked up and saw Bachmann, surfboard under her arm, and a big smile on her face, approaching. She looked even better in the red bikini she was wearing than she had in the tailored black suit she was wearing the previous Friday when he met her for the first time. She had it all—ample breasts, a flat stomach, curvy and perfectly symmetrical hips, and shapely, toned legs. The little, triangle-shaped patch of fabric at the front of the bikini bottoms left little to the imagination. He could also tell by the cut of the bottoms that if she were walking away from him rather than approaching, he'd see only a narrow strip of red material between her buttocks. Her hair still looked great, even wet, not something every woman could pull off. He had to admit. Reyes was right. Older or not, she was definitely hot.

"Hey Malone," she said.

"Hi, Vanessa," he said.

Bachmann turned the board upright and expertly jammed it into the sand so that it remained standing upright.

"How was the surfing?" Malone asked.

"Awesome," she said. "Sorry I'm late, but I was catching some great waves. Hey, my stuff is just over there. I'll grab it and be right back."

Malone watched as she walked away. The sway of her hips seemed slightly exaggerated, perhaps for his benefit. He visually verified the narrow strip of red material between her buttocks that he had expected to see. About a hundred feet away, she stopped, bent forward, and pull a towel from a beach bag she used to dry her hair. She remained bent at the waist for another long moment while she dug through the bag and then stood upright and put on a pair of sunglasses. Then she scooped up the beach bag and walked back towards him with the towel over her shoulder. Vanessa dropped the bag on the sand next to him, unfurled the beach towel on the sand, and then sat down with her legs crossed, facing him.

"So, how's it going?" she asked.

"Good," he said. "I was a little tired when I woke up this morning, but had coffee on the way over and feel a lot better now."

"Nice," she said. She leaned over and patted him on the upper thigh with her palm and then let the hand linger there for a moment. It felt cool against his warm skin.

"I'm so glad you came," she said. "I enjoyed our chat Friday, and well, just thought you were an interesting guy I'd like to get to know better."

"In what way?" he asked with a grin.

She smiled broadly and removed her hand from his thigh.

"Well," she said. "I've always got my eyes open for talented investigators to add to Special Assaults Section. And we have an opening right now."

"So, you invited me here for an impromptu interview this morning?" Malone asked.

Bachmann's smile broadened.

"Well, maybe that was part of the reason," she teased. "But honestly, I made some calls and checked you out Friday afternoon after the meeting. What I learned impressed me. You have an admirable case clearance track record and an excellent reputation as an investigator. You seem the exact type of detective I enjoy having in my unit. And I think you would be a great fit."

"I'm flattered, of course," Malone said. "But I'm not sure I want to live under the PAB microscope any longer than I have to. I'd like to get back to Hollywood Division."

"I'd still appreciate it if you would consider it," she said. "You're going through a bit of rough patch now with the shooting incidents, but that will pass. With all the 'hands up, don't shoot' bullshit going on these days, every OIS gets intense scrutiny from the press, the public, the feds, and the asshole activist agitators. It's no surprise that LAPD and every other law enforcement agency in the country are in full-on cover their asses mode. Spending a year, maybe two, in special assaults could be exactly what you need to weather the storm career-wise. Your talent is just being wasted in the cold case section. You would work on active cases again."

"Okay," he said. "I'll think about it, but no promises."

"That's all I'm asking," she said. "Just consider it. Who knows? You might find you like working cases in special assaults. Maybe you would decide you don't want to go back to division, and honestly, building an exemplary reputation in special assaults could be an eventual stepping stone to Homicide Special."

"It's something to think about," Malone agreed.

"So what did you and Reyes get up to on Friday after I kicked you guys out of the conference room?" she asked.

"We spent a little time on the case Reyes spoke about," he said. "We had nothing else going, so it was the only game in town until your meeting finished, and we could get back to work on the files."

"So, did you come to any conclusions as far as the viability of reopening it?" Bachmann said.

"Nothing definite," Malone said. "It's honestly only a gut feeling now, but there is a lot about that case that seems weird to me. Reyes feels the same. I don't like unanswered questions, and there are a lot of them in that case. If it were my call, then yes, I'd re-open it. But Turner has given gave us strict guidelines to go by. So far, we have found nothing that would convince him it's worth re-opening."

"Well," she said. "You know my opinion on the subject. As a supervisor, just like Jim Turner, I must look at the big picture, things like the best and most efficient use of our finite resources. I can't imagine an upside to delving into a case almost twenty-five years old. Hell, the killer may have died or they're already incarcerated for some other crime. You know? Like the one case, you guys cleared where the guy died in prison, serving time for another offense that Reyes mentioned. Technically, the Elizabeth Short murder is still an open case, but we won't see anyone reopening that one."

"Well, the case Reyes and I are looking at isn't nearly as old as The Black Dahlia," Malone said with a wry laugh. "But I see your point, at least looking at it from a supervisor's perspective. But to me, it represents a challenge, and I love a challenge. I'm confident that Reyes and I could clear that case if we could pursue it. I'm sure of it."

"But there is another thing you have to consider. You're not the subject of official disciplinary action, of course, but based on what I know of the circumstances, you are under a cloud at the moment. You said there were some weird things about the case. And who knows why? But it isn't exactly rocket science to figure that maybe someone somewhere in the command structure may not want old bones dug up by revisiting that case. As an example, you might step on some toes you don't want to be stepping on. Rocking the boat, so to speak, you know? That's not something that would be a brilliant career move right now."

"So, what you're saying is someone in the department might have covered up something they don't want exposed?"

"Well, I didn't mean something as sinister as someone covering up something in a criminal sense."

"Then what did you mean?"

"Well, just as an example," she said. "Let's for a moment assume that the original detectives totally screwed up, that they missed something they shouldn't have, maybe out of negligence, incompetence, or plain old laziness. It wouldn't be good for the LAPD for something like that to surface, to come to the attention of the press and the public. Like it or not, public relations are as important these days to the LAPD as good police work. We must have the trust and support of the community, or our job gets that much harder, and it's already tough enough. There are political realities that a bureau level detective just doesn't see or understand because they are things dealt with far above his pay grade."

"So, you think we should just drop the case, then? Drop it on the chance there may be some dirty LAPD laundry involved. Walk away even if we feel there might be evidence we could find that would justify reopening it?"

"I'm saying I can't imagine an upside for you and Reyes and your respective careers from pursuing a case that old," she said. "I think you have to consider what is in your best future interests and the best interests of the department."

"So, we sweep it under the rug and deny a victim justice for the good of the LAPD?"

"Look, Ben, the LAPD needs no more scandals or any more federal oversight. And the city needs no more civil lawsuits. The lawsuit filed in connection with your last shooting incident is a big part of the cloud I mentioned that you have hanging over you at the moment."

"But that lawsuit is bogus. I did nothing wrong."

"I'll be honest here, Malone. I believe you did nothing wrong. But people's perceptions are their reality. That you have done nothing wrong isn't the perception some people in the department have. So the reality is you're on something of a bubble here. If you go rocking the boat or stepping on someone's toes now, even though you may have the best and most honorable of intentions, you could find yourself out of the LAPD. The same goes for Reyes, who I understand has his own little dark cloud to contend with."

"Still, it just seems wrong to turn a blind eye, even in the interest of self-preservation," Malone said. "If there was an intentional cover up going on with this case, an active attempt to suppress the truth, I'm not sure I'd even want to continue as part of an agency that would condone something like that."

"I applaud your ethics, Malone. I really do. And I admire that you've remained so idealistic when most of us lost all that after just a few years on the street. But you need to grow up. I don't think you're looking at things realistically here. That's all I'm saying."

"Yeah, I get it. I just don't particularly like it. It makes me feel like I need a shower just thinking about the possibility that what you've said might be true."

"Well, that's enough shop talk," Bachmann said, smiling. "Tell me more about you."

"Not much to tell. We've already covered my military background and time on the job."

"Yes, but I know nothing about your personal life. Married? Girlfriend? Kids?"

"None of the above. I was married once, but not anymore. We divorced. And I'm not seeing anyone at the moment. I haven't been looking, frankly, because I'm still a little emotionally drained after the divorce thing. Not that I was unhappy about the divorce. It was unavoidable. But my ex-wife made things way more difficult and bitter than they had to be. Thankfully, there were no kids involved."

"So, any curiosity about my situation in that regard?"

"Well," he said. "Obviously, you're a Latina, and your last name isn't one I associate with a person of your heritage. I assumed it is your married name."

Bachmann laughed.

"Yes, accurate enough. It is my married name. The most recent one."

"So, you are married?" he asked.

"Sort of," she said.

"How can a person be sort of married?" he asked.

"I'm married, but things have been pretty rocky for quite a long time," she said. "So, we separated three months ago, and I don't expect we will reconcile. This marriage is number two for me. I married for the first time during my second year on the job. It only lasted a couple of years. So, guess I'm headed for my second divorce."

"What happened this time, if it isn't too personal?" he asked.

"He wanted children," she said. "As a lot of women have done, I made my career my top priority before I thought much about things like marriage and having children. Ironically, just about the time I married my husband, and we decided it was time to start a family, a doctor diagnosed me with cervical cancer. I had surgery, chemo, and radiation. I beat it, and after five years of complete remission, my doctor has declared me cured. But the downside to all that was I couldn't have children. My husband took it very hard. We adopted a daughter, and she's an amazing kid, but I guess she has never been enough for him. So we started drifting apart, as people often do in such circumstances. Then I found out he was cheating on me. So we separated."

"Sorry to hear that," Malone said. "I can imagine how hard all that must have been."

"Yes, but I've always been a forward-looking person," she said. "I don't dwell on the past."

"Great outlook," Malone said. "I guess I haven't mastered that approach myself."

Bachmann put her hand back on his thigh, allowing her palm to slide down his inner thigh and then up a little higher toward the point where his thighs met at the apex.

"So, can I ask a personal question?" she said.

"Sure," he said. "I'm an open book."

"Okay," she said. "It's something I need to know the answer to before I commit to the other reason I invited you to meet this morning. Obviously, I have some years on you. Quite a few, I guess, if we're honest about it. Here's the question. Could you see yourself getting involved with someone my age?"

She moved her hand further up his inner thigh until it reached the apex.

"If you mean do I find you attractive, then yes, it's probably obvious at this point that I do," Malone said. "But I suppose I need you to define what you mean by getting involved."

"Well," she said. "I'm not talking about genuine commitment at this point. As you now know, I've tried marriage twice. So I'm not looking for husband number three at the moment. But I'm going to be really forward now and tell you what I am looking for. You're an attractive guy. I like attractive guys, and I like great sex a lot. What I'm looking for is a guy I find attractive guy who finds me attractive and likes great sex too. I'm speaking of a mutually beneficial arrangement here with no strings attached beyond those we decide to tie."

"That sounds like a definition of involvement that could work for me," Malone said with a grin.

Bachmann gently squeezed before pulling her hand away and grinned wickedly.

"I hoped that might be the case when I saw you checking out my ass when I went to collect my stuff earlier," she said. Her voice had taken on a little huskiness.

"Oh, you saw that, huh?"

"Yeah, and just now I was hoping you weren't carrying a concealed weapon in there, but are just glad to see me."

"Oh no," Malone said with a laugh. "Do you realize how old that line is?"

Bachmann laughed too until she had to remove her shades and wipe her eyes. "Yeah, it's a paraphrase of an old Mae West line from a play she did in the forties. But trust me, I'm not old enough to have seen it."

"Good to know," Malone chuckled.

"Well, what about lunch?" Bachmann said. "Feeling hungry?"

"Yes," Malone said. "I could eat."

"Let's have lunch at my place," she said. "I live close by."

"Okay, works for me."

Ever the gentleman, Malone grabbed her surfboard while she collected her bag and towel. They walked together to the parking lot, and he helped her secure the surfboard to the rack on her red Honda SUV. He assumed red must be her favorite color, considering the vehicle and her bikini. She climbed in behind the wheel while he folded himself into the front passenger seat.

"I'll drive you back to pick up your car after," she said.

"After lunch?" he asked.

"Just after," she said with another laugh.

After a 10-minute drive, they pulled into the driveway of a small but tidy bungalow, off the beach but with the ocean only a couple of miles away. It was still Malibu, and it seemed a pleasant neighborhood. She pushed a button on a remote clipped to the sun visor, and the garage door opened.

"I'm just leaving it in the driveway since I'll be driving you back, but I want to get my board out of the sun," she said.

Malone helped remove the surfboard from the rack and then carried it inside the garage in her wake. Together, they lifted it and placed it on a rack attached to the wall. She led him to the door entering the house, pushed it open, and invited him inside. He turned and shut the door behind him.

As he turned back, she placed both hands on his chest and shoved him forcefully until his back was hard against the door. She grabbed his face in her hands and pulled it toward her, her lips hungrily seeking his. They kissed passionately for several minutes, her tongue invading his mouth and seeking his. Her lips were soft and warm, and Malone felt the familiar ache he hadn't felt in a long while.

He felt her fingers untying the laces of his board shorts. Then her thumbs slipped inside the waistband. Her hands moved down, causing the shorts to fall to his ankles. He wasn't wearing anything underneath. She pulled her mouth away from his lips, rested her forehead on his chest, and looked down.

"I guess you are glad to see me," she said, looking up at him, her wet lips curled into a mischievous grin. "So, let's have lunch after dessert."

Then Bachmann slipped down to her knees.

"Works for me," Malone croaked.

After the spur-of-the-moment foreplay, things progressed rapidly. Leaving a trail of hastily removed clothing in their wake, they were soon both naked in Bachmann's bed, making love for the first time. Malone meant to be gentle at the start, but she wanted no part of that. She preferred it raw, gritty, and rough. She was completely uninhibited and passionate, her excitement matching his own.

Malone thought the first time was amazing. The second time, he thought, was mind-blowing. Lying on his back, with her in his arms and her head resting on his chest, sweaty and spent after the second time, he thought about Reyes' words from Friday. Reyes, he thought, was only partly right. She hadn't shown him anything he hadn't ever imagined, but she had certainly shown him many things he had never experienced.

Afterward, they got up and showered together. Bachmann dressed in a pair of cut-offs and singlet, and Malone put his boardies and tank back on. She made them Caesar salads with grilled chicken for lunch, and they traded a few war stories, cop to cop. She laughed easily and often, which Malone found infectious. Then she told him she needed to drive him back to his car because she had to pick up her daughter.

When they arrived, they sat in her Honda and talked a while longer. She made him promise to give serious consideration to her offer of a transfer to her unit.

"How would that work, being involved with my boss?" Malone asked.

"I definitely want the involvement to continue," she said, smiling. "Do you?"

"Definitely," he said. "It was amazing being with you today."

"Then we'd just have to be discreet while at work, is all," she said. "No one needs to know about us."

"So we would have to sneak around," he said. "I'm not sure I like that idea."

"No, not sneak around exactly," she said. "But we can't advertise it. The department frowns on relationships between those of unequal rank. Department policy wouldn't allow you to work under my supervision if it became common knowledge that we were sleeping together. The reality is if we both want to continue what we started, and I want you in my unit, we have to be discreet. That's all."

"Sure, I get it."

They said their goodbyes, and Malone opened the door to get out. She grabbed a handful of his shirt and pulled him back in. When he turned, she leaned over and kissed him deeply.

"I can't see you tomorrow," she said. "Although I want to. Let's plan something for next weekend, though. Call me later."

"Okay," he said. "Sounds great."

He got out and closed the door. Bachmann waved, and he watched her drive away. He found he really liked her and looked forward to seeing her again.

7

Turning Over a New Leaf

Monday morning started vastly differently for Malone than had the previous Friday. Different like that between night and day. On the way home from the beach Saturday afternoon, he had found a barber and got the long-overdue haircut. The barber, following his instructions, cut Malone's hair the way he had formerly kept it during his army days. High and tight. A single strip of thick hair centered on top with the sides and back of his head buzzed with a short setting on the clippers.

He had then picked up some dry cleaning that had been languishing in the shop for weeks. After waking early Monday morning and showering, he dressed in a starched white shirt, a maroon-colored tie, and a freshly dry-cleaned conservative gray pinstripe suit. He left his apartment in plenty of time to grab a large paper cup of coffee from the shop near his apartment before getting on the freeway for the drive downtown. It was the house blend without a shot of espresso. He'd had plenty of sleep and didn't need the extra caffeine.

What a difference a pleasant weekend sometimes made. Malone felt a lot better about many things after having spent time with Vanessa Bachmann on Saturday. He had spoken to her by phone late Saturday evening and again on Sunday. She had said that her daughter would spend the night with a friend the following Saturday. So they had made plans to have dinner on Saturday evening. Afterward, maybe they would see a movie, or maybe they would do something else. Malone hoped it would be the something else.

The biggest change the previous weekend had brought was that Malone had not had a drink since Friday evening. That, in part, explained why he arrived in the PAB parking garage forty-five minutes early on Monday morning rather than twenty-five minutes late, as he had the previous Friday morning. He rode the elevator up to the fifth floor and walked directly to the conference room, carrying the rest of his coffee. He had beaten the boss to work. Turner's door was closed, but the blinds were open, and the lights were off. Reyes hadn't arrived either.

Malone lifted the file box from the floor and placed it on the long wooden table. Pulling the Anderson file from it, he set the coffee cup within easy reach, and then sat down at his end of the table. He opened the file and flipped through the pages of statements where Detective Myers had recorded the results of his interviews. He started reading them, one by one.

Sunday Malone had spent some time thinking about a couple of things. He had considered Bachmann's invitation to transfer to special assaults. That decision was relatively easy. He would turn it down. He truly didn't like the "under the microscope" vibe at the PAB, so the prospect of working long-term in a unit based there wasn't very appealing. Plus, the character of his current involvement with Bachmann made the idea of working for her in the unit she commanded completely untenable, as far as Malone was concerned. It simply would make things far too complicated.

Malone was not a man for lengthy reflection and rumination. When faced with a situation requiring a decision from him, he quickly defined the issues as completely as possible, given all the data available to him. Then he mentally ticked off the pros and cons of binary alternatives. Then he decided and went with the decision, never second-guessing himself. That approach had served him well, both during his time in the military and his time with the LAPD.

Considering Bachmann's job offer, he saw a lot of cons and only a few pros. He decided quickly and easily. He would weather the balance of his temporary assignment to the cold case unit and return to Hollywood Division when the brass finally relented.

He hoped Bachmann would understand. Even more, he hoped his decision would not upset the delicate balance of their budding relationship. So he would have to make her understand. He wasn't a headquarters kind of cop. And he needed to be on the mean streets, where the metal met the meat, as they used to say in the army. Far away from any limelight, political correctness, and budgetary concerns. That was the environment where a cop like Malone could make a difference, because it was the environment in which he excelled.

Malone had also spent a considerable amount of time thinking about the Anderson murder case over the weekend. He understood he had linked the two decisions in a way. Bachmann seemed to care about him, at least superficially. She had done her best to discourage him from pursuing the Anderson case because she obviously believed it was not in his best interests or the department's. She believed following that path could hurt his career and possibly embarrass the LAPD. And maybe from her supervisor's perspective, she really believed in the greater scheme of efficient deployment of resources, and that there was no real benefit to solving a 23-year-old homicide. She had said as much about the 10-year-old case that Malone and Reyes had already solved.

As far as Bachmann was concerned, his second decision would be an even harder sell than the other. But he had also made that one. The die was cast, and there would be no looking back for Malone.

He intended to work the case and find Mary Beth Anderson's killer, come what may. He had a keen, analytical mind and was supremely confident that he would succeed where Myers had failed all those years ago. Besides, what was the point of the LAPD throwing any resources at fielding a cold case homicide section if the department didn't want the old murder cases solved?

Malone had no way of knowing it, but his decision to go forward with the cold case investigation would turn out the most significant of the two, one that would prove dangerous and fraught with peril. Malone intended to pursue the case investigation on the books and out in the open, if possible. But if Lieutenant Turner refused permission for him and Reyes to reopen the case, then with or without Reyes' help, he would work on it off the books if that proved to be the only option.

Malone took out his memo book and pen. He jotted notes as he read through the witness statements. The first was that of Robert Thames, Mary Beth Anderson's husband, at least until the day she died. The identifying information in the file clarified that Mary Beth had chosen not to adopt her husband's last name. Not unusual in modern-day America. He knew she had been an orthodontist. Perhaps she already had an established practice when she met and subsequently married Robert Thames. A surname change might have confused things as far as her profession went. Or maybe she had simply been a garden variety feminist who saw taking a husband's last name as bowing to the pressure of patriarchal society. Or perhaps she just liked her maiden name better and didn't wish to give it up. Regardless, Malone wondered if the surname Thames, in this case, was heterophonic, like the River Thames in England. Brits pronounced the Thames as "Tims," a pronunciation counterintuitive to its spelling, rather than phonetically as "Thames."

Robert Thames had stated that he left for work in his wife's car a little before seven-thirty that morning. After he had dropped his wife's car off at a Van Nuys BMW dealership for servicing, a dealership employee had driven him to work as a courtesy. He had arrived at work and had a series of appointments with customers until leaving for lunch at one in the afternoon. He stated he had telephoned his wife at home after lunch to check on her and to see how she was feeling. But she hadn't answered. Since the answering machine hadn't picked up, he assumed she was sleeping because she always turned the machine on when leaving the house.

Thames had told Myers he left work at around five. Then that afternoon, he had stopped off at the dry cleaners and supermarket before arriving home at around six. A short time later, he had discovered his wife's body on the floor of the living room at their townhouse.

The next three witness statements were from interviews conducted by Myers that had obviously been the primary basis of excluding Robert Thames as a suspect in his wife's murder. At least it ruled out any possibility the husband could have killed her himself. There was no opportunity because the three witness statements provided Thames an ironclad alibi.

The coroner had estimated Mary Beth Anderson's time of death at between eight and ten o'clock the morning she died. In the first interview, the service manager at the BMW dealership, where Thames had taken his wife's car for servicing, stated that Thames arrived at the dealership at seven thirty-five that morning. He had entered the time on the service order. Thames then left the car at the dealership for servicing, and an employee had then given Thames a courtesy ride to work.

The second statement recorded an interview with a receptionist from Thames' place of employment, Pacific Bank & Trust in Van Nuys. At the time of the murder, Thames worked there as a loan officer. The receptionist said that Thames had arrived at the office at about fifteen minutes after eight, before his first scheduled appointment of the day with a bank customer that had been at eight-thirty. The receptionist also stated that Thames had similar appointments with customers until one o'clock in the afternoon when he had left for lunch with a co-worker, another loan officer.

The last of the three statements was from an interview with the co-worker who had gone to lunch with Thames. After lunch, the associate had dropped Thames at the BMW dealership to pick up his wife's car. Thames had driven directly back to work with his associate following.

Malone knew that a time of death was always an estimate. It was impossible for a coroner to fix an exact time. Based on many variables, an experienced pathologist arrived at a reasonable estimation of the time of death, usually given within a range of hours. The process was subject to error, especially if the pathologist overlooked some crucial piece of information. However, the estimated time of death certainly represented more than just an educated guess. Time of death was a scientifically derived opinion based on a totality of specific factors distinctive to each case compared with ordinary time factors attributed to pathological changes that occur in a human body at death. In Malone's experience, the time of death estimates given by pathologists were reasonably accurate.

While it may have been possible for Thames to have killed his wife before leaving home that morning, it seemed highly improbable. The witness statements had apparently satisfied Myers that Thames was on the way to his office or already there when some unknown suspect killed his wife.

Malone thought about the statistical data again. A spouse or ex-spouse killed twenty-four percent of female homicide victims. So despite Meyers' conclusion, Malone wasn't ready to rule out the husband just yet. He wanted to interview Thames himself first. Obviously, he wouldn't have the advantage that Meyers had, the opportunity to assess Thames' emotional state and behavior on the very day of the murder. But even twenty-three years after the fact, Malone believed he would get a read on Thames that would enable him to make up his own mind about Thames' innocence or guilt after speaking with him personally.

Reyes walked into the room carrying his own cup of coffee. Malone glanced up at the clock on the wall, eight o'clock. Right on time.

"Bro, outstanding," Reyes said. "You got to work before I did for a change. That is the first time that has happened since they assigned us to work together. And just look at you, dude. You actually look like an LAPD detective instead of a homeless person."

Malone laughed. "Yes," he said. "I turned over a new leaf."

Reyes looked at the file on the table in front of Malone. "Working the case already, I see."

"Yes, checking some details," Malone said. "I've been reading some of the witness statements."

"Which ones?" Reyes asked, removing his jacket and hanging it on the back of his chair before sitting down.

"The ones establishing the husband's alibi," Malone said.

"Yeah, I read those," Reyes said. "Pretty solid, I thought. You ruling out the husband?"

"Not until we've interviewed him," Malone said. "But given the time of death and the witness statements, I think it's unlikely the husband did it."

"I agree," Reyes said. "I don't like him for it, at least based on what is in the file."

"How was your weekend?" Malone asked.

"Excellent," Reyes said. "Which reminds me, bro, Saturday night, I ran into an old-timer at Van Nuys at a bar where we all hang out sometimes. He is a patrol sergeant now, but was a patrol officer back in the day when Myers was there."

"So you asked him about Myers' reputation?" Malone asked.

"Yeah," Reyes said. "It surprised me to hear what he had to say. He said Meyers was a squared away dude, a real straight arrow. According to my guy, probably one of the best investigators they had there back then."

"Interesting," Malone said. "Also, a little problematic. That kind of rep doesn't line up very well with what we know about his investigation of the Anderson murder. If it wasn't incompetence, it had to be something else that made him stick with a theory that even back then wouldn't have made much sense."

"Possibly," Reyes said. "But like we discussed on Friday, there were a lot of murders back in 1992. Van Nuys probably had its share. The caseload was probably worse than it is now. Maybe Myers had other irons in the fire that he thought had higher priorities than the Anderson murder."

"Could be," Malone said. "Makes me want to look up Myers and ask some questions."

"So, what's the plan for today?" Reyes asked.

"I want to get out to SID," Malone said. "I want to find out what they processed from the murder scene back then. Especially since all the physical evidence seems to have gone missing."

"Definitely," Reyes said. "When are we doing it?"

"This morning," Malone said. "Right after the weekly status meeting with Turner. We can get him to sign off on a request to process the DNA evidence from that murder with the sexual assault you found Friday afternoon. Then we can hand carry it out to SID."

"Yeah," Reyes said. "Gives us a good reason to go out to SID."

Less than an hour later, the six detectives permanently assigned to the cold case homicide unit drifted into the conference room and took seats around the table. Malone had put the Anderson file away when they started arriving. Reyes had moved down the table to sit beside him. A couple of minutes after the last detective had sat down, Lieutenant Turner walked in, shut the door behind him, and moved to the chair at the end of the table where Reyes worked.

Turner had paired the six permanently assigned detectives up into three teams. Malone and Reyes listened as each team took their turn to brief Turner on the cases they were currently working. After asking some questions and offering a few comments at the end of the briefing from the last team, Turner turned his attention to Malone and Reyes. Instead of allowing them to provide him with a briefing like the other teams had, probably because of their temporary assignment status, Turner instead asked questions.

"How many cases did you two review last week?"

"Seventeen, lieutenant," Reyes said.

"Only seventeen?" Turner asked. "It seems you aren't getting through them very quickly."

Tuner's tone seemed to suggest that he viewed Malone and Reyes as slackers. Malone didn't appreciate that and spoke up.

"The early part of the week, we were wrapping up the 10-year-old homicide we cleared. There were a lot of meetings last week. We didn't have optimum access to our workspace."

"We're pressed for space," Turner said. "The circumstances aren't ideal, but we have to make do. Still, I expect more production out of you both. So, from this point forward, when the conference room is unavailable, find desks out on the floor that aren't being used at the time and keep working on the files. This section has over 6,000 cases. I want to get maximum use out of you both while you're assigned here. I sure as hell expect over seventeen cases a week to get reviewed."

Turner placed his elbows on the desk, steepled his fingers, and leaned forward, awaiting a reply. When neither Malone nor Reyes spoke, he leaned back in his chair and then dismissed the other six detectives. They stood up and filed out of the room. The last in line closed the door on the way out.

Turner looked at Malone and Reyes, then continued. "To prevent any misunderstandings, allow me to review what you were told when you joined this section. Your primary responsibility is to review cases, to identify those with unprocessed DNA evidence and those that do not, and then to bring to my attention to those that do. In hindsight, it was probably a mistake to allow you two to work that 10-year-old case. I think it distracted you from your primary responsibilities. So for the duration, you will both confine yourselves to reviewing cases, not working cases. Are we clear?"

"Yes, sir," Reyes said.

"Crystal," Malone said.

"What resulted from the seventeen cases?" Turner asked.

Reyes answered. "Sixteen had no DNA evidence, and we returned them to the records division. The other, a case we reviewed Friday, concerns a homicide that included a rape. There is a rape kit that was never analyzed, evidently because of a backlog. We planned to ask you to sign a request for analysis, and we were going to walk the request through, out at SID this morning."

Turner asked a few questions about the case and then said, "No point in wasting the morning driving out to SID. Give me the file. I'll fax over the request. Then I'll assign the case to a team."

Reyes stood up. He walked over to the file box on the floor in the room's corner. Bending over, he thumbed through the files in the box, retrieved a file, and returned to the table. He placed the file on the table in front of Turner, returned to his chair, and slumped into it.

Turner flipped open the file, glanced at Reyes' notes, and then closed it. He stood up and left the room, leaving the door open.

Reyes looked ruefully at Malone. "There is no way the lieutenant is going to let us re-open the Anderson case, bro."

"Nope," Malone agreed. "Or any other case, it seems."

"So, now what?" Reyes said.

"We work on the files until lunch," Malone said. "We can drive out to SID then. He can't dictate where we choose to spend our lunch hour."

"Dude, after what he just said, he will have our asses if he finds out we're investigating that case," Reyes said.

"Then he better not find out," Malone said. "We'll forget about signing out a pool car and just use mine."

Reyes looked thoughtful. "I don't know, bro. I'm hoping to get out of here and back to Van Nuys. Sooner rather than later. I'm not sure challenging Turner's authority is a great idea. Maybe we should just keep our noses clean and do what he says. It shouldn't be more than another week or two before we're out of here and back at our divisions."

"If you're that worried about it, you don't have to help," Malone said. "But I'm not dropping it. To hell with Turner. He's a bean counter, just like the rest of the brass. All he cares about are budgets and numbers."

"Well, I'll ride along with you to SID," Reyes said. "I'm curious to see if they have anything. Maybe if we find something, then we can talk to Turner again and try to change his mind."

Malone nodded. He got up and grabbed the file box from the corner and set it on the desk. Both detectives pulled a stack of files and started reading. They worked steadily until 12:30, and then they left the PAB for lunch.

8

Evidence and Relationships

Malone exited the San Bernardino Freeway and swung the car into a parking space in the lot at the Hertzberg-Davis Forensic Science Center a little before one o'clock. He and Reyes went inside the building, a large, multi-floored, modern-looking concrete structure. They headed for the Forensic Science Center (FSD).

Construction of the regional crime laboratory state-of-the-art facility finished in 2007. In response to the increased emphasis on forensic evidence by the criminal justice system, SID had expanded dramatically by September 2015. That's when the department split into two entities: the Technical Investigation Division (TID) and the Forensic Science Division (FSD). FSD comprised the Questioned Documents, Serology/DNA, Trace Analysis, Firearms Analysis, Field Investigation, Quality Assurance, Toxicology, and Narcotics Analysis Units.

The detectives made for the centralized records department to make their inquiries. On arrival, a civilian clerk greeted them, an attractive Asian woman with long black hair and large brown eyes. Malone identified himself and Reyes, and then provided the clerk with the Anderson case file number. She input the information on her desktop computer.

"Sorry, detectives," she said. "FSD has processed no evidence from that case."

Malone said, "There was a swab of a bite wound done during the autopsy of the victim. If they have not analyzed the swabs, is it possible you would still have that type of evidence stored here?"

"No," the clerk replied. "No evidence gets directly booked here. It's only submitted here for analysis by the custodial agency. Once processed, we return the evidence to them. Since FSD has processed nothing connected with your case, no one ever submitted anything for analysis. The logical assumption is that since the coroner's office collected the evidence at autopsy, those swabs are probably still in the custody of the Los Angeles County Coroner. The evidence collection section there receives and manages all evidence collected that coroner cases generate from submission to final disposition."

"Okay, thanks for your help," Malone said.

"My pleasure," the clerk replied.

Malone and Reyes walked back to the parking lot, got into Malone's car, and drove away. They grabbed burgers and fries from an In-N-Out Burger restaurant before getting back on the freeway. Then they wolfed down lunch while sitting in the car before heading back downtown to the PAB. They arrived back in the conference room just before 1:30.

"Another dead end," Reyes lamented.

"Yes, but we got some useful information," Malone said. "If the medical examiner's office kept the evidence they collected, that's good news. It means that they won't just have the bite wound swabs. They should also have swabs of the blood smear on the VCR that we saw in the crime scene photos. And according to the report, they recovered one bullet from the body at autopsy. They might have even more evidence. So only what they booked into the property division went missing."

"So, we going to the coroner's office for lunch tomorrow, bro?" Reyes asked.

"No," Malone said. "I've got a mandatory appointment with a department shrink tomorrow afternoon. I'm taking the afternoon off for that. So I'll drive over to the coroner's office after the appointment. I'll let you know Wednesday what I find out."

"You still see a shrink in connection with the last OIS incident?" Reyes asked. "Dude, I thought that was over within a few weeks of the incident, a month tops."

"Yeah, tell me about it," Malone said. "Evidently not after incident number three during an eleven-month stretch. I've got mandatory bi-weekly appointments until they tell me otherwise."

Reyes laughed. "That sucks, dude." "But you plan for the coroner part of it sounds good, bro. A regular diet of burgers and fries in the car isn't really my idea of a satisfying workday lunch."

The rest of the afternoon passed unremarkably. No one disturbed their work, and by the end of the day, they had already well surpassed their production of reviewed cases from the previous week. They had worked through twenty-three files, identifying three that had unprocessed DNA evidence. They left the building at five, went their separate ways, and headed to their respective homes in the Los Angeles rush hour traffic.

* * *

The idea of stopping by a liquor store to get a fresh bottle of Jack Daniels tempted Malone, but he resisted. Instead, he stopped at a supermarket near his apartment and picked up something for dinner, along with a six-pack of beer in place of the bourbon.

After arriving home, he changed into a pair of jeans and a tee-shirt, opened a beer, and started dinner. He scrambled a pound of ground round in a skillet and placed the skillet on the stove to brown the meat. He chopped an onion and dumped it in the skillet with the meat. Meanwhile, he chopped lettuce, a tomato, and grated some cheddar cheese. Once the meat had browned, he stirred in chili powder and a cup of water. He stirred the mixture and lowered the heat to let it simmer. He arranged some hard taco shells on a cookie sheet and shoved the sheet into his preheated oven.

Once the water in the skillet had cooked off, he removed the skillet from the stove and spooned it into a bowl. After removing the taco shells from the oven, he filled them with meat, lettuce, tomatoes, and cheese. Then he placed the tacos on a plate, grabbed another beer from the fridge, and carried everything to the living room. He sat down, turned on the television, and found the Dodger game. The bottom of the first inning had just started. He watched the game while he ate dinner.

A few minutes before nine, Malone had cleaned the kitchen and loaded the dishwasher. He picked up the phone and returned to his living room chair. He muted the volume on the television and dialed Bachmann's number. She answered on the third ring.

"Hey Malone," she said. "I was wondering if you were going to call or if I'd have to call you."

"I just finished dinner and cleaning the kitchen," he said.

"Oh my," she said. "A man that can cook and clean. Be still my beating heart."

"Yeah, well, I'm not exactly a gourmet chef, but I get by," Malone said.

"So, how was your day?" she asked.

"Outstanding," he said. "Turner chewed on our asses for a while after the Monday status meeting."

"What?" she said. "How come?"

"He evidently wasn't any more impressed than you were with our clearance of that 10-year-old murder case," Malone said. "And also, he was less than impressed with the number of cases we had reviewed last week."

"Oh, I'm sorry to hear that, babe," she said. "But he is under a lot of pressure, I'm sure, with the thousands of cold cases he's saddled with. It probably never seems to get any better, only worse."

"He seems to believe we've been dogging it. So he restated our primary responsibilities, and more or less said we wouldn't be working cases at all, just doing the damn case reviews."

"All the more reason you should think seriously about my offer," Bachmann said. "There isn't any telling when they will allow you to go back to Hollywood. I'm confident I could get you out of the cold case section much sooner."

"Well, that's part of the reason I called," Malone said.

"You've decided already?" she asked.

"Yes," Malone said. "I truly appreciate the offer and the confidence you seem to have in me as an investigator. But I'm going to have to turn down the offer. I want to go back to Hollywood."

Bachmann was quiet on the other end of the line for several moments. When she finally spoke, he could hear the disappointment in her voice.

"I wish you would take a little more time to think about this," she said finally. "It's only been a couple of days, and honestly, I think it will be a big mistake to turn down the opportunity I'm offering you."

"I'm just not cut out for working under the scrutiny that comes with an assignment at the PAB," he said. "I'm good as a bureau detective. So I feel like I make a real difference there. It's what I'm best suited for."

"Well, I still think you're making a mistake," she said. "But it's your career."

"Thanks for understanding," he said.

"I didn't say I understood," she said. "Only that I'll accept your decision, even if I don't agree you've made the right choice."

"You will find someone who is a much better fit."

"Well, I won't pretend I'm not disappointed, but maybe it will make the other thing less complicated."

"Yes," Malone agreed. "That was something that weighed heavily on my decision. I don't want to risk losing that part of it."

"I'll admit I'm relieved to hear what Turner told you guys today," she said.

"What do you mean?" he asked.

"I mean, since he more or less put you guys on notice that you won't be working any cases, that should be the last nail in the coffin for that old homicide case. It has concerned me you two might do something foolish, like trying to pursue that investigation out of stubbornness, even though it doesn't come close to meeting the criteria to reopen."

"Frankly, Reyes and I haven't exactly decided not to continue looking into it," Malone said.

"I hope you're kidding," she said. "That would just be insane, Ben. You mean that you and Reyes are seriously thinking about challenging Turner's authority? You're contemplating disobeying a direct order?"

"If we drop it now, it might be another 23 years before anyone looks at that case again if anyone ever does," Malone said.

"Ben, you need to forget all about that case. Just ship that file right back to the records division," she said. "I'm telling you as a friend and as someone who cares about you. Digging into that old case could end up costing you and Reyes your jobs."

"I'm just not sure I can let it go, even if Reyes pulls out," Malone said.

"I think you must let it go. If you don't, I'm not sure we can continue what we've started."

"What?" he said. "How would my decision about that case affect our relationship?"

"If you continue trying to work a case after Turner told you officially that you will not work cases, then you will disobey a direct order. Turner is no idiot. He will eventually find out. Don't think for a moment he would let that slide."

"I get that," Malone said. "But that's all on me. Even if I end up in trouble at work, why would that impact on our relationship?"

"Because I have to think of my career," she said. "Who I associate with has a direct bearing on my reputation. I worked hard to get where I am, and I'm set on making captain before I pull the pin. If you get yourself jammed up and thrown out of the department, I couldn't afford to be associated with you. It would reflect negatively on me if people found out about us."

It was Malone's turn to go silent.

"Look, Ben," she said. "I'm sorry, but I'm just honest here. I'm trying to make you see what a mistake it would be to risk your career over an old case that you probably would get nowhere on, anyway."

"Maybe we should just cancel our plans for Saturday," Malone said. "If you're that worried associating with me would be such an embarrassment, then maybe we should just end things right now."

"Ben, don't be that way. I don't want to cancel Saturday, and I don't want to end things right now. Look, I care about you, and I'm only trying to stop you from throwing your life away with a crazy decision. I won't apologize for not pretending that wouldn't affect me if you did that or that it wouldn't negatively affect our relationship."

"I should go," Malone said. "I need to get some sleep."

"Ben, let's not leave things like this," Bachmann said. "Let's talk in person again first. I think you're just being stubborn and not seeing things clearly. Let's go for a drink after work tomorrow and talk."

"I can't," Malone said. "I've got a mandatory appointment with a department shrink tomorrow, so I'm taking the afternoon off. So I won't be there when you finish up."

"In that case, let's leave our plans for Saturday intact then," she said. "Don't just throw us away without a fight. Ben. We need to talk."

"Okay," he said. "We're still on for Saturday, and we will talk. But I've got to get some sleep now. Goodnight, Vanessa."

"Goodnight, Ben," she said.

Malone hung up the phone. Things had seemed so good just that morning. Now, not so much. He had another beer, all the while wishing it was bourbon. As bad as things seemed to Malone on Monday evening, things were about to take a turn for the worse.

9

Suspended

Malone had slept fitfully but was awake before his alarm sounded. He dressed for work, stopped for coffee, and still arrived at work fifteen minutes early. When he got to the conference room, he grabbed the Anderson file and copied down some names and contact information for some individuals he wanted to interview. He realized the information might be out of date. Over the years, addresses and telephone numbers would have changed. Some would have moved on to new jobs or perhaps retired since 1992. But it was a start. He had just finished when Reyes arrived for work.

Both men grabbed a handful of files and got to work, determined to complete the review of as many files as possible since Malone was working only a half-day. At just past ten o'clock, the first shoe dropped for Malone. His cell phone rang. He fished it out of his pocket and saw "City of Los Angeles" on the screen. He pressed the answer button and put the phone to his ear.

"Malone," he said.

The voice on the other end said, "Malone? Brad Fulmer, city attorney's office."

Fulmer was the assistant city attorney charged with defending the wrongful death lawsuit filed on behalf of the common-law-wife of the last suspect Malone had shot and killed.

Obviously, the city had the deep pockets, the sweet spot that ambulance-chasing shyster lawyers working on a contingency-fee-basis always aimed for. The bigger the damages if the plaintiff prevailed, the larger the fee the attorney received off the top.

Knowing a cop living in an apartment, driving an older model Toyota, and paying a hefty monthly alimony payment wasn't flush with cash, the plaintiff's attorney had naturally named both Malone and the City of Los Angeles as defendants in the lawsuit. With the city as a defendant, the city officials naturally would not trust the defense of the case to a lawyer chosen by Malone. Instead, the city attorney defended against the suit.

"I hope you've called with good news, Brad," Malone said. He knew that once the lawsuit went away, his circumstances were bound to improve.

After a pause, Fulmer replied. "No, Malone. I'm afraid not. It looks like we're going to trial."

"But the last I heard, they had nothing, and we figured the judge would dismiss the case," Malone said.

"Things have changed," Fulmer said. "A new witness has come forward."

"A new witness?" Malone asked. "A witness to what?"

"A witness to the shooting, Malone, the entire incident," Fulmer said. "It changes everything."

"Impossible," Malone said. "The patrol units that responded rounded up everyone in the vicinity. They only found three people who said they saw anything. Internal affairs interviewed them all and got nothing that contradicted my statement."

"This guy says he was sitting in a parked car across the street waiting for a buddy to get off work," Fulmer said. "He claims he saw Reid exit the convenience store and turn north. Then heard you shout Reid's name. He says when Reid turned toward you, you shot him twice. Claims the only gun he saw was yours and that you didn't identify yourself as a police officer. You just started shooting."

"He's lying," Malone said.

"We deposed him this morning, Malone. His testimony was very compelling. The guy described the scene, and he described Reid. Then he accurately described you and your partner down to what you were both wearing. He even described your gun and knew things that the LAPD never made public or released to the media. He certainly convinced me he must have been at the scene. And it gets worse."

"Worse?" Malone asked. "How?"

"He stated that after Reid had gone down, he saw you walk over to him before your partner made it around the building. Says he saw you bend over, remove something from Reid's waistband, and drop it on the ground beside the body."

"He's saying I staged the gun?" Malone asked. "That's crazy. Reid pulled the weapon. He was bringing it up when I shot him."

"I know your version, Malone," Fulmer said patiently. "I'm just relating the new witness' version."

"It's a frame job," Malone said. "Don't you see that? How much do we ever get from an eyewitness at a shooting scene? That's way too much detail. I can't explain it, but I know he's lying. Someone coached him, provided him all those details along with a different ending to the story that makes me look guilty."

"Believe me, Malone," Fulmer said. "I'd love to have evidence that's all true. The city is on the hook here for potentially a very large judgment if we lose this case. But we can't just claim liar, liar, pants on fire and have this all go away. We would have to prove he wasn't there, or that even if he was, he is lying about the key elements."

"So why is this guy just now coming forward after all this time if he's legitimate?" Malone asked.

"He claims he didn't know it was the police involved," Fulmer said. "Says it looked like an organized crime hit to him, and he got scared and drove away. He said he only came forward when he saw an ad the plaintiff's attorney published in the paper seeking witnesses to a police-involved shooting at the store he had parked across the street from. Says he contacted the attorney who convinced him it would be safe for him to come forward and tell what he saw."

"Yes, and he also probably learned it would improve his financial condition considerably if he came forward," Malone said. "Assuming that part of his story is even true."

"I just called to give you a heads up, Malone. This is bad. Bad for the city and terrible for you. Our problem is the potential financial liability exposure, but that's the least of your worries."

"What do you mean by that?" Malone asked.

"What I mean is I know enough about your financial circumstances that with a civil lawsuit, you're effectively judgment proof. It's not like you have a house or a bunch of stocks and bonds they could get at. But your real problem is going to get a lot worse when the DA gets wind of this new eyewitness."

"They cleared me on the criminal side," Malone said. "They can't charge me criminally now."

"That's not factually true, Malone," Fulmer said. "No court tried you and found you not guilty. The DA presented the evidence to the grand jury. They failed to indict. The DA then decided not to prosecute because he accepted your story that you acted lawfully and in self-defense. This new witness represents fresh evidence. The DA can take the case back to the grand jury or even just decide to file a criminal complaint against you. They never charged you in connection with Reid's death. You could very well end up facing a murder charge now. There is no double jeopardy involved."

"It's a setup," Malone insisted. "I told the truth. This is all bullshit."

"I hope so, Malone," Fulmer said. "I really hope so. But I've got to go now. Take care."

Fulmer ended the call, leaving Malone staring at his phone in disbelief.

"What the hell, bro," Reyes asked. "You look like someone just stepped on your grave. Did someone die?"

"Yeah, someone died," Malone said. "But that's not the worst of it."

Reyes pressed for details, and Malone summarized the phone conversation with Fulmer.

"Jesus!" Reyes said. "Who would set you up like that?" he asked.

"No clue," Malone said. "Unless that damn attorney manufactured the whole thing just to win the civil case."

"Damn lawyers," Reyes said. "Why don't they just stick with suing the pharmaceutical companies and driving the cost of medical care into the stratosphere for all of us?"

* * *

Bad news always travels fast. It didn't take long for the other shoe to drop for Malone. It dropped like an anvil on the head of Wylie Coyote in the old Road Runner cartoons. He didn't even have time to finish his conversation with Reyes. Lieutenant Turner appeared in the doorway, looked at Malone, and said, "Come with me."

Malone got up and followed Turner down the hallway to the elevator. Turner pushed the call button, and when the doors opened, they got in. Turner pressed the button for the tenth floor, and they rode up together in silence. Malone followed Turner to the office of the chief of police. As they entered the office, the secretary stood up, stepped to the inner door, opened it, and ushered them both inside.

Malone had never met the chief personally, but recognized him from the photograph he had seen on the first floor of the PAB. That he was the guy seated behind the enormous desk in the room was also what the police might call a clue that he was the chief. But the chief wasn't the only one in the room.

Also present were two other men Malone recognized. Seated on a couch was the Los Angeles County District Attorney, Raymond Burkett. In an overstuffed side chair across from him sat Nathan Martinez, the Los Angeles Police Protective League attorney. The latter had represented Malone during the various investigations into the shooting incident that culminated in the death of one David Allen Reid.

The chief told Turner and Malone to sit, and they did, side by side, on the couch next to the DA. The chief then turned to the DA and nodded. Malone assumed the nod was the signal he should begin.

Burkett leaned forward on the couch so that he could see around Turner and look directly at Malone while speaking.

"Detective Malone, it came to my attention this morning that a new witness to the David Allen Reid shooting incident has come forward. I've learned that this witness claims to have seen the entire incident from start to finish. His recollection of the events seems to differ substantially from the account provided me by the police department and that which is contained in your sworn statement."

Malone nodded his understanding. The DA continued.

"This new eyewitness testimony places me in a rather difficult position, Detective. My office is under a good deal of pressure at the moment. Pressure from the community, civil rights organizations, and last but not least, the U.S. Department of Justice. Pressure to prosecute any police officer deemed to have unlawfully used deadly force against a citizen, especially in an instance where the application of such force resulted in the death of a citizen."

Malone again nodded his understanding, prompting the DA to

continue.

"Can you explain why this witness's version of the circumstances of the death of David Allen Reid differs so substantially from your own, Officer Malone?"

Before Malone could even form a reply, Martinez spoke up.

"My client chooses not to make any statements or answer questions concerning this matter at this time on the advice of counsel."

"Very well," Burkett said. "Considering the recent developments, it pains me to inform you, Detective Malone, that I am compelled to file a criminal complaint against you under California Penal Code Section 187, specifically on the charge of Second Degree Murder. Do you understand?"

"My client understands the charge," Martinez said.

"Given the unique, dangerous circumstances a police officer would face if incarcerated in the county jail that an ordinary citizen would not face, after consultation with the presiding judge of the Superior Court of Los Angeles County, we have agreed to an alternative arrangement. Instead of the immediate delivery of a warrant for your arrest, I have arranged for you to surrender yourself to the Los Angeles County Sheriff at nine o'clock tomorrow morning. They will then take you immediately before the superior court for arraignment. If you enter a plea of not guilty, the judge will set bail. Do you understand the arrangements, Detective?"

Malone looked at Martinez. The attorney nodded to him, showing that he could answer.

"Yes, sir," Malone said. "I understand."

"Very well," Burkett said. "However, I must warn you if you fail to appear as agreed, the court will immediately issue a warrant for your arrest. Should that become necessary, the deal is off. If you must be located and arrested, once taken into custody, no special treatment will continue. You will become the same as any other criminal defendant."

"My client will appear as stipulated by the agreement," Martinez said.

With his part of the unpleasantness concluded, Burkett stood up. He nodded to the chief and walked out of the room. Everyone remaining then turned their attention to the chief of police.

The chief said, "Beyond your painfully obvious and unfortunate penchant for getting involved in fatal shooting incidents, you have a fine record, Detective Malone. I stand behind the integrity of the findings of the investigations conducted by this department into the circumstances of Reid's death. Personally, I feel you are innocent of any unlawful actions in connection with that incident. Personal feelings aside, however, given the gravity of the circumstances we face and the fact that the DA has charged you, I have no choice but to take certain actions. I'm placing you on administrative suspension pending the outcome of the legal matter. And I need you to surrender your badge and sidearm."

Malone stood up, pulled the Glock Model 23 pistol from the holster on his belt, and dumped the magazine. After ejecting the chambered round, and catching it in his hand, Malone laid the pistol, magazine, and single bullet on the chief's desk. Pulling the leather case containing his shield and identification card from his inside jacket pocket, he laid it on the desk next to the weapon.

"Your assigned place of duty for the duration of the suspension is your home address," the chief said. "Your duty hours will be from 8:00 a.m. to 5:00 p.m., Monday through Friday. You are not to leave your place of duty during duty hours except in the event of an emergency, medical appointments, or appointments with your legal counsel. During duty hours, you must always be available for contact by the department, whether in person or by telephone. For the duration of the suspension, you may not leave the County of Los Angeles for any reason without authorization from me or my designee. Do you understand the terms of your suspension as I've outlined them?"

"Yes, chief," Malone said.

"Questions?" he asked.

"No, sir," Malone said.

"Lieutenant Turner remains your supervisor. Should you have questions later, you can contact him by telephone," the chief said.

"Yes, sir," Malone said.

"Dismissed," the chief said.

* * *

Turner led the way out of the office, followed by Malone and Martinez. They walked single file down the corridor to the elevator. After pushing the call button, Turner turned to Malone.

"I know you have the appointment with the department psychiatrist this afternoon. That's department mandated, so you can keep the appointment. Call me for any future appointments so that I'm aware of your whereabouts. Same goes for any appointments with Martinez here away from your home."

"Okay, Lieutenant," Malone said.

The elevator arrived, and the doors opened. All three men got in and rode down to the fifth floor. After stepping out of the elevator, Turner turned to Malone.

"Good luck, Malone. Hope this all works out. For what it's worth, I think you're a good cop, and I'd be glad to get you back."

"Thanks, Lieutenant," Malone said.

The doors closed. The elevator continued its downward journey to the first floor of the building.

"Try not to worry too much, Malone," Martinez said. "We will find out about this new surprise witness and his story. This whole thing stinks to high heaven."

"Yes, putting it mildly, it sure does," Malone said.

The elevator arrived on the first floor. The doors opened. Martinez placed an enormous hand on Malone's shoulder.

"I'll meet you at the sheriff's office at nine in the morning, Malone," he said. "In the meantime, call me if you need anything."

"Thanks, Nate," Malone said.

The men shook hands, and Malone walked across the lot to his car in a daze, wondering what the hell had just happened. It was like a bomb had just gone off, and he was at ground zero.

10

Sara Bernstein

As he pulled out of the parking garage and drove away from police headquarters, Malone's mind was racing. He was searching for answers. How had things so suddenly gone to hell? He briefly entertained skipping the appointment with the shrink. Just as quickly, he dismissed the idea. She would be obligated to report it to the department if he didn't show up. Perhaps a minor issue compared to the problems he now faced. But he knew the last thing he needed now was more trouble of any stripe, minor or otherwise.

Malone took the westbound ramp to the I-10 towards Brentwood, specifically the Ronald Reagan UCLA Medical Center. Sara Bernstein's office was in a single-story medical office complex a couple of blocks west of the medical center. It was lunchtime, and traffic was heavy on the freeway. Still, Malone arrived a few minutes ahead of his scheduled appointment. He dumped the Toyota in the parking lot and walked into the office. He gave his name to the receptionist. She smiled and checked her computer to verify the appointment, smiled again, and asked him to take a seat. She picked up the phone and spoke briefly. A few moments later, an inner office door opened, and Bernstein appeared.

"Hello, Detective Malone," she said. "Come on back."

Malone stood up and walked to the door. He followed Bernstein down a short hallway and then into her office. He remembered being surprised when he had arrived the first time and hadn't found a therapeutic couch in the room—a couch like those often seen in the movies. There was a black leather couch in the room, but the type designed for seating, not for lying on. It seemed too short for that. There were two matching overstuffed leather chairs in the room, arranged so that they were facing. Dr. Bernstein had already sat down in one of them, her back to the window. She gestured to the other.

"Please have a seat, Detective," she said. "Make yourself comfortable."

Malone sat down in the chair facing her and leaned back, his forearms resting on the arms of the chair. The chairs were close together. His knees were almost touching hers. The doctor began the conversation.

"I'd like to thank you for coming in today and giving us time to go over some things," she said.

Malone assumed she intended the comment as an icebreaker of sorts to help him feel relaxed. She had said something different, but similar, during his first appointment.

"No problem," Malone said.

"So how has your day been, Detective?" she asked.

"Not great," he said.

"Really?" she asked. "Why? What has happened? You seem tense."

"It's not something I wish to talk about at the moment," Malone said. "It hasn't much of anything to do with the reason the department requires me to continue seeing you."

"I see," she said. "Still, it might help to talk about it to someone, and that is what I'm here for."

Malone watched as she jotted down something on the pad she held in her hands. She noticed he was watching her write.

"Don't worry about the note-taking," she said. "I simply write some things down so that I can recall the specifics of the things we discuss."

Malone nodded.

"I understand that you presently work at the department's cold case homicide unit," she said.

"Yes, that's correct," Malone said. Technically not true at the moment, because the chief had suspended him, but he didn't feel like getting into all that with the shrink.

"Could you tell me a little about what you do there?" she asked.

"Sure," he said. "I read old unsolved homicide cases all day, looking for those where there is unprocessed DNA evidence the crime lab might analyze that could provide leads to a suspect."

"How do you feel about your job?" she asked.

"I don't find it particularly interesting," he said. "I'd rather be doing what I was doing before, working cases in Hollywood."

"I'm just curious about something," she said. "Don't you feel it worthwhile to do what you are doing, perhaps helping to bring those to justice who, for years, I suppose have gotten away with a heinous crime?"

"I don't think there is anything wrong with the concept of working and trying to solve cold cases," he said. "It's just that my specific part in it doesn't involve working cases. It's only administrative work."

"So, if I understand you correctly, you feel the work is beneath you?" she asked.

"Not beneath me exactly," he said. "I'm just saying I don't think the work I'm doing requires my training and skills as an experienced investigator. I think a record clerk could do what I'm doing just as effectively."

"I see," she said. "So, you feel your potential isn't being fully used."

"Something like that," Malone said.

Bernstein made more notes on the pad.

"What sense do you make of the reason you're here today, Mr. Malone?" she asked.

"I'm here because the department requires me to be here," he said.

"All right," she said. "But why do you feel the department has decided you need to be here?"

"I think they feel there is a problem, given that I was involved in three fatal police-involved shootings in less than a year. I think that made the brass feel uncomfortable, and they felt they had to do something. Sending me to a shrink was doing something."

"How does that make you feel?" she asked.

"Annoyed," he said. "Frankly, I think this is a waste of time. There isn't any problem here that needs solving. I have done nothing wrong. I've just done my job. Three armed criminals provoked violent confrontations with the police, with predictable results. So they got what they got."

"But can't you see things from the perspective of your superiors?" she asked. "Couldn't it be that there is a basis for finding it at least a little alarming when one police officer seems to use deadly force again and again, almost routinely? Doesn't it make sense they might view the circumstances as problematic?"

"If you choose to interpret it that way, then sure," Malone said. "But the flaw in that interpretation results from looking at it from the perspective of all three incidents at the same time. As if they are linked when that's not the way it was."

"How do you mean?" she asked.

"They were three separate incidents involving three different individuals. The only thing they have in common is that three separate individuals in three separate circumstances made similarly poor decisions with similarly negative consequences for each of them."

"How does it make you feel when you think about being responsible for taking the lives of three men?" she asked.

"I don't really think anything about it," he said. "Do I take any satisfaction in it? No, of course not. I'm not a psychopath or sociopath. Killing those individuals doesn't make me feel bad about myself or feel guilty. I don't have any trouble sleeping at night because of them. In the first place, I didn't set out to kill any of them. I defended myself in all three situations. That's all. They were all armed. They each tried to use their weapons to shoot me. So I simply reacted to the threats, as the department trained me to react. I used my weapon to stop them from using their weapons against me. I aimed center mass as I learned at the academy, and fired. Unfortunately, each of the individuals died of their wounds. End of story."

"I see," she said. She scribbled some notes and continued. "I understand you served in the military before you became a police officer. The army, wasn't it?"

"Yes," Malone said. "I was in the army for six years before joining the LAPD."

"Can you tell me a little about what you did in the army?" she asked.

"I was an infantry officer, assigned to a Ranger battalion," he said.

"Did you see action in the army?" she asked.

"Yes, I did a couple of tours in the Middle East," he said.

"Were you at genuine risk of danger or injury back then?" she asked.

"Yes, sometimes," he said.

"Did you see things in battle, for example, things like other soldiers being hurt or killed in action?" she asked.

"Yes," he said. "A few times."

"Were you ever forced to kill or hurt enemy combatants?" she asked.

"Yes," he said. "That's what happens in war, doctor. You try to kill the enemy. They try to kill you."

"Do you view the dangers and risks involved in working as a police officer in similar ways to the experiences you had as a soldier?" she asked. "Does it sometimes seem a little like a war zone? Does your work on the streets sometimes remind you of the things you experienced during your combat tours?"

"I suppose there are certain similarities," he said. "But of course, it isn't the same. There are no IEDs on the streets of LA, at least not yet. You don't have to worry constantly about snipers. Not everyone is out to kill you. But, yes, sometimes you must deal with desperate individuals who don't want to be arrested, who maybe have already been to prison and who are determined not to go back."

Bernstein made more notes on the pad.

"Is it upsetting when you experience something as a police officer that somehow reminds you of things you saw or experienced on the battlefield?" she asked.

"That rarely happens," Malone said. "Those are two different environments. They aren't actually all that similar."

Bernstein looked thoughtful; she jotted down a few more notes.

"Doctor, would you mind if I saved us both a lot of time?" Malone asked.

"How do you mean, Mr. Malone?" she asked.

"It seems pretty clear to me from your line of questioning that you think I might suffer from PTSD because of my army experiences, and that PTSD may explain why I shot and killed three individuals. That simply isn't the case."

Bernstein nodded, "Please continue, Mr. Malone."

"There are some smart people in the army. They have shrinks of their own. It's a fact that after you leave a combat zone, the army gives you a psychological battery aimed at predicting whether you suffer from or may later suffer from PTSD. A psychologist interprets those test results and then talks with you. I got a clean bill of health twice. After both tours, I was told there were no indications that I suffered any negative psychological effects from my combat experiences. But to be on the safe side, they always advised me to be mindful of certain symptoms that might show problems later. The army even provided me with a list of things to watch for: feeling upset by things that reminded me of what happened in combat. Having nightmares, vivid memories, or flashbacks of some event that made me feel like it was happening all over again. Feeling cut off emotionally from others. None of that has ever applied to me."

"You're correct in assuming I was checking for symptoms of PTSD, Mr. Malone," she said. "Not diagnosing, as you seem to assume, but checking. I don't approach any patient with any preconceived notions that there is anything wrong with them psychologically. But especially in cases like yours, referred by a police agency because of serious incidents like those you've been involved in, my job is to investigate and rule out the existence of any psychological defects."

"So how many appointments is it going to require for you to arrive at a decision, doctor?' he asked.

"There isn't any specific number of appointments or sessions involved," she said. "I just know when I know. Partly, it depends on how open a patient is with me and how willing he or she is to talk candidly with me."

"Can I ask you a personal question?" Malone asked.

"Certainly, you may ask Mr. Malone," she said. "But of course, depending on how personal the question is , I may choose not to answer."

"Fair enough," Malone said. "I easily imagine that it would be unethical for a therapist to date a patient she was treating. But assuming a patient needed no therapy and the doctor-patient relationship ended, would it still be unethical or inappropriate for the therapist to date the now former patient?"

"That doesn't seem a patently personal question unless, of course, you are specifically asking about my opinion regarding the ethics of dating a former patient of mine," she said.

"Yes, that's what I'm asking," Malone said.

"I'm just curious about something here," she said. "Are you interested in dating me, Mr. Malone? Is that the motive behind the question you've posed?"

"Perhaps," Malone said cautiously.

"Do you find me attractive, Mr. Malone?" she asked. "Sexually attractive? Do you think you have, on some level, developed feelings of affection toward me?"

"Do you always answer questions with questions, doctor?" Malone asked.

"Sometimes," she said. "But only because I'm trying to get a complete picture of the question posed, including the motivation behind the question. Did my questions make you feel uncomfortable?"

"Maybe a little," he said.

"You needn't feel uncomfortable," she said. "I asked because if you felt some sexual attraction and perhaps feelings of affection toward me, it's nothing to be ashamed of. It is quite normal and frequently happens with patients. A patient even sometimes falls in love with his therapist. It is far more common than you might suspect for patients to develop romantic feelings for a therapist."

"Seriously?" he asked.

"Yes," she said. "And there is nothing shameful or crazy about it. Therapists expect it will happen from time to time. Perhaps it's a pattern in your life that you always fall in love with people who are circumstantially or emotionally unavailable, and a therapist is just another example of one of those people. Or perhaps you have never had the sincere warmth of unconditional acceptance from someone. The first experience of that can feel intoxicating to you. That makes perfect sense since, as human beings, we all need someone to care about and who accepts us. There is a term in psychoanalysis that refers to a patient's feelings about his or her therapist. It's called transference when a patient's feelings for a former authority figure get transferred onto a therapist. The feelings feel very real to you. I'd never attempt to invalidate them. But neither would I ever consider reciprocating them."

"Perhaps none of what you just said really explains it," he said.

"Then what do you feel explains it?" she asked.

"Maybe at the root of the issue, an unresolved Oedipal complex motivates my feelings, and that produces dynamic sexual repression mixed with a little psychosomatic erectile dysfunction," he said.

"God, I hope not. That could require years of therapy to overcome." Bernstein stifled a giggle. "Are you poking fun at psychoanalysis, Mr. Malone?"

"Maybe a little," he said. "But, on a more serious note, you wouldn't ever consider dating a former patient?"

"It is crucial to understand that romantic relationships are always inappropriate between therapist and patient, even a former patient. It is completely the responsibility of the therapist to uphold the boundary. Therapy is largely one-sided, unlike most other relationships in life. By sharing your emotional experiences and sometimes secrets with me, you are opening yourself up and being vulnerable, which is crucial in getting the most out of the therapeutic process. If, however, as your therapist, I was to take advantage of that vulnerability and reciprocate in any way the feelings you've expressed, it would be a very clear ethical violation, whether you are a current patient or a former one. I'm flattered, of course. I don't see the harm in admitting that I find you both an intelligent and physically attractive man, the type of man I might be interested in dating under other circumstances. But to answer your question directly, no, I wouldn't consider seeing a former patient socially because it would be unethical."

"That's disappointing," he said.

"Perhaps," she said. "But I feel it is very positive that you brought up the topic. I can certainly imagine that the idea of professing an attraction for your therapist is far easier said than done, and since you dared to do it, I think it's important for us to discuss it openly. So I am willing and able to help you explore those feelings in the sessions, as I believe you will probably grow through the process and learn from it. Hopefully, you won't think me narcissistic, but candidly, I was already aware of your feelings. I am a therapist, but I'm a woman above all else and am as intuitive as the next woman. Also, I've noticed how you have looked at me during our first session as well as how you've looked at me today. And of course, what parts of me you've been looking at. So what you've shared today did not come as any surprise. I'm neither dismayed by it nor offended."

"I'm happy about that part of it, at least," he said. "That I haven't offended you, I mean."

"We can, of course, talk about this more in future sessions, but I see our time today is almost gone, so let's wrap up," she said. "I am satisfied that there is no underlying, sinister pathology behind your involvement in the unfortunate incidents that ultimately brought you to me. I'm ready to recommend to your superiors with no reservations that they return you to your normal duties. That said, it's clear that you're facing some problems today that you find very stressful. It's equally apparent that you aren't ready to talk to me, or perhaps talk to anyone about those problems at present. The LAPD has already paid me for four sessions, so two remain. While they won't likely make it mandatory for you to keep the other two appointments once they receive my report, I'd encourage you to return voluntarily for the remaining sessions. If you decide to do so, you will no longer be an involuntary but a voluntary patient. Thus, I will have no ethical responsibility to inform your superiors that you are still seeing me. And, of course, whatever you choose to share with me will always be completely confidential and protected by the doctor-patient privilege.

We've already scheduled the sessions, so you need only show up at the appointed time in two weeks if you decide to continue."

"Thank you, doctor," he said. "No promises, but I'll seriously consider coming back."

They stood up, shook hands, and Bernstein escorted him back to the waiting area, where they said goodbye.

Malone admitted to himself that he felt somewhat better after talking with Sara Bernstein. But despite her words, he felt the sexual tension and the chemistry between them. She had let down her guard at the end and was relating more to him as a woman than as a shrink. He couldn't help wondering just how committed she really was to her ethical views. But Malone knew he wasn't ready to give up on Sara Bernstein just yet.

11

Jane Kroft

Malone sat in his car in the medical office complex parking lot for several minutes, deciding what to do. Yesterday he had intended to pay a visit to the Los Angeles County Coroner's office after his shrink appointment. But that could be perilous now. It was two in the afternoon. Based on the chief's instructions, he assumed they expected him to go directly home and remain there until five o'clock. But if he did that, most of the staff at the coroner's office would have left work before he could get there and he wouldn't accomplish anything by going there later.

Finally, he decided. He would take the risk. If they caught him out, he could always claim he thought the terms of the suspension started the following day. After all, the chief had said, "Dismissed." He could argue that he interpreted that to mean they had dismissed him for the day. He started the car, backed out of the parking space, and pulled out of the lot. He jumped back on the I-10, eastbound this time towards downtown. Arriving downtown, he saw the Staples Center in the distance to the north as he passed over the 110. Traffic wasn't bad, by LA standards. He pulled into the parking lot of the Los Angeles County Medical Examiner-Coroner on North Mission Road at a little past three.

Malone had been there many times. Like most homicide detectives had he had been to the coroner's office to view autopsies. He went directly to the Evidence Control Section, where a civilian clerk greeted him.

"I'm Detective Malone, LAPD robbery-homicide," he said. "I'm working a cold case homicide from 1992 and need to check on what evidence is in custody here relating to the case."

He obviously looked and sounded like a cop. Evidently to the twenty-something female clerk, if it looks like a duck and sounds like a duck, you got a duck since she didn't ask to see a badge. She just typed in the case number he had given her and then picked up a phone and called someone who could provide the information Malone wanted.

The clerk related his request to someone on the phone and then hung up. She looked at Malone and said, "A criminalist will be here in a moment to help you, Detective." She then went back to what she had been doing before he had interrupted her. Probably watching the clock, wishing five o'clock would arrive so she could leave work for the day.

After about fifteen minutes, another civilian woman entered the reception area through an inner door. Although air conditioned against the Southern California summer heat, it wasn't as cold in the evidence section as in the other parts of the coroner's complex that Malone had visited in the past. But when the door opened, the familiar chemical odors that belied the function performed by the pathologists at the medical examiner's office wafted into the room where Malone was standing, leaning against the counter.

The second woman was older than the clerk he had spoken with initially, closer to mid-thirties. She wore a navy blue pantsuit with a violet-colored blouse beneath her jacket. She had a plain, but not unattractive oval-shaped face, with a prominent nose, wide-spaced and half-lidded gray eyes, and a small mouth with unsmiling lips. The woman parted her sandy-brown straight hair on the left and wore it longer than collar length. She looked serious and completely business-like.

"Detective Malone?" she said. It seemed more of a statement than a question.

"Yes, LAPD robbery-homicide," Malone said.

"Thought you were Hollywood Division," she said.

"Have we met?" Malone asked.

"Not really," she said. "I just recall seeing you at an autopsy once with your name on it, maybe around a year ago. I'm Criminalist Jane Kroft."

"Oh, I see," Malone said. "Yeah, I'm still permanently assigned to Hollywood, but at the moment I'm temporarily on loan to the robbery-homicide cold case homicide unit downtown. But anyway, good to meet you, Jane."

"Likewise," Kroft said. He wasn't sure if she meant it or not.

Kroft was carrying a file folder.

"Since I know you, I don't need to see your badge," she said. "But I need the badge number for the file."

Malone nodded and recited the number while she copied it on a printed form inside the file jacket. He was relieved she hadn't asked to see his badge since he didn't have it now, but a little uncomfortable with the fact that a paper trail of his visit to the coroner now existed.

"You were inquiring about case number 92-014387?" she asked.

"Yes, the victim's name was Mary Beth Anderson," he said.

"I wouldn't know," Kroft said. "We don't use names. We file and store everything by case number only here."

She looked at the documents in the file for a couple of minutes and then looked up at Malone.

"You wanted to know what evidence we still have in custody related to this case?" she asked.

"Yes," he said. "It's an old case. I found that there was stuff missing from the murder book. Specifically, there were no evidence logs in it. I've already got copies of the log from our property division on the evidence booked in there. So I wanted to touch base here to find out what the medical examiner collected in connection with the autopsy."

"I see," she said. "If you don't mind me saying, it's a little sloppy losing stuff connected with a homicide case, even an old one."

Malone decided she was a little smug already, so he certainly wouldn't tell her about the evidence that had gone missing.

"Well," he said, "it was just paperwork. You know how it is."

"No," Kroft said. "I don't."

She continued, "So you want to see the evidence?"

"That would be outstanding," he said.

"Okay, follow me," she said.

He followed her through the same door she had previously exited. They followed a long corridor, then made a right-hand turn into another and walked halfway down it. She stopped in front of a heavy door made of blonde wood with a small metal wire reinforced window in the top. It reminded Malone of the door to his high school chemistry classroom. She punched a series of buttons on the security lock keypad and then opened the door and walked inside with Malone in tow.

Kroft walked over to a large cage made of heavy wire that took up a good part of the large room they were in. She punched another series of numbers into another keypad, turned a handle, and swung open a gate made of a steel frame and covered in the same heavy gauge wire as the cage itself. Inside were long rows of steel shelving with five shelves. The bottom shelves were at floor level, and the top ones were just above eye level for Malone.

Malone followed Kroft down the narrow passageway between two rows of shelves. There, she examined labels that someone had affixed to the front edges of the shelves. She found one labeled "92-014387" on a middle shelf near the end of the passageway. Kroft pulled out a cardboard file box with a lid on it. Then she carried it to the end of the passageway and placed it on a stainless-steel table that was against the painted concrete block wall. After removing the lid and setting it on the table beside the box, she looked at a list in the folder she was carrying and then reached inside the box. She withdrew a small manila envelope, closed and sealed with evidence tape. On the tape were initials and a date.

"This is a .38 caliber projectile removed during autopsy," Kroft said. "It says here it's a hollow point projectile which mushroomed when it struck the victim and then lodged in the decedent's spine. I can remove it from the envelope, but if I do, you must reseal it with new evidence tape and write your initials and today's date on it to preserve the chain of custody."

"Unnecessary," Malone said. "You obviously run a tight ship around here, and I'll take your word for what's in the envelope. I just needed to know if it was here."

"Okay," Kroft said. "Next, we have the decedent's clothing removed at autopsy. One pair of women's panties and one tee shirt with traces of blood on it. She removed a larger manila envelope, also sealed with evidence tape and held it up."

"Okay, no need to open it," Malone said.

Kroft pulled a large folded butcher paper package from the box.

"This is a paper bindle containing trace evidence at autopsy that fell off while the decedent's clothing was being removed," she said.

"Noted," Malone said. "Obviously, we don't want to open that one and lose stuff."

"That's it as far as in the cage," she said. "There is one other item of biological evidence, but it has to be stored under refrigeration."

Kroft put everything back inside the box and put the lid back on. She retraced her steps and returned it to the shelf where she had taken it. She started back towards the entry gate, with Malone following. After exiting the cage, she shut the gate, which locked automatically. She then led Malone to the other side of the room, where large stainless steel refrigeration units stood like sentinels against another painted concrete block wall.

Kroft looked at placards inside little metal frames affixed to the doors of the refrigeration units. She located the one she was looking for and entered another series of numbers on a digital keypad. She then pulled a lever, and the door opened, allowing frosty cold air to billow out. The refrigerator had several wire shelves inside. The unit was deep. It looked like a residential refrigerator except for being far larger, both in height, width, and depth.

Kroft sorted through some manila envelopes on the second shelf from the top. After several moments, she turned and glanced at Malone with a look of puzzlement on her face. Eventually, she started searching through manila envelopes of various sizes on the remaining shelves, looking intently at the labels affixed to them. Finally, she stopped, shut the door to the unit, and then turned to face Malone.

"Houston, we have a problem," she said.

"What kind of problem?" Malone asked.

"An anomaly," Kroft said.

"An anomaly?" Malone asked.

"Yes," Kroft said. "Nothing goes missing here. Nothing. Never. But something has gone missing."

"What's missing?" Malone asked.

Looking at a sheet inside her folder, Kroft recited, "A small manila envelope containing two small glass vials with rubber stoppers containing two biological evidence swabs from a bite wound."

"Damn," Malone said.

"Yes, damn," Kroft said. "That just doesn't happen here."

Her smugness had evaporated faster than water droplets on a hot skillet.

"It's likely just out of place in that unit somewhere," she said. "I'm sure it we haven't actually lost it. That just doesn't happen here."

Malone assumed she was in denial. It certainly seemed it had gone missing to him.

"Rest assured I'll get to the bottom of it," Kroft said. "I will find it."

"Okay," Malone said. "But there was one other thing I had expected to be here."

"Like what?" Kroft asked.

"Swabs from a blood smear on a piece of electronic equipment from the crime scene," he said.

Kroft inspected her folder.

"Oh, that," she said.

"Yeah, that," Malone said.

"The lab discarded those swabs after they analyzed and typed the blood."

"Why didn't they keep the evidence?"

"Because the blood was Type AB negative," she said. "AB negative is the rarest of all blood types. Less than one percent of Caucasians have it. It is even rarer in people of color. The evidentiary blood swabs matched the blood type of the decedent. Type AB negative. Chances that the person who committed the homicide had the same rare blood type as the decedent are so astronomical that for all practical purposes, it is non-existent. DNA analysis wasn't commonly available in 1992. There was no reason back then that justified taking up the space to store those swabs."

"But they kept the bite wound swabs, well, allegedly they did, since they seem to have gone missing," Malone said.

"Not missing," Kroft said. "Temporarily misplaced. Not the same thing. But to answer your question, those swabs were different."

"Different how?" Malone asked.

"I said DNA analysis wasn't commonly available in 1992," she said. "I didn't say it didn't exist. It was expensive, and it was rudimentary compared to now, but DNA analysis has been around since 1986. DNA evidence was first used in a criminal case in the United States in 1987 when a Florida court convicted Tommy Lee Andrews of rape after DNA tests matched his DNA from a blood test to that of semen traces collected from the victim. So we knew cheaper and more advanced DNA analysis was coming back in 1992. The policy then was to collect and store any biological samples that might contain DNA for future testing."

"Interesting," Malone said. "I hope we can find it."

"I said I would find it," she said. "Don't worry about it."

"Well, if that's it, I guess I'll be going," Malone said. "I certainly appreciate not only your help but the education on DNA analysis."

"You're welcome," Kroft said. "But if you don't mind me saying so, as a detective, you should have already known all that. You need to up your game, Detective."

"Point taken," Malone said.

Kroft escorted him back to the lobby. He thanked her again and turned to go out of the exit.

"Wait for a second," Kroft said.

Malone turned back toward her. She was writing something on a business card. When she finished, she handed it to him. He looked at the front. It had three lines of black text. "Los Angeles County Medical Examiner-Coroner" was on the first line. "Evidence Control Section" was on the second line. "Jane Kroft, Criminalist" was on the last line. Malone flipped it over and saw a number written on the fact. He recognized it from the area code as a Los Angeles County cellular telephone number. Beneath the number, Kroft had drawn a little smiley face, two dots for eyes with a half moon mouth. He looked at Kroft.

"You can call me to find out if I've located those swabs if you wish," she said. "Sometimes I can't get to the desk phone if I'm in the cage or lab, so instead I gave you my cell phone number because the cell phone is always in my pocket."

"Oh, great and thanks," Malone said.

"But feel free to call me anytime," she said. "Like if you want to have a drink or something. I'm here from 8 to 5, Monday through Friday. I'm on call every other weekend. So if you want to call me, we can work something out."

"Outstanding," Malone said. "I'll definitely keep that in mind."

Kroft finally smiled and then said goodbye.

Malone walked out and back to his car. He got inside and started the motor. "Hm, he thought. Bernstein insisted she was unavailable, even though the chemistry in her office suggested differently. Jane Kroft, on the other hand, had sent an unmistakable message that she was not only interested, but ready, willing, and able. Women. They were all different, which always kept you guessing."

Malone pulled out of the lot and headed back to the I-10 and home. His duty hours would be over by the time he got back to West Hollywood. So he stopped for Chinese takeout on the way to his apartment.

12

Seeking the Source

Malone arrived home with the Chinese takeout. The Dodgers were playing at home, so he couldn't watch the game on television because of professional baseball's blackout policy. Instead, he tuned in the game on the radio and listened as he ate dinner at the dining room table. He couldn't concentrate on the baseball game, so he turned off the radio and retired to the living room with a beer afterward to think. He hadn't even thought about stopping at a liquor store on the way home. Maybe he was over the booze obsession.

Malone never considered himself the smartest man in the world. He knew better than that. But, well educated and relatively intelligent, like most people, he could add two plus two and usually get four. Something explained why the sky had come crashing down on him. After mulling it over for a while, he became certain he knew what that something was. Only one thing had changed materially in his life during the past few days, his decision to pick at a 23-year-old homicide. Someone was trying to shut him down, someone who didn't want the case re-opened or the truth about what happened to see the light the light of day.

His problem was he did not know who that person was. What he knew was that he had a good reason to believe that person was a cop or someone that had a connection inside the LAPD. The revelations from Brad Fulmer told him that much. The mysterious witness knew things that only someone with either direct or indirect access to LAPD files could know.

Malone knew the mysterious witness was a fake. He knew there had been no vehicle parked across the street from that convenience store on the side he was on. He'd checked. Based on intelligence, he knew Reid was probably armed. He also knew that there was a good chance Reid would try to shoot it out with police to avoid arrest. Malone had made certain there were no civilians in his background, just in case Reid got off a shot at him.

It was clear then that whoever wanted to shut down his investigation into the Anderson murder was also the person who manufactured the so-called witness. That had certainly shut him down. It could shut him down permanently if he didn't find a way to impeach the false witness. But who felt so certain he was going to work on the Anderson case that they had gone to such considerable effort to derail him?

The only person in the position to know for sure that the case was actively being worked was Reyes. Malone had told no one else. He and Reyes hadn't even discussed it with Lieutenant Turner. Vanessa knew only that he was seriously considering it. He hadn't ever told her he was definitely going to pursue the case. That's why she had still been trying to talk him out of it, because she was so concerned about his career. At least until what had happened that morning, he had expected she would continue trying to discourage him when they got together on Saturday. Given that he was now accused of felony murder, he seriously doubted that she would see him Saturday after all. She would obviously be too concerned about her own career and reputation to risk that.

Malone wasn't ready to believe Reyes was behind his problems. He had only known the guy for a couple of weeks, but he seemed a straight-arrow type. Plus, it had been Reyes who had pushed him into reading the case to begin with. Why would he have done that if he had some reason to not want the case re-opened, or if he had a connection with someone who didn't want it investigated? That just made no sense.

But by a simple process of elimination, Malone concluded it had to be Reyes. Not in a direct sense. He didn't think Reyes was out to set him up for a murder charge. But Reyes must have told someone they were working on the Anderson case who didn't want it investigated. Reyes was bad about that. He was the one who first told Vanessa about the case, trying to impress her. So he needed to talk to Reyes, to find out who else Reyes had told.

Malone and Reyes had exchanged cell phone numbers when they found out they were being partnered up in the cold case unit. He dialed Reyes' number. He answered on the second ring.

"Hello?"

"Reyes, it's me, Malone."

"Bro! What the hell happened this morning?"

"Long story, Reyes. The short version is a new witness in the wrongful death suit I'm involved in came forward. The witness claims to have seen the shooting go down, and his story is very damning. Says I basically executed David Allen Reid. So, it looks like the city is now facing a monster judgment. As icing on the cake, the DA got wind of the new civil case witness. As a result, he has re-opened the criminal side of the shooting. I got suspended, and I'm being arraigned on a murder charge in the morning."

"Dude, you're fucking kidding me, right? Please tell me you're kidding."

"Wish I was Reyes, but no, I'm not kidding. It's definitely not a joke."

"But I thought the DA already cleared you and that the civil thing was going nowhere," Reyes said.

"Yeah, well, all that has changed with the appearance of this new witness," Malone said.

"So, it's legit?" Reyes asked.

"No, it's a setup," Malone said. "The so-called witness is lying. The guy was never there. But someone inside the LAPD has funneled some information to him that the department never made public. So, he is telling a convincing story that has some people, including the DA, believing he was really there and saw the whole thing go down."

"Jesus Christ, bro!" Reyes said. "Someone is trying to frame you for murder?"

"Yeah, couldn't be any other way, Reyes."

"Well, I got your back, bro. You need anything. I'm your man. All you have to do is ask."

"There is something you can help me with now," Malone said.

"Name it bro, anything you need."

"I think this is all somehow connected with us working the Anderson case."

"The Anderson case?" Reyes asked. "How?"

"I can't explain it yet. I haven't figured out what the link is yet," Malone said. "But I don't believe in coincidences. All the stuff that happened today had to result from something I've become involved in recently. That is the only thing that could explain it. Otherwise, why would this witness show up now? The civil case has been dragging on for months. The Anderson case is the only thing of substance that I've become involved in recently that could explain it. So that has to be it, the reason someone has manufactured this fake witness. Someone is trying very hard to shut down the Anderson investigation before we ever get started."

"I can't believe that someone is so against re-opening that old case that they would frame you for murder," Reyes said. "Especially someone inside the LAPD."

"It isn't necessarily a cop," Malone said. "Could be a civilian employee with access to the investigative files from the shooting incident. A friend, a partner, or a relative of someone outside the department who doesn't want us digging around in the Anderson murder."

"Yeah, bro, I hear you. I can see how it could be something like that."

"So here is what I need from you right now, Reyes," Malone said. "You and Lieutenant Bachmann are the only two people I've talked to about working the Anderson case. You know for sure it's happening because you've been helping. Bachmann only knows we're thinking about working on the case, not that you and I have already started working on it. So what I need to know is this. Who else have you told we're working on the case?"

"Oh shit, bro."

"What, Reyes?"

"It's in the wind, dude. Remember, I told you I ran into that Van Nuys old timer, the sergeant in patrol that knew Myers. When we were talking about Myers, he asked why I wanted to know about him. I told him, dude. I told him we were working on one of Myers' old cases that had gone cold and that Myers' case theory had been total crap. That was why I wanted to know what kind of detective he had been. Dude, you know how cops gossip. We're worse than old church ladies. It's probably all over Van Nuys by now and spreading fast. I'm really sorry, bro. I never even dreamed something like this would happen. Dude, who would have ever thought that? But the information is out there now. It's in the wind."

"Don't worry about it, Reyes," Malone said. "I'm not pissed at you. Like you said, who could have imagined that the information getting out that we were working on an old cold case was going to cause me this kind of problem? But that blows up my plan to figure out who manufactured the witness by isolating the source of the leak. With about 9,000 cops and 3,000 civilians in the LAPD and the story spreading fast, sounds like I'll have about 12,000 suspects for the leak."

"So, what are you going to do, bro?" Reyes asked.

"I'm going to have to work it from the other direction," Malone said. "I've got to prove the witness is lying."

"How are you going to do that?" Reyes asked. "Bro, if you go near him, they will probably put an intimidating a witness charge on top of the murder charge."

"Yeah, I know that," Malone said. "As much as I'd like to confront the lying bastard myself, I know that would just get me into more trouble. I'm going to call a friend for help."

"Who?" Reyes asked.

"Jack Bright," Malone said. "Jack was my first partner at Hollywood when I made detective. He taught me the ropes. He retired and set up shop as a private investigator in West Hollywood."

"So, you think he can find someone to discredit the guy?" Reyes asked.

"Yeah, Jack still has informants and contacts from his days with the LAPD. If anyone can, Jack can get the real skinny on this new witness."

"Hope you're right, bro," Reyes said.

The two detectives talked a while longer. Malone filled Reyes in on what he had learned from his visit to the coroner's office. Then Malone ended the call so that he could try to reach his old partner.

Malone dialed Bright's cell phone number. Bright picked up, and Malone identified himself.

"Well, well, if it isn't make my day Malone," Bright said. "At least that's what I hear they have taken to calling you over in Hollywood these days. I also heard you got your tit in a wringer over that last scumbag you popped. Reid, wasn't it?"

"Yeah, Jack," Malone said. "I'm sort of up chocolate creek without a popsicle stick at the moment."

"I thought that was a done deal," Bright said. "What the hell happened?"

"Someone came forward claiming to have witnessed the shooting and says I gunned Reid down as soon as he walked out of the convenience store, with no warning."

"Without so much as a come on punk, make my day?" Bright said with a laugh.

"That's his story," Malone said. "But I'm not finding any humor in it, Jack."

"Yeah, I can imagine," Bright said. "So why did you call? Need a shoulder to cry on?"

"Not exactly," Malone said. "I need a favor."

"That figures," Bright said. "That's the trouble with you kids today. You never write. You never call. Unless you need a favor."

"Come on Jack," Malone said. "I'm in deep shit here."

"Okay, okay, Malone," Bright said. "I'm just busting your balls a little. What do you need?"

"The whole thing is a fabrication, Jack," Malone said. "I know for a fact there was no witness where this guy claims he watched the shooting from. But I need proof he is lying. If I can't discredit him, I'm going to be tried for murder."

"Does this character have a name?" Bright asked.

"His name is Eddie Romano," Malone said.

"Got any details?" Bright asked. "Date of birth, physical descriptors, address?"

"Nothing yet," Malone said. "My lawyer is supposed to be tracking that down."

"Not a hell of a lot to go on, with only a name, Malone," Bright said. "Romano is a common a surname around here. Might as well be Eddie

Jones or Smith. Probably plenty of guys named Eddie Romano in the valley alone, not to mention the state."

"I'm seeing my lawyer in the morning," Malone said. "Hopefully he will have the details then."

"Okay, Malone. Let me know. The sooner we get this turd out of the frame, the better."

"Yeah, and the sooner I get my life back," Malone said.

"Dollars to donuts, the civil attorney cooked the whole thing up. We find something to prove this witness didn't see what he claimed, and the lawsuit gets blown up too."

"That's what I'm hoping, Jack," Malone said. "That's what I'm hoping."

"Okay, Malone. Call me tomorrow."

"Roger that," Malone said. "And thanks, Jack."

"You can thank me later, Malone, if I solve your problem. Catch you later."

Bright clicked off.

Malone stared at the phone. It was already late, but he thought about calling Vanessa. Then decided he'd worry about it later. He went to bed to get some sleep instead.

13

Arraignment

Malone woke early the following morning. After getting showered and dressed, he drove downtown to the Los Angeles County Sheriff's Department Men's Central Jail on Bauchet Street to surrender as agreed. He skipped the coffee shop drive thru and arrived well before the nine o'clock deadline. He parked the Toyota in the public lot and then waited outside the lobby entrance until his lawyer arrived. Nathan Martinez drove into the lot and parked at a quarter to nine.

"How are you holding up, Malone?" Martinez asked.

"I'm okay," Malone said.

"Nothing to it," Martinez said. "They will formally arrest and book you. Then they will transport you to Central Arraignments Courts and hand you off to the bailiffs. You will get arraigned, enter a plea, and then the judge will set bail. I'm expecting something in the ballpark of $500,000. The protective league policy you pay dues for will take care of that. Then the judge will release you pending trial, and I'll drive you back here to pick up your ride."

"Okay," Malone said. "Never expected I'd be on this side of things."

"Yes, I can imagine," Martinez said. "Ready?"

"Yeah, ready as I'm going to get, I guess," Malone said.

The men walked into the jail lobby and two county detectives met them. Malone didn't know either of them. They escorted him and Martinez to an interview room. One detective read Malone the Miranda and then they arrested him. He declined to make any statements or answer questions.

Martinez left for the courthouse. A deputy booked, printed, and photographed Malone. Then he took his property and placed in a plastic property bag. The detectives handcuffed him and walked him over to the Central Arraignments Courts.

At the courthouse, the detectives left Malone in the custody of a couple of bailiffs. They didn't lock him in a holding cell. His case was the first on the docket, so they escorted him directly upstairs to the courtroom. Martinez already sat at the defense table. After Malone sat down beside him, the bailiffs walked to the side of the courtroom and took positions along the wall with arms crossed.

A young female assistant district attorney walked in and sat down at the prosecution's table. Malone had met her in the past, but couldn't recall her name. Some deputies brought in a group of inmates from the county jail, all dressed in orange coveralls and shackled. The inmates sat in the jury box. Some spectators filed in and took seats on the wooden benches, probably family members of the inmates. A bailiff stepped in front of the bench, told everyone to rise. A gray-haired judge, clothed in a black robe, swept into the courtroom from a side door. He took his seat on the bench.

The bailiff said, "Central Arraignments Court for the State of California, County of Los Angeles, is now in session. The Honorable Judge Mark Davis presiding. Be seated."

The judge examined some papers in front of him for several minutes, reading through a pair of half-glasses perched on the end of his nose. He then looked up and said, "Good morning, ladies and gentlemen." He gave a brief explanation of the arraignment process and then nodded to the bailiff.

The bailiff called the first case, reading from a docket form in his hand. "The People of California versus Benjamin J. Malone."

"Are both sides ready?" the judge asked.

"Ready for the people," said the assistant DA.

"The defense is ready," said Martinez.

"Defendant, please rise," the bailiff said.

Malone and Martinez stood up. Martinez leaned over and whispered, "I'll do all the talking." Malone nodded.

The judge read the criminal complaint aloud. "Mr. Malone, do you understand the charge against you?" he asked.

"The defendant understands the charge, your honor," Martinez said.

"How do you plead to the charge of murder in the second degree?"

"Not guilty, your honor," Martinez said.

"Trial by judge or trial by jury?"

"Jury trial, your honor," Martinez said.

"So noted," the judge said.

The judge then turned to the assistant DA. "What say the People, Ms. Morgan?"

"Based on defendant's employment and lack of any criminal convictions, we are agreeable to minimum bail. Provided that the defendant agrees not to absent himself from the County of Los Angeles pending trial."

"I set bail at $500,000," the judge said. "The court orders the defendant to remain within the confines of Los Angeles County pending trial. Any objections from the defense?"

"No objections, your honor," Martinez said.

Martinez had spoken with the assistant DA in advance. She stood and addressed the court. "If it pleases the court, the People are satisfied that appropriate arrangements for bail have been made."

"Very well," the judge said. "The defendant is released on bail pending trial, which I'm tentatively scheduling to commence three months from today."

Turning to the bailiff, the judge said, "Next case."

Malone stood up, and a bailiff came over and removed his handcuffs. He and Martinez walked out of the courtroom. Martinez led Malone to the stairway and then out to a rear exit. "Reporters are waiting out front," he said.

They walked to his car, got inside, and drove away.

"Did you get the information on the witness?" Malone asked.

"Yes, I got a copy of the affidavit from the DA's office," Martinez said. "But I'm not giving you the information until you swear you won't try to contact him. You're in deep enough already."

"In for a penny, in for a pound," Malone said.

"Take this seriously," Martinez said. "It isn't a joking matter."

"Okay, Nate, I swear," Malone said. "I will do nothing stupid."

"I know you're going to do something," Martinez said. "So, convince me it won't be anything stupid."

"I know better than to contact the dirtbag myself," Malone said. "I've asked a PI friend to check him and his story out. He is retired from LAPD. There won't be any connection to the department or me."

"That could work if he is any good," Martinez said.

He then gave Malone a paper with Eddie Romano's identifying information and address on it.

Martinez dropped Malone at his car. "I'll be touch," he said. Malone nodded and got out of the car. He closed the car door, and Martinez drove out of the lot.

Malone figured that since it was his arraignment day, he didn't have to go directly home. If the department checked on him, he believed he could probably explain away a couple of hours. Spending a couple of hours with his lawyer after court seemed reasonable. He needed to work. If he sat at home thinking about the legal mess, it would just drive him crazy. He decided it was time to interview some people connected with the Anderson case. So he pulled out the memo book he had stashed in the glove box and flipped to the pages where he had copied the information from the case file. He looked at the list.

He wasn't ready to start with the victim's husband or family. He wanted to get more of a feel for the case first. Especially where the family was concerned. He didn't want to raise false hopes.

He zeroed in on Marilyn Baker. She had worked at Anderson's clinic as a dental hygienist. It seemed they had been close friends since their college days at USC. Meyers had interviewed her. Malone was under no illusions that she would recall anything over twenty years later that she hadn't thought to tell Meyers. But maybe Meyers had missed something. That's why Malone wanted to interview Marilyn Baker himself, along with some other key people who had been part of Mary Beth Anderson's inner circle.

He punched the number from the file into his phone, all the while wondering what the odds were that she still had the same phone number. A woman answered.

"Hello, this is Detective Malone, Los Angeles Police Department. I'm trying to reach Marilyn Baker."

After a pause, the woman said, "This is Marilyn Baker."

"Ms. Baker, I'm with the cold case homicide unit. I'm looking into the murder of Mary Beth Anderson. I believe you knew her."

"Yes," she said. "I worked with Mary Beth at her clinic until they killed her. We met in college at USC. We had been close friends ever since. Do I understand this correctly, Detective? Is the case being re-opened after all these years?"

"Not officially. We have certain criteria we must meet before reclassifying a cold case as an active investigation. I've seen some things in the file, despite how old the case is, that lead me to believe the case deserves further investigation. I'm doing some preliminary inquiries at the moment, hoping to uncover something that warrants re-opening the case."

"So, what can I do for you, Detective?" she asked.

"I'd like to speak with you in person about the case," Malone said.

"I don't recall his name, but I spoke to a detective right after it happened. I told him everything I knew. Nearly over twenty years after the fact, I'm certain I have nothing new to add."

"I'm sure that's probably true, Ms. Baker. I don't expect to hear anything new, especially after so many years have passed. What I'm hoping is something you told Detective Myers twenty years ago, that he didn't recognize as important, might turn out to be important."

"I'm available this morning, but I have an appointment this afternoon," she said. "How soon could you be here?"

"Do you still live at the address in Van Nuys?" Malone asked.

"Goodness, no, I've moved several times since Mary Beth died," she said. I live in Sherman Oaks now."

"I could be there in an hour," he said.

"All right, Detective," she said. She gave him the address.

Malone disconnected the call. He tried Jack Bright's cell phone, but the call went to voicemail. He left Romano's identifying information on the recording. Malone put away the phone and started the car. He drove out of the parking lot, headed for the the 101 and Sherman Oaks.

* * *

For once, the LA traffic cooperated. Fifty-five minutes after the phone call, Malone parked in front of the Sherman Oaks address Marilyn Baker had given him. It was an older but well maintained single-story ranch in the middle of the block. A couple of large, mature live oaks nicely shaded the carefully manicured green grass of the front yard.

An abundance of colorful flowers of various hues filled the planting beds along the front of the house. Malone walked up to the front door and pushed the doorbell button.

After a few moments, the door opened. A green-eyed woman of about fifty appeared, framed by the open doorway. She was of average height with a nice figure. Her short blonde hairstyle stressed the graceful curve of her head. Her hair was longer in the front, sweeping across her face and tucked behind an ear on one side. She wore a pair of jeans and a pink top.

"Ms. Baker, I'm Detective Malone. We spoke on the phone earlier."

"Yes, Detective," she said. "Won't you come in?"

She stepped aside to allow him to enter and then closed the front door.

"Would you care for some coffee?" she asked.

"That would be great if it isn't any trouble," Malone said.

"No trouble at all," Baker said. "I was just having some. Follow me. We can talk in the kitchen."

Malone followed her down the hallway and into the kitchen, which was at the back of the house.

"Please sit down," she said, gesturing towards a wooden pub table with four matching tall, high-backed chairs positioned in front of a large bay window that looked out on the backyard.

Malone sat down and looked out the window. The backyard was as impeccably landscaped as the front. Baker filled two white mugs from a drip coffeemaker and carried them to the table.

"Cream or sugar?" she asked.

"No thanks, I take it black," Malone said.

"All right," she said, sitting in a chair across from Malone. "Were the burglars identified?" she asked. "Is that why you're looking into Mary Beth's case again?"

"No, ma'am," Malone said. "Actually, based on what I know from reviewing the case file, I don't believe burglars killed her. I feel it was something more personal than that."

"But that other detective seemed so certain burglars had done it when she surprised them," Baker said. "He mentioned they had disconnected some electronics and put them near a back door. Are you saying now it was someone else?"

"There are some things I've found that strongly suggest that someone staged the murder scene to make it look like a burglary to mislead the investigators," Malone said. "Were you aware of anyone that she may have had a problem with back then, someone that might have had a grudge against her and may have wanted to harm her?"

"I can only tell you the same thing I told the police back then," she said. "Mary Beth was a confident woman. She could be assertive, but not in a manner that might rub people the wrong way. I think everyone who knew Mary Beth loved her. Friends, co-workers, and even her patients. I only witnessed Mary Beth at odds with someone on one occasion the entire time I knew her."

"Can you tell me about it?" Malone asked.

"It happened just after Mary Beth opened the clinic," Baker said. She and Robert were engaged at the time but hadn't yet married. A woman came in and demanded to see Mary Beth. I was in a treatment room next to the reception area and could hear her talking to the receptionist. The woman seemed very agitated and angry from the moment she came in. She was speaking loudly, almost shouting."

"Was she a patient?" Malone asked.

"No, she wasn't," Baker said. "That became clear afterward, but at the beginning of it, I overheard the receptionist ask her if she had an appointment. The woman told her she didn't, that she wanted to see Mary Beth about a personal matter. Mary Beth evidently overheard the conversation, too. She came down the hallway and stepped out into the waiting room."

"Then what happened?" Malone said.

"Mary Beth seemed to know the woman. I remember hearing her say to the woman something like, 'what are you doing here?' The woman said they needed to talk. Mary Beth led the woman down the hall to her office. They went inside, and the door closed. The woman raised her voice even more, and Mary Beth raised hers. Soon they were having what sounded like a pretty heated discussion."

"Could you hear what they said?" Malone asked.

"Not much of it," Baker said. "The door was closed, and I wasn't attempting to eavesdrop or anything. But as I said, the discussion seemed heated, so I moved down the hallway closer to the door. I didn't know what was going to happen. If things seemed to get out of control, I wanted to either try to intervene or at least call the police."

"So, did you hear anything that was said?" Malone asked.

"A little. I heard the woman accuse Mary Beth of stealing Robert from her and demanding that she leave him alone. I also clearly heard the woman say that if she could not have Robert, no one could."

"So, she was threatening Mary Beth?" Malone asked.

"Actually, that wasn't the impression I got," Baker said. "It sounded more like the woman was threatening to do something to Robert, not threatening Mary Beth personally. The woman said, 'you will be sorry if you don't leave him alone because I won't let him get away with dumping me' or something very close to that."

"Then what happened?" Malone asked.

"Mary Beth screamed at the woman to get out and threatened to call the police. I went to the phone and call the police myself, but then the door opened. The woman came out of the office and stormed down the hallway. She was obviously leaving. Mary Beth came out of her office and shouted after her she better not come back or she would call the police. The woman turned briefly and glared at her, saying 'I'll make you sorry bitch' and then she turned away and left."

"Did you talk to Mary Beth about what had happened?" Malone asked.

"Not right away. I'd never seen her so angry. She went back into her office and shut the door. A few hours later, after she had calmed down, she told me a little about it."

"Who was the woman?" Malone asked.

"Mary Beth said the woman was someone Robert dated in college before she and Robert had met and that the woman evidently just couldn't accept it when Robert had ended the relationship. She said the woman apparently hadn't known that Mary Beth and Robert were already engaged to be married, so she had set her straight."

"Did she tell you the woman's name?" Malone asked.

"No, and I didn't press it," Baker said. "It was very clear that just talking about the woman was making Mary Beth upset all over again. She dropped it, and I didn't press her for any details."

"Was that the end of it?" Malone asked.

"Well, the woman never came back to the clinic, but Mary Beth told me about a week later that she was seriously thinking about breaking off the engagement with Robert because she wasn't sure what was going on between him and the ex-girlfriend."

"But she didn't break the engagement?" Malone asked.

"No, a while later, she told me she and Robert had talked it out. She said the ex-girlfriend was just crazy, and that Robert had promised her she would not bother them again."

"I know she has changed over the last twenty-three years, but what did the woman look like back then?" Malone asked.

"I'd say middle to late-twenties. She looked Hispanic, with dark hair and brown eyes. Perhaps it was just the circumstances, but to this day, I still remember she had crazy eyes. That certainly made sense later when Mary Beth said she was a compulsive-obsessive nut case. She certainly had the eyes for it. At least she did that day she came into the clinic."

"Was she tall, short, thin, heavy-set?" Malone asked.

"I think she was about average as far as height. She was athletic looking. Not heavy but not thin either. I'd describe her as muscular. Like athletic. She was attractive, I guess, apart from her demeanor that day. But it was really just the crazy eyes that stood out to me."

"You don't know of anyone else Mary Beth might have had a problem with?" Malone asked.

"No, not at all," Baker said. "As I told you, most everyone who knew Mary Beth absolutely loved her, other than that one woman evidently, who I just mentioned. She just had that kind of personality. That's why her death was such a shock. I would never have imagined someone murdering her."

"Thinking back on it, do you think that Hispanic woman may have wanted to harm Mary Beth?" Malone asked.

"She was obviously furious, but even to this day, I don't think so. As I said, the impression I got from it all was that the woman was threatening Robert, not Mary Beth. If someone had murdered Robert, then it wouldn't have surprised me in the least if that woman turned out to be the killer."

"You said that you and Mary Beth were close friends. Did she ever share things with you about her marriage?"

"Yes, Mary Beth always talked with me about everything," Baker said.

"So how would you characterize her marriage at the time of her death?" Malone asked.

"Like just about any new marriage," Baker said. "They had only been married a few months when she died. They were still acclimating to married life and living together. But she seemed happy. I think they were both deeply in love."

"Did you ever suspect Robert may have killed Mary Beth?" Malone asked.

"Oh no, not at all," Baker said. "I'm certain Robert had nothing to do with it."

"What makes you feel so certain about it?" Malone asked.

"First, I saw Robert at the funeral. The murder devastated Mary Beth's family, of course, but Robert was beyond devastated. He fell apart, utterly and completely. His grief was literally palatable. He was so emotional he couldn't even speak coherently to anyone at the funeral. I've never seen a man cry like that, either before or since. It was hard to watch. No one could have faked the raw emotions I saw in Robert that day."

"You said first, so was there something else that made you so sure Robert wasn't responsible?" Malone asked.

"Yes," Baker said. "I almost hate to say this because it will probably seem quite rude."

"It might be important," Malone said. "Please continue."

"Well, as I told you, Mary Beth could be quite assertive. Nowhere was that more clear than in her relationship with Robert. He was a nice man, as far as I know, probably still is. But he was quiet and shy, I think. And Mary Beth was two years older than Robert. Pardon my French, but Robert just didn't have the balls to do something like that. I don't think he could have hurt a fly."

"Is your opinion based on knowing him well?" Malone asked.

"No," Baker said. "I only saw Robert a few times. But as I shared, Mary Beth talked with me about everything. They had arguments sometimes, disagreements over silly little things like new married couples often do. I know that Robert always deferred to Mary Beth in the end. She was the dominant force in their relationship. As the saying goes, she wore the pants in that family."

"Okay," Malone said. "Anything else you can think of that might help us with the investigation?"

"No, I don't think so," Baker said. "Well, on second thought, maybe one more thing."

"What's that?" Malone asked.

"It's about that Hispanic woman. Robert's ex-girlfriend."

"Yes?" Malone asked.

"That was the one thing that Mary Beth didn't seem willing to talk with me about much. She and her sister Rebecca were very close. I know Rebecca was her closest confidant. If you want to know more about Robert's ex-girlfriend, if anyone knows more about her, it would be Rebecca."

"Yes, I had planned to speak to her too," Malone said. "I only have phone numbers and addresses from twenty-three years ago. Do you know where she lives now?"

"Yes, she moved to San Diego," Baker said. She got up from the table and retrieved an address book from a kitchen drawer. She opened it and read off an address and telephone number while Malone copied it down in his memo book.

"Do you remain in close contact with the family?" Malone asked.

"Not really, not anymore," Baker said. "I stayed in contact with them at first. I suppose it was an attempt to hold on to Mary Beth. But life happens, people move on, even from tragedies as profound as the loss of your very best friend. My contact with her family became less and less frequent over the years. We still exchange Christmas cards. That's why I have Rebecca's address. But I haven't seen her or any of the family for years and years."

"Well, thank you for your time, Ms. Baker. You've been very helpful," Malone said. He stood up, reached inside his coat, and pulled out a business card. He handed the card to Baker.

"If you should think of anything else, please call me. I spend little time in the office, so my mobile number is the best one to call."

"Thank you for looking into Mary Beth's case," she said. "I know it won't bring her back, but if you find and punish the killer, I think it would really help her family. Even after all the years that have passed. It might finally give them some closure. I really don't think her parents or her sister ever got over it."

"Yes, I can imagine," Malone said. "By the way, I mentioned I'm just making preliminary inquiries at present. We haven't re-opened the case officially. So I must ask you not to discuss what we've talked about with anyone. If it got back to the family that we were investigating the case, but my supervisors ultimately decide it doesn't meet the criteria for re-opening it, it might just cause them more anguish and disappointment."

"Doesn't the police try to solve all the cold cases?" Baker asked.

"Theoretically, homicide cases remain open forever unless cleared," Malone said. "That's because there is no statutory limitation on prosecuting someone for murder. In a perfect world, of course, we would try to solve every single one of them. Unfortunately, in the real world of budgetary and manpower constraints, we must concentrate our limited resources on those cases that offer the most realistic chance we can identify and arrest a suspect. That's the reason for the criteria I mentioned we must satisfy before reclassifying a cold case as an active one."

"I see," Baker said. "And that's only logical, I suppose."

"I better be going," Malone said. "I've already taken up a lot of your time."

"Yes, I must get ready for my afternoon appointment," she said. "Let me show you out."

They walked to the door. Malone thanked Baker again for her help and cooperation. He walked back to his car and got in. He started the car and drove away, threading his way through Sherman Oaks to the on-ramp for the 101.

14

Out With the Old

Malone walked into his apartment a few minutes before 1:00 o'clock. The light was blinking on his answering machine. The interview with Marilyn Baker had taken longer than he had expected. So he hoped Turner hadn't called to check whether he was at home as the terms of the suspension dictated. When he checked the machine, he saw he had three messages. He pushed the button to play them.

The first message was from Jack Bright. Bright confirmed he had received the message Malone had left on his voicemail earlier. He said he was working on it and he'd be in touch.

The second message was a reminder about his next appointment from Sara Bernstein's office. That reminded him he still needed to work out a strategy concerning the good doctor.

The last message was from Vanessa Bachmann. It wasn't really a message, but a question and a statement.

"Where the hell are you? You're supposed to be at home during duty hours." Vanessa sounded irritated. He was trying to decide whether to call her back when the phone rang, startling him. He picked up the receiver.

"Malone," he said.

"I understood from Turner that you are supposed to be at home during duty hours while you're suspended," Vanessa Bachmann said.

"Roger that," Malone said. "Unless I have legal or medical appointments."

"So where were you?" she asked.

"After court, my lawyer and I drove back to his office for a strategy meeting," Malone fibbed.

"Just be glad it was me that called and not Turner," she said. "You should have cleared that with him if he wasn't aware of it. Telling him after the fact wouldn't have excused you for disobeying a direct order. If you screw up during this suspension, they will start termination proceedings."

"Well, you know Vanessa, at the moment I'm dealing with a couple of problems that are just a little more serious than the stupid suspension," Malone said.

"Yes, I heard," she said. "That's why I called when I didn't hear from you yesterday."

"It's all bullshit," he said. "There was no witness at the scene that we didn't know about. It's a frame job. The guy is claiming he saw the shooting from a place that I know no one was at."

"I hope that's all true, for your sake," she said.

"It is all true, and I'm going to prove it," Malone said.

"Don't do anything stupid, Malone," she said. "You're in deep shit as it is."

"I'm not going to," he said. "I've got someone helping with it unconnected to me, or the department."

"Okay," she said. "You can tell me about it later. I have a meeting in a few minutes. But I wanted to talk to you about Saturday."

"Let me guess," Malone said. "You have to cancel."

"I'm sorry, Ben," she said. "I really want to see you. But I just can't risk it right now. Please understand the murder charge makes you something of a pariah at the moment. I can't risk it getting out that we see each other until you resolve the legal complications."

"So you're dumping me then?" Malone asked.

"No, Ben," she said. "Please don't say that. I've developed some genuine feelings for you. I want to be with you, but that's just not feasible right now. You know how things are with my career."

"I'm not exactly a member of the mob," Malone said.

"Just be patient, Ben," she said. "I believe you, and I believe in you. And I accept that the new witness isn't legit. I'm sure the truth will come out, and they will exonerate you. Once that happens, and they drop the charges, once you're back from on the beach, then we can reboot what we started. But I can't see you until this mess gets resolved."

"Well, when that happens, I'll consider it, Vanessa. But I'm already having doubts about the wisdom of being involved with a woman already married to her career."

"That's not fair, Ben, and you know it," she said. "You can't imagine what I've been through to get where I am. I'm not risking that for you, or for anyone. But it doesn't mean that I don't care about you or that we can't have a future together. But look, I'm already late for the meeting, and I have to go. Please, just try to see things from my perspective. Be fair about it."

Before Malone could respond, she continued, "I really have to run, Ben. You can still call me. Call me tonight after work if you can. We can talk things out then. Bye Ben."

Bachmann hung up, and Malone put down the receiver. He was feeling certain that things with Bachmann were over, at least as far as he was concerned. He wasn't feeling support from her and he sure as hell wasn't feeling the love. In fact, she was reminding him of his ex-wife. So they had sex twice. Big deal, he thought. It had meant nothing.

Malone went to the kitchen and opened a cabinet. The bottle of Jack Daniels was nearly empty. He took it down and set in on the counter. He was about to reach for a glass, but changed his mind. Instead, he put the bourbon back in the cabinet and made himself a sandwich for lunch. Then he grabbed a beer from the refrigerator. He sat down on a stool at the breakfast bar. He ate the sandwich and sipped the cold beer and tried to stop thinking about Bachmann.

He thought about Rebecca Anderson. San Diego was 120 miles away. Too far for him to think about traveling while he was on the beach. Not to mention, confined to Los Angeles County under the terms of his bail. He definitely couldn't screw that up or his next stop would confinement at the Los Angeles County Jail. The slam was definitely not a healthy place for any cop to find himself. Rebecca Anderson and San Diego would have to wait until some other things got cleared up. He could call her, but he preferred face-to-face interviews. You could miss too many things talking to someone by phone.

That decided, his thoughts turned to Sara Bernstein. The seed of a strategy developed. He got up and went back to the phone.

Malone dialed Sara Bernstein's office number.

"Doctor Bernstein's office," said the receptionist in a cheery voice.

"This is Ben Malone," Malone said. "I need to speak with Dr. Bernstein, please."

"Hello Detective Malone," the receptionist said. "She has been in session. Let me check to see if she is available."

The receptionist put him on hold, and some elevator music played. After several minutes, the music stopped, and the phone clicked.

"Sara Bernstein."

"Hello, Doc, Ben Malone here."

"Hi, Detective," she said. "How are you?"

"Honestly, I'm not feeling great, Doctor. That's why I called."

"That's not good," she said. "What's going on?"

"Things have gotten a little worse," he said. "I mean, those things I wasn't ready to talk with you about during our last session."

"So, do you feel like talking to me about it now?" she asked. "I think that would be a very positive step. I could certainly tell that something was weighing heavily on you when we spoke last time."

"Yes, I am ready to talk about it," Malone said.

"But you don't feel it can wait until your next appointment?" she asked.

"No, I really don't, Doctor," he said. "Actually, I'm feeling a little depressed right now, and I'm worried it will only get worse."

"I can check with the receptionist for an earlier appointment," she said. "When did you want to come in?"

"I just don't think this can wait, Doctor," he said. "I was hoping you could see me today."

"I'm sure that's impossible, Detective Malone," she said. "It's late afternoon already, and I know I've got patients booked through the end of the day. There isn't a place to squeeze you in, and I wouldn't want you to feel limited by time constraints, anyway."

"I was hoping maybe you could see me after hours," he said. "Maybe you could just drop by my place on your way home."

"I'm sorry, Detective," she said. "I really don't do house calls."

"But this is important, doctor. I feel ready for a breakthrough, and there is another complicating factor as well that may make it impossible for me to see you at your office again."

"Complicating factor?" she asked.

"Yes, doctor," he said. "The department suspended me from work. I'm not supposed to leave home during the duty hours specified under the suspension. Unfortunately, those hours coincide with your office hours."

After a pause, Bernstein said. "Detective Malone, may I ask you a question and expect a truthful answer?"

"Sure, Doctor," Malone said.

"Would this attempt to coerce me into visiting you at your home have anything to do with the infatuation we spoke about during the last session?" she asked.

"Of course not, Doctor," Malone said. "I really have some problems that I need to talk to you about it. It just won't wait. Maybe you can recommend another shrink if you don't have the time to help."

"All right, but let us be clear," she said. "I'm willing to make this one exception to my no house calls rule simply because you seem so adamant about needing to talk, but only if you agree to a few ground rules."

"Anything you say, Doctor," Malone said. "I'm just really feeling desperate to talk to someone about what's going on and about my depression."

"Fine. Here are the ground rules. This home visit will not be a social call. It will be strictly a professional therapist-patient interaction. If I feel you are attempting to deviate from that, I'll immediately leave. That includes any feeling on my part that you are attempting to press forward on any agenda not directly related to your mental health, including the feelings of attraction you expressed to me during our last session. I think I made my position on that perfectly clear when we last talked. And if this should go awry, I will never again consider seeing you outside my office. Do we understand each other?"

"Of course, Doctor," Malone said. "There is no hidden agenda. I just need your professional help."

"All right, Detective Malone," she said. "My last appointment should end at five o'clock. Give me your address."

Malone gave her the address and some rough directions to his apartment from her office.

"I have GPS in the car," she said. "So I'm sure I can find it. I should be there by six o'clock."

"That's great, Doctor," Malone said. "I can't thank you enough for doing this for me."

They said goodbye, and Bernstein hung up. Malone put down the phone and grabbed his car keys from the kitchen counter. He needed to pick up some things from the supermarket and a nice bottle of wine. There were still another couple of hours before his duty hours ended. Technically, he shouldn't be away from home. But surely the LAPD didn't expect him to starve to death, and he needed food. He already knew what he was making for dinner. Lasagna, his specialty. Sara Bernstein would love it.

* * *

An hour later, Malone was back from the supermarket. He had picked up some sweet Italian sausage, ground beef, lasagna noodles, mozzarella, parmesan, ricotta, onion, garlic, and fresh parsley. Everything else he needed for the lasagna was in the cupboards. He had also picked up fresh veggies for a garden salad, a loaf of fresh crusty bread, and a bottle of Chianti, a fruity Tuscan red that Ted at the supermarket recommended. According to Ted, the rich flavors of lasagna required an assertive red wine and Chianti was just the ticket.

Malone placed a chopping board on the counter and went to work on the onions, garlic, and salad fixings. Next, he grabbed a Dutch oven, set it on the stove over medium heat, and browned the sausage and ground beef. He stirred in crushed tomatoes, tomato paste, tomato sauce, and water. He seasoned the mixture with sugar, basil, fennel seeds, Italian seasoning, salt, pepper, and some freshly chopped parsley.

Having about ninety minutes to kill while the marinara sauce simmered, he tore iceberg and romaine lettuce into bite-sized pieces until he had filled a large salad bowl. Then he tossed in some diced fresh tomatoes, chopped carrots, green onions, radishes, and celery. He added some sliced cucumbers for good measure and then tossed the salad. He grated some fresh Parmesan on top before stowing the salad in the refrigerator. Next, he went to work on his signature homemade raspberry vinaigrette.

Malone placed a dozen lasagna noodles into a pot of boiling, lightly salted water. While the pasta cooked, he mixed the ricotta cheese with an egg, more chopped parsley, and a little salt. After ten minutes, he drained the noodles and rinsed them in cold water. Then he set the oven to 375 degrees to preheat.

While he waited for the sauce to finish, Malone opened a beer and sipped it while he checked his email. Forty-five minutes later, he was back in the kitchen, assembling the layers of lasagna in a baking dish. He topped it off with the rest of the grated mozzarella and Parmesan. He covered the dish with foil and slid the dish into the oven. It would be ready in about a half an hour, which he hoped would be a few minutes before Sara Bernstein's expected arrival. He sliced along the length of the fresh bread and spread the inside with a generous amount of garlic butter. He wrapped it in foil so that it was ready to go into the oven as soon as the lasagna was done.

Sara Bernstein didn't miss her estimated arrival by much. There was a knock on at his front door at seven minutes past six. He opened the door and invited her in. She brushed the hair out of her eyes and stepped into his apartment. She was wearing a silky white top, a tight black skirt, black stockings, and medium heels. Had she not lectured him about keeping the visit purely professional, he might have suspected that she had used the extra seven minutes to freshen her makeup before getting out of the car and walking to the door of his apartment.

"Have you been cooking?" Bernstein asked.

"I have," Malone said.

She stared at him a moment, clearly looking as if she was trying to decide about something.

"Did you cook me dinner, Detective?" she asked. "I believe I mentioned that if it appeared this visit veered from a professional therapist-patient interaction towards a social one, I'd immediately leave. I think cooking me dinner might very well qualify."

"Oh, heavens no," Malone said with a grin. "Believe it or not, many people have the habit of eating dinner at this time of the evening. I merely prepared my dinner while I was waiting for you to arrive."

Bernstein looked skeptical.

"But now that you mention it, I made lasagna, and there is more than enough for two," Malone said. "Would you care to join me in breaking bread?"

"I'm not having dinner with you, Mr. Malone," she said. "I think I've been very clear about the ethical boundaries we must observe as therapist and patient."

"How could having dinner be an ethical violation?" Malone asked. "It's dinnertime. I'm hungry. You're probably hungry. There is plenty of food for both of us. Civilized people often share a meal while talking together. You're here at my request so that we can talk together. I've imposed on you by asking you to come here. Obviously, the imposition will delay your dinner. The least I could do in return is feed you while we talk."

"You're trying my patience," Bernstein said.

"Okay, fine," Malone said. "I'm won't force you to dine with me. But I'm hungry. So I'll eat my dinner while we talk. You can watch. Surely that won't violate any professional boundaries."

"All right, Detective Malone, but this is your final warning. One more step towards socializing and I'm leaving."

"You're the doctor, Doctor," Malone said.

Malone went to the kitchen. After plating a healthy portion of lasagna and putting a serving of salad into a bowl, he drizzled some of the vinaigrette on the salad and then carried the food to the dining room table. He grabbed a wine glass and retrieved the bottle of wine from the refrigerator.

Malone knew enough about wine to know most people served red wine at room temperature, but he also knew what he liked. He preferred red wine slightly chilled, regardless of the opinions of a bunch of snooty wine connoisseurs.

By the time Malone had returned to the dining room table with the wine, Bernstein had taken a seat in the chair across from where he had set his service for one. Malone sat down, poured a liberal serving of wine, and picked up his fork. As he dug into the lasagna, Bernstein spoke.

"You made lasagna."

"Yes, it's my specialty," Malone said.

"I love lasagna," she said. "Homemade marinara sauce?"

"Yes, I always make the sauce from scratch," Malone said.

"Frankly, I have to admit I had you pegged as more of a spaghetti from a box kind of guy."

"Looks can deceive," Malone said.

"Know what? I changed my mind. I'll have some lasagna."

"But won't that leave you squarely on the horns of an ethical dilemma?" Malone asked.

"I'll rationalize it," she said. "I'm a shrink after all. We know all about that sort of thing. Besides, I'm starving now after smelling lasagna since the moment I walked in the door."

"You sure?" Malone asked. "I wouldn't want you struggling with guilt later, tossing and turning, unable to sleep."

"Please, just serve me some lasagna. I am a woman, and I'm sure you must have heard that it's always a woman's prerogative to change her mind."

Malone got up from the table to get Bernstein's lasagna and salad. He brought it back a few moments later, along with the hot, crusty garlic bread. Bernstein took a couple of bites before speaking again.

"This is delicious. I'm impressed."

"Thank you."

"So what did you wish to talk with me about?" Bernstein said. "I'm fully committed to salvaging this session despite your determined efforts to make something else of my visit."

"Ben," Malone said.

"Pardon me?" Bernstein said.

"You can call me Ben."

Bernstein raised an eyebrow, then sighed.

"Detective Malone...," Bernstein began before Malone interrupted.

"Ben," he said.

"To maintain a professional therapist-patient environment, I think it best if I continue to address you as Detective Malone," Bernstein said. "Or Mr. Malone, if you prefer."

"You know, doctor," Malone said. "When I was soldiering in the Middle East, we usually referred to enemy combatants as hajjis, which isn't unusual. In Somalia, we called Somalis skinnies. Soldiers in Vietnam from my father's generation used words like gooks and dinks to refer to their enemy. As far back as World War II, soldiers in the Pacific called the Japanese Japs or Nips and soldiers in the European theater called Germans Krauts, among other things. From a psychiatric perspective, why do you think soldiers in wartime refer to enemy combatants with derogatory slurs?"

"Most psychiatric professionals would say they do it to overtly dehumanize the enemy, Mr. Malone," Bernstein said. "It may be an attempt to cope with the cognitive dissonance many soldiers experience when thrust into war. On the one hand, most men are raised to believe that taking human life is inherently immoral and wrong. But then in the military, after being told it is not only okay to kill all their lives, the military says killing is fine and in combat it's okay, and that it's also their patriotic duty to kill the enemy. It's far easier to visit violence upon a group viewed as creatures warranting separation, suppression, and even annihilation because they are somehow different, somehow less than human."

"I see," Malone said. "Would you view that as something of an analogy for the way people overtly keep others at arm's length by addressing them in a formal rather than informal way?"

"I see where you're going with this," Bernstein said. "And to answer your question, no, I don't consider that a good analogy at all. I'm not attempting to dehumanize you, Detective Malone. It is simply a fact of life that formality rather than informality best lends itself to establishing and observing the professional boundaries between therapist and patient. That is what the ethical standards demand."

"Okay, I can see that," Malone said. "But would it be a fair statement to say that I am not suffering from any psychiatric problems and, in reality, never actually needed therapy? After all, you said you were going to recommend to my superiors that they return me to regular duty."

"Yes, I suppose that would be a fair statement," Bernstein said. "You don't appear to suffer from any psychological problems connected with the shootings you were involved in. And in our sessions, I have found no reason to believe you suffer from any diagnosable pathologies requiring treatment. Still, that doesn't mean that you can't benefit from therapy or counseling if you prefer that term."

"So would agree then, Doctor, that the only reason I came to be your patient is that my superiors, out of an abundance of caution, required it?" Malone said.

"Yes, I suppose I agree with that statement," Bernstein said.

"Then perhaps you can see things from my perspective on some level," Malone said. "Theoretically speaking, had my superiors not compelled me to become your patient, and we had met under different circumstances, at a coffee shop, a shopping mall, or even on an online dating site, then perhaps we may have developed a mutual attraction and interest. That might have naturally evolved into a dating relationship."

"I'm willing to agree with your premise, yet the reality we face is we met as therapist and patient," Bernstein said. "It isn't possible to turn back time and imagine that didn't happen, despite how it came to be. So you have been my patient, and once you stop seeing me professionally, you will forever more be my former patient. Those facts are simply incompatible from an ethical perspective. And the reason we cannot see each other socially. I am not saying that it is so, but theoretically speaking, if I felt any attraction or interest in you, ethical considerations would prevent me from acting on those feelings."

"Sara, I won't ask you to sacrifice your ethical ideals," Malone said. "Obviously, those are very important to you. However, I am going to ask you to look at our circumstances in the light of objective logic. If I didn't have psychological problems that required treatment, then how can you logically claim to have treated me? All we've done is discuss some things and discuss them in quite the same way that we might have as friends or two people seeing each other socially. If I never needed treatment and if you've never treated me, then does it make sense to insist we've had a therapist-patient relationship?"

"I have to admit you make somewhat of a compelling argument," Bernstein said. "But let's say I could agree with all of what you have just said. What if I simply don't reciprocate the feelings you obviously have developed toward me? Must things be as you wish them to be just because it's what you want?"

"No," Malone said. "If you tell me right now, you don't feel any attraction to me as a man and you have no interest in exploring a dating relationship with me, then I'll drop the subject and never speak of it again. But if you're honest, I don't think you can say that."

Bernstein stared at him pensively for a few moments before speaking.

"So tell me something," she said. "Did you invite me here this evening and make dinner for me, intending to seduce me?"

"No Sara, I didn't," Malone said. "Inviting you here wasn't the ruse you seem to believe it was. I really need to talk, but to tell you the truth, I'd much rather talk with a friend than a shrink. No offense intended. I'm already starting to see you as a friend. I was just hoping that you might start to see me that way instead of as a patient you have to keep boundaries up for."

"Fair enough," she said. "If you need to talk, I'm ready to listen. But let me say something first. Let's assume for the moment I have similar feelings to those you've expressed for me. Based on that assumption, I feel I have to be completely candid about something. I'm not looking for a man to just have some fun times with and perhaps enjoy some no strings attached sexual adventures with. I'm certainly not suggesting that is wrong for those who may find that to be what they want and need. But that isn't me. If I am to date someone, I have to feel confident that he is genuinely open to the possibility of a committed relationship. I'm not saying I am looking for a proposal. Honestly, I haven't even decided about whether I want to be married. But I need the potential of a committed relationship part. So if you and I are going to consider seeing each other, it's only fair that you understand I'd be looking for a committed relationship."

"That would be perfect," Malone said with a smile. "I'd be looking for exactly the same thing. I know there are no guarantees, but I want someone who is at least open to the possibility of a relationship developing."

Bernstein stared down at her hands, folded on the table, for the moment. She then looked up at Malone. He saw a single tear trickle from the corner of her eye down her cheek, but she was smiling.

"In that case, at the risk of sounding bold, I'm free Friday evening," she said.

Malone smiled back.

"Perfect," he said. "But I'm in something of a jam at the moment, so I suppose we better have that talk. You might change your mind about seeing me after you hear about the mess I'm in."

Malone then told her the entire story about the cold case investigation, the appearance of the mystery witness from the last shooting, his suspension at work, and finally his arrest and arraignment on a murder charge. Bernstein listened intently, stopping him now and again to ask a question or two. After he had finished, it was her turn to speak.

"Ben, I'm completely confident that you are not a cold-blooded killer," she said. "So I know there is no way that the witness against you is telling the truth. I just hope your friend can help you prove that. I'm also so sorry to learn that they have subjected you to such stressful circumstances, with seemingly a complete absence of support from your department and superiors. You can rest assured that you have my complete support and nothing you have shared with me changes anything. In fact, I'm really excited about Friday evening and truly looking forward to spending time with you."

"Thank you, Sara," he said. "That means a lot. You've already proven to me you are everything I believed you were."

Bernstein helped him clear the table, and together they put the dishes in the dishwasher, and the leftovers put away. Sara then said she had to get home. Malone walked her to her car. She turned to him, kissed him lightly on the lips, and put her arms around him. He embraced her, enjoying the subtle smell of her perfume. They parted after several moments and Bernstein got into the car.

"I'll see you Friday then," she said. "Around seven?"

"Yes, seven is great," he said. "I'll be out of detention by then."

Bernstein laughed.

"I really do like you, Ben Malone," she said.

"And I really like you too, Sara Bernstein," Malone said. "Louie, I think this is the beginning of a beautiful friendship."

Bernstein laughed.

"And who knows, maybe more," she said. She grinned widely. "Of all the psychiatric clinics in all the world, you had to walk into mine."

Malone laughed and said, "Here's looking at you, kid."

Sara laughed again and then she closed the car door, started the engine, and drove away.

15

Vasily

The next day passed uneventfully for Malone until just before five in the afternoon when his cell phone rang. He picked it up and saw "Bright Investigations" on the caller ID. Malone pushed the answer button and put the phone to his ear.

"Malone," he said.

"Malone, Jack Bright."

"I know it's you, Jack," Malone said. "I have caller ID like most everyone else in the world."

"Aren't you a little ray of sunshine?" Bright said with a laugh.

"Yeah, sorry Jack," Malone said. "I'm getting a little tired of the suspension and the rest of the crap. But what's up? Did you find out something?"

"Maybe," Bright said. "Just on my way to see a guy and find that out. I thought you might want to take a ride and hear what he has to say firsthand."

"Sure," Malone said. "Where are you?"

"About five minutes away," Bright said.

"See you in five, Jack," Malone said.

Malone pulled on a pair of jeans and put on a navy polo shirt. He put on a pair of New Balance sneakers and tied the laces. He grabbed his blue Dodgers cap and settled it on his head. When he stepped out the door, Jack Bright pulled into the lot. Malone got in, and Bright's Crown Vic roared out of the lot.

Jack Bright had retired after thirty years with the LAPD. Almost sixty now, he kept his longish steel-gray hair impeccably styled, reminiscent of the look made famous by former Dallas Cowboys coach Jimmy Johnson. Bright had softened a little with age since the days he had broken Malone in as a rookie detective, but still looked like a man who could take care of himself. With all the attention he paid to his grooming, Bright's clothing was another matter. His cheap, rumpled suit looked as if he had slept in it. He looked like the old television detective Columbo, minus the trench coat.

"Who are we going to see?" Malone asked.

"A guy named Vasily Dmitriyev," Bright said. "Vasily is Russian mafia, a brodyaga. Pretty much the same as a soldier in Italian-American mafia crime families."

"And he knows something that could help me?" Malone asked."

"Looks that way," Bright said. "But I only talked with him a couple of minutes on the phone. He prefers face to face. That's why we're going to see him."

"But if he is a criminal, why would he be willing to do anything to help a cop?" Malone said.

"Because it has nothing to do with his business," Bright said. "This mystery witness, according to Vasily, has some kind of connection to the Italian mob."

"Still, it makes little sense why he would help me," Malone said.

"He doesn't have any skin in the game, Malone," Bright said. "He is the Russian mafia. They are Italian mafia."

"What about honor among thieves?" Malone said.

Bright laughed. "That was always bullshit, Malone," he said. There has never been any honor among thieves. They may be in the same business, but only as competitors."

Bright took the southbound 710 exit off the 405 towards Long Beach. He followed the 405 south until they exited onto the Pacific Coast Highway and headed east across the Los Angeles River. They left the freeway at Oregon Avenue. After two blocks south, Bright turned right onto West Esther Street. He pulled to the curb in front of an old and dilapidated red brick warehouse building in the middle of the block filled with similar buildings. The area looked like a perfect site for some much needed urban renewal efforts. Some boarded over windows faced the street. Rusted iron bars covered the rest, along with the glass door at the center of the building. But the barred, gate-like enclosure for the door was standing open.

They got out of the car, and Malone followed Bright to the door. Bright pushed inside. The door opened onto a dusty reception area that looked as if they had decorated it in 1950. They had furnished the room with an ancient looking wooden desk, and a half dozen gray painted metal framed chairs with worn padding that looked like they had come from a surplus junk sale.

A large, barrel-chested man with broad shoulders and a thick neck leaned against the edge of the battered wooden desk. Malone guessed the man's height to be about six foot four. He appeared to be every bit of 250 pounds. His salt and pepper hair was closely cropped. His hairline in front had obviously been receding for a few years. Malone figured him to be mid-forties. He had gray eyes and a prominent nose that looked as if someone had broken it for him more than once. The man wore shiny black dress shoes, dark slacks, and a crisply starched light blue long-sleeved dress shirt. The most noticeable thing about his overall attire was a leather shoulder holster rig that held a large square-framed semi-automatic pistol.

"Hello Vasily, it's been awhile," Bright said.

"Hello Jack," Dmitriyev said. "I don't see so much of you since you left the cops."

"Vasily meet Malone, Malone meet Vasily," Bright said. "I've known Vasily a long time."

Dmitriyev pushed off the desk, stepped towards Malone, and extended a hand. Malone took it, and they shook.

"A pleasure I'm sure," Dmitriyev said. "Jack tells me you have trouble."

"Yes, a little legal matter," Malone said.

"On the phone, you said you might know something that could help Malone," Bright said.

"Perhaps," Dmitriyev said. "Let us sit and talk about it."

Bright and Malone sat down on a couple of the metal-framed chairs. Dmitriyev grabbed the back of the third from the line and pulled it around in front of Bright and Malone. He sat down facing them with his chair turned backward, his muscular forearms resting on the back of his chair.

Dmitriyev looked at Malone appraisingly, and then he began.

"As businessman, I make it my business to know the activities of my competitors. Word came to me that some competitors from Cleveland were looking to establish themselves in Los Angeles. That does not worry me. Their interests differ from mine and no threat to my business. They sell a little coke and make a few loans. What is that to me? Nothing. They are, as you Americans say, small potatoes."

"So what does that have to do with my situation?" Malone asked.

"The loan sharking part of their business, it explains your difficulties," Dmitriyev said."

"How so?" Malone said.

"The attorney who files the civil case against you, he borrowed money from my competitors. He needed money to finance the upfront expenses of the lawsuit. He believed he had a sure thing, a wrongful death lawsuit involving a policeman who had killed three suspects in less than one year. But he cannot finance expenses of the case himself, so he borrows money. The City of Los Angeles has history of settling such lawsuits. Certainly, they would not wish such a case as this to go to courts. So attorney thinks he would get quick settlement worth millions. He would pay out a few thousand to his client, explain the rest of settlement represented legal fees and expenses. He could then repay loan and pocket the rest, a substantial profit."

"But the city refused to settle," Malone said.

"Exactly," Dmitriyev said. "Plan go awry when city refuse to settle. City attorney believe the past practice of settling such lawsuits make city easy mark for crooked attorneys. The settlements had become too costly. City attorney believes the lawyer has weak case and refuses to consider settlement. He will take chances in court."

"So now the shyster lawyer is in a jam with his creditors," Malone said.

"Yes, exactly," Dmitriyev said. "They expect repayment of loan and the vig, of course."

"Of course," Malone said.

"With loan coming due, the lawyer is forced to reveal his problem to my competitors," Dmitriyev said. "They offer solution, but at a price. They tell lawyer to publish advertisement in LA newspaper seeking witness to police shooting. Then they tell lawyer a witness will come forward."

"But how could they know someone would read the ad and come forward?" Malone said.

"Simple," Dmitriyev said. "Advertisement was smoke screen for sake of appearances. My competitors provide the witness."

"How?" Malone said.

"Again, simple," Dmitriyev said. "They have another man who owes them money, who cannot pay. This man has habit of living beyond means. He enjoys gambling but has no luck. They offer this man deal. Instead of a bullet and shallow grave in desert, they will forgive his debt if he agrees to testify in civil case. They give him story to tell, confidential facts that they get from a source in the LAPD, so he is credible witness. He agrees, of course."

"So the lawyer places the ad, and the witness comes forward," Malone said.

"Exactly," Dmitriyev said.

"You've told us where the witness came from, Dmitriyev," Bright said. "But we already knew the witness was bogus. Malone needs a way to prove the witness is bogus."

"Patience Jack," Dmitriyev said. "I get to that. So I make some calls to inquire about Eddie Romano. And I learn things about his finances and habits. I learn when Romano has money, he spends more time in Las Vegas than LA. I call an acquaintance in Nevada who works in banking. She finds transactions from Las Vegas ATMs where Romano takes cash advances on credit card, two transactions the same day. That seems interesting because transactions occur same date as shooting that Romano claims to witness. ATMs have security cameras. My acquaintance sends me still photos from videos recorded at the time of Romano's transactions. Photos are good. Excellent likeness. Photos time-stamped. Show that Romano was in Las Vegas within minutes of shooting, he claims to see. How can Romano be in Las Vegas and over 250 miles away in LA at the same time? Impossible, no?"

"You have the photos?" Malone said.

Dmitriyev produced a thumb drive from his shirt pocket.

"Photos here," he said. "But also more on this drive. Informant tells me Romano is well known in Las Vegas casinos. I make another inquiry. I call someone who works security in a casino my employers have financial interest in. He is familiar with Romano. Says Romano regular customer there. He reviews casino security videos from dates of interest. He finds Romano on videos the day before the shooting, the day of shooting, and the day after. Impossible that Romano could have been in LA to witness shooting. Casino videos, also time-stamped, also on thumb drive."

Dmitriyev handed the thumb drive to Malone.

"This should be enough to discredit witness. But if needed, I also have records and security video photos from the hotel where Romano stays in Las Vegas."

"I really appreciate this, Vasily," Malone said. "But if you don't mind me asking, why did you go to all this trouble for me?"

Dmitriyev smiled. "In my country, we have saying," he said. "When someone gives you a free horse, you don't look at teeth."

"I think he is saying don't look a gift horse in the mouth, Malone," Bright said.

Dmitriyev looked at Bright, nodded, and then continued. "But I give you the answer. Jack did me big favor long time ago. He asked me to help with your problem. Could I say no? I return the favor to Jack. You get benefit. Who knows? Maybe someday you do favor for me."

Malone nodded. "Maybe so," he said. "Thanks, Vasily. I owe you."

The three men talked for a few more minutes, and then Bright and Malone left and started the drive back to Hollywood.

"Thank you, Jack," Malone said. "Send me a bill for your time. You saved my ass."

"Don't worry about it, Malone," Bright said. "Vasily did all the legwork. I'm just glad he had the juice to get the goods on Romano."

"I never dreamed I'd end up in the debt of a Russian mobster," Malone said.

"There are more things in heaven and earth, Horatio, than are dreamt of in your philosophy," Bright said with a grin.

They both laughed at the reference to Hamlet.

"Sometimes, you find a friend where you least expect it," Bright said.

Bright dropped Malone off at his apartment. Malone went inside and wasted no time calling Nathan Martinez. He told Martinez about the proof he had gained that discredited Romano as a witness. His lawyer agreed to come by first thing the following morning to pick up the thumb drive.

For the first time in a long while, Malone's life seemed to be headed in a more positive direction.

16

A Damning Lead

Malone awakened bright and early on Friday morning. He was relieved to have the evidence that Romano was a fraud. But he was really looking forward to his first date with Sara Bernstein that evening.

Martinez arrived after Malone had showered and dressed and was enjoying his second cup of coffee.

Malone filled a cup with coffee for Martinez, and the men sat down at the dining room table. Malone had set up his laptop on the table, and he inserted the thumb drive. Everything Dmitriyev had described was on the thumb drive, which wasn't a surprise to Malone because he had reviewed the data on the thumb drive the night before.

"How did you get this?" Martinez said.

"Bright got it from an old acquaintance of his," Malone said. He then summarized for Martinez the meeting with Dmitriyev.

"Okay," Martinez said. "I'm sure a Russian mobster has no plans to testify on your behalf, but we can definitely use this. I recognize Romano in all the photos. His California license photo was in the discovery file the assistant district attorney showed me. I'll just need to get affidavits from the bank, casino, and the hotel to support the photos."

"So what's the plan?" Malone asked.

"I'll contact them all today and ask them to fax me the affidavits," Martinez said. "As soon as I get them, I'll schedule a meeting with the assistant district attorney to get the criminal charge dismissed. Without Romano, they have no case. Then I'll see the assistant city attorney and provide him with this information. That will torpedo the civil case. With any luck, you should be free and clear of your legal problems by close of business on Monday."

"What about Romano and the crooked civil attorney?" Malone said.

"I'm pretty sure the DA will file a perjury charge against Romano," Martinez said. "But I think the lawyer covered his ass by publishing the advertisement in the paper. That gives him plausible deniability. It would be difficult, if not impossible, to prove he was in on the conspiracy. He will claim he took the witness at face value in good faith since Romano knew details that the LAPD had never made public outside the department, details he will claim that even he didn't know beforehand."

"I guess I'll just have to be satisfied with that," Malone said.

"Well, if it makes you feel any better, the lawyer's investors will not be thrilled with him," Martinez said. "If they really are a criminal syndicate like Dmitriyev says, then the lawyer may be the one with a bullet to the head and a shallow grave in the desert in his future. Romano might end up the fortunate one if he only goes to jail on the perjury beef."

"Yeah, until he gets shanked," Malone said. "He won't have exactly paid his debt to them, either."

"True," Martinez said.

"I suppose I should feel some sympathy for them, but I don't," Malone said.

"Can't fault you for that," Martinez said.

Martinez finished his coffee and then left for his office to get to work. Malone changed into shorts, a tee shirt, and his running shoes and went for a 3-mile run.

After the run and his second shower of the day, Malone worked on the Anderson case. He had accomplished nothing since he had interviewed Anderson's friend Marilyn Baker. Baker had suggested that he contact Anderson's sister Rebecca if he wanted more background on Robert Thames and his Latina ex-girlfriend from college. The problem was Rebecca now lived in San Diego, and until Martinez solved his legal problems, it wasn't feasible for Malone to travel to San Diego to interview her.

Initially, he had waited until he could interview her in person, but he changed his mind. She was the next logical person to talk with, and so he decided he would try to reach her by phone.

Malone got out his memo book where he had copied Rebecca Anderson's information given to him by Marilyn Baker. He dialed the number.

"Hello?" said a female voice.

"I was calling for Rebecca Anderson," Malone said. "I was told I could reach her at this number."

"Who is this?" the woman said.

"Detective Malone, Los Angeles Police Department," Malone said.

"Oh, hello, Detective," the woman said.

"Anderson is my maiden name," she said. "Larson is my married name. What's this about?"

"If you could spare me a few minutes of your time, I wanted to ask you a few questions about your sister, Mary Beth," Malone said.

"Have the police re-opened the investigation of her murder?" Larson said.

"Not officially yet," Malone said. "But I'm making some preliminary inquiries to determine whether circumstances warrant returning the investigation to active status."

"Okay," Larson said. "Please hang on just a moment."

Malone heard Larson telling someone to hold her calls and then heard a door being closed. Larson picked up the phone.

"What is it you wish to know?" she said.

"I spoke to Marilyn Baker a few days ago," Malone said. "She told me you were Mary Beth's closest confidant, and I had some questions Ms. Baker couldn't answer, but believed you might be able to. Specifically, questions relating to Robert Thames and an ex-girlfriend."

"My parents and I have prayed for over 20 years that Mary Beth's murder case would get re-opened," Larson said. "But we had just about given up hope that was ever going to happen. I'd be more than happy to help in any way possible to make that happen, Detective."

"Great," Malone said. Then he asked a few preliminary background questions and received similar answers to those that Marilyn Baker had given.

Mary Beth had been a wonderful person, admired and adored by practically everyone who knew her and a person with no enemies. Thus, Larson echoed the sentiments of Marilyn Baker in that Mary Beth's murder had been a complete and utter shock that just had made no sense. While not as direct about it as Baker had been, Larson expressed the same opinion as Baker had, that Robert Thames had simply not been capable of killing her sister under any circumstances. The conversation then turned to Thames' former love interest, beginning with the testy confrontation between the ex-girlfriend and Mary Beth Anderson that took place at Anderson's clinic after she and Thames had become engaged.

"Yes, Mary Beth told me about that," Larson said. "And that wasn't the only clash that occurred between them."

"What else happened?" Malone said.

"After the argument at the clinic, Mary Beth told me that the woman stalked her for months," Larson said. "It seemed like no matter where she went, the woman was always there."

"Were there more arguments?" Malone said.

"Not during the stalking thing," Larson said. "The woman kept her distance but made sure Mary Beth saw her. A few times Mary Beth tried to confront her, but the woman always disappeared into a crowd."

"Anything else?" Malone said.

"Yes, one more face-to-face confrontation that Mary Beth told me about," Larson said. "The woman was evidently a surfer, and when they were together, Robert always waxed her surfboard for her. Mary Beth told me that one day out of the blue after she and Robert had married, the woman showed up at their townhouse with her surfboard. She asked Robert to wax it for her."

"What happened?" Malone said.

"Mary Beth was livid," Larson said. "She told Robert there was no way in hell he was waxing the surfboard. But Robert wasn't exactly what you would call a forceful man. He told Mary Beth there wasn't any reason to cause a scene, and he agreed to take the surfboard and wax it. That only made Mary Beth angrier. She told the woman she was not welcome at their home and to never come there again. She said if Robert didn't have the balls to refuse, he could deliver the damn surfboard when he finished waxing it. So the woman left."

"Sounds like the woman caused a few problems for their marriage," Malone said.

"Yes, she did," Larson said. "Mary Beth almost called off the engagement after the woman came to her clinic. But then it almost became a test of wills between her and Robert's old flame. Despite her suspicions that Robert had somehow stayed involved with the woman after he and Mary Beth were engaged, she became determined that the woman would not break up their relationship."

"You said Mary Beth suspected that Robert and his ex-girlfriend were still involved," Malone said. "Do you mean romantically?"

"Well, Mary Beth believed they still saw each other on the sly," Larson said. And once after they were engaged and after they had an argument, Mary Beth told me she believed Robert had recently slept with his ex-girlfriend. That's when she gave him an ultimatum. Either the former girlfriend disappeared from their life, or she was going to end things with him."

"So did she disappear?" Malone said.

"She did until she showed up uninvited at their home with the surfboard," Larson said. "But Mary Beth was true to her word. She made Robert return the surfboard to her and, as far as I know, that unwelcome visit to her home was the last time Mary Beth ever saw the woman. Robert must have convinced her to leave them alone."

"It just occurred to me I haven't asked you the woman's name," Malone said.

"Oh, it was Alvarez," Larson said. "I mean, that was her last name. I think her first name may have been Essa or Essie? Something like that. But I only heard Robert call her by her first name once. Mary Beth only ever referred to her as Alvarez, or 'that woman' or 'that slut', if she was particularly angry at the time."

"So no one in your family ever suspected Robert Thames had anything to do with your sister's death?" Malone said.

"Absolutely not," Larson said. "If you had seen him afterward, especially at the funeral, you would have seen the same thing we saw. Mary Beth's death practically destroyed him. Robert acted like it was his fault. He acted like he had failed her by not protecting her. Then he started drinking heavily, and I heard he even became an alcoholic. He ended up getting fired by the bank, and I heard he really hit bottom before he finally turned his life around. Besides, as I mentioned, Robert was truly harmless. I don't think he could have harmed a fly, much less murdered someone. And he had a solid alibi, from people who had no real reason to cover for him if they had thought he had killed his wife. The police eliminated him as a suspect right away."

"Yes, that's what the file showed," Malone said.

"So what about Robert's ex-girlfriend?" Malone said. "Any feeling she might have killed your sister?"

"Of course," Larson said. "Haven't you talked with the original investigators?"

"Not yet," Malone said. "As I told you, I'm just making some preliminary inquiries at this point."

"Personally, I can't claim to know anything that proves she did it," Larson said. "But apparently Mary Beth had shared some things with our dad that she hadn't even told me about. As a result, he was adamant that Robert's ex-girlfriend had killed Mary Beth, and he told the detectives that from the beginning. And he kept telling them when they didn't seem to want to hear it."

"What made your father feel like they weren't interested in hearing it?" Malone said.

"Because she was a cop," Larson said. "Evidently, the LAPD hired her right out of college. My dad told the detectives 'that cop lady did it' and he still says it today."

"What did the detectives tell your father about it?" Malone said.

"They kept telling him it wasn't possible Alvarez had killed Mary Beth. They said they had checked it out, and that she was on duty the day Mary Beth died. I think they said she worked at Hollenbeck and that she was already at work at the time of the murder."

"But your father didn't believe it?" Malone said.

"No way," Larson said. "He has always believed the LAPD covered it up because they didn't want it known that one of their own had committed cold-blooded murder."

"And what's your opinion about it?" Malone said.

"Well, given the scandals the LAPD has been involved in, it wouldn't surprise me if it turned out that it was a cover-up," Larson said. "Besides Alvarez, there is absolutely no one that Mary Beth ever had a problem with that might have made someone want her dead."

Malone asked a few more questions and then gave Larson the same speech he had given Marilyn Baker. He asked her not to tell her family that they had talked until the LAPD decided whether to re-open her sister's case. Again, he had used the excuse that he didn't want to get their hopes up and leave them disappointed if his superiors didn't decide the case warranted re-opening. She agreed, and they hung up.

Malone was now very interested in learning a lot more about Thames' ex-girlfriend, LAPD Officer Alvarez. He wasn't ready to buy the cover-up story. He didn't want to believe that anyone associated with the department would bury a murder by a cop just to avoid embarrassment. Maybe that happened in the old days like they had depicted it in movies like LA Confidential, but things had changed a lot even by 1992 when Anderson died.

What Malone wanted to know before forming any conclusions was Officer Alvarez's whereabouts. Was she still with the department or had she left under a cloud of suspicion after someone killed Mary Beth Anderson? If she had resigned or they had terminated her shortly after that, then that might be a reason to believe there had been a conspiracy. He picked up his phone and punched in Jack Bright's number.

"Bright Investigations," Bright said.

"Jack, I have another favor to ask," Malone said.

"Jesus Christ, Malone," Bright said. "I'm trying to make a living here. What now?"

Malone ignored the jibe. He knew Bright was just giving him a hard time.

"Know anyone who worked at Hollenbeck in 1992?" Malone asked.

"Yeah, I know some guys," Bright said. "Probably all retired now. Why do you ask?"

"You know the Anderson case I've been looking at?" Malone said. "There wasn't anything in the murder book about it, but I just learned from the victim's sister that the family pointed the finger at a Hollenbeck cop by the name of Essa or Essie Alvarez when it happened. She was the ex-girlfriend of the victim's husband and seemed to be on the outs with the victim. I was hoping you knew someone I could get some background on her from."

"Didn't the original homicide dicks look at her?" Bright said.

"Yeah, but they brushed it off pretty quickly, it seems," Malone said.

"You aren't becoming another one of those LAPD conspiracy theorists, are you Malone?" Bright said.

"No, of course not," Malone said. "The detectives said they checked it out, and she was on duty when Anderson died. But mistakes happen. We both know that."

"So assuming I find someone who knew her, what do you want to know?" Bright said.

"I want to know her background, from 1992," Malone said. "I especially want to know if she left the department after the murder and if so, how long afterward."

"Yeah, I can guess why you would want to know that," Bright said. "Okay, I'll make some calls and get back to you."

Malone thanked Bright, and they disconnected. Malone hoped that the original investigators had been right. He didn't want to find out a cop had committed murder, much less that she had gotten away with it because the department had buried it. That could only have happened if some ranking officer or officers in the department had intentionally covered it up. Despite his own problems with the LAPD, Malone just didn't want to believe that had happened.

17

Date Night

Malone had offered to pick up Sara for their date, but she had insisted on driving herself and meeting him at the restaurant. Malone assumed it was because she didn't want to be held captive by depending on him for a ride if the date didn't come off well. He couldn't blame her. He could understand how a psychiatrist might view him as a little manipulative considering how he had parlayed a request for an in-home psychiatric session into a date with the therapist.

Given the suspension from duty without pay, Malone's bank account had reached a dangerously low level, but he had credit cards to finance a date. He planned on impressing Bernstein with his extravagance. He had chosen MW Restaurant, a pricey Asian fusion eatery on the 25th floor of the Palisades Hotel on Olympic Boulevard, near the Staples Center. It had a reputation for magnificent views of the nighttime LA skyline, a romantic atmosphere, and a refined wine list, not to mention an extended menu of craft cocktails. There was also a trendy theater just a block away if Sara was up for catching a movie after dinner.

Malone selected a nice dark blue suit with a plain white shirt and a conservative print tie. His black oxford shoes, polished to a nice shine, completed the ensemble.

Malone parked the Camry in the Staples Center parking garage and made the five-minute walk on South Figueroa to the Palisades. He found Sara waiting in the lobby near the elevators, and he thought she looked absolutely beautiful. She was wearing a form-fitting, emerald-green A-line skirt with a mid-thigh hem and fitted with a wide black belt at her natural waistline. She had paired the skirt with a fitted cream-colored blouse and had topped off her outfit with diamond stud earrings, a sparkling diamond pendant, heels, and a black clutch handbag. The shortness of the skirt emphasized her long and shapely legs. Her light brown hair was up, pulled back in a layered bun at the back of her head.

"Hello, Ben," Sara said.

"Hi Sara, you look stunning," Malone said.

"Well, thank you," she said. "You clean up pretty well yourself."

They joined several other couples in the elevator and headed up to the 25th floor. The entrance to the restaurant was directly across the corridor when the elevator doors opened. They stepped up to a hostess and Malone gave her his name, confirming that they had a reservation. Moments later, the hostess seated them at a table, looking out at the brightly lit LA skyline from high above. An attractive dark-haired server wearing a black skirt, white blouse, and bow tie appeared at the table to take their drink orders. Malone ordered a gin and tonic for starters, and Sara a glass of Chardonnay. They then perused the menus.

"Nice place you chose," Sara said. "Have you been here before?"

"No," Malone said. "But I've read some excellent reviews and hoped you might like the view and the food."

"Actually, I've been here before, and the food is marvelous," she said. "And yes, the view is fabulous, too. It's quite romantic here."

Malone stifled the urge to ask who she had been there with. He didn't want to appear a possessive jerk on the first date.

"There has been a positive development, and I have some news," he said.

"What news?" Sara said.

Malone gave her an abbreviated version of the visit he and Jack Bright had made to a man named Vasily Dmitriyev in Long Beach the previous day and how Dmitriyev had provided the hard evidence needed to expose that the surprise witness behind Malone's legal problems was a fraud.

"That's wonderful news, Ben," she said.

"Yes, if all goes according to plan, my lawyer says the DA should drop the criminal charge by Monday afternoon, and they should clear everything up."

"So you should be off suspension and back on duty soon," she said.

"Yes, hopefully by the middle of next week at the latest," Malone said.

"I can just imagine how relieved you are," Sara said.

"I'll say," Malone said. "This has been like living in a nightmare that I can't wait to wake up from."

"I'm very pleased for you, Ben. Not to mention relieved personally. I wasn't looking forward to the possibility of having to introduce my parents to a hardened criminal beau. I think they would be far more impressed by a police detective suitor."

They both laughed.

"Surely they have received my report by now, so I suppose you will return to Hollywood Division," Sara said.

"That's what I'm expecting," Malone said. "I should know more by Tuesday."

"Then tonight should definitely be a celebration," she said.

"Yes," Malone said. "But what I'm celebrating is the chance to be on a date with such a beautiful and intelligent woman."

"Aren't you sweet," Sara said, beaming.

The server returned for their dinner order, interrupting their conversation. Malone ordered crab shrimp sushi, and Sara ordered a hamachi salad and spring rolls. When their plates arrived, the portions were generous, and they shared. An hour after they had arrived, Malone was on his third gin and tonic, and Sara hadn't yet finished half of her first glass of white wine. After dinner, they sat and talked while they enjoyed the views of LA.

"Want to see a movie?" Malone said.

"Sure," Sara said. "Have one in mind?"

"No," Malone said. "I picked the restaurant, so you get to pick the movie. We can walk over to the Royal and see what's on."

"Okay, sounds good," Sara said.

They walked the block from the hotel to the theater. Malone reached for Sara's hand, and she allowed him to take it. When they arrived hand-in-hand at the theater, they checked out the movie listings displayed on the marquis. On a whim, Sara chose a romantic comedy called "Aloha." The movie was about a military contractor returning to the site of his greatest career achievements where he attempted to reconnect with a long-lost love while unexpectedly falling in love with the attractive, hard-charging female Air Force watchdog assigned to keep tabs on him. They enjoyed the movie and had a lot of laughs.

It turned out that Sara had parked at the Staples Center too, so after the movie, Malone walked her back to her car. Based on the discussion they had at his apartment previously, he hadn't expected that they would spend the night together. When they arrived at her car, she thanked him for a lovely evening and gave him a chaste kiss on the lips. She then opened the door and got into her car.

"I really had fun," she said. "And I think I'm past the ethical dilemma."

"I had fun too," Malone said. "Spending time with you was everything I imagined it would be, better even."

"I'm thrilled that things are working out for you, Ben," she said.

"Thanks," he said. "Me too. It will make a lot of things less complicated."

"Thanks again," she said. "Call me."

"Count on it," he said.

She smiled and started the car. Malone watched as she backed out, waved, and drove away. He wasn't feeling disappointed that the evening had ended as it had. Since his divorce, it was the first date he had been on that hadn't ended in sex. But with Sara, he found he was almost happy the evening hadn't ended that way. It just gave him something to look forward to because he felt certain they had really clicked. If so, then sex would be in their future when both of them felt the time was right. He walked to his car, left the Staples Center, and started the drive home to his apartment.

When Malone arrived home, he found the light blinking on his answering machine. He picked up the phone, hit the button, and listened to the recording. The message was from Jack Bright. He said he had some information on Alvarez and to call him when he could. It was almost one o'clock in the morning, so Malone decided it had to keep until morning.

Malone grabbed a beer from the refrigerator, sat down in his chair, and switched on the television. He tuned into ESPN to see how the Dodgers had done against the Padres. Apparently, the game had been a pitcher's duel, but LA had come out on the short end of a 2-1 final. Unless the Dodgers turned things around soon, they were going to miss the chance to win their third consecutive NL West Championship and the chance to make the playoffs for the third year in a row for the first time in team history.

He watched Sports Center until he finished the beer and then turned off the television. He headed to bed. Mostly, thoughts of Sara Bernstein filled his mind. He couldn't help wishing she was in his bed waiting for him.

18

Evidence Found

Jack Bright didn't wait for Malone to return his call from the previous evening. He called Malone first thing Saturday morning and early. Malone had planned to sleep in and hadn't set the alarm. Nevertheless, when the phone rang, arousing him from a deep sleep, he automatically started flailing at the alarm clock, thinking it was the source of the irritating racket that was disturbing his sleep. Finally, he realized it was the phone ringing, not the alarm, and he grabbed the receiver.

"Malone," he said groggily.

"Good morning, sleeping beauty," Bright said cheerily.

"Jack?" Malone said. "What time is it?"

"Time to wake up, pal," Bright said. "I have some information for you on Alvarez."

"I was going to call you back," Malone said. "I got home late last night."

"Hot date, Malone?" Bright said, laughing. "I called you seeing as how I have a tee time at the club in forty-five minutes. I didn't want you ringing my cell phone and spoiling a putt."

Malone sat up on the edge of the bed and rubbed his face, struggling to clear his mind of drowsiness.

"I found a guy that remembered Alvarez," he said. "He knew her pretty well. He was one of her training officers after she finished the academy."

"So what's the story?" Malone said.

"He didn't remember much," Bright said. "It was over twenty years ago, so that's understandable. But he said he remembered her as a decent boot. There was a problem, though. When she went hands-on with a suspect, she seemed prone to forget all about the concept of reasonable force. In fact, he finally threatened to wash her out of training if she didn't get it under control. She got with the program after that and completed training with no more problems. Once she was out on her own, she turned out to be a solid cop and had a good rep with the other troops."

"So what happened with her, especially after around January 1992?" Malone said.

"Nothing special apparently," Bright said. "The guy I talked with retired in 1998. The guy said Alvarez made detective and then they promoted her to sergeant just before he pulled the pin. He didn't keep in touch after he took his pension, but said she was still at Hollenbeck in 1998 when he left. Also, he said she was definitely a career girl with high aspirations. He said he would surprise him to learn she wasn't still a cop."

"Anything else?" Malone said.

"He said he remembered she had a brother, a banger, who got into some serious trouble while she was in training. One day, she got a call. She told him there was a problem with her brother. She said her parents were very worried and asked if they could stop by their house on East 27th Street for a few minutes so she could try to calm them down. He said it was slow, so he told her okay. He said there were a couple of Newton Division black and whites at the house when they arrived. They had her brother handcuffed in the back of one of them.

He said Alvarez got out, walked over to the car, opened the back door, and went bat-shit crazy on her brother, punching and screaming at him until the Newton guys pulled her off."

"I'm seeing a pattern here," Malone said.

"No shit, Sherlock," Bright said. "At least back then, Alvarez seemed to have some violent tendencies. Probably to be expected from someone who grew up in South Central. Probably needed that to survive."

"Was he able to confirm her first name?" Malone said.

"He said her name was Essie. At least, that was what everyone called her. He said that was a nickname, though, not her actual name. But if he ever knew her given name, he had forgotten what it was."

"If I could track down her parents, I could find out the name," Malone said.

"So, are you asking for yet another favor, Malone?" Bright said. "Now you want me to track down Alvarez's parents for you?"

"Only if it wouldn't be too much trouble, Jack," Malone said. "You have access to the databases, which I don't until I get off the beach."

"Well, would it be okay with you Malone if I enjoyed the rest of my weekend and started on Monday?" Bright said.

"Come on Jack," Malone said. "I can tell you're hooked on this case now. You want to find out if Alvarez did it as much as I do."

"Yeah whatever, Malone," Bright said. "But okay. I'll see what I can find out. I'll let you know. But now I got a golf game to get to."

Bright hung up, and Malone put down the phone, laughing. Bright could be ornery as hell, but he was a good friend.

Malone decided he might as well start his day, since he was already fully awake. He could always sleep in on Sunday. He went for a run, showered, and made himself eggs and bacon for breakfast. After he had finished eating, he took his coffee out on the patio and thought about what he should do next. A lot would depend on what happened with work. If Martinez had been right, he might have to return to work as soon as Tuesday. By Wednesday, he might be back at Hollywood Division with a normal heavy caseload. That would make it a challenge to find time to work on the Anderson murder.

It also occurred to him that a move back to Hollywood would complicate even more the possibility of getting permission to re-open the case. The legal realities demanded that at some point he had to be working the case in an official rather than unofficial capacity. He wondered whether Jim Turner would even consider giving permission to a detective from an outside bureau permission to open and investigate a cold case. Members of the LAPD command staff could be obsessively protective of their turf. Some would never allow an outsider near a case under their personal jurisdiction.

Malone decided there were too many moving parts at the moment to worry about how things were going to shake out. He would just take it a day at a time and not worry about what he could not influence or control. Instead, he would do what he could do. He decided it was time to talk with Kenneth Myers.

Malone knew that the reports in the murder book that Meyers had written were like all official police reports. They were sterile and concise distillations of all the facts and impressions that Myers had uncovered during the original investigation. Reading them was no substitute for talking to the man who had likely summarized the reports from literally hundreds of pages of field notes.

At the very least, Malone wanted to hear directly from Myers about Officer Alvarez and why he had excluded her as a suspect. He decided he would track down Myers on Monday and try to arrange a meet. If he got lucky, maybe Bright would turn up an address for Alvarez's parents early on Monday, and he could talk with them, too. He would play Tuesday by ear and wait to make any plans until he found out more about work. Even if Martinez cleared up the legal mess Monday, it might still take the department more than a day to react. He had a sneaking suspension that the brass was a hell of a lot more efficient with handing out suspensions than they were in unsuspending people. Even for those who hadn't deserved to be suspended in the first place.

Just after three o'clock in the afternoon, Malone's phone rang. He picked up.

"Malone," he said.

"Detective Malone, this is Jane Kroft from the coroner's office," the caller said.

"Oh yes, hello Jane," Malone said. "How have you been?"

"Good thanks," Kroft said. "I thought you were going to call me."

"I'm sorry Jane," Malone said. "I've just been crazy busy and haven't had a chance. Anyway, what's up?"

"I just wanted to let you know I found the missing swabs from your case," Kroft said.

"Did you?" Malone said. "That's great news."

"Yes, everyone in my section pitched in. We cleaned out and searched every nook and cranny of every evidence refrigeration unit. Somehow, the envelope containing the swabs from the bite wound had fallen into a small space behind one shelf in the unit we stored it in. Over time, moisture had faded the printed case number until it was completely unreadable. Luckily, the victim's name had also been printed on the label and was still legible. So anyway, mystery solved. I've properly repackaged the evidence, labeled it, and safely stored it for retrieval."

"Now we just need a DNA analysis from those bite wound swabs," Malone said.

"All I need is a signed request from the cold case unit supervisor, and I can submit them for analysis," Kroft said.

"You can't just submit them on my request as the investigator?" Malone said.

"No," Kroft said. "Policy requires a signature from a unit supervisor. It's a budget issue. DNA analysis costs money. That money has to come out of the budget of the requesting unit. So someone with the authority to approve the expenditure has to sign the request. Here, that would be the supervisor of the cold case homicide unit."

"Look, Jane, I'm in something of a Catch 22 here," Malone said. "I really need that evidence analyzed. But I don't exactly have a firm suspect for comparison. I'm close, but I'm just not there yet. I'm certain my supervisor won't sign a request for analysis until I can tell him I have a suspect ready to be hooked and booked. But having the analysis could point me in the right direction. It could even give me some leverage to use when I identify a firm suspect. Isn't there anything you can do?"

"No, there isn't," Kroft said. "And given what you've just told me, your supervisor would be right to refuse to authorize the expenditure without a viable suspect. DNA analysis isn't useful without a sample from a viable suspect that the lab can compare against the evidentiary sample."

"At least in this specific case, that isn't true," Malone said. "The analysis would reveal whether the killer was male or female. That is a piece of information that would help my investigation right now. Doesn't your section sometimes request DNA analysis on evidence collected at autopsies or the scene by medical examiner investigators?"

"Of course we do but only on county cases," Kroft said. "This is an LAPD case, and the cost of the analysis should come from your department's budget."

"Please Jane, can't you find a way to do this for me?" Malone said. "Getting the DNA analysis from those swabs could be crucial. It could help break the case wide open."

"If my supervisor found out I authorized the expenditure of county funds on a city case, I could get into a lot of trouble, Malone," Kroft said.

"You have a perfect explanation that would cover you even if your supervisor found out," Malone said. "The evidence envelope got temporarily lost. The information printed on the label faded until it was illegible. You could just say it accidentally got submitted for analysis with another case and it wasn't possible to know that had happened until the results came back and you realized the evidence was from a different case."

"Well, I suppose that might work," Kroft said. "But I'd still be taking a risk. My supervisor knows I don't make mistakes like that."

"Yes, but knowing something and proving it are two very different things, Jane," Malone said. "You would still be covered. Your supervisor would just have to take your word for what happened. Won't you do this for me? Please submit the swabs for analysis for me. I'll be so grateful, and I'll owe you big time. After all these years, Mary Beth Anderson deserves justice."

"You'll owe me, huh?" Kroft said.

"Yes, I will," Malone said. "You get me that analysis and I'll buy you lunch or drinks, whatever you want."

"Okay, I'll do it," Kroft said. "I'll submit the swabs today. But Malone, I'm holding you to your promise."

"Oh thank you, Jane," Malone said. "I appreciate it. And of course, we'll get together for lunch or drinks just as soon as I hear from you. Count on it."

Kroft said goodbye, and they disconnected. Malone knew he was going to have to have a discussion about the case with Lieutenant Turner very soon. But at least the DNA analysis of the swabs would already be a done deal. With that already accomplished, it might be enough to convince Turner to re-open the case if Malone had a viable suspect to collect a DNA sample from for comparison. And he was confident he would have a suspect soon.

Malone decided he should call Sara Bernstein to tell her how much he enjoyed their date on Friday evening. He had heard somewhere that it always impressed women when a guy called them the next day after a date and improved the chances of getting another date. She had given him her cell phone number the previous evening, so now he didn't have to wait to reach her at the office. He punched the number into his cell phone. She answered on the second ring.

"Hello?" she said.

"Hi Sara, Ben here," Malone said.

"Hi there, Ben," she said. "It's great to hear from you."

"I was just thinking of you, and I just wanted to call and tell you how much I enjoyed spending time with you last night," Malone said.

"I enjoyed it very much too, Ben," she said.

"I'm thrilled to hear that," Malone said. "So I thought maybe we should make a plan to do it again next weekend."

"Sounds great," Sara said. "I have nothing planned for next weekend. Were you thinking about Friday evening again or Saturday?"

"How about both?" Malone said.

"Both?" Sara said. "Don't you think you might grow tired of my company if we spend too much time together?"

"I'm pretty certain I couldn't grow tired of you if I saw you every single day," Malone said.

"That's so sweet, Ben," Sara said.

"Just telling it like is," Malone said.

"So what did you have in mind, then?" Sara said.

"Well, Friday I thought we could have dinner again and maybe see a concert at the Microsoft Theater afterward," he said.

"That sounds fun," she said. "I'd been thinking about how much I'd like seeing something at the Microsoft. It would be great going with you."

"Terrific," Malone said. "That takes care of Friday evening, then."

"And Saturday?" Sara said.

"I thought we could have brunch and then catch the Dodgers game," Malone said. "That is, if you like baseball."

"Honestly, I haven't been to a baseball game since I was a teenager," she said. "But yes, it might be fun seeing a game with you."

"That's great," Malone said. "After the game, if you're up for it, we might have dinner again."

"You want to make a full day of it, then?" Sara said with a chuckle.

"Sure, if it works for you," Malone said. "I just really like spending time with you."

"I enjoy spending time with you too, Ben," she said. "So sure. I'm up for Friday evening and for making a full day of it on Saturday."

"Wonderful," Malone said. "I'll peruse the reviews and find great restaurants for both days."

"Awesome," Sara said. "I'll leave it to you. You picked a great one for last night. But please know I don't expect you to take me to expensive places all the time. There are tons of wonderful restaurants in LA that don't cost an arm and a leg."

"I'll keep that in mind," Malone said. "But I do like taking you to nice places."

"Thank you, Ben," she said. "I appreciate it, but you don't have to spend a lot of money on me to get my attention. You already have it."

"Good to know," he said. "I'll see you Friday then. But I'll call you during the week to work out the details."

"Sounds good," Sara said.

They said goodbye and hung up. It occurred to Malone that he was feeling fantastic about things in general for the first time in a long while. He knew that Sara Bernstein was a big part of that.

19

A New Theory

Malone slept in, waking just before ten o'clock on Sunday morning. The phone rang as he was about to start his third cup of coffee after eating breakfast. He picked it up and saw "Bright Investigations" on the caller ID screen. So he took the call.

"Malone," he said.

"Up already, Malone?" Bright said. "It isn't even noon yet."

"Yes, I'm up Jack," Malone said. "You know me. Early to bed, early to rise."

"Yeah, whatever Malone," Bright said. "I had some time this morning and checked the databases for a line on Alvarez's parents. There was only one Alvarez listed in the property tax records on East 27th Street, Ramon Alvarez. I checked the California license database and found a driver's license issued to Ramon Alvarez, listing the same address. He is in his seventies, so I'm pretty sure it has got to be her father. How about we take a ride over there and talk to Ramon this afternoon after lunch?"

"Sounds like a plan," Malone said.

"Okay, I'll pick you up at your place around noon," Bright said.

"See you then, Jack," Malone said.

Bright hung up, and Malone headed for the shower. It had been a while since he had been to South Central LA, which comprised much of the city south of the 10 freeway.

South Central had a reputation as one of Los Angeles's most dangerous neighborhoods. For many Angelenos, South Central was shorthand for "ghetto." Malone knew from experience that mostly hard-working, blue-collar people populated South Central. But without a doubt, since the eighties, there had been an enormous increase in the number of gangs in South Central.

The influence of the gangs spiraled out of control with the beginning of the crack epidemic in the nineties. Beginning in 2000, the LAPD became intensely focused on the South Central gang problem in efforts to reduce the crime rate. The emphasis had achieved positive results, reducing both the number of gang-related homicides in the neighborhood and decreasing the overall number of gangs when they arrested scores of gang members, charged them with various crimes, and sent them to prison. Still, gangs remained a problem in South Central LA. Every block, street, school, park, apartment complex, and housing project had some degree of gang influence. The violence might have become more sporadic, but it still existed. There were a lot of homeless people around, revealing the poverty that existed in the neighborhood. It was simply a fact of life that where there was poverty, there was crime. The same was true of every large American city, not just LA.

Realistically, Malone didn't expect to learn much from Ramon Alvarez. The residents of South Central LA didn't cooperate with the police as a rule. They simply didn't trust cops, believing that the officers who patrolled the streets of the gang-heavy neighborhood engaged in brutality, fabricated evidence, and told outright lies in criminal investigation reports. There were even accusations that narcotic officers stole money and drugs from the drug dealers in the neighborhood. Still, he hoped he could learn something about Essie Alvarez's background from her father before he spoke with Kenneth Myers about her.

Malone was sitting on his second story patio when he saw Bright's car pull into the lot. He donned his Dodger's cap, went downstairs, and got into the passenger seat of Bright's car.

"You think Alvarez is going to tell us anything useful?" Bright asked, by way of a greeting as he drove out of the parking lot.

"Let's just say I'm cautiously optimistic," Malone said. "At least I think it's worth finding out."

"Yeah, we don't have any leverage with him," Bright said. "He will probably just tell us to take a hike."

"Only one way to find out," Malone said. "Let's go see him."

Bright took to the entrance ramp to the 101 and drove south to the 110. After exiting onto the 110, he followed it to the East 17th Street exit. Leaving the freeway, Bright took South Central Avenue to East 27th Street. They arrived about 30 minutes after leaving Malone's apartment at the address listed on Alvarez's driver's license. It was a small, white-framed house badly in need of a fresh coat of paint, surrounded by a cyclone fence. Bright stopped the car in front of the house, and the men got out. As they approached the gate, a large brindle and white colored pit bull dog charged the gate barking ferociously, and the men took a step back.

"You go on in and knock on the door, Malone," Bright said, laughing. "I'll wait here."

"Like that is going to happen," Malone said. "We would have to shoot that son of a bitch before I'd take a step inside that fence.

The two stood on the sidewalk outside the fence while the dog growled, barked, and lunged against the fence. The front door eventually opened, and an elderly Latino man stepped out onto the porch to see what had the dog stirred up. He eyed Malone and Bright suspiciously, but he said a few words in Spanish to the dog, and it reluctantly left the gate and sauntered over to the porch. The man spoke another couple of words to the dog in Spanish, and the dog went through the door into the house. The man closed the door and then walked out to the gate.

"Mr. Alvarez?" Malone said.

"Cops?" the man asked.

"Yes, I'm Detective Malone, LAPD," Malone said. He introduced Jack as Detective Bright, not making the distinction that Bright was a PI and letting the man draw his own conclusions.

"Yes, I'm Ramon Alvarez," the man said. "If this is about Javier, I have not seen him since he went to prison the last time."

Malone assumed Javier must be Alvarez's son, Essie's brother.

"Is he still in prison?" Malone said.

"As I have said, I have not seen him," Alvarez said. "But I have heard rumors he received a parole a few months ago. He is not welcome here. He would not come here."

"We aren't here about Javier," Malone said. "If you could spare me a few minutes of your time, I'd like to ask you a few questions about your daughter."

"Essie?" he said. "What questions could you have about my Essie? She is like you, no? LAPD."

Malone quickly fabricated a story, not wishing to disclose the real reason he was interested in Essie Alvarez.

"Essie is being considered for a promotion," Malone said. "They have assigned me to do a background check in connection with the promotion."

"She has been a police officer for many years now," Alvarez said. "What more is there to know than is already known? Cops came around and asked many questions before they hired her and she went to the academy."

"All I know is my superiors assigned me to speak with her family members and ask some questions," Malone said. "I'm just doing my job."

"These questions, what is it you wish to know?" Alvarez said.

"Over twenty years ago, not long after Essie completed the academy, there was a woman who complained that Essie stalked her and harassed her," Malone said. "Do you recall anything about that?"

"I don't have to answer your questions," Alvarez said. "I think I will tell you nothing."

"You're right, Mr. Alvarez," Malone said. "You don't have to talk with me. But I'm sure you care about your daughter's future, and you would like to see her promoted as any father would wish the best for one of his children. If you choose not to cooperate, it could cause her to not get the consideration she deserves for a very important promotion."

"Perhaps your superiors are seeking an excuse not to promote her," Alvarez said.

"No, that's not true," Malone said. "It's just that the position she has applied for is sensitive where she would be in the public eye. My superiors just want to be certain that the incident from the past isn't something that someone might use to discredit the department."

"Then why do you not talk to Essie about it?" Alvarez said.

"We have," Malone said. "We're simply verifying the information by speaking with family members who might have known about the incident I mentioned. It's necessary to corroborate Essie's recollections. You know, to make sure that everyone tells the same story. If you help me with this, it will only help Essie's chances."

It was obvious from Alvarez's facial expressions that he was struggling with the decision over whether to tell Malone what he wanted to know. Finally, his concern over possibly harming his daughter's career won out.

"I know of what you speak," he said. "It was all lies, the accusations made by that woman. Essie spoke of it to me. The problem was not Essie. Essie had ended a relationship with the woman's fiancé before the woman became engaged to him. But he would not leave Essie alone. He kept calling, coming to see her. So she went to the woman only to ask her to reason with him, to persuade him to leave her be. The woman did not believe her. She became angry and tried to make trouble for Essie."

"The man who was involved, that was Robert Thames?" Malone said.

"Yes, that is the one," Alvarez said. "Even once he was married, he kept trying to be with Essie."

"Do you recall anything about the relationship when Essie and Thames were together?" Malone asked.

"Yes, of course," Alvarez said. "Essie met him in college. They dated for over two years. He proposed to Essie. My wife, may she rest in peace, and I was against the proposed marriage. He was an Anglo, and my wife longed for Essie to meet and marry a nice Latino man. But Essie, she believed she was in love. She accepted his proposal. They were engaged. But he was not a good man. I knew this after meeting him only one time. Eventually, Essie discovered he was cheating on her, seeing that woman behind her back that he eventually married. Essie was heart-broken, but she ended the relationship when he disrespected her, and violated her trust."

"So Essie was pretty upset about how things turned out with him?" Malone said.

"Yes, of course," Alvarez said. "We all were. After accepting that she was going to marry him despite our feelings, we gave her our blessing, only for him to break her heart and dishonor her that way. Javier was so angry he threatened to kill him."

"Really?" Malone said. "Why was Javier so upset?"

"Essie is his older sister," Alvarez said. "He worshiped her and admired her in every way. He could not stand to see her dishonored that way and Javier has always had problems controlling his anger."

"He actually threatened to kill Thames?" Malone said.

"He did not go to him and threaten him personally, no," Alvarez said. "He only said to us, to Essie, what he planned to do."

"What happened then?" Malone said.

"Essie demanded that he stop speaking like a fool," Alvarez said.

"So he dropped it?" Malone said.

"Not really," Alvarez said. "Javier had become involved with the gangs in the neighborhood. He got a gun. One day, he got drunk and pulled out the pistol here in this house. He said he was going to go to Thames and kill him for dishonoring his sister and family. I was at work and my wife, she could not talk sense to him. While he was getting dressed, she called the police. The police came and disarmed him. They arrested him. My wife called me at work, and I came home. After I had arrived, Essie showed up with another cop. She confronted Javier, and she beat him a little until he promised not to go near Thames."

Suddenly Malone felt he might have learned something very important.

"How old was Javier back then?" Malone asked.

"He was about twenty," Alvarez said. "Maybe nineteen. Anyway, it was the year before Essie talked him into enlisting in the Marines."

"Do you have a photo of Javier from around that time?" Malone said.

"Perhaps," Alvarez said. "Why do you ask about photos? You said you were not here about Javier."

"Do you know what happened to Thames' wife?" Malone said.

Alvarez was quiet for a long moment before speaking.

"I know she died," Alvarez said finally. "Essie spoke of it when it happened, that she someone killed her during a burglary. It was a tragedy."

"Yes," Malone said. "And the investigators never identified or arrested a suspect. What was Javier in prison for?"

"He has been in prison three times," Alvarez said. "I had such hopes for him when he joined the military. I thought the Marines would make him grow up and help him develop self-discipline. But after he finished his training, he got into a fight in a bar in San Diego and almost beat a man to death. The Marines kicked him out with a bad conduct discharge. When he arrived home, he took up with the gangs again. He got into more trouble. The first time it was drugs. He went to the county jail for one year. Then the police arrested him for burglary. He went to prison, to San Quentin for two years before they paroled him. He did not learn. His rage became worse. He shot someone in another gang last time. The man lived, so they charged Javier with attempted murder. His attorney arranged a plea bargain. Javier pled guilty to attempted voluntary manslaughter. He got eleven years at Pelican Bay."

"When did they arrest him for burglary?" Malone said.

"It was a long time ago," Alvarez said. "I think maybe 1992, 1993 perhaps."

Malone felt his pulse quicken, the way it always did when he knew he was getting close to solving a puzzle or learning a truth he had been searching for. Maybe he was about to discover the identity of Anderson's killer, a potential suspect with a history as a burglar and for violent assault. A suspect that had once threatened to kill Robert Thames for shaming his sister. Maybe Myers hadn't been completely wrong after all. Maybe Mary Beth Anderson had died during a burglary gone sideways. But maybe she had never been the intended victim. Maybe the motive had been revenge, a plan aimed at settling an old score. Maybe it had been Thames who was the intended victim, and Mary Beth had simply made the mistake of taking a sick day on the worst possible day.

"So, what about the photo?" Malone said.

"After they sentenced him to prison the first time, I told Javier he had shamed our family. I told him he was no longer welcome in this house. But he is still my son. I will not help you implicate him in that woman's murder," Alvarez said.

"Not even to help your daughter?" Malone said.

"What do you mean?" Alvarez said.

"I shouldn't tell you this, but you seem like a good man and a good father, so I'm going to break the rules," Malone said. "I'm going to confide in you. Your daughter was a suspect in the murder of Thames' wife twenty-three years ago. But she had enough of an alibi that they didn't arrest or charge her. However, suspicion has hung over her, and her career like a dark cloud since the murder happened, especially since they never identified the killer. That is the real reason they sent here me to talk with you. My supervisors want to promote her to a key position in the department, but only if they can clear up the suspicions once and for all. It's the one thing standing in Essie's way of getting the promotion. One black mark against an otherwise exemplary record as a police officer."

Alvarez remained silent for several moments, looking thoughtful. Malone could see that he was clearly torn between doing something that might help his daughter's career, but at the price of possibly betraying his son to the police. Finally, he spoke.

"I will save us trouble," Alvarez said. "I would have to search through many boxes containing my wife's things to find a photo of Javier. You want to know if Javier appears to match the drawing that the police circulated after the woman was murdered? No?"

"Yes, I am curious to know that," Malone said.

"I saw the drawing in the newspaper," Alvarez said. "Do not think I did not spend many sleepless nights wondering about the very thing you are now curious about. I will save us the time it would take to find a photo from back then. Instead, I will say this. Yes, there were similarities. I never spoke of it to Javier. I feared the answer given his threats. But you must know that drawing was merely an image of a Latino man in his twenties. It could have been Javier. But it could have been the likeness of a thousand Latinos in Los Angeles back then, perhaps ten thousand. It is not proof that Javier did this evil thing."

"The detectives assigned the case believed there were two men involved," Malone said. "Perhaps Javier was a part of it, but he wasn't the killer. Perhaps we could learn that by speaking with him."

"I think he will say nothing to you. No matter whether he had involvement or not," Alvarez said. "He is even more distrustful of the police than me."

"Well, thank you for your cooperation, Mr. Alvarez," Malone said. "I can appreciate this conversation has been very uncomfortable for you."

"I only hope your superiors make the right decision," he said. "My Essie is an excellent police officer. She has escaped from this neighborhood and made a good life for herself. It is not only the pride of a father speaking when I say she would do well if she received the promotion. She has always excelled in all that she has ever done."

"I'm sure you're right, Mr. Alvarez," Malone said. "She has an impressive record and an outstanding reputation as a Los Angeles police officer."

Bright interrupted, speaking for the first time when it seemed the interview of Alvarez was ending.

"Excuse me, Mr. Alvarez, but I have just one question before we let you go," Bright said. "It's just something I'm curious about, if you wouldn't mind telling me the answer."

"What is it you wish to know?" Alvarez said.

"I know Essie is a nickname," Bright said. "But who came up with it? Who first started calling her Essie? Was it you, a father-daughter thing?"

Alvarez laughed.

"I do not mind clearing away the mystery for you," he said. "It was Javier who started calling her Essie when he was very young. He could not pronounce 'Vanessa' and instead produced a name he could pronounce, 'Essie.' Soon we all adopted the name. It seemed to fit her."

"Delightful story," Bright said.

Malone thanked Alvarez again for his time, and he and Bright returned to the car. As they were driving away, Malone looked at Bright and grinned.

"Well played, Jack, well played," he said.

Bright laughed. "Well, after the fairy tale you spun for him about her big promotion opportunity, he sure as hell would have become a little suspicious if we had revealed we didn't even know her damn name."

"Yeah, you're right about that," Malone said. "The whole time I was trying to think of some way of finding out her real first name, but nothing was coming to me. Your idea was brilliant, and it worked so smoothly."

"I am the expert detective here, after all," Bright said with a grin. "You're learning, but you're still a little wet behind the ears, Malone."

"It's funny," Malone said. "I went there looking for a reason to believe Essie or Vanessa Alvarez killed Mary Beth Anderson. Now, after talking with Ramon Alvarez, I'm leaving, really liking his son Javier for it. It seems like some pieces of the puzzle have fallen into place."

"Yeah, there are sure a lot of things that seem to point to old Javier," Bright said. "I guess when you go see Myers, you're planning to give him an apology."

"Apology?" Malone said.

"Yeah," Bright said. "It seems his burglar theory wasn't as screwed up as you thought, and maybe he wasn't as stupid or lazy as you've been giving him credit for."

Malone laughed. "Yeah, you might be right, Jack. But I don't think I'll be mentioning any of that to Myers."

A half-hour later, Bright dropped Malone at his apartment and drove away. Malone felt as if he was getting somewhere. He was even more impatient to get the results from the DNA testing on the bite wound swabs that Kroft was taking care of.

Malone knew that from 2004 to 2014, it had been standard procedure in California county jails to take DNA samples from all adults booked into jail who and charged with a felony. The collections involved just a simple swab inside the cheek. The crime lab processed the swabs. Then they submitted the DNA profiles to CODIS, the national law enforcement database of non-medical DNA profiles.

The database also contained DNA profiles from evidence collected from crime scenes across the nation submitted by law enforcement agencies. The samples collected from inmates were automatically compared against the evidentiary profiles in the electronic database. Malone knew the system had cleared many cold cases. It was a very effective tool for California law enforcement until 2014, when the California Court of Appeals ended the practice in California of collecting DNA samples from every inmate charged with a felony. The CCA ruled that collecting DNA from someone only suspected, not convicted of a crime, violated an individual's constitutional rights.

But Malone knew from the interview with Ramon Alvarez that chances were good that Javier Alvarez's DNA profile was already in the system. It would be a simple matter of submitting the profile yielded from the bite wound swab analysis to get a hit on Javier's profile.

Malone figured he might now not only be able to bring Lieutenant Turner a DNA evidentiary profile, but might just be able to hand him a solid suspect at the same time. That should certainly be enough to get the case re-opened.

The rest of Malone's weekend passed uneventfully. He went to bed feeling good about the progress made on the Anderson case and feeling hopeful his legal problems would be over sometime on Monday afternoon. Then he could put it all behind him and get back to work. Unfortunately, while there was no way Malone could know it when he dropped off to sleep, things were about to get worse before they got better.

20

An Unexpected Development

Malone woke up early on Monday morning. He was so eager to learn the outcome of his legal mess that he hadn't been able to sleep well during the night. After breakfast, he sat down at the dining room table with another cup of coffee and his laptop. He wanted to locate Kenneth Myers, the retired Los Angeles detective who had worked the Anderson case over twenty years before.

All he knew about Myers was that he had retired after almost thirty years with the department in 2004, a dozen years after Mary Beth Anderson's murder. Malone figured Myers must be in his mid-fifties now.

Malone had considered calling Jack Bright to ask if he could get a line on Myers' whereabouts, but decided against it. He had already asked Jack to do too much. He started with Facebook and got lucky.

There were several Kenneth Myers profiles, but it was obvious when he had found the profile he was looking for. There were lots of references to the LAPD, particularly the Van Nuys Division. Malone learned several useful facts. Myers evidently lived in Westwood. He worked in some security capacity for a large, well-known aerospace corporation in El Segundo, a Los Angeles County city on the Santa

Monica Bay. El Segundo had long been the home to many aviation-related industries and operations.

Malone hoped to speak with Myers today. Given that it was a Monday, he was likely to be at work, so contacting him there seemed the best option. He looked at the clock and saw it was just before eight o'clock. Malone wanted to go for a run. Afterward, he would call Myers at work and try to arrange a meeting over lunch. Before shutting down the computer, he pulled up the website of Myers' employer and copied down the main telephone number.

After his morning run and a shower, Malone dialed Myers' work number. A pleasant sounding female answered the phone and asked how she could direct his call. Malone identified himself as a Los Angeles police detective and asked to speak with Kenneth Myers in security. The operator transferred the call. A secretary answered, and Malone repeated his spiel and asked to speak with Myers. Again, the call was transferred, and then Meyers came on the line.

"Kenneth Myers," he said.

"Mr. Myers, this is Detective Malone, LAPD," Malone said.

"Hello," Meyers said. "What can I do for you, Malone?"

"I'm working a cold case, one of your old cases," Malone said. "And I was hoping to speak to you about it. Today, if possible. I'd be happy to buy you lunch if you could work me in this afternoon."

"Which case?" Myers said.

"It's a homicide case from 1992," Malone said. "The victim's name was Mary Beth Anderson."

There was nothing but silence from Myers' end for several moments.

"Have you read the murder book?" Myers said.

"Yes," Malone said. "But I have a few questions I'd like to ask you to clarify a few things."

"If you've read the files, I don't know what more I can tell you,"

Myers said. "It's been what, twenty years since that murder? I mean, I have some recollection of the case, but that happened a long time ago."

"Yes, it happened twenty-three years ago, to be exact," Malone said. "While I have read all of your reports, there are still a few things I'm curious about that I hope you might shed some light on."

"I have a few minutes now," Myers said. "Can we just handle this on the phone? My schedule is pretty full today, and I already have lunch plans."

"I'd rather speak to you face-to-face," Malone said. "You were a murder cop, so I'm sure you understand that."

"Yes, I guess I do," Myers said. "But the fact remains, my plate is pretty full today. I just can't fit anything else in, not even with a shoehorn. So if it can't wait, handling it now on the phone is the best option I can offer you."

"I'd rather talk to you in person," Malone said. "Could you spare me a few minutes after work? I could buy you a drink."

"You're a persistent sonofabitch, aren't you Malone?" Myers said.

"Is there some reason you don't want to talk with me about the Anderson case?" Malone said.

"Look, I did everything that I could do when I worked that case," Myers said. "There just weren't many leads, and the investigation stalled in a hurry. The case went cold. It happens that way sometimes. No offense intended, but in my opinion, some young hotshot detective looking into it again after all these years will change nothing. If I couldn't clear it back then, I sure don't think you're going to. Talking with you would just be a waste of time for both of us."

"I think you're wrong about that, Myers," Malone said. "DNA analysis wasn't an option for you back then. It is now. We still have the swabs from the bite wound. That evidence is being analyzed as we speak. Also, I think I have a lead on one of your burglary suspects from back then. He's a convicted felon, and his DNA profile may already be in the system. We could get a CODIS hit any day now."

"Who is the suspect?" Myers said.

"His name is Javier Alvarez," Malone said. "Ring any bells?"

"Now I remember," Myers said.

"What, something about the case?" Malone said. "You've heard of Javier Alvarez?"

"No, not about the case," Myers said. "Your name. It sounded familiar, and I just realized why. Aren't you the Hollywood dick that got himself jammed up over an OIS? I seem to recall reading somewhere that they recently charged you with murder in connection with the shooting. It seems to me the department probably suspended you, and you're cooling your heels on the beach right now. Now I'm wondering why you're calling me on the pretense of working a cold case homicide."

"It's a long story, but yes, you're right about some of it," Malone said. "The short version is a false witness came forward, and the DA put a murder charge on me based on his statements. But his story was impeached, and the DA will officially dismiss the charge this afternoon. I was working on the Anderson case before all that happened. And I'll be back at work before the end of the week. I'm just playing catch up and trying to do what I can on the case until then."

"Again, no offense intended, but I don't know you from Adam," Myers said. "Maybe you're on the up, and up, maybe you aren't. But the bottom line is this. I will not talk to you, Malone. This is what I'm going to do. Before I hang up, just on the off chance you are legitimate, as one cop to another, I'm going to give you a piece of friendly advice. Detectives kick rocks over to see what's underneath. That's the nature of the job. But there are some rocks you don't want to kick over Malone, because if you do, something just might crawl out that ends up biting you in the ass. Digging around in the Anderson case is one of those rocks you don't want to kick over, in my opinion. If I were you, I'd drop it and drop it right now. It's ancient history."

After he had offered the cryptic piece of advice, the line went dead. Myers had hung up.

Malone couldn't figure it out. The longer Myers had been on the phone, the more unfriendly he had become. But there at the end, when parting with his piece of "friendly advice," from one cop to another, it seemed to Malone that Myers had actually sounded panicky. Myers was obviously hiding something. The problem was, Malone did not know what it was.

Malone decided there didn't seem any point in trying to call Myers back. He'd probably just get a brush-off from the secretary if he tried. With nothing better to do, Malone decided to call Jack Bright to bounce his conversation with Myers off him, just to see what Jack made of it. He punched Bright's phone number into his phone. After four rings, the call went to voicemail, and he got the familiar "Bright Investigations" message. Malone assumed Jack was busy with something, so he left a message at the beep, asking Jack to return his call as soon as possible.

Just after three o'clock in the afternoon, Malone got the call from Nathan Martinez that he had been waiting for impatiently. For once, it was a piece of good news.

Martinez told him he had met with the prosecutor and with the Los Angeles District Attorney himself. The attorney said that he had shown them the evidence that impeached Romano's story by proving that he had not even been in LA on the day of the shooting Malone had been involved in. Martinez said that he had raised the specter of a possible civil suit against the County of Los Angeles for malicious prosecution. He had threatened the lawsuit based on negligence by the district attorney's office for failing to properly vet the so-called witness before filing a murder charge based on his testimony.

The district attorney had quickly agreed to move to dismiss the case with prejudice. The charge would get dismissed permanently, and they could never again charge Malone with murder in connection with that shooting incident. Martinez said that he waited until they had prepared and filed the motion with the court before leaving.

Last, Martinez told Malone that after the city attorney reviewed the evidence that impeached Romano's false testimony, he told the assistant handling the case to file a motion in civil court Tuesday morning, asking the judge to dismiss the civil suit against Malone that also named the city.

Martinez told him he was confident his criminal and civil legal troubles would be over by the end of the week. With the official dismissal of the criminal part of it, he said that he felt sure Malone would be off the beach and reinstated to full duty, perhaps as early as Wednesday. Martinez mentioned he had already made an appointment to see the chief of police on Tuesday morning to bring him up to speed on the pending dismissal of the criminal charge, adding that Malone needed to attend the meeting.

After Martinez had hung up, Malone breathed a sigh of relief. It felt someone had suddenly lifted a great weight from his shoulders. He hadn't realized the stress he had been living under since they had filed the murder charge. He wondered if everything went as Martinez expected, whether he would return to work at the cold case homicide section briefly or would return directly to Hollywood Division.

While he missed his old division, Malone hoped he would remain assigned to the cold case section for a while longer. He knew it would be much easier to continue working the Anderson case if he continued in the temporary assignment than if he returned immediately to Hollywood. He felt quite certain that even if he convinced Lieutenant Turner to re-open the case, it would be unlikely Turner would allow him to continue working on it once he no longer worked in Turner's section. No point in worrying about it until the Tuesday meeting with the chief, Malone reasoned. Until the meeting with the chief, it was impossible for him to guess what the immediate future might hold for him.

An hour after dinner, Malone still hadn't heard from Jack Bright. He speculated Jack might have stopped off after work for drinks at his favorite hangout, Patrick Delaney's, an Irish pub on Hollywood Boulevard, a couple of blocks from Bright's office. Malone was eager to learn whether Bright had found out where Vanessa Alvarez currently worked within the LAPD or had gotten a line on the whereabouts of her brother Javier. He knew that Bright often stopped at Delaney's after work, intending to have only a drink or two. But invariably he would run into some old friends and end up staying until closing time. It was still early evening, so Malone took a drive over to Delaney's to see if Bright was there.

Malone walked inside Patrick Delaney's a few minutes after eight o'clock to the sound of the U2 song "Vertigo" blaring from the jukebox. The bar was popular with Hollywood Division cops. It was packed, especially for a Monday night. He looked around the familiar room. The walls were painted a medium shade of brown with green and cream accents. There were dark wood chair rails along the walls, with dark wood paneling along the lower half of the walls. A rugby union game was showing on the many flat-screen televisions placed strategically around the bar. There was a square-shaped bar in the middle of the room with seating on all four sides. The walls were decorated with a prominent flag of Ireland, the expected shamrocks, and Celtic symbols, along with posters depicting popular Irish alcoholic beverage brands.

Malone pushed his way to the bar and found an empty stool. Paddy Delaney himself and three bartenders were behind the bar, efficiently keeping up with the orders from their thirsty clientele. One bartender

Malone knew, Mickey, came to get his order. Malone ordered a pint of Guinness. He glanced around, but Bright wasn't at the bar or at any of the tables Malone could see from his place at the bar.

Paddy Delaney finished washing some glasses in the large sink behind the bar. Then he stacked the glasses on a shelf, and after drying his hands on a bar towel, he turned in Malone's direction and caught sight of him. Paddy grinned widely, his face lighted by recognition. He made his way over to Malone, weaving and dodging around the other busy bartenders. He leaned in to shout over the cacophony, the music blasting from the speakers around the room, and the boisterous chatter of the bar patrons.

"Malone!" Delaney said. "Haven't seen you about in a long while, lad."

"Yeah, I've been working downtown for a few weeks, Paddy," Malone said. "Haven't been in the neighborhood."

"Busy, eh?" Delaney said. "Well, it's grand to see you again, boyo."

"Paddy, has Jack Bright been in this evening?" Malone said.

"No, haven't seen the puss of that chancer about since Saturday," Delaney said.

"Okay, Paddy, thanks," Malone said. "I thought he might have come by after work."

"No, not this evening, lad," Delaney said. "I best be getting back to it. Good seeing you, Malone. The drink is on me. Now be a good lad and don't be such a stranger."

Malone said, "I'll do my best, Paddy, and cheers."

Malone finished the last of the Guinness and left the bar. He couldn't imagine that Jack was already at home for the day. He thought maybe Bright was burning the midnight oil at the office. Bright's office was only a couple of blocks away at the corner of Cahuenga and Hollywood. He walked over to see if Bright was still there.

Less than five minutes later, Malone arrived in front of the massive seven-story limestone building, constructed in the Italian Romanesque style, where Jack kept his office. Bright had a two-room office suite on the sixth floor at the front. Malone entered the building, nodded to the security guard at the desk inside the front entrance, and walked directly to the elevators. He pushed the call button, and the doors on one of the elevator cars opened immediately. He walked inside and pushed the button. Moments later, the elevator doors opened on the sixth floor. Malone stepped out. He turned right and followed the corridor, walking on the threadbare carpeting until he arrived in front of the door with "Bright Investigations" painted in gold leaf on the glass. The door was standing open a crack. Malone pushed it open and walked inside.

There was a desk that ordinarily Jack's secretary Rhonda occupied during business hours. The coat rack behind the desk was empty, showing that Rhonda at least was already gone for the day. The door to Bright's office was also partially open, but the lights were off, and Malone couldn't see far into the gloomy interior. He pushed the door open, stepped inside, and felt for the light switch.

At first, he couldn't find the switch, and he took another step inside, only to stumble over something and almost fall just as his hand found the light switch. Malone looked down and stared at the body of Jack Bright. There were two neat bullet holes in the center of his chest. What appeared to be powder burns encircled both of the blackened holes in Bright's starched white dress shirt. Blood soaked the front of the shirt. Bright lay face-up on the floor, his gray, lifeless eyes open, staring upward sightlessly at the ceiling. Instinctively, Malone knew Bright was dead, but still he knelt down and touched his fingertips to the side of his friend's neck, checking for a pulse. Not finding one, Malone remained kneeling beside Bright's body for several minutes, absorbing the shock of finding his friend dead.

Finally, Malone got shakily to his feet. His knees felt rubbery. He stumbled forward and leaned heavily against the desk. Given the position of the body, it looked to Malone as if Bright had opened the door of his office and someone waiting on the other side had immediately shot him two times. Malone ran a hand through his close-cropped hair, still not wanting to believe what his eyes were seeing. He glanced wildly around the room, trying to think. For the first time, he noticed that the computer that usually occupied a corner of Bright's desk lay smashed on the floor beside it. It was the computer Bright had used to access the various databases from which he gleaned much of the information for his investigations.

The shock of finding his friend dead receded a little. Malone detached himself emotionally from the scene and thought like a cop. The first thing was to notify the police. He took a handkerchief from his back pocket and lifted the receiver from the phone of Bright's desk. Using the knuckle of the bent index finger on his right hand, he punched in the three numbers, 911. He was careful not to contaminate the scene with any of his fingerprints. When the emergency operator answered, he gave his name, the address of Bright's office and told the operator there had been a murder. He told her he would wait until the police arrived and hung up.

Less than five minutes later, two uniformed patrol officers from Hollywood Division showed up. After a few questions, the one with "Day" engraved on the silver nameplate pinned to his blue uniform shirt and two silver chevrons on his sleeves keyed his portable radio and requested that a supervisor respond to the scene.

21

Hollywood Station

Soon the patrol supervisor, a sergeant named McLemore, arrived at Bright's office. Officer Day filled him in, and the sergeant made some calls on his mobile phone. A crime scene evidence collection team arrived, followed shortly afterward by two Hollywood dicks and an investigator from the coroner's office. While the crime scene team processed Bright's office, everyone else had gathered in the outer office. Malone knew the two detectives. The senior detective was a tall, thin black man named Denny Washington. His partner was Jimmy Chang.

Malone told the detectives how he discovered Bright's body, how he had been expecting a call from Bright and when the call never came he had gone looking for him, first at Patrick Delaney's and later his office when he hadn't found Bright at the bar. Washington asked Malone if he knew who might have wanted Bright dead. Malone said he did not know, as he knew nothing about the investigations Bright might have been working on. Of course, that was only partly true.

Secretly, Malone felt guilty because he believed involving Bright in his investigation of the Mary Beth Anderson murder might have gotten Bright killed. But he didn't mention any of that to the two detectives. After all, it was just speculation on Malone's part, speculation that he hoped was wrong.

Over two hours after Malone had found Bright's body and had called 911, the Hollywood detectives finally allowed him to leave the scene. By that time, a two-man transport team from the coroner's office had arrived. They had bagged Jack Bright's body and had left with it for the county morgue. Washington had asked Malone to come to the Hollywood station the following morning to give a written statement. Malone agreed and then wearily left the office building to go home, feeling the numbness that accompanies the loss of a close friend. It was hard for him to get used to the idea that Jack Bright was gone forever. He just hoped that he hadn't been responsible for his friend's death.

Malone woke up Tuesday morning before his alarm sounded, drenched with sweat. He vaguely recalled having nightmares about Jack Bright's murder that had disturbed his sleep on and off the entire night. He hardly remembered the drive home late the previous evening or finally getting into bed.

A deep sadness enveloped him. Jack Bright had been more than his closest friend. Malone acknowledged to himself that Jack had been a father figure to him. Losing his friend hit him like a hard blow to the gut. Malone had never felt so alone. He forced himself to get out of bed. He had a lot to do. The day demanded that he get an early start.

Malone didn't feel like eating, so he skipped breakfast. Instead, he showered and got dressed. He decided that instead of making coffee at home, he would just grab a cup from the shop near his apartment on the way downtown.

A few minutes after leaving his apartment, he arrived at the shop with the familiar green and white logo. He gave his order to the barista and then walked over to the newsstand and scanned the front page of the morning edition of the Times. He saw nothing about the murder of Jack Bright. The media probably discovered it too late the previous night to cover it in the morning edition. He grabbed his espresso and headed back to the car.

Malone had made meeting Jack's secretary Rhonda, his priority. He didn't want her arriving at the office only to be greeted by yellow crime scene tape blocking the door. Not knowing what time she arrived at work, he decided he would station himself in the building's lobby by seven o'clock. He wanted to intercept her and break the news about Jack.

Malone arrived at the office building at five minutes before seven. He parked in the building's lot. Then he walked into the building through the rear entrance and made his way to the elevators. He loitered there, drinking his espresso, waiting for Rhonda to arrive. Thirty-five minutes later, he saw her approaching. He hadn't visited Jack's office much, but he had met Rhonda and recognized her immediately. She was a sturdy-looking woman in her fifties with graying hair. She was stylishly dressed and attractive for a woman her age. Rhonda recognized Malone too, as evidenced by the fact that she deviated from her course towards the elevators and walked directly up to him.

"You're Malone," she said. "Jack's friend."

"Yes, I am," Malone said.

"Are you waiting for Jack?" she said. "He rarely gets here until at least nine. But you can come up and wait in the office. I'll put the coffee on."

"I'm not waiting for Jack," Malone said. "I came to see you."

"Me?" Rhonda said.

"Yes, I'm afraid I have some bad news, Rhonda," He said. "I've never really been good at this sort of thing, so I'll just say it. Jack is dead."

"Dead?" Rhonda said. "Are you sure?"

"Yes, I'm sure," Malone said. "I found him."

"What happened?" she said.

"Someone murdered him," Malone said. "I found him last night on the floor in his office. They had shot him."

"Oh my god," Rhonda said. "Jack dead?"

She started to tear up, but at least she didn't have a complete breakdown. Malone appreciated that because comforting hysterical women was another thing he didn't feel that he was good at. Rhonda dug into her handbag and pulled out a tissue and began dabbing at her eyes.

"Who would kill Jack?" she said. "He hasn't been working on anything dangerous."

"We don't know yet," Malone said. "But you can be sure that I'm going to find the person who did it."

"So I suppose I'm not to go upstairs?" she said.

"Crime scene processed the office last night," Malone said. "There isn't anything stopping you from going up there. It's up to you. But if you do, don't go into Jack's office."

"Okay," she said. "I need to go up and find the telephone number for Jack's sister. She is… was Jack's next of kin. Do you think the police have contacted her yet?"

"I don't know," Malone said. "They didn't ask for a next of kin last night when I was here. Maybe they don't know about her yet."

"Well, I'm going to phone her," Rhonda said. "If she doesn't know, I'll tell her. Probably be better coming from me, anyway."

Rhonda dabbed at her eyes again. She seemed to hold up better than Malone had expected, but he presumed she was still a bit in shock, just as he had been the night before when he first discovered that Jack was dead.

"Will you go up with me?" she said.

"Sure I will," Malone said. "Anything I can do, just ask."

They walked over to the elevators, and Malone pushed the call button. The doors opened, and he followed Rhonda inside the car. She pushed the button for the sixth floor, and they rode up together in silence. The door to the office was closed. Two lengths of yellow crime scene tape, which covered the door in an X pattern, barred it. Malone reached out and pulled down the tape. He tried the doorknob and found the door unlocked. Evidently, the police hadn't found a key inside to secure it.

Malone entered first and saw that the door to Jack's office was closed. He turned and motioned Rhonda inside. She removed the light outer jacket she was wearing and hung it on a hook on the coat rack behind her desk. She placed her handbag in the bottom drawer of her desk.

"I'll make coffee while I try to compose myself," she said. "Then I'll try calling Jack's sister."

She picked up the glass carafe from the drip coffee maker on a table behind her desk.

"I'll be back in a moment," she said.

Rhonda opened the entry door and walked out into the hallway, shutting the door behind her. A couple of minutes later, she came back with the water in the carafe. She poured the water into the drip coffee maker, placed a white paper filter in the basket, and filled it with coffee from a canister beside the machine. She switched it on and then walked behind her desk and collapsed in the chair. Malone stood quietly and uncomfortably beside her desk.

"Jack thought a lot you, Malone," she said. "He talked about you all the time. Almost like a father speaking of a son that he was very proud of."

"I thought a lot of him too," Malone said. "My father and mother died in a plane crash when I was only thirteen. Jack became almost like a father to me, and he was a damn good friend."

"I expected to work here until Jack retired," she said. "When that happened, I planned to retire too. I never expected to be looking for another job at my age. But even thinking of that makes me feel selfish at a time like this."

"It's not selfish," Malone said. "Just realistic. Jack would have understood that."

Rhonda took a couple of white porcelain cups from a shelf above the coffee maker and filled them from the carafe. She handed one to Malone.

"Do you take sugar or cream?" she said.

"Just black," Malone said.

Rhonda added sugar and a packet of creamer to her cup. They both sipped the hot coffee without speaking for a few moments, lost in their own thoughts. Rhonda was the first to speak.

"I suppose I should try Jack's sister now," she said.

"Karen, isn't it?" Malone said.

"Yes," Rhonda said. "Karen Milner. Do you know her?"

"I met her once when she was in LA visiting Jack," Malone said.

"She is a very nice lady," Rhonda said. "Like Jack in some ways, but different in others."

"I suppose that's the way it usually is with brothers and sisters," Malone said.

"I'll need to find out what she wants to do about the agency," Rhonda said. "Jack had several cases going. I'll need to bill the clients for the work he put in on them and let them know they will need to find someone else to finish their cases."

"Yes, I expect you have at least a couple of weeks before you need to worry about looking for another job," Malone said. "It will probably take at least that much time to wind down Jack's affairs."

"I suppose so," Rhonda said.

"I better be leaving," Malone said. "I've got to get down to Hollywood to write out a statement for the detectives investigating Jack's murder. Will you be okay here alone?"

"Yes," Rhonda said. "You said I shouldn't go into his office. Is there a mess in there?"

"Yes, some blood," Malone said. "It stained the carpet where he fell after they shot him."

"After I call Karen, I'll call a cleaning company," she said. "Then I think I'll go on home. I need some time to process this. Then I'll start on winding things down here tomorrow after I discuss it with Karen and find out what she wants to do."

"Good idea," Malone said. "By the way, whoever killed Jack busted up his computer. I suppose there isn't any way of finding out what he was working on before they killed him."

"Actually there is," Rhonda said. "Jack only used that computer to search the databases he used for investigations. He was very mindful of security. For example, he didn't keep any files, reports, or client information on his computer. All of that is on my laptop, which I lock in that file cabinet before leaving at the end of the day."

She nodded towards a gray file cabinet against the wall. Malone saw that there was a tumbler in the center of the top drawer, similar to the type safes had.

"I can also access Jack's databases using the laptop, and I can search the histories to see what he had been looking at," she said.

"That could be helpful in finding out who killed him," Malone said. "If you wouldn't mind, I'd like to come by again tomorrow and see what you find out about what Jack had been working on last night."

"Of course," she said. "I know it won't bring Jack back, but I'll be glad to do anything that might help get the person who killed him."

Malone finished his coffee. They said their goodbyes. Malone then left Jack's office and headed to the Hollywood station to give his statement. He had scratched one thing off his list, but he had several more things that he had to attend to before the end of the day.

Malone arrived at Hollywood station at eight-thirty. He dumped the Toyota in the public lot and went inside the lobby. The desk guy recognized him, and they chatted a few minutes. Malone told him he was there to see Washington, and the guy called upstairs. A couple of minutes later, Washington came through a glass inner door and met Malone in the lobby. Malone followed him inside through the door and then they took the stairs to the second floor, where the detective bureau was located. Malone glanced at his old desk as they passed by. Washington's partner was at his desk when they walked over. He looked up, nodded at Malone, and then returned to typing on his computer keyboard.

"We've got you set up in an interview room," Washington said. "You can write your statement in there."

"Okay," Malone said.

He followed Washington to the room. There was a small stack of witness affidavit forms and a pen in front of one chair at the table inside the room. Malone sat down in the chair.

"I'm going to get coffee," Washington said. "Can I get you some?"

"Sure, just black," Malone said.

Malone picked up the pen and a form and started writing. Washington returned a few minutes later. He set a plastic cup in front of Malone and sat down in a chair across the table from him. Fifteen minutes later, Malone put down the pen and pushed the completed statement across the table to Washington. Washington drained the last of the coffee from his cup. He set the empty cup on the table. He picked up the statement and read it. Once he had finished reading it, he took a pen from his shirt pocket and signed the witness section at the bottom of all three pages.

"That establishes for the record how you came to find the body," Washington said. "You sure you can't think of anyone who might have wanted to kill Bright?"

"Yeah, about that," Malone said. "I might have a person of interest for you."

"Who?" Washington said.

"It's a long story," Malone said.

First Malone told Washington about the background information, about the cold case homicide he had been working on while temporarily assigned to the cold case unit. He related the story about the alleged witness to his on-duty shooting coming forward that had led to him getting suspended and charged with murder. He explained how Jack Bright had helped him discover the information that ultimately impeached the witness' story and had exonerated him.

"That's how I first got Jack involved in the case I was working," Malone said.

"Go on," Washington said.

"Once the chief suspended me, I still couldn't let the case go," Malone said. "I wanted to find out more about a female cop, the ex-girlfriend of the victim's husband, who the victim's family had believed was involved in her murder. The detective that had the case evidently eliminated her as a suspect. Or maybe he never took seriously what the family told him in the first place. At any rate, there was nothing of substance about the female cop in the case files. All I had was a name and the fact that she had been working at Hollenbeck at the time the victim died. I asked Jack to track down someone who might have known her at Hollenbeck. To make a long story short, that led us to identify and locate her father, Ramon Alvarez."

"Let me get this straight," Washington said. "You think this female cop might be involved in Jack Bright's murder?"

"No, that's not it," Malone said. "Let me finish the story. This past Sunday, Jack and I paid Ramon Alvarez a visit. In the course of the interview, we learned some things about his son, Javier Alvarez, the Hollenbeck cop's brother. Javier Alvarez is a banger and an ex-con who did time for burglary and attempted murder. Ramon Alvarez told us some things that made Javier look good as a suspect in the cold case murder. It seems to be too much of a coincidence that Jack Bright gets killed the day after we talked with Javier's old man."

"So you think Javier Alvarez found out the cold case was being investigated and eliminated Jack Bright to shut down an investigation that might link him to that murder?" Washington said.

"I think it's definitely a possibility," Malone said. "I talked with Jack's secretary this morning, and she told me that none of his current cases involved anything that might have caused someone to want to kill him. It certainly seems like a coincidence that Jack gets murdered the day after we interviewed Ramon Alvarez. And personally, in police work, I don't believe in coincidences."

"So you think the old man warned Javier after you and Bright visited him?" Washington said.

"Ramon Alvarez told us he hadn't seen or heard from his son since he went to prison last time. But Javier is his son. Maybe he had an attack of conscience after talking with us. Maybe he felt like he had implicated his son in the murder. I think it's possible he got word to Javier that the police had been around and were looking at him in connection with the old murder. I sure think it would be worthwhile to talk with Ramon Alvarez to find out who he told about the visit from Jack and me."

"Yes, I agree," Washington said. "What about Javier Alvarez? Do you know where to find him? I'm definitely interested in talking to him and finding out where he was last night."

"No, that's what Jack was working on," Malone said. "All we had on Vanessa Alvarez was that she used to work at Hollenbeck and was still with the LAPD. Jack was trying to find out where she works now and he was trying to locate Javier. I hadn't spoken to him since Sunday afternoon, so I don't know what he found out, if anything."

"Well, maybe we can find out something from Ramon Alvarez that will help track down his son," Washington said.

"I could go with you to talk to him," Malone said. "He wouldn't try to deny anything he already told Jack and me if I were there."

"No, I can't let you do that," Washington said. "Sounds like you are about to get out of the mess you've been in, but technically, you're still suspended. No way am I taking you along to see Ramon Alvarez. And let me make something clear, Malone. I know Bright was a close friend but stay out of this investigation. Don't try to find Javier Alvarez. Chang and I will take care of that. And we'll find out who killed Jack Bright."

"Speaking of that, I'd appreciate it if you kept everything I've just told you to yourself for the time being," Malone said. "I'd just as soon the brass didn't find out that I've been working that cold case off the books while on suspension."

"Yes, I can imagine why you would like to keep that on the down-low," Washington said. "If Javier Alvarez turns out to be our suspect in Bright's murder, then we will have to establish how we developed him as a suspect. It will have to come out at that point that you pointed us at him. But I'll keep your involvement confidential for the time being."

"That's all I'm asking," Malone said.

Malone looked at his watch. It was after ten o'clock, and he had to meet Nathan Martinez at the Police Administration Building in less than an hour for the appointment with the chief.

"If there isn't anything else, I have to get down to the PAB," Malone said.

"We've got everything we need for the moment," Washington said. "If there is anything else, I know where to find you."

"Yes, hopefully, I'll be back here working before the end of the week," Malone said.

The men stood up, and Washington escorted Malone back downstairs to the lobby. They shook hands and Malone left through the front entrance. He got into his car, drove out of the lot, and headed to the PAB.

22

Back to Work

Malone arrived at the Police Administration Building at ten forty-five. He parked in the public lot down the street and made his way into the first-floor lobby. Nathan Martinez was already waiting at the elevators, his briefcase in hand.

"Hello, Ben," Martinez said, pushing the call button. "Hopefully, this thing will be behind you in another half hour."

"Yes, I sure hope so," Malone said. "I'm ready to get back to work."

The elevator doors opened, and the two walked inside. Martinez pushed the button for the tenth floor. On the ride up, Malone briefly told Martinez about the murder of Jack Bright, how he had discovered the body, and that he had just come from Hollywood Division, where he had given his formal statement.

"That's tough," Martinez said. "It's always hard losing a close friend. Especially under the circumstances."

After the elevator stopped, the doors opened. The men walked down the hallway to the chief's office and went inside. The chief's secretary had them sit while she called the chief to tell him they had arrived. A few minutes later, she ushered them into the chief's office.

The room wasn't as crowded as the last time they had been there, but the chief wasn't alone. Malone's current supervisor of record, Lieutenant James Turner, was in attendance along with Captain Steven Davis, Hollywood Division's commanding officer. The chief told them to have a seat. Martinez and Malone sat down together on the leather couch to the left of the chief's desk.

"Sounds as if you may be out of the woods, Detective Malone," the chief said.

"I sure hope so, Chief," Malone said. "I'd like to get back to work."

"What have you got for me, counselor?" the chief said, directing his attention to Martinez.

Martinez opened his briefcase and retrieved a document. He closed the briefcase and set it on the floor. Then he stood up, walked to the front of the desk, and handed the document to the chief of police.

"That's an order of the superior court dismissing the charge against Officer Malone," Martinez said. He then returned to the couch and sat down.

The chief picked up a pair of reading glasses from the desk and perched them on his nose. He spent several moments reading the court order. He then removed the glasses and placed the document on the desk before looking at Malone.

"The DA dismissed the criminal charge with prejudice, so I'm rescinding your suspension," the chief said.

The chief opened a desk drawer, reached inside, and then placed Malone's service pistol and badge on the front edge of the desk. Malone wasn't certain if he should go over and retrieve them, so he waited.

"Go ahead, take them," the chief said.

Malone stood up, walked over and picked up the Glock and the badge. He then returned to the couch and sat back down.

"Now I just have to decide what to do with you," the chief said. "Captain Davis, you're up."

Davis cleared his throat. "I received a report from Dr. Sara Bernstein, the psychiatrist who has been seeing Officer Malone," he said. "She has cleared Malone to return to regular duty."

Malone felt relief washing over him like a flood.

"But…," Davis continued. "I'm sorry, Ben, but I can't take you back at Hollywood. At least not right away."

"Why captain?" Malone said. "They have exonerated me. I think I've done a good job at Hollywood Division."

"I'll answer the question," the chief said. "There has been a great deal of noise from the police brutality conspiracy crowd since they indicted you. The media has already reported the DA dropped the charge against you. Activists have already started pressing complaints with the mayor's office and mine, alleging that the district attorney and the LAPD are covering for a rogue cop too quick to use deadly force. They have threatened to picket the Hollywood station. I think it would be unfair to the rest of the officers at Hollywood to return you to duty there until this all blows over."

"So am I going back to the cold case section?" Malone said.

"That's what we've been discussing this morning while we were waiting for you and counselor Martinez," the chief said. "Lieutenant Turner tells me your performance while assigned to his section was satisfactory. He is willing to take you back. But after talking it over, we think perhaps temporary assignment to a training post at the academy might be in everyone's best interests until this blows over. Then in a month or two, when something else has come along to grab the attention of the activists and the media, we can find a detective position to put you back into."

"If it's all the same to you, chief, since Lieutenant Turner apparently has no objections, I'd rather go back to work in the cold case homicide section instead of hiding out at the academy. At least I could continue doing the job they have trained me for."

"I'm simply not convinced that is any better a choice than sending you back to Hollywood," the chief said. "It will probably just focus their attention here instead of there. I'm inclined to believe a temporary post to the academy, where you will be out of sight and out of mind, would be best both for you and for the department."

"Permission to speak candidly, chief?" Malone said.

"Go ahead," the chief said.

"While I strongly disagree with a bunch of activists dictating assignment decisions for the police department, I can understand why you and Captain Davis won't allow me to return to Hollywood Division. But you've already given me one temporary assignment while ordering me to see a psychiatrist over incidents where the department had already me, both by internal affairs and the board. I'm sorry, but I feel like the department has punished me enough already when I did nothing wrong in the first place. Then some shyster lawyer produces a fake witness, and I end up getting charged with murder. We've cleared that up. The shrink's report makes it clear I shouldn't have ever been pulled out of Hollywood Division to start with. Now you want to stick me in a training assignment where I will be 'out of sight and out of mind' for the benefit of a bunch of bleeding heart activist fruit loops who don't have a clue about police work. To be perfectly honest, Chief, I'm a little tired of being punished for nothing but trying to do my job."

"Take it easy, Malone," Martinez said.

"No, I won't take it easy," Malone said. "I'm sick to death of politics screwing with my career."

"Watch your tone, Officer Malone," the chief said. "There is a bigger picture here that you obviously aren't seeing. The LAPD cannot function effectively without the trust and support of the community. If maintaining that trust and support means I must subject the rights of one police officer to an inconsequential and temporary imposition, then that's just a decision I have to make and that you have to live with. I certainly can understand the feelings you've expressed, but I can't simply think about you at the exclusion of the rest of the department."

"I meant no disrespect, Chief," Malone said. "I'm just really frustrated with this whole thing. Looking at yet another temporary assignment and the interruption of my career as a detective is really hard to take."

"If I could interject something, chief," Lieutenant Turner said.

"Go ahead, Jim," the chief said.

"I can see the wisdom of posting Malone to the academy," Turner said. "But I can sympathize with Malone's view. The fact is, someone is always protesting something in front of the PAB, so I think it's a totally different situation compared to activists picketing the Hollywood station. Picketing here is so commonplace, the media barely pays any attention to it. So even if they make good on their threats by picketing here, it will not have any serious impact. I'm willing for Malone to return to work in my section. He won't be working the street, and there is virtually no chance of him being involved in any further controversy. It's just my two cents, but I vote to allow Malone to return to his assignment in the cold case homicide section until you deem it appropriate to reassign him to a field bureau."

The chief leaned back in his chair and drew a meaty hand down his face. Finally, he leaned forward, looking at Malone.

"You said you felt like the assignment to the cold case homicide section was punishment," he said. "You think you are going to feel any more satisfied returning to that temporary assignment than one somewhere else?"

"Yes sir," Malone said. "I regarded my assignment there as punishment in the beginning. But once I started reviewing cases there, I understood it was some very important work. Sure, it isn't the same as working active cases out of Hollywood, but it is actual police work. I'd be happy to continue working there until you decide it's appropriate for me to return to Hollywood or some other field division assignment."

"Okay, Officer Malone," the chief said. "At least for the interim, I'm going to allow you to go back to work in the cold case section. But I'm not making any promises. If I get too much heat from the mayor's office, I'm reserving the right to revisit the decision."

"That's more than acceptable," Malone said.

"You can take the rest of the day off, Malone," Turner said. "Be at work at seven tomorrow morning."

"Okay, Lieutenant," Malone said.

"Remember one thing, Officer Malone," the chief said. "Trouble is trouble, regardless of whether it is of your own making. Police all over this country are under a microscope right now over the use of force, particularly deadly force. Do yourself a favor and stay out of trouble and out from under scrutiny."

"I plan on it, chief," Malone said.

"You're dismissed," the chief said.

Malone and Martinez stood together and walked out of the office. They followed the corridor back to the elevators.

"You pushed a little hard back there," Martinez said.

"Maybe," Malone said. "But a posting to the academy just didn't fit my vision for my immediate future. Especially now, after what happened to Jack Bright."

"Ben, you've got to learn to accept the reality of politics if you plan to have a full career with the LAPD," Martinez said.

"I've thought a lot about that, Nathan," Malone said. "After everything that has happened, I'm no longer confident that a full career with the LAPD fits my vision for my future, either."

The elevator doors opened, and the two men got in for the ride down to the lobby. The elevator stopped on the first floor, and they got and walked to the front entrance. Once they were outside the building, Malone turned to Martinez and extended his hand, and they shook.

"Thank you, Nathan, for all you've done for me," Malone said. "I owe you big time."

"Glad I could help, Ben," Martinez said. "I hope things go smoother for you in the future."

"Thanks," Malone said. "I'll see you around."

The men parted company. Malone drove back to Jack Bright's office to check in with Rhonda Freeman. He wanted to find it if she had contacted Jack's sister and whether she had learned anything about what Jack had been working on Monday evening. He had planned to do that the following day, but since he would report back to work on Wednesday, it might not be possible.

Malone parked at Jack's office building a little before noon. He took the elevator up to the office. When we walked in, Rhonda Freeman looked up from her computer.

"Well hello," she said. "I wasn't expecting to see you again until tomorrow."

"Yes," Malone said. "I don't know whether Jack mentioned my recent difficulties, but the chief suspended me from duty for a while. But I was just reinstated and will return to work in the morning. I wasn't sure I could come by tomorrow, so I thought I might as well stop back by on my way home. I wasn't sure you would still be here."

"I hadn't planned to be," Freeman said. "But I got busy after I called and talked with Karen. I called and scheduled a cleaning crew for Jack's office, and they should be here at one o'clock. I also telephoned a few of Jack's current clients with the news to let them know their investigations can't be completed. Then I started checking the database queries from Monday afternoon and evening to see what Jack had been working on."

"You *have* been busy," Malone said. "How did Karen take the news?"

"Pretty well under the circumstances, I suppose," Freeman said. "It was a terrible shock, of course, but she is a strong woman. She sounded tearful, but she didn't break down."

"That's good," Malone said. "I assume she will come to LA."

"Yes, she said she would book a flight and should be here tomorrow afternoon to make the funeral arrangements. She also asked me to stay on until we wind down Jack's affairs."

"It's still hard to believe Jack is really gone," Malone said. "The worst of it is that I think they killed him over something he had been helping me with. I really am feeling a lot of guilt over that. If I hadn't asked him to help, Jack would still be alive."

"You can't look at it that way, Ben," she said. "One thing I admired most about Jack was his willingness to help his friends. If he had known you needed help, he would have insisted on getting involved even if you hadn't asked him to. He wouldn't have wanted you to feel guilty."

"You're probably right," Malone said. "But I just hate the thought that he died because of doing something I asked him to do."

"Bad things happen to good people all the time, Ben," she said. "That's just life. We don't have to like it, but we have to accept it. All we can do now is whatever we can to help see that they find the person who killed him and that justice is done. Speaking of that, I've been able to learn a little about what Jack was looking into Monday evening."

"What did you find out?" Malone said.

"Evidently, Jack was trying to locate someone named Javier Alvarez," she said. "Does that mean anything to you?"

"Yes, Javier Alvarez is a suspect in a case I'm working, and locating him was one thing Jack was working on for me," Malone said. "We interviewed Alvarez's father Sunday afternoon and developed some information that made him look good for a murder that happened a long time ago."

"I see," she said. "Well, Jack queried the DMV database and found a driver's license and a car registration issued to Javier Alvarez. He was looking for an address, obviously. Both records returned the address 1905 East 27th Street."

"Yes, that's his father's address," Malone said. "But at least according to the father, he doesn't live there. I guess he just used it as a permanent address."

"Jack found another address for him," Freeman said. "I also checked Jack's email and found one from a friend of his who works for a large telecom. There was a cell phone number with an address in the email. It mentioned no name, but given what Jack had been searching for, it's a good bet that the phone number and address belong to Javier Alvarez."

"What's the address?" Malone said.

"1366 East Vernon Avenue," Freeman said. "I looked it up, and it's an old apartment complex with a dozen one-story units."

"Yes, I'm familiar with that neighborhood," Malone said. "It's the kind of area I'd expect to find Alvarez living in, and it's close to the old neighborhood where his father lives. No apartment number?"

"No, just the primary street address," Freeman said.

"Well, it shouldn't be hard to find out which apartment he lives in," Malone said. "What kind of car is registered to him?"

"A 1971 Chevrolet Monte Carlo, California license plate 5X21206," Freeman said. "The record says the color is blue, but that might mean nothing. A car that old could have been re-painted many times."

"Yes, that's true," Malone said. "I'll pass on the information to the detectives working Jack's murder. I've already given them Alvarez's name."

"Might save them some work, assuming they haven't already found the information on their own," Freeman said.

"They may have checked the DMV already, but I doubt they have the address from the cell phone records," Malone said.

There was a knock at the door. The door opened, admitting two guys wearing gray coveralls with a patch reading "Bio Clean Up" sewn on them. They were carrying a variety of janitorial equipment and supplies.

"We're here to clean the office," one man said.

Freeman stood up and walked around her desk.

"This way please," she said. She ushered them to the closed door of Jack's office and opened the door. The men went inside, and Malone could hear them setting down their equipment. He noticed that Freeman had avoided looking inside the office. The cleaners went to work, and she returned to her desk.

"I should get going," Malone said. "I have some things to do before going back to work in the morning."

"I know I'm not Jack, but I have done a lot of the database searches for his cases in the past," Freeman said. "As long as I'm still here, if you need anything, please ask."

"I appreciate that, Rhonda," Malone said. "But after what happened to Jack, I don't want to get you involved in this."

"Well, the offer stands if you change your mind," she said.

"Thanks," Malone said. "I'm sure you will have enough to do winding down Jack's business affairs. You have my number. I'd appreciate it if you would call me about the funeral arrangements once his sister has made them."

"Of course I will," Freeman said.

"Okay, I'll be seeing you," Malone said.

"Take care of yourself, Ben," she said.

Malone walked out of the office and headed back to the lot where he had parked the car.

23

DNA

Malone sat in his car for several minutes with the motor running. His first instinct was to go to Alvarez's apartment to confront him. The grief he felt over Jack Bright's death had moved past shock and disbelief to anger. Convinced that Javier Alvarez had gotten word about Jack's involvement in the Anderson murder investigation, and had killed him in an attempt to shut it down, Malone wanted nothing more than to avenge his friend's murder. But the rational part of his brain took over. He knew that if he involved himself personally by confronting Alvarez, he could taint the case. Alvarez might eventually walk on a technicality. So instead he did what he had told Rhonda Freeman he was going to do with the information she had given him. He took his cell phone out of his pocket and called Washington. Washington answered.

"Washington, this is Malone," he said.

"Malone, please tell me you aren't going to be calling every few hours for a progress update," Washington said.

"I'm not calling for an update," Malone said. "I have some information for you on Javier Alvarez."

"I told you that you couldn't be involved in this," Washington said.

"I'm not pursuing anything on my own," Malone said. "It's some information that Jack discovered on Monday evening. His secretary just gave it to me."

"Okay, what is it?" Washington said.

Malone told Washington about the cell phone number and the address it came back to. He also gave him Alvarez's vehicle information.

"The cell phone information could really be useful," Washington said. "We already checked the DMV and found out that his license and registration show his father's address. Now we have his address. We can get the apartment number from the landlord. But where the phone might help is we can get his telephone records from the service provider and see what towers it was pinging off of Monday evening. We could get lucky. If he is the killer and he had his phone turned on, with triangulation, we might be able to place him at the scene of the murder at the time it occurred."

"Did you talk with Ramon Alvarez yet?" Malone said.

"No," Washington said. "We went to his house this morning, but evidently he had already left work. There wasn't anyone there."

"Anything from the coroner yet?" Malone said.

"Malone, this conversation is sounding an awful lot like a progress update request," Washington said.

"Okay, Washington, I'm sorry," Malone said. "Jack was a close friend, and I want his killer hooked and booked. Sooner rather than later."

"Understood," Washington said. "But you know these things take time. Give me time to do my job. But, yes, I have the preliminaries from the coroner. They shot Bright with a nine. They recovered three nine-millimeter slugs from the body. Two of them are in good shape. We can match them to the weapon if we find it."

"Hopefully it wasn't tossed in the Pacific after the murder," Malone said.

"Yes, there is that," Washington said. "Since I'm giving you an update,

I might as well tell you this. We got the oldest booking photos of Alvarez from the county and a copy of the composite drawings of the burglary suspects they distributed back in 1992 from the cold case you're working. Javier was a dead ringer for one suspect. He may be your suspect, too."

"Now we just need to nail it down that Ramon Alvarez told Javier about the interview with you and Bright and that he mentioned the Anderson murder," Malone said. "If you can get Ramon to admit to that, you should have enough to get a search warrant for Javier's apartment, and you might find the gun."

"Yes, we're going to work on that," Washington said. "We're going back to the old man's house to catch him after he returns from work. I'll threaten him with a conspiracy charge on Bright's murder if he is uncooperative."

"Then I'll let you get back to work," Malone said. "I'm off the beach and going back to work tomorrow morning. I've got some loose ends to tie up before the end of the day."

"Just remember what I said, Malone," Washington said. "Stay away from my case. And don't be calling me ten times a day. If something breaks, I'll let you know."

"Fair enough," Malone said. "Talk to you later, Washington."

Malone disconnected the call, drove out of the lot, and took a left on Hollywood Boulevard. He was hungry after skipping breakfast and drove home to have lunch. He was thinking about going for a run afterward. But Malone was about to get a phone call that would change his early afternoon plans.

A few minutes after leaving Jack Bright's office building, Malone's cell phone rang. He fumbled the phone out of his pocket and answered.

"Malone," he said.

"Malone, this is Jane Kroft."

"Hello Jane," Malone said. "I was just thinking about calling you."

"Sure you were Malone," she said. "But anyway, I got a CODIS hit on the DNA profile from the bite wound swabs."

"Seriously?" Malone said. "Javier Alvarez?"

"The short answer is no," Kroft said. "No one named Javier Alvarez bit your victim. But there is an interesting connection."

"What connection?" Malone said.

"It's a little complicated to get into on the phone, Malone," she said. "Especially since I'm guessing you don't know all that much about deoxyribonucleic acid profiles and markers. Have you had lunch?"

"Not yet," Malone said. "I was just headed home for lunch when you called."

"You like Mexican?" Kroft said.

"Sure, love it," Malone said.

"Okay, then meet me at the Camino Viejo Restaurant on Marengo Street," she said. "You can buy me lunch, and I'll give you the scoop."

"Okay, but where exactly is it?" Malone said.

"Where are you now?" she said.

"Just got on the 101 at Hollywood Boulevard," Malone said.

"Okay, take the 101 to North Mission. Take North Mission east to Marengo Street. Go right on Marengo and just past the USC Medical Center, you will see Camino Viejo on the right at the corner of Marengo and North Cummings Street."

"Okay, I should be there in about half an hour," Malone said.

"I'll be waiting, Malone," Kroft said. Then she disconnected.

Kroft had given good directions, and Malone drove into the parking lot at the restaurant less than a half hour after she had hung up. He walked inside the cozy little Mexican eatery and spotted Kroft in a corner booth at the back. She smiled brightly when she saw him approaching. Malone slid into the booth opposite her.

"Jeez, Malone, the things a girl has to do to get you to buy her lunch," she said.

"Sorry Jane, I've had a lot on my plate lately," Malone said. "Someone murdered a close friend of mine Monday night."

"Oh my god," Kroft said. "I'm so sorry Malone. What happened?"

Malone told her the story, including how Jack Bright had been helping him on the cold case and why he suspected that Javier Alvarez had been the killer.

"I'm sorry about your friend," Kroft said. "Alvarez might be good for that murder, but I don't think he is a suspect in the Anderson murder. At least he didn't inflict the bite wound."

"But you said there was a connection?" Malone said.

"Yes, I'm getting to that," Kroft said.

A server who came over to take their order interrupted them. Kroft ordered chicken enchiladas with green sauce and Malone, the Camino Viejo super burrito. After the server had left, with their order, Kroft continued.

"The CODIS hit I received was a partial match of Alvarez's DNA profile and the unknown profile from the bite wound swabs. In technical parlance, we term a partial match a moderate stringency candidate match between two single source profiles, having at each locus all the alleles of one sample represented in the other sample. A partial match is not an exact match of the two profiles. When evaluating whether a candidate match is viable and should be processed through to confirmation, a forensic scientist needs to determine whether there is a reason to exclude the candidate offender profile as the probable source of the profile obtained from crime scene evidence."

"So how does that help us, if it's only a partial match with Alvarez's DNA?" Malone said. "What's the connection?"

Kroft continued, "Because of a similarity in alleles between the forensic unknown and Alvarez's DNA profile, we can conclude that it is extremely likely that a close biological relative of Alvarez is the source of the forensic unknown. It looks like Alvarez's profile contains about 50 percent of the markers present in the unknown forensic profile, which allows us to conclude that the person who bit your victim is Alvarez's sibling. Do you know whether he has brothers or sisters?"

Malone was so astonished it left him speechless for a moment.

"What is it, Malone?" Kroft said. "You know anything about his siblings?"

"Sibling, singular," Malone said. "He has only one, a sister."

"That's great then," Kroft said. "There is your suspect."

"Yes, but things are about to get complicated," Malone said.

"Complicated how?" Kroft said.

"His sister was a patrol officer at Hollenbeck in 1992 when the murder occurred. She was the ex-girlfriend of the victim's husband, and the family claims she was harassing the victim before the murder. But the detectives looked at her as a suspect back then but excluded her. And that's not all. She still works for the LAPD, probably in a senior position."

"Holy shit, Batman!" Kroft said. "Are we talking about another LAPD scandal in the making?"

"It's possible," Malone said. "If she killed Anderson, it wasn't job-related. It was a personal deal. And given her connection to the victim back in 1992 and the fact they excluded her so quickly as a suspect, it's reasonable to assume that there was some kind of cover-up by someone in the department."

"Who is she?" Kroft said.

"I don't know yet," Malone said. "All I have is her maiden name, Vanessa Alvarez. Apparently, she married and goes by her married name now. I can get with personnel and find out, though."

"And you also need a DNA sample from her," Kroft said. "Since she is a cop, you can bet she won't be giving you one without a court order."

"Yes, I know," Malone said. "And even with what you've just given me, I don't have enough yet to get one."

The server brought their food, and they continued the conversation about the case while they ate.

"So what's the motive for Javier Alvarez killing your friend if he wasn't the Anderson murderer?" Kroft asked.

"It actually makes me like him more for the murder," Malone said. "Jack and I interviewed the father, Ramon Alvarez, the day before Jack's murder. We learned Javier has always been fiercely protective of his sister. He must have known she killed Anderson, and he was trying to derail the investigation by killing Jack."

"If that's true, you had better watch your back, Malone," she said. "If he is trying to shut down the investigation, he likely intends to eliminate you, too. It wouldn't do him much good just to kill your friend."

"That's a possibility," Malone said.

They finished lunch. Malone paid the check, and they walked outside the dimly lit restaurant into the bright Los Angeles sunshine. Malone walked Kroft to her car, a newer model Toyota Prius Hybrid. The car fit her, Malone thought.

"So, what are you going to do now?" Kroft said.

"First, I'm going to find out what Vanessa Alvarez calls herself these days," Malone said. "Then I'll talk to my boss in the morning about formally re-opening the Anderson case. After that, I'll have to figure out a way to get a DNA sample from the former Vanessa Alvarez. Hey, Jane, I owe you for this."

"Damn right, Malone," she said. "You owe me big time. First, I stuck my neck out for you getting that forensic DNA sample analyzed on the county dime and got it submitted to CODIS. Now I've broken the case for you. Sex may be the only way for you even things up now."

Malone laughed.

"Hang onto to that thought," he said. "But I have to tell you I'm in a new relationship, so that's not an option at the moment. Not that the possibility doesn't appeal to me."

"Well damn, Malone," she said. "Just when things were getting interesting, you tell me you're in a relationship."

"Don't give up hope," he said. "Unfortunately, my track record with relationships is rather bleak."

"Okay, I'll keep my fingers crossed," she said. "But you better not wait too long. Some other guy may come along any day now and sweep me off my feet."

"Wouldn't surprise me," Malone said. "And that definitely would be my loss."

They said goodbye. Kroft got into the Prius and drove away. Malone got into the Camry and headed home.

24

Shot At

On the drive back north on the 101 to his apartment, Malone's mind was racing. He was mentally preparing for the discussion he planned to have with his boss, Lieutenant Turner, the following morning, and the push to get the Anderson murder case officially re-opened. With the DNA evidence, Kroft had gotten him, the case now met the criteria for return to active status.

Malone was also thinking about what his next moves would be. Of course, he first had to find out the last name that the former Vanessa Alvarez was going by, but more importantly, he had to come up with a plan to get a DNA sample from her. He knew Kroft had been right when she said that would not be easy. Once she knew she was again a suspect in the Anderson murder, she would likely keep her mouth shut and lawyer up. No defense attorney was going to allow her to give up a DNA sample, even if she was willing to.

Malone decided the best tactical approach would be to get the sample surreptitiously. He knew there were legal ways to do it because he knew other investigators who needed a DNA sample from an uncooperative suspect had done it.

Once he had a DNA sample from Vanessa Alvarez and had her

profile compared to the forensic sample, he was certain he would get a match. Then it would just be a matter of pulling her in for questioning to nail down the case. As a cop, she would certainly know all the tricks detectives used when questioning suspects and would try to stonewall. In his wildest dreams, he certainly wasn't expecting a confession. But Malone was a skilled interrogator. He wouldn't bother with trying to trick Alvarez into overtly implicating herself. Instead, he would simply make her commit to a story. Then he would try to take the story apart piece by piece by finding inconsistencies. He knew from experience that whenever a person was attempting to be deceptive, there were always inconsistencies.

Deep in thought, Malone hadn't noticed the black tricked-out, older model Chevrolet Caprice that pulled alongside the driver's side of his Camry and that was keeping pace. It was only when the heavily tinted passenger side window of the Caprice started down that he picked up the movement in his peripheral vision and noticed the car. He glanced over and saw the male front seat passenger was wearing a ski mask and was extending a semi-automatic pistol out the window, pointed at him. The car in front blocked Malone from speeding up, so he instinctively jammed on the brakes. That forced the car behind him to brake suddenly and veer to the left to avoid colliding with Malone's Toyota. But it caused the Caprice to bolt ahead just as the gunman fired, causing the bullet aimed at Malone to miss. Unfortunately, the sudden evasive action taken by the vehicle behind Malone's started a chain reaction of squealing tires and panicked maneuvers that predictably culminated in the deafening sound of multiple metal-on-metal collisions.

After locking up the brakes to allow the Caprice to shoot past his car, Malone immediately sped up and shot the narrow gap between the two cars in the adjacent right lane. Miraculously, he had avoided getting into a collision himself. He got his car safely onto the shoulder without getting struck by the cars crashing behind him. He stopped the car on the shoulder to put more distance between him and the Caprice. Unless the occupants stopped on the shoulder ahead to wait for him to catch up, they couldn't get to him now. There was no chance that they could exit, do a U-turn and come back at him from behind as the many vehicle wrecks that now littered the freeway behind him had effectively turned that portion of the 101 into a parking lot. Horns were already blaring in evidence of the frustrated drivers already caught behind the wreckage.

Malone couldn't see the Caprice on the shoulder ahead of him, so he put the car in gear and cautiously drove along the shoulder. Then he decided the best option was to get off the freeway at the next exit and to continue towards West Hollywood on the surface streets, just in case the Caprice was waiting up ahead. He made it to the North Western Avenue exit without incident. He scanned left and right but saw no sign of the black Caprice.

He followed North Western all the way to Hollywood Boulevard, where he could turn west towards his apartment. After the turn, he found a parking spot across from a coffee shop. After parking the car, he got out. While locking the car, he noticed the bullet hole in the side molding just in front of the driver's door. He headed into the coffee shop. He needed a drink, but he would settle for coffee. Mostly, he wanted to call Washington.

After getting a large coffee, Malone sat down at a table and pulled out his cell phone. He punched in Washington's number. Washington answered on the third ring.

"Washington, it's me again," Malone said.

"Malone, what a surprise!" Washington said, his voice dripping with sarcasm. "I thought we agreed you wouldn't keep calling me."

"Something just happened," Malone said. "Someone just took a shot at me on the 101."

"You hit?" Washington said.

"No, but my car took a bullet," Malone said.

"Thank goodness," Washington said. "If they had shot you, my luck the lieutenant would have stuck me with the aggravated assault and I'd be hearing from you even more often than I already do."

"Thanks for your compassion," Malone said. "It had to be Alvarez. He is trying to shut down my investigation. He killed Jack and now he wants to take me out."

"How do you know it was Alvarez?" Washington said. "Did you see him?"

"No, the shooter was wearing a ski mask," Malone said. "But who else could it have been? I have made no other recent enemies as far as I know."

"Was it his car at least?" Washington asked.

"No, it was a black older model Caprice," Malone said. "A tricked-out banger car with rims and limo tinted windows. The shooter was riding in the front passenger seat."

"Did you get a look at the driver?" Washington said.

"No, Washington," Malone said. "I was a little busy trying to keep from getting shot. And before you ask, I didn't get the license plate either."

"You know, Malone, you aren't very observant for a cop," Washington said.

"Spare me the criticism," Malone said.

"So, are you the one responsible for the multi-vehicle accident on the 101 south of Western that just came out a few minutes ago?" Washington said.

"It depends on how you define responsible," Malone said. "I had to take evasive action to avoid getting killed, but I haven't been involved in an accident myself. I have to say that the drivers behind me at the time are responsible because of the faulty evasive action they took."

"Nevertheless, I expect the CHP would sure like to talk with you right about now," Washington said. "Maybe I'll dime you out to them. Might get you out of my hair for a while."

"Enough with the jokes," Malone said. "I've got a serious problem here."

"Okay, Malone," Washington said. "Where are you now? Can you come to the station?"

"Yes, I'm not far away," Malone said.

"Good, then come here, and we'll get a technician to pull the slug out of your car," Washington said. "If it isn't too badly deformed, they might match it up to the slugs they recovered from Jack Bright's body. Then if we find the weapon and connect it with Alvarez, that will prove he was the person who shot at you. Since you won't leave me alone anyway, when you get here, I'll fill you in on some new information we just got."

"Okay," Malone said. "I'll be there in ten minutes."

Malone backtracked south on Western Avenue to Sunset Boulevard. He took Sunset to the Hollywood Community Station and arrived at ten after four. Washington met him in the lobby with a crime scene technician. Malone gave her the keys to his Camry, and she went out to drive the car into the sally port to work on recovering the spent bullet from it. Malone followed Washington upstairs to the detective bureau. Washington pulled another chair over from an unoccupied cubicle, and the two sat down at Washington's desk. Washington began the update.

"We got Alvarez's phone records faxed over this afternoon," he said. "We triangulated the towers his phone was pinging off of Monday night and can put him near Jack Bright's office building at 7:10 p.m. He has an iPhone, so the location function is very accurate. According to the records, he was there for a little over five minutes before the phone moved away. The coroner established Bright's time of death at between seven and eight o'clock. That's close enough to put Alvarez at the scene at the relevant time. So we've got the opportunity part of it. According to what you've told me about your case and Alvarez's connection, I think we have a plausible motive. Now we just need to find the murder weapon and connect it to Alvarez, and we'll have the means nailed down."

"It's all circumstantial at the moment, but that's a good start," Malone said.

"Yes, and there is more," Washington said. "Chang and I went back to Bright's office building and talked to the security guard. He showed us the security video recordings from Monday night. We have Javier on video entering through the front door at eleven minutes after seven. The guard locks the rear entrance that leads to the parking lot at five. But the front doors remain unlocked until he goes home at nine. It's the only way into the building after five o'clock."

"But he didn't see Alvarez come in?" Malone said.

"No, there is only one guard, and he leaves the desk in the lobby for things like restroom breaks or to get coffee from a room off the lobby. Alvarez could have watched him until he left the desk for something and could have then made it to the elevators or stairs without being seen."

"He would have had to have been awfully lucky to miss being observed both when he arrived and when he left a few minutes later after shooting Jack," Malone said.

"That's where it gets interesting," Washington said. "The guard said he got a telephone call around seven-fifteen. A male caller said that there was an unconscious woman lying in the parking lot in back of the building. The guard said he hustled to the back door, unlocked it and went outside to check the parking lot. He didn't find anyone in the parking lot and went back inside. He figured he was back at the desk around seven-twenty."

"Plenty of time for Alvarez to shoot Jack, go back downstairs, and exit the front doors while his ruse kept the guard distracted," Malone said.

"Yes, and it explains why he didn't hear any gunshots," Washington said. "It's a solid old building, and someone outside might not have heard them."

"We have Alvarez at the scene," Malone said. "But it's still circumstantial with no witnesses or physical evidence."

"That's why we have to find the murder weapon," Washington said. "But what we have is enough probable cause for a search warrant, and a judge signed a warrant this afternoon. Right now Chang is sitting on Alvarez's apartment. We want to serve the warrant while he is at home, just in case he is carrying the gun around with him. If it was Alvarez that took the shot at you, that seems likely."

"So the plan is, you wait to hear from Chang if Alvarez shows up at the apartment and then you're going to serve the search warrant?" Malone said.

"Yes, that's about it," Washington said. "If I hear from Chang, we'll roll the SWAT team and serve the search warrant. Then, if we find a nine millimeter on him or in the house, we'll bring him in for questioning while we run the ballistics. If we get a match, he's toast."

"And if you get his phone, you can check the locator function and see whether he was riding down the 101 this afternoon," Malone said.

"Yes, that too," Washington said.

The crime scene technician walked in and handed Malone his keys. She held up a clear plastic evidence bag containing a spent nine-millimeter projectile that looked to be in remarkably good condition.

"The good news is I recovered the round," she said. "It passed through the side molding and then through mostly plastic until it lodged in the dash. Shouldn't be a problem getting a good comparison with the other spent rounds recovered from the victim's body."

"You said 'good news', which has me concerned that there might be some bad news," Malone said.

"There is," the technician said. "I'm afraid the shooter killed your CD player. I recovered the bullet from the chassis."

"Better it than me," Malone said ruefully.

Malone and Washington got up and headed downstairs to the lobby. They shook hands, and Malone turned towards the exit door.

"Hey Malone," Washington said.

Malone stopped and turned towards him.

"Don't call me, I'll call you," Washington said.

They both laughed, and Malone walked out the door. He fired up the battle-weary Camry and headed towards his apartment, hoping against hope that he would actually make it there this time.

25

An Active Case

Malone awoke immediately when the alarm sounded on Wednesday morning. Washington hadn't called in the middle of the night, so Malone assumed that Javier Alvarez was still in the wind. He scrambled out of bed, went to the kitchen, and got the coffee started. Then he went to the bathroom to shower while he waited for the coffee maker to do its thing. Malone dressed in a navy, pin-striped suit, and a clean starched white dress shirt. He selected a tie in a lighter shade of blue and a pair of black loafers to complete the outfit. Satisfied after checking himself in the bathroom mirror, he returned to the kitchen for coffee.

Malone was eager to get to work, but knowing he had plenty of time, he forced himself to relax while he drank the coffee. Then he rinsed the cup after he finished and placed it in the sink. He filled a travel mug from the pot before switching off the coffee maker. He clipped his badge holder on his belt on the right side and then the holster holding his Glock semi-auto behind it. After grabbing his keys and wallet, he headed for the front door.

After opening the door, he scanned the parking lot. After the incident on the previous day, he had vowed to be more alert until they took Javier Alvarez into custody. Malone knew he had been lucky, and knew he couldn't depend on always being lucky. He needed to be more vigilant. Seeing nothing suspicious, Malone locked his apartment door and walked to his car. He got inside, fired up the Camry, and headed downtown.

When Malone got off the elevator on the fifth floor of the PAB, he walked to the conference room. The door was open, but the lights were off. He switched on the lights and saw that someone had removed all the cardboard case file boxes. He switched off the lights and headed down to Lieutenant Turner's office to see what was up. As he approached the office, he could see the lights were on through the open window blinds of Turner's office. Just as he got to the door, it opened, and Vanessa Bachmann came out of the office.

Bachmann paused and glared at Malone for a moment and then turned and walked away without saying a word. Malone had seen that same menacing look in her dark eyes that he had noticed for a millisecond the first time they had met. But this time, the look hadn't quickly evaporated. It hadn't evaporated at all.

When Malone turned back to the door of Turner's office after watching her stalk away, Turner was standing in the doorway looking at him.

"Morning boss," Malone said. "I saw that someone removed the case files from the conference room and I was wondering where I'll be working."

"A couple of desks came open for you and Reyes while you were away," Turner said. "I'll walk you over in a minute, but first we need to talk. Come in and shut the door."

Turner turned and walked back into the office. Malone followed. Turner walked around the desk and sat down in his chair. He didn't offer a seat to Malone, which left him with the distinct feeling that he was being called on the carpet for something.

"I just had an interesting conversation with Lieutenant Bachmann," Turner said. "I take it you and she know each other?"

"Yes sir," Malone said. "I'm acquainted with Lieutenant Bachmann."

"You're too modest, Malone," Turner said. "Not the type to kiss and tell? At least according to Bachmann, you two have been a lot more than just acquainted. She just told me that the two of you have slept together."

Malone could feel the heat rising into his cheeks and knew his face had reddened.

"Yes, sir," he said. "We had casual sex once… well, twice actually… but both times on the same day."

"I don't care about Bachmann's sexual exploits, or yours," Turner said. "But that wasn't all Bachmann had to say this morning. She told me she decided things would not work out with you and her and broke things off, but that you seem unwilling to let it go. She claims you've been calling and trying to see her, basically harassing her to the point where she is considering getting a restraining order against you. Malone, I really hope I didn't make a big mistake going to bat for you with the chief yesterday and getting you re-assigned to the section."

"Lieutenant, we were intimate one time, on a Saturday after she invited me to go to the beach with her, but that was the extent of it," Malone said. "The rest of it is nothing by lies. I've neither seen nor spoken with Vanessa Bachmann since the day I got arraigned on the murder charge. She distanced herself from me because she feared if it got out that we were seeing each other, with my legal issues, it might negatively impact her career. I haven't tried to see her, and I haven't called her. As a matter of fact, I'm seeing someone else now. I damn sure am not obsessed with Vanessa Bachmann."

"I hope that's true, Malone," Turner said. "The last thing you need right now is Bachmann making an official sexual harassment complaint against you. But she also said something else I found troubling. She claims that you're also trying to frame her brother for murder to spite her for breaking off the relationship."

Malone was stunned. *"Her brother!" he thought.* Uninvited, he dropped into a chair.

"Her brother is Javier Alvarez?" Malone said.

"Yes, Alvarez was her maiden name before she married the first time," Turner said.

"Then her brother murdered Jack Bright Monday night, and I'm pretty sure that he tried to take a shot at me yesterday on the 101," Malone said.

"What?" Turner said. "Jack Bright is dead? That's the murder Bachmann claims you're trying to frame her brother for?"

"It's probably what she was talking about," Malone said. "But Lieutenant, that's not the only murder, and we really need to talk."

"Christ, Malone," Turner said. "What have you got yourself into now? Sit down and tell me what you're talking about."

Malone started at the beginning. He told Turner about reviewing the Anderson murder cold case and how he just couldn't ignore it, even though initially it didn't meet the criteria for re-opening as an active investigation. Then he explained how he and Reyes had worked the case off the books until the chief suspended him. Next, he admitted that he had continued working the case even while on suspension and parts of the puzzle had fallen into place. Finally, he revealed that Jack Bright had been helping him with the case and had gone with him to interview Ramon Alvarez, the father of Vanessa and Javier. The results of the interview had given him reason to believe Javier Alvarez had been involved in the Anderson murder.

Malone continued by telling Turner that Jack Bright's murder happened at his office the day after he and Malone had spoken with Ramon Alvarez and that he suspected Javier Alvarez had killed Bright to shut down the investigation. Then he dropped the bombshell.

He told Turner about the DNA evidence that the coroner's office misplaced but later found and analyzed, and about the CODIS hit on a partial match with Javier Alvarez's DNA profile."

"A partial match?" Turner said.

"Yes, and a criminalist over at the coroner's office told me that the comparison of Alvarez's profile to the profile of the forensic sample collected from a bite wound suffered by Mary Beth Anderson twenty-three years ago strongly suggest that a sibling of Javier Alvarez inflicted the wound."

"Are you telling me what I think you're telling me, Malone?" Turner said.

"If you think I'm going to tell you that Vanessa Bachmann is Javier Alvarez's only sibling, then yes, that's what I'm telling you right now," Malone said. "She was also the ex-girlfriend of Mary Beth Anderson's husband, who many believed was stalking and harassing Anderson shortly before the murder. At least briefly, the Van Nuys detectives looked at her as a suspect, although from what I've been able to find out, they excluded her rather quickly. I talked to the original lead detective in the case, but he was less than cooperative. He did, however, give me a rather cryptic warning which seemed to suggest that someone told him, perhaps ordered him to exclude Vanessa Alvarez, now Bachmann, from the list of suspects. Someone back then with the LAPD may have intentionally covered up her involvement."

"Christ, Malone," Turner said. "You're just a regular shit-storm magnet, aren't you? You're telling me you've not only disobeyed my direct orders, and disregarded my explicit instructions on the protocol to be used when processing cold case files, but you've broken perhaps an incalculable number of department policies along the way. Not the least of which include working a homicide investigation while on suspension and conspiring with an employee of Los Angeles County to ignore policies for the submission of forensic DNA evidence for analysis. Hell, Malone. You may have even broken a few state and federal laws along the way. Then to top it all off, you've apparently dug up another LAPD scandal in the making that implicates at least one senior LAPD officer and that will probably bury us both under an avalanche of shit once it rolls downhill from the top floor of this frigging building."

"Yes lieutenant, I think you've pretty fairly summarized it," Malone said. "The only thing you left out, and thanks for that, was that I got Jack Bright killed in the course of an unauthorized criminal investigation."

"Yeah, there is that," Turner said, his elbows on the desk and his face cradled in his hands. "What the hell were you thinking, Malone?"

"I just read the file, lieutenant, and I couldn't let it go," Malone said. "I felt like Mary Beth Anderson, and her family deserved to get justice, and I believed I could get it for them."

"And you got yourself charged with murder and apparently shot at in the process," Turner said. "How the hell am I going to spin this to the chief? I've got to tell you, Malone. If I had heard this story and it involved anyone else but you, I'd never have believed it. So now I suppose you need a DNA sample from Vanessa Bachmann. I don't think there is a snowball's chance in hell that you're going to get that sample, do you, Malone?"

"Well, sir, if you mean, do I think she will voluntarily give a sample? The answer is no," Malone said. "Once she knows for sure she is a suspect again, I think she will lawyer up and won't cooperate at all."

"But you have a plan, don't you, Malone? I almost forgot. Minor inconveniences like regulations, policies, and constitutional rights concerns don't apply to you. Do they Malone? You've got to be kidding me, Malone. Who do you think you are? You think you're Philip fucking Marlowe?"

"No, Lieutenant," Malone said. "But I think I have a plan for getting a

DNA sample from Vanessa Bachmann that doesn't require her consent or cooperation, but that is still perfectly legal."

"Jesus, Malone," Turner said. "Don't even think about telling me about it. I don't want to know. I want a fighting chance to claim plausible deniability. If you wind up in federal prison on a civil rights violation beef, I sure as hell don't plan on sharing a cell with you."

"So, can I have your permission to re-open the Anderson case for active investigation?" Malone said.

"Permission?" Turner said. "Permission! Since when did you ever need permission, Malone? It seems to me you've been actively investigating the case for what, at least several weeks now?"

"I'm sorry about that," Malone said. "I just thought you would tell me to drop the case if I came to you with this before I had some hard evidence."

"You're damn right I would have told you to drop it, Malone," Turner said. "And you knew that, and still you keep at it. That's the part that pisses me off the most. It wasn't just ignorance. You intentionally went around me and circumvented policy because you thought you knew best. Malone, tell me something. Were you born stupid, or did you have to work at it?"

"Probably a little of both," Malone said.

"Well, it is what it is," Turner said. "You identified a viable suspect, maybe two. Javier could have still been involved in the murder of Anderson, even though he evidently didn't inflict the bite wound. There is no way in good conscience that I can tell you to drop the case now. But I'm telling you one thing, Malone. This may turn out one of those times when you may have won a battle, but end up losing the war. But in answer to your *request*, sure you have my permission to return the case to active status."

"Thank you, Lieutenant," Malone said. "I know I'm going to clear this with an arrest."

"I sincerely hope so, Malone, for your sake," Turner said. "If you decide to accuse a senior LAPD officer of murder, you better be able to produce the evidence to make it stick, or your career with this department is likely going to come to an abrupt and inglorious end. Not to say that might not end up as one of the likely outcomes of all this anyway, before all gets said and done."

"Understood," Malone said.

"Tell me this," Turner said. "What's the status of the investigation of Jack Bright's murder where Javier Alvarez is concerned? No doubt you have your big fat thumb in that pie as well. There isn't any point in me going to the trouble of talking to the actual investigators. I'll just cut out the middleman and get the scoop directly from you."

"The Hollywood dicks can put Javier at the scene. They have solid circumstantial evidence and a video recording of him inside Jack's office building. But they don't yet have enough to make the arrest. They are sitting on a search warrant, trying to catch Alvarez at home. But he hasn't been back to his apartment since they set up surveillance on him. Since he took a shot at me, they feel he is walking around with the murder weapon from Jack's murder. They don't feel confident they would find it if they hit the apartment while he was away."

"You're sure it was Javier who took a shot at you?" Turner said. "You positively identified him?"

"No, the shooter was wearing a ski mask and was a passenger in someone else's car," Malone said. "But I know it was him. If you wake up and the ground wet, you know it rained overnight whether or not you actually witnessed it. It's just common sense."

"Knowing and proving are two different things, Malone," Turner said. "You've been a cop long enough to know that much. You better hope those Hollywood dicks find that murder weapon."

"Yes, that would certainly simplify a lot of things," Malone said.

Turner got up from his chair and, taking the cue; Malone stood up, too.

"Well, let me show you to your desk. Reyes is probably in the office by now. I'm sure you and your partner in crime must have a lot of catching up to do. I suppose I should take some solace from the fact that you two characters became cops. You're both big enough pains in the ass as it is. I shudder to think of how much trouble you might have caused the LAPD if you two had gone to the dark side and become real criminals."

Malone followed Turner to his newly assigned workspace. He saw Reyes sitting at a desk next to a vacant one, reading a case file. Turner pointed to the vacant desk.

"Go forth and make us all proud, Malone," he said. "Now all I have to do is figure out what I'm going to tell the chief."

With that, Turner turned and walked away.

"Well, that went better than I expected," Malone thought.

He then headed for his desk.

Reyes looked up as Malone approached. He smiled broadly and jumped up from his desk. Reyes seemed genuinely pleased to see him.

"Dude!" he said. "I heard you were coming back today!"

Reyes grabbed his hand and shook it, slapping him on the back at the same time.

"Good to have you back, bro."

"Good to be back," Malone said. "And do I have some news for you."

"What news?" Reyes said.

"Turner just gave us permission to re-open the Anderson case," Malone said. "Put away the files. We have an active case to work."

"Are you kidding me?" Reyes said.

"No, I'm not kidding," Malone said.

"So what happened?" Reyes said.

"Sit down, my friend," Malone said. "I'll tell you all about it."

Malone then told Reyes the entire story, much in the same way he had told it to Turner. But this time, he had a far more receptive listener. Reyes had wanted to work the case as badly as Malone had. It blew Reyes away to learn that Lieutenant Vanessa Bachmann was the prime suspect in the Anderson murder. But once he heard all the details, it made perfect sense. Once Malone had finished the story, Reyes had a score of questions.

"So how are we going to get a DNA sample from Bachmann?" he asked.

"Here is what I think we should do," Malone said. "I think we keep her under surveillance here at work. We follow her whenever she leaves the building. I hope we can be there when she goes to lunch or gets coffee. If we see her leave something behind or discard something like an empty cup or eating utensil, we snag it. Anything she uses to drink from or eat with will have come into contact with her saliva and should provide us with enough of a sample for analysis and comparison to the forensic sample."

"That might work," Reyes said. "Why not just see if we can snag a coffee cup or empty water bottle from the trash in her office?"

"That could work too," Malone said. "But she probably locks the door when she leaves the office. Especially now because she knows Hollywood is looking at her brother for the murder of Jack Bright. She probably also knows I suspect a connection to the Anderson case, so she will probably be even more cautious than usual. It won't surprise me if she takes her trash bag with her when she leaves at the end of the day. She is a detective, and I've heard a good one. So she probably knows what we're after."

"So say we get the sample, and her profile turns out to be a match for the forensic sample profile," Reyes said. "Then what?"

"Then we pull her in and interrogate her," Malone said. "We make her commit to a story, and hopefully we tear the story apart piece by piece to prove she is lying. That's really all we have to go on besides the DNA evidence. I'm sure the gun used to kill Mary Beth Anderson is long gone by now."

"That gives me an idea," Reyes said. "No doubt she wasn't stupid enough to use her duty weapon to shoot Anderson. But she probably had a backup weapon and might have used that. Like you said, chances are she was smart enough to get rid of it. But think about it, dude. She had been on the job for what, a little over a year? I don't know about you, but when I was on for the first year or two, I really had to stretch my paycheck. I sure would have had a tough time deciding to throw a pistol worth several hundred dollars into the ocean. Maybe she sold it. A lot of weapons change hands among cops. She might have sold it to someone at Hollenbeck."

"Or she might have dumped it and then reported it stolen and collected insurance on it," Malone said.

"I like that idea even better," Reyes said, moving to his computer. "And to do that, she would have needed a police report. Let's see if she reported the theft of a firearm back there in 1992."

His fingers flew over the keys for a few moments, and then he queried the department's theft report database. A record popped up. They both scanned it.

"Look at that!" Reyes said. "There it is. In 1992, the same month someone killed Anderson, Vanessa Alvarez reported the theft of a Model 36 Smith & Wesson .38 revolver."

"Good work, Reyes," Malone said. "You just found another piece of the puzzle. Bachmann reported the theft of the same caliber weapon used to kill Mary Beth Anderson. What a coincidence and we both know that in police work there is no such thing as a coincidence. She probably collected the insurance and then tossed it into the ocean. The lab experts could probably testify that the suspect fired the bullets recovered from Anderson's body from a snub-nose as opposed to a weapon with a longer barrel because of the difference in the rifling grooves. That would make this even a more damning piece of evidence, circumstantial or not."

"What else do we need to be looking at?" Reyes said.

"I want to get the Hollenbeck duty roster from the day of the murder," Malone said. "First to see if Vanessa Bachmann was actually on duty that day, as the case file says. And if the roster does show she was on duty, I want to see who certified it because that is the person who would have been in the best position to cover it up if she wasn't on duty."

"Good plan," Reyes said. "So, how are we going to handle the surveillance?"

"I think one of us should stay downstairs where we can see the police parking lot," Malone said. "Just because she leaves the floor doesn't mean she is leaving the building. Plus, to stay covert, we can't exactly ride down the elevator with her. If she goes down, by the time we get to the ground floor, we could lose her. She could already be gone. She has an assigned unmarked. I'll find out which one it is and where she parks. Then we'll take turns surveilling it. If she leaves the PAB, whoever is watching will immediately tail her and call the other."

"Sounds like a plan, bro," Reyes said. "So you taking the first watch?"

"Yes, I'm going down now and scope out the unmarked she drives," Malone said. "I'll call your cell phone and give you the scoop as soon as I have it spotted. Then I'll stay and watch it until say one o'clock. You can grab lunch before one and then relieve me."

"Okay, dude," Reyes said. "While you're doing that, I'll put in a call to records and see about getting that Hollenbeck duty roster."

"Sounds good," Malone said. "See you at one then, unless she makes a move before then."

"Okay, bro," Reyes said.

Malone then headed to the elevator and took it to the ground floor. He walked around the police lot and noticed for the first time that the parking spaces in the back had designated spaces for the senior officers. He quickly found the space assigned to Bachmann. They had assigned her a black Ford Crown Vic. He jotted down the license plate number to pass on to Reyes. He then counted the spaces from left to right so that he and Reyes could keep track of the right vehicle from a distance since there were several black Crown Vic unmarked vehicles parked in the lot. Malone supposed that made sense because they handed down as unmarked cars, older high mileage patrol black and whites. It was probably just easier, not to mention cheaper, for the city garage to paint over the white parts of a retired patrol cruiser to match the black parts than to repaint the whole car.

Malone then found a shady area about a hundred yards from Bachmann's assigned parking space where he could observe her police vehicle without being obvious about it. He pulled out his cell phone and called Reyes. Then he gave Reyes the information and told him where he was so that Reyes would know where to come to relieve him later. He then settled down to watch, hoping Bachmann would leave the building soon and give them a chance to get something with her DNA on it. He'd always hated stakeouts, and this one promised to be a particularly boring one.

26

Evidence Collection

Luckily for Malone; he didn't have long to wait. It began with a phone call from Reyes telling him he had just seen Bachmann headed for the elevator. Malone looked at his watch and saw that it was almost noon. Bachmann was probably on her way to lunch. So he hoot-footed it to his car so that he would be ready to follow her. He jogged to the police lot and got into the Camry. Then he backed out of the parking space and drove to a position where he could see Bachmann's unmarked car. Just as he arrived there, he observed her walking toward the black Crown Vic. She got in, started the car, reversed, and headed to the exit. Malone drove slowly through the lot until he arrived at a spot where he could see which way Bachmann turned onto Spring Street.

He watched as she turned and then sped out of the parking lot exit and followed. Malone drove out of the lot just in time to see Bachmann's car, a block ahead and turning right onto West Third Street. He fumbled for his phone and called Reyes. Reyes told him that because it had been almost noon, he had already hurried downstairs on the chance Bachmann was going to lunch and was already in his car. Malone told him he was behind Bachmann's unmarked on West Third and Reyes said he would head that way.

Malone stayed on the phone to provide Reyes with location updates. He was three cars behind Bachmann's car in moderate traffic as they continued west on Third Street. Bachmann stopped her car for the traffic light at South Figueroa Street and then turned left when the light changed. Malone followed, still three cars behind, and gave Reyes an update.

After passing West Fourth Street, Bachmann pulled to the curb in the middle of the block and parked her car. Malone continued past. Watching in his rearview mirror, he saw Bachmann get out of the unmarked and walk towards Las Brisas, an informal Mexican food eatery offering patio dining. It was almost always outdoor dining season in LA, so there were lots of eateries like Las Brisas around the city offering al fresco dining. Malone knew the place. He had eaten lunch there a few times with Reyes since they had been working together at the PAB. Speaking into his phone, Malone told Reyes that Bachmann had stopped there.

"Looks like lunchtime," Malone said. "She is at Las Brisas."

"Where do you want me?" Reyes said.

"Take Figueroa to West Sixth and turn right," Malone said. "I'm parked here just past the corner, and there is a space for your car in front of mine. When you get here, we will walk back down to Las Brisas."

"Okay, be there in two minutes," Reyes said.

Malone waited on the sidewalk while Reyes parked his car. When Reyes joined him there, they walked around the corner and up Figueroa to the restaurant. They stopped near the restaurant where they could see the patio. Bachmann was standing beside a table occupied by a bald and tanned broad-shouldered man wearing a dark suit.

"Is that who I think it is?" Reyes said.

"It is if you think it is Deputy Chief Thompson," Malone said.

They both knew that Brad Thompson was the commanding officer of the LAPD Employee Relations Group, which represented the Office of the Chief of Police in all employee relations matters, including investigations of grievances.

"Is she having lunch with him?" Reyes said.

"I guess we're about to find out," Malone said.

They watched as Bachmann spoke briefly with Thompson and then walked to the counter to order lunch. She returned to Thompson's table carrying a paper plate of food and a drink cup. Thompson already had a plate in front of him. Bachmann sat down in the chair across from Thompson, and they began chatting while eating lunch. Malone and Reyes were too far away to overhear the conversation, but it appeared from the way they interacted that Bachmann and Turner were old acquaintances. From time to time, when Bachmann laughed at something Turner said, she would reach over and touch his hand. It seemed evident that it was lunch between two friends, not a business meeting. There was intimacy between them.

"Wonder what she is talking about to Thompson?" Reyes said.

"I haven't told you yet, but when I arrived for work Turner informed me that Bachmann had come to him this morning alleging that I was sexually harassing her," Malone said.

"What!" Reyes said. "Get out of here. You serious, bro?"

"That's what Turner told me," Malone said. "Maybe that's what she is doing here with Thompson, making a formal complaint."

"A complaint like that sort of implies you two must have been doing the nasty at some point," Reyes said, clearly interested in hearing every juicy detail.

"It's a long story," Malone said. "I'll have to tell you later."

They watched as Bachmann wiped her mouth with a napkin and then picked up her drink cup, taking a long pull on the straw.

"Malone, you dog you," Reyes said with a big toothy grin. "How was it? Was it everything I've been imagining?"

"I said I'll tell you later," Malone said. "We've got to figure out some way to get the plastic fork she is using or the straw from that cup. I sure hope she finishes the drink and leaves it behind."

"Yeah, that would be sweet," Reyes said. "We could get the DNA sample today and be done with it. Dude, this is making me hungry watching them eat. I love the tacos at this place, and now my stomach is growling."

"It shouldn't be much longer," Malone said. "It looks like they are almost finished eating. Unless they hang around chatting, they should leave soon and when they do, we can have lunch."

Fifteen minutes later, Thompson and Bachmann stood up. They embraced for a moment. Then Bachmann gave Thompson a kiss on the cheek. They laughed about something and then they both walked to the exit and up the sidewalk. They stopped briefly at Bachmann's car, said a few words, and then Thompson continued to his car.

Malone and Reyes watched until Bachmann got into her car, pulled away from the curb, and drove away. They then sprinted for the restaurant patio, arriving at the table where Bachmann and Thompson had been sitting just ahead of an employee intent on clearing the table. Malone grabbed his badge holder from his belt and held the badge out to the employee.

"Hold on a second, LAPD," he said. "We need to collect some evidence before you clear this table."

"*Okay*," the guy said.

"And we could use your help," Malone said. "Do you have any bags, like for to go orders?"

"Sure," the guy said.

"Great, can you get me a couple?" Malone said.

"Okay," the guy said. He sauntered back behind the counter, ducked behind it, and moments later returned with two white paper bags.

Malone took the bags from him.

"Hey, thanks a lot," he said. "We'll be out of your way in just a moment."

Malone grabbed a clean napkin from the dispenser on the table and used it to pick up the fork from Bachmann's plate. He dropped it into one of the paper bags and handed the bag to Reyes. He then used the napkin to pick up Bachmann's drink cup, grasping it near the bottom. With his other hand, he pulled another napkin from the dispenser and used it to pull the plastic top holding the straw off the cup. He walked to a nearby trash bin and dumped the ice and remaining liquid inside the cup into the bin. He gingerly replaced the plastic top on the cup and then deposited the cup, lid, and straw into the other paper bag.

"I thought we just needed the straw," Reyes said.

"No, we need the whole thing," Malone said. "At the moment, all we have is our testimony that Bachmann used these items. Hopefully, the lab can lift her prints from the fork and the cup and then we will have some physical evidence linking her to the items so that a defense attorney can't claim this evidence is just trash we randomly picked up from a restaurant table."

"Good thinking, Bro," Reyes said.

"I thought you guys were supposed to use rubber gloves to collect evidence," the employee said.

"That's just on television, kid," Malone said. "Sometimes we just improvise, like with the napkins. Okay, the table is all yours now."

"*Gee, thanks,*" the guy said, with a smirk.

Malone turned to Reyes.

"Okay, we've got the evidence," he said. "I'll take the bags and lock them in the trunk of my car, then we can eat. After lunch, we will run it down to the lab."

"Works for me, bro," Reyes said. "I'm starving."

"Get me an order of the fish tacos and a soda," Malone said. "I'll be back in a couple of minutes."

Malone left with the bags for the car, and Reyes went to place their food orders. When Malone returned after securing the evidence they had collected, he found Reyes sitting at a table already eating. Malone sat down and picked up a taco.

"How long you think it will take to get the stuff processed?" Reyes said.

"Maybe a day or two," Malone said. "I'm going to ask Turner to get them to expedite it."

"Okay, bro," Reyes said. "Now tell me your long story about banging Bachmann. And leave nothing out."

While they ate their lunch, Malone recounted the story about meeting Bachmann at the beach and then going to her house afterward. Reyes was more than a little impressed, not to mention more than a little envious of Malone's good fortune.

"I thought you had said before she wasn't your type," Reyes said.

"She seduced me, Reyes, that's what she did," Malone said.

"Oh, so she took advantage of you," Reyes said, laughing.

"Yes, you could say that," Malone said, grinning.

After lunch, Malone followed Reyes back to the police parking lot. After parking, Reyes got into Malone's Camry, and they headed over to the Hertzberg-Davis Forensic Science Center. When they arrived, Malone collected the paper bags from the trunk of his car.

The first stop was at the Forensic Science Division, where Malone convinced a criminalist to swab the fork and drinking straw for DNA evidence. He telephoned Lieutenant Turner while he and Reyes waited and requested that Turner immediately fax over a request for expedited processing. Turner asked a few questions and then said he would take care of it right away. He instructed Malone to see him as soon as he and Reyes returned to the PAB.

Malone and Reyes then walked the evidence over to the Technical

Investigation Division to have the fork and drink cup dusted for latent prints. Malone convinced a criminalist there to drop everything and to process the items immediately. They followed her back to the lab and watched as she developed prints from both items and then lifted them with transparent fingerprint tape. She placed them on white fingerprint cards and labeled them.

"Now I'll submit the prints to AFIS," the criminalist said. "Might take a while to get the returns, assuming the person's prints are on file."

"Let me save you some time," Malone said. "Just query the law enforcement applicant database."

Malone knew that every person who applied for a law enforcement job got printed as part of the application process, and law enforcement agencies uploaded the fingerprints to the national law enforcement fingerprint database.

"Do you know the agency?" the criminalist said.

"Yes, LAPD," Malone said.

"Great, that will speed things up even more," she said. "I should have the results for you in five minutes. Maybe sooner."

The criminalist walked to a terminal in the back of the lab and scanned the newly developed prints into the machine. Four minutes later, the laser printer next to the terminal came to life and spat out two printed pages. The criminalist looked at them and then walked back to where Malone and Reyes were waiting.

"The prints came back to a female named Vanessa Marie Alvarez aka Vanessa Marie Sandoval aka Vanessa Marie Bachmann," the criminalist said.

"Good enough," Malone said. "We really appreciate your help."

They collected the latent print cards and the documents and walked back over to the Forensic Science Division. Malone confirmed they had received the faxed request from Turner. The criminalist there told him they would probably have the profile from the samples by the following Monday. Malone told her they needed a comparison of the profile from the evidence with a forensic sample in the custody of the Los Angeles County Coroner. He told her that a criminalist there by the name of Jane Kroft had recently submitted the forensic sample for analysis and gave her the case number. The criminalist typed the case number into a computer and pulled up the profile from the forensic sample. She said she would make the comparison as soon as the samples collected from the cup and drinking straw were processed.

Malone and Reyes left Hertzberg-Davis and drove back to the PAB. On arrival, they went directly to Lieutenant Turner's office to bring him up to speed. They found Turner there waiting.

27

A Suspect Arrested

Malone knocked on the door frame and stuck his head into Turner's office. Turner looked up from his desk and waved them in.

"Sit down," he said.

Malone and Reyes sat down in the chairs in front of the desk.

"How did you get the samples?" Turner said.

Malone walked him through it, how that watched Bachmann at the restaurant and then collected the plastic fork and the drink cup after she left.

"Sounds okay," Turner said. "It falls under the plain view exception, and when she abandoned the stuff in public, she had no expectation of privacy. I think you're good. It should be admissible in court if it turns out the profiles match. You sure you can link her to the items?"

"Yes, Reyes and I had her under observation the entire time," Malone said. "No question that she had used the fork and the drinking straw. Plus, we have these."

Malone tossed the fingerprint cards and computer printout on Turner's desk. The lieutenant picked them up. He looked at the latent prints and then dropped them on his desk. He read the document.

"How did you get these?" he asked.

"We took the stuff to the Technical Investigation Division after a criminalist swabbed the fork and straw for DNA," Reyes said. "They lifted the prints from the fork and the cup and then ran them through AFIS. Those are the results."

"Huh," Turner said. "So you've also got affirmative physical evidence to go along with the surveillance. That works. You guys aren't as dumb as you look. So what else you need?"

"We are trying to get the Hollenbeck patrol duty roster from records to determine whether Bachmann was actually on duty the day of the Anderson murder," Malone said.

"You have a reason to believe it will show she was on duty but wasn't?" Turner said.

"Just speculation at the moment," Malone said. "But the cryptic thing the original lead detective said to me left me with the impression that someone at Hollenbeck falsified the duty roster so that it would appear Bachmann had been on duty that day."

"Yes, it might be obvious someone changed the duty roster after the fact," Turner said. "Anything else?"

"I just have a question," Malone said.

"So ask it, Malone," Turner said.

"Did Bachmann tell you she was going to make an official sexual harassment complaint against me?" Malone said.

"You sure you want to discuss this in front of your partner?" Turner said.

"Yes, I have nothing to hide," Malone said. "I already told him all about it, and it's all bullshit, anyway. Never happened."

"No, she didn't say she was definitely going to make a complaint," Turner said. "She just said she was considering it if you didn't back off. Knowing what I know now, I'm inclined to believe your version of it, since she obviously has an ax to grind here. So I wouldn't worry about it."

"That isn't why I asked," Malone said.

"So why did you?" Turner said.

"Because she had lunch with Deputy Chief Thompson today," Malone said. "I figured he would be the person she would take a complaint to. And another thing. They seemed awfully friendly."

"Christ, Malone," Turner said. "The hits just keep coming with you, don't they?"

"What do you mean, Lieutenant?" Malone said.

"First, none of what I'm about to tell you leaves this room," Turner said. "You both got that?"

Malone and Reyes nodded in unison.

"Brad Thompson is an old and close friend of mine," Turner said. We went through the academy together, and we worked together at Rampart. They promoted us both to sergeant off of the same exam in 1989. I stayed on at Rampart, and he transferred to Hollenbeck. Brad was a patrol watch commander at Hollenbeck when Bachmann was there. Now here is the part that doesn't get mentioned outside this office. Brad and Bachmann, Alvarez back then, had an affair. It broke up Brad's first marriage. If what you believe is true, if someone falsified the patrol roster to cover Bachmann's ass, chances are Brad was the one who did it. Bachmann probably asked for a meeting today to tell him what was going on and maybe to ask him to help squash your investigation. For his sake, I sure as hell hope he told her no."

"Yes, well, from what Reyes and I saw of their lunch meeting, I kind of doubt that he said no if she was asking him for help," Malone said. "They looked pretty chummy."

"Christ, I have to go to the chief with this now," Turner said. "I was planning to wait until the DNA comparison came back, but I can't wait to put the chief in the loop now. Brad might plan to do something else stupid. Stupid enough to get his dumb ass arrested and thrown in the slam. Tell you what. You two get back to work. I'm going upstairs to see the chief."

"Okay boss," Malone said.

"And listen, Malone," Turner said. "I have no plans to throw you under the bus, but I'm going to have to tell the chief most of what you told me this morning. Some of it I have a feeling he will not like very much. But it is what it is. Come what may, you're just going to have to accept the consequences of your actions. I understand you had good intentions, but we all know what road they pave with those."

"Understood boss," Malone said. "I knew there was a certain amount of risk involved when I continued working on the case. I accepted that."

"Okay," Turner said. "Make sure you two keep me in the loop from this point forward. After our conversation today, I'm certain the chief is going to be expecting regular updates from me, so neither of you better be doing anything that I don't know about. Now get back to work."

Malone picked up the latent print cards and the paperwork from Turner's desk. He and Reyes left Turner's office. They headed over to the property division to book the cards and documents as evidence. Turner's office door was closed, and lights were off when they returned to the fifth floor. He still hadn't returned when four o'clock rolled around, and it was time to call it a day.

Malone and Reyes walked out together, said their goodbyes in the parking lot, and left for their respective homes.

Malone arrived at his apartment at around five-thirty. He prepared dinner and was just sitting down to eat when his phone rang. He picked it up and answered.

"Malone."

"Malone, Denny Washington. We just caught a break."

"What happened?" Malone said. "Did you get Javier?"

"Yes, but not the way we expected," Washington said. "The Newton

Division gang unit was looking for the shooter in a drive-by. One of their snitches told them the Chacales Locos gang had done the drive by and the shooter was a guy named Victor Perez. They found out there was already a felony arrest warrant out for Perez on an unrelated assault with a deadly weapon charge. So they got patrol to set up a perimeter on his house and called for SWAT to serve the warrant. Someone called and tipped Perez just as SWAT was getting into position to hit the front door. A guy ran out of the back and tried to flee on foot. A couple of uniformed officers on the perimeter gave chase. They saw him toss something over a fence into a backyard while they were chasing him down an alley. They finally caught the guy and got him into custody. The guy turned out to be our very own Javier Alvarez. One of the patrol guys went back to see what he had tossed over the fence. It was a Beretta 92F. Chang and I went to the Newton station and picked up the weapon. The lab is doing the ballistics comparison as we speak."

"How did you find out about it?" Malone said.

"A friend of mine is one of the gang guys at Newton. I had a couple of beers with him Tuesday night and had told him about my case. He knew I was looking at Javier Alvarez for Bright's murder and that a nine millimeter was involved. He called me right after they identified Alvarez and recovered the weapon."

"Are you going to interview Alvarez?" Malone said.

"Not until morning," Washington said. They are transporting him to the county for evading and unlawfully carrying and possessing a firearm as a convicted felon. He isn't going anywhere."

Malone started to ask another question, but Washington interrupted.

"Hang on Malone. Chang has got the lab on another line."

Malone heard Washington put the phone down. He could hear talking in the background, but couldn't make out what was being said.

Moments later Washington came back on the line."

"We got him, Malone," Washington said. "The ballistics were a perfect match. The Beretta was the weapon used to kill Jack Bright, and the weapon used to shoot at you on the 101. It looks like old Javier is about to catch another couple of felonies."

"That's great," Malone said. "I won't have to keep walking around looking over my shoulder."

"Chang and I will go see him at the county jail in the morning," Washington said. "I'll call you with an update after we interview him."

"Okay, and thanks for letting me know, Washington," Malone said.

"No problem, Malone," Washington said. "I'm glad we got him. Catch you later."

Washington disconnected. Malone put his phone down and resumed eating, even though his dinner had gone cold. He was feeling pretty good about things now. Jack's killer was in the slam, and hopefully, by Monday, he would have the evidence he needed to arrest Vanessa Bachmann for the murder of Mary Beth Anderson.

Malone had received one more call before we went to bed on Wednesday night. Rhonda Freeman called to tell him that Jack's sister had arrived in LA and had made the funeral arrangements. She told him that there was only going to be a graveside service, and they set it for two o'clock on Saturday afternoon. Malone told her he would be there. It had been a full day, and Malone went to bed exhausted.

28

Meeting With the Chief

Malone arrived at work wearing a clean suit and starched long sleeve shirt, freshly removed from the protective plastic coverings from the cleaners. Having had coffee at home, he had skipped the coffee shop, but by the time he arrived at the PAB, he was ready for another cup. He stopped at the break room and grabbed a cup on his way to his newly assigned desk. Reyes arrived a few minutes later carrying his own cup of coffee.

"Anything from records on the duty roster?" Malone asked.

"Not yet, bro," Reyes said. "I don't think they bring around the inter-office mail until around nine, though."

"The roster may not give us anything," Malone said. "If she was not on duty that day, but the roster says she was, it depends on how much effort they put into doctoring it."

"Yes, but it's still worth looking at," Reyes said.

Malone felt driven to continue building on the progress they had already made, but he accepted the fact that they were in something of a holding pattern while they waited for the analysis of Bachmann's DNA sample. He knew that Washington and Chang would interrogate Javier Alvarez that morning at the Los Angeles County lockup and they might get lucky. But given his experience with ex-cons, he wasn't optimistic. Alvarez would probably refuse to talk and lawyer up. Still, he hoped to hear something from Washington before lunch.

Given that Javier had been willing to commit murder out of his radical devotion to his sister, it wasn't likely he was going to turn on her now. Not even for a chance to save himself from the needle if they convicted him of murdering Jack Bright. Not that Alvarez had to worry that much about the death penalty. Malone knew that since Californians had voted to reenact the death penalty in 1972 with the passage of Proposition 17, the state had carried out only thirteen executions, the last one in 2006. Malone had read somewhere that there were nearly 750 offenders on California's death row. Some of them had tortured their victims before killing them, some had murdered children, and others had killed police officers. But their sentences remained mired in appeals, and there had been no executions carried out in almost a decade.

Malone was ambivalent about the death penalty. He wasn't quite certain that it served as the effective deterrence that death penalty advocates argued it did. But he knew one thing for sure. Death penalties certainly provided no deterrence when the state never carried them out.

The first several hours of work passed slowly for Malone and Reyes. They spent the morning working through another stack of cold cases, a flashback to their first days in the cold case homicide section. On another trip to the coffee maker in the break room, Malone saw that Lieutenant Turner was in his office, but he hadn't even looked up when Malone passed by.

Washington called at ten-thirty. He told Malone what he had expected to hear. Alvarez denied he had killed Jack Bright and claimed the cops had planted the Beretta to frame him. He had also denied knowing anything about the murder of Mary Beth Anderson. After that, he asked for a lawyer and clammed up. There was a little good news, though, at least as far as the Jack Bright murder case. Washington told Malone that the lab had pulled Alvarez's fingerprints off the gun so his claim that it wasn't his wouldn't hold up in court.

At a quarter to noon, Malone and Reyes were debating on where to go for lunch when the phone on Malone's desk rang. He picked it up. It was Turner summoning them to his office. They walked to his office and found him sitting at his desk. He waved them in and told them to sit.

"We're going up to see the chief," Turner said. "I gave him a thorough briefing yesterday afternoon, so I'm not clear about what the meeting is about. Maybe he has some questions, or maybe he just wants to hear from you directly about the Anderson case. Guess we will find out when we get there. Let's go."

The men got up and left the office. Malone and Reyes followed Turner to the elevator. They got off on the tenth floor and made their way to the chief's office. When they arrived, his secretary stood, opened the inner door, and waved them in. The chief of police was behind his desk. No one else was in the room. He told them to sit and then, looking directly at Malone, he began speaking.

"Any fresh developments on the case?" he said.

"The Hollywood detectives interrogated Javier Alvarez at the county jail this morning," Malone said. "Mostly they were there for their case, the Jack Bright murder. But they asked Alvarez about the Anderson murder. All they got were denials, and then he asked for a lawyer and clammed up."

"Pretty much what you would expect," the chief said. "So now you're just waiting for the DNA analysis and comparison?"

"Yes sir, that's about the size of it," Malone said.

The chief nodded absently.

"I've got something that should help your investigation," the chief said. "But first I have something to say to you both."

His eyes drifted from Malone to Reyes and then back again. Then he continued.

"Initiative is a positive trait that can be useful in doing good police work. Generally, it's something worthy of commendation. But in this instance, both of you, especially you Malone, went far beyond the pale of exercising initiative. To some degree, both of you have ignored department regulations and policies while working on this case. The rules, policies, and procedures in effect at this department exist for some very good reasons. They are not suggestions. We expect officers of this department to follow them to the letter, not ignore them when it seems convenient no matter what their intentions may be. Since it is my responsibility to promulgate the rules, policies, and procedures, it also falls to me to see that members of this department follow them. And to take appropriate action when it comes to my attention that any officer under my command intentionally ignored any of them. Do we understand each other?"

"Yes, chief," Malone and Reyes answered in unison.

"There will be appropriate disciplinary action taken at a later date for your transgressions," the chief said. "But the seriousness of the information you've uncovered while working this case demands that the case receives the priority at present. Consequently, I've postponed deciding about what I will do with you two until we have concluded the case."

The chief leaned forward in his chair, to emphasize the gravity of what he intended to say next.

"I called Deputy Chief Brad Thompson and the commanding officer of Internal Affairs into my office this morning. After questioning Deputy Chief Thompson thoroughly, by the end of the meeting, I felt satisfied that he had been truthful. He made two admissions pertinent to your case. He admitted that then Officer Vanessa Alvarez was not on duty the day of Mary Beth Anderson's murder. She was on the duty roster but called in sick. Deputy Chief Thompson admitted he had covered for her by altering the duty roster to make it appear that she had been on duty that day. When the time comes, he will testify to those facts in court."

"So he actively took part in trying to cover up her involvement in the murder?" Malone said.

"I'm satisfied that was not the case," the chief said. "If you're not aware of it, Thompson was having an affair with Vanessa Alvarez in 1992. The day after the murder, she went to him. She told him she was terrified that the Van Nuys detectives would consider her a suspect because she was a recent former girlfriend of the victim's husband and because the victim had been spreading lies about her, claiming she had been trying to break up their marriage. She said that it wouldn't look good that she hadn't been on duty the day the murder occurred and that she didn't want to be forced to reveal the reason she had taken a sick day. If that happened, she told Thompson it would embarrass both of them. She told him she was pregnant and had taken a sick day to go to a clinic to arrange for an abortion, claiming the child was his. Deputy Chief Thompson told me she convinced him she was telling the truth. Since he didn't believe she was capable of murder, he changed the duty roster, making it appear that she had been at work to alibi her. He was married at the time and didn't want it to come out that he had impregnated Alvarez."

"Did he say why he and Vanessa Bachmann met for lunch yesterday?" Malone said.

"Yes, he did," the chief said. "Vanessa Bachmann called him and asked to meet. Over lunch, she told him that the Anderson case was being investigated again and that the investigation was unauthorized, that Lieutenant Turner wasn't aware of it. And she asked Thompson to intervene, to talk to Lieutenant Turner to get the investigation shut down. She told him she was afraid if the investigation continued, it would come out that she had not been on duty the day the murder occurred and that he had falsified the duty roster. She said that the investigation was ridiculous, but if that should come out, it could be very damaging to both their careers."

"So Commander Thompson agreed to get the investigation shut down?" Malone said.

"Yes, he did," the chief said. "The affair between them had ended decades ago, shortly after Thompson's divorce. But he and Bachmann have remained on good terms, and of course, Thompson wanted to protect his career. That was the primary motivation behind his agreement to help her."

"So he not only provided an alibi for Bachmann back in 1992, but he conspired to help her get our investigation quashed," Malone said.

"I know where you're going with this, Malone," the chief said. "So let's be clear about something. Deputy Chief Thompson exercised extremely poor judgment when he falsified that duty roster in 1992. But aside from that one, albeit serious transgression, he has since served this department and city with distinction. He is a highly decorated officer with an exemplary record. The bottom line is I will not refer him for prosecution. I'm confident he was unaware twenty-three years ago that he was helping to provide an alibi for a murder suspect."

"But chief, by providing Bachmann an alibi that got her excluded from the suspect list, he materially interfered in a murder investigation," Malone said. "Had he not done that, the original detectives might have cleared the murder back then, and we wouldn't even be having this discussion."

"You're not getting Deputy Chief Thompson," the chief said. "And it's not only because I've given him the benefit of the doubt in recognition of an otherwise honorable thirty year career. There was no official conspiracy. If Vanessa Bachmann killed Mary Beth Anderson, it was not the act of a Los Angeles police officer. It was the act of an individual employed as a police officer. Falsifying that duty roster was not an act of a corrupt LAPD official. It was the act of an individual LAPD watch commander protecting someone he was romantically involved with at the time. I will not allow the reputation of this department to be sullied by another scandal."

"So he gets a pass?" Malone said.

"No, he is not getting a pass," the chief said. "I accepted his retirement request this morning at the conclusion of our meeting. He is no longer with the Los Angeles Police Department. His career is over as the consequences of his actions. I feel that adequately addresses his breach of department regulations. And if it turns out that Vanessa Bachmann did indeed murder Mary Beth Anderson, as it is certainly appearing she did, we will arrest her for murder and prosecute her to the fullest extent of the law."

Looking from Malone to Reyes and back again, the chief continued.

"For now, you may proceed with your investigation. But you should give some serious thought to Deputy Chief Thompson's fate. When this is all over, there will be consequences for your actions as well. You should not have undertaken an investigation without the knowledge and approval of Lieutenant Turner. And you, Malone, should never have continued working the case while you were on suspension. Once you wrap up the investigation, rest assured I intend to take appropriate disciplinary actions that will hopefully dissuade you both from intentionally ignoring the policies and procedures of this department in the future."

Turning to Turner, the chief continued. "I can't find fault with you, Lieutenant. I can't assess any responsibility to you for the actions of these officers when obviously they intentionally concealed their activities from you. However, in the future, you might wish to exercise more vigilance in the supervision of those under your command, especially officers temporarily assigned to your section."

"Understood, Chief," Turner said.

"That will be all for now," the chief said. "Turner, keep me posted on any fresh developments. I expect to be the first to know when the results of the DNA comparison come through."

"Certainly," Turner said.

"Very well, you're all dismissed," the chief said.

Turner, Reyes, and Malone stood up and filed out of the office. They walked down the corridor to the elevator.

"Well, that went better than I expected," Malone said.

"Don't kid yourself, Malone," Turner said. "The old man is going to hammer you when the investigation is over. If you escape termination, at the very least, you will probably be back in uniform. I warned you he would not overlook your cavalier attitude toward policy and procedure."

"I'm willing to accept the consequences," Malone said. "The only thing I'm concerned with right now is nailing Bachmann and getting long-delayed justice for Mary Beth Anderson and her family."

They rode the elevator down in silence. Turner got off on the fifth floor. Malone and Reyes continued to the ground floor to head for lunch.

"Think we will really get busted back to patrol?" Reyes said.

"When the time comes, I'll take full responsibility," Malone said. "I'll tell everyone I talked you into helping and that you did nothing wrong."

"I knew what I was doing," Reyes said. "I don't expect you to take the rap for both of us."

"I know your career with the LAPD is important to you," Malone said. "So I will not allow your career to be comprised because I became a little obsessed with solving this case. I'm the one who violated the most serious rules, and I'm taking full responsibility for that."

"But what about your career?" Reyes said. "If you try to take all the blame, the chief might fire you."

"I've been thinking about that a lot," Malone said. "The lack of support after the shootings I was involved in, the politics of it all, had already left a nasty taste in my mouth. And now looking at the fact that the chief intends to discipline us for cutting through a bunch of bureaucratic bullshit to clear a decades-old murder is sort of the proverbial last straw. We only did what we had to do. If we had talked to Turner from the get-go, he would have nixed the investigation, and a murderer would have gone free. I've thought maybe I should consider a career change, anyway."

"Seriously, bro?" Reyes said.

"Yes, I'm dead serious," Malone said. "I think after we have wrapped this up, I'm going to resign."

"I hope you change your mind, dude," Reyes said. "You're a good cop and a hell of an investigator. I hated being assigned to the cold case section until we partnered up. Now I've started to like it because you're a great partner."

"I appreciate that," Malone said. "I enjoy working with you, too, Jaime. But I'm just not sure I want to continue with the LAPD once this is all over."

Malone and Reyes went to lunch at a sandwich place a few blocks from the PAB. After lunch, they returned to work, reviewed another stack of cold case files, and then left for the day.

29

A Second Date

Friday came with Malone and Reyes still waiting on the results of the DNA profile comparison between Bachmann's sample and the forensic sample. They were impatient to get that last piece of the puzzle that they expected would break the case wide open. But at least they wouldn't have much longer to wait, fully expecting the results sometime on Monday. They were thankful that Turner had expedited the analysis request. Otherwise, they would have faced weeks of waiting rather than just a few days.

They spent Friday reviewing more cold case files, although it was difficult to concentrate on that task with the Anderson case at the forefront of both their minds. Despite that difficulty, by the end of the workday, they had identified several cases that met the criteria for re-opening. They had flagged those for Lieutenant Turner's attention and had returned the other stacks of files to the cardboard storage boxes.

Malone had the hardest time focusing on the case reviews. Not only was his mind on the Anderson case, but he also spent the greater part of the day thinking about and eagerly anticipating his second date with Sara Bernstein. They had talked by phone a few times during the week. He had told her about the murder of Jack Bright, and he had kept her up to date on the developments in the Anderson case. Now he was really looking forward to spending time with her again in person.

They were still planning to have dinner, but there had been nothing playing at the Microsoft Theater that they wanted to see. Sara had suggested that instead, they go back to her place after dinner to watch a movie. Malone wasn't sure what all that might entail, but whatever she had in mind, he was all for it. Jack Bright's funeral had nixed their plans to see a day game at Dodger Stadium on Saturday. Sara had surprised Malone by offering to go with him to the funeral, even though she had never met Jack. He had accepted her offer, feeling like he could probably use the moral support.

Mercifully, five o'clock finally came, signaling the end of the workday and the end of a long week. Malone and Reyes headed home.

Malone was due to pick up Sara Bernstein at her place for dinner at seven-thirty. He rushed home, showered, and dressed in clean clothes. He left his apartment at a few minutes past seven and arrived at Bernstein's house right on time.

She met him at the door, and Malone thought she looked absolutely stunning. She wore a little black dress with heels; her attractive outfit accented with a pair of diamond stud earrings and a matching pendant. Her hair was different, a new layered cut that she had gotten since he had seen her the previous week. Malone liked it. After she closed and locked the front door, he took her by the hand and escorted her to the car. She forced him to detour to the driver's side of the Toyota so that she could see the bullet hole he had told her about.

"You were lucky, Ben," she said. "Just a few inches further back and it might have been you getting shot instead of the CD player."

"I would never have let that happen," Malone said. "Nothing could have kept me from our date tonight."

Bernstein smiled and allowed Malone to lead her around to the passenger side. He opened the door for her, and she got into the front passenger seat. For dinner, Malone had chosen an old favorite, Marty's. Marty's was a romantic Mediterranean restaurant in Marina Del Rey, with views of the harbor and marina.

They arrived at the restaurant around eight-thirty. After being seated, they ordered drinks. Malone ordered a Blue Moon beer and Sara a glass of white wine. When the server returned with the drinks, Sara had decided on the shrimp bucatini and Malone, the aged rib eye steak that Marty's was famous for.

"So," she said, "if I understand it. You are just waiting for the DNA test results to finish up the case you've been working so hard on."

"Exactly," Malone said.

Sara took a tiny sip of her wine. The glass was down perhaps an eighth of an inch since the server had set the glass in front of her. Malone, on the other hand, was already looking for the server to order another Blue Moon.

Malone caught the server's attention, and she brought him another beer. Minutes later, their dinner arrived.

They started eating, Sara eating slowly, and in tiny bites.

"And if the profiles match, you will arrest the female police lieutenant?" Sara said.

"That's the plan," Malone said. "We'll bring her in for questioning first and try to find discrepancies in her answers that we can use to show she knows things about the victim that she couldn't unless she was the killer. We will look for indications that she is being deceptive that may suggest guilt."

Sara took another tiny bite of shrimp.

"And will you be able to link her to the murder of your friend and the attempt on your life?" Sara said.

"I think it's unlikely," Malone said. "Her brother isn't talking. He idolizes his sister, and I'm sure he will say nothing to implicate her. Besides, my gut feeling is that it was his idea to kill Jack, an attempt to protect her by stalling the investigation. It would surprise me to learn she asked him to do it. As a cop, she would have known that it would have only drawn more attention."

"How will you feel afterward after arresting another police officer?" Sara said.

"It won't make me happy," Malone said. "But cops are subject to the same laws as everyone else. If a cop commits a murder, he or she can't expect to be treated any differently than any other person who commits murder. If she is guilty, and I believe she is, she will have to face the consequences of her actions like anyone else."

"It just all seems so dreadful," Sara said.

"Dreadful?" Malone said.

"Someone in her twenties, probably in a fit of rage and feeling rejected, makes a horrible decision and kills someone out of jealousy. And she snuffs out an innocent young life. The murder goes unsolved for over two decades. The victim's family suffered all those years terribly. And the killer goes on with her life as if nothing happened. Assuming this Bachmann was the killer and given what you've told me, she evidently went on to have a full and exemplary police career. Now twenty some odd years later, she gets exposed. It ruins her career and her life, the result of a rash decision she made in her twenties. Another innocent person, your friend Jack, gets murdered. Her brother commits murder trying to protect his sister and will probably spend the rest of his life in prison. The father likely will have to see both of his children go to prison, convicted of murder, perhaps society's most heinous crime. So many lives wasted."

Sara took another bite of shrimp. A sailboat tacking into the wind sailed into their view, a young girl at the tiller. A man stood next to her, probably a father giving his daughter sailing lessons. They watched as the boat passed.

"Wow," Malone said. "You shrinks really know how to put things in perspective. I think I'm depressed now."

"I'm sorry," Sara said. "But this whole thing plays out like a Greek tragedy. And I didn't even touch on how it's affected you. How did your superiors react when they learned you had been working on the case without their knowledge?"

Malone took a bite of his steak and considered how to best answer the question. He didn't want to alarm her.

"They weren't happy about it," he said. "I think Lieutenant Turner understood at least a little why I did what I did. But the chief has promised disciplinary action once we wrap up the case."

Sara said, "But none of that changes how you feel about it. You still feel you were right to do what you did."

"Of course," Malone said. "If I'd followed the rules, followed the policy, Lieutenant Turner would have nixed the investigation at the start. Bachmann would probably have gotten away with the murder and Mary Beth Anderson would likely never have received justice."

"Do what you have to do, and let the chips fall where they may, and then move on?" she said.

"Yep," he said.

"They build organizations like police departments on rules and policies," she said. "You will always find yourself at odds with your superiors unless you find a way to stop chafing against the rules. But you won't change."

"Won't I?" Malone said.

"Nope," she said.

"You shrinks think you know everything," he said.

"Am I right?" she said.

"Yes," he said.

Sara took another sip from her glass of wine. When she set the glass back down, Malone couldn't tell that she had even drunk from it. It seemed about as full as it had when the server first brought it. He downed the last swallow of his second beer and considered ordering another.

Sara said, "You're something of a knight errant, traveling through life in search of adventures, wrongs that need righting, and damsels in distress in need of rescue. You will always take the shortest route between two points. The rules be damned."

"What's your diagnosis doctor?" he said. "Do you feel I have repressed emotions and experiences that I need to release to help me learn to work and play well with others?"

"Probably," she said, with a big grin. "I hope you don't think I'm being critical. The things you do are simply because of who you are and how you are. It's what in psychoanalysis we term characterological. When you pick something up, you simply can't put it down until you have imposed your will upon it. Your psyche simply won't allow you to approach things like this investigation differently than you have, whether or not you wished to."

"Sounds serious," Malone said. "Tell me, doctor, is there a cure?"

Sara smiled and said, "You don't need a cure."

"You sure?" he said.

"Yes."

"Because as my former therapist, you know me so well?" he said.

She smiled wider.

"Because how you are is what makes you good at what you do," she said. "You ignore the rules to cut through the bullshit and do what needs to be done to solve the puzzle or fix the problem. For you, I think following the rules rather than bending the rules would make you far less effective as an investigator. But the reality is your superiors have the expectation that you will comply with the policies and follow the rules the same way other police officers do. Despite your accomplishments, they will always feel it necessary to discipline you whenever you choose not to do so."

"I suppose they feel the rules and policies are necessary that order doesn't turn into chaos," Malone said.

"Exactly," she said. "I think to a degree they view someone like you as a bit of an anarchist."

"Interesting perspective, doctor," he said.

They finished their dinner. Sara, at long last, finished her glass of wine.

"I've never seen a person take more than an hour to finish a glass of wine," Malone said. "I can see now that my plan to ply you with liquor will not work."

"Hardly," she said, laughing.

"Ready to go home and see a movie?" she said.

"We'd be fools not to," Malone said.

An hour later, they arrived back at Sara's place. He followed her inside.

"What movie have you chosen for us to watch?" Malone said.

"I haven't selected one," she said. "But I'm sure we can find something on Netflix."

"Netflix?" he said. "I had you pegged as a conventional DVD kind of girl."

"Did you?" she said. "Perhaps I'm full of surprises."

"Perhaps," he said. "Are you serving popcorn and sodas with the movie?"

"Do you want popcorn and a soda?" she said.

"Well, I do like having the whole traditional theater experience when I watch a movie," Malone said.

"I see," she said. "Unfortunately, I haven't any popcorn, but I might have a diet soda in the fridge."

"That's very disappointing," Malone said. "No popcorn and I hate diet soda. I prefer the real thing."

"I see," she said.

"Is there any other way that I could help you have the whole traditional theater experience in the absence of popcorn and soda that isn't the diet variety?" she said.

"Well, sometimes instead of popcorn and sodas, people make out in a movie theater to achieve the whole traditional movie experience," he said.

"Do they?" she said. "It seems intuitive that kissing while engaged in various acts of rubbing, touching, and, dare I say, groping, would distract them from watching the movie."

"There is that," Malone said. "But it's still an alternative way of getting a full traditional theater experience."

"I see," she said. "So, if I understand it, you're saying that you would be willing to miss seeing the movie to kiss while we engage in rubbing, touching, and groping?"

"Well, yes," he said. "But only in the interest of having the whole traditional theater experience, of course."

"Of course," she said. "In that case, perhaps you would prefer just to skip the movie then and go directly to bed."

"We'd be fools not to," Malone said.

Sara agreed, and so that's what they did.

30

Changes

Malone awakened to find Sara lying on her side facing him, her beautiful face cradled in a hand propped by her bent elbow. She was looking at him and smiled brightly when he first opened his eyes.

"Good morning, sailor," she said.

Malone smiled back and said, "Good morning."

He stole a glance at her exposed, perky breasts and then looked into her soulful brown eyes. He felt himself stirring.

"Ready for breakfast?" Sara said.

"I was hoping we might do something else first," he said.

"Were you?" she said coyly, her smile even wider. "Last night didn't satisfy you? We were awake half the night."

"I was more than satisfied," Malone said with a grin. "I just need a little reminder that it wasn't all just an amazing, delicious dream."

"I see," she said.

He felt her soft, warm hand on his chest beneath the sheet. The hand slowly and inexorably traveled down his chest and across his stomach until she found what she was seeking.

"You're incorrigible," she laughed.

Malone embraced her and pulled her to him. He kissed her deeply on the lips.

"Well, if you insist," she said.

"I do," he said.

And he did.

An hour later, they were in the kitchen, freshly showered. Malone sipped coffee while Sara prepared ham and cheese omelets for breakfast. They lingered over breakfast for a while, talking, until Sara announced she needed to get dressed. They had decided that after she dressed, she would accompany him to his apartment so that he could get dressed for the funeral. Then they would drive to the service from Malone's apartment, and he would drive her home afterward.

Sara dressed modestly in a conservative and simple, knee-length black dress with a pair of two-inch heels. Her make-up was minimalist, and she omitted jewelry altogether except her wristwatch. Malone still found her stunning.

After they had arrived at Malone's apartment, he took less than twenty minutes to dress, since he had already showered at Sara's place. He shaved, brushed his teeth, and then dressed in a black suit, white shirt, black tie, and black dress shoes. They were on the road by one o'clock, giving them plenty of time for the drive to the cemetery in Glendale, where they would bury Jack.

Once they had driven through the gate into the cemetery, Malone followed the directions Rhonda Freeman had given him. The California sun was shining brightly against a deep blue cloudless sky. Malone thought it would have been a good day for a funeral if only there were such a thing.

Malone parked the Camry on the side of the road behind a relatively long line of cars. It seemed to him from the number of cars that Jack's funeral had attracted a large turnout. He parked, and then he and Sara walked the short distance across the manicured lawn to the gravesite. As Malone expected, there was a rather large gathering of mourners in attendance.

As he looked over the crowd, Malone recognized a few faces but saw many belonging to people he didn't know. They had positioned a row of chairs before the casket at the front of the green awning. He recognized Rhonda Freeman sitting near the middle of the row. He assumed that the woman sitting next to her must be Jack's sister, although he had only met her once before and wasn't sure. Malone knew Jack had only a small immediate family. He guessed the others seated in the chairs were family friends or distant relatives.

A youngish minister wearing a black suit and starched white collar stood in front of the crowd. The shiny bronze-colored coffin gleamed in the brilliant sunshine in the background behind him, perched on the rails they would use to lower it into the ground at the conclusion of the service. The murmuring in the crowd immediately grew silent when the minister spoke.

Malone disliked funerals. Not only because they were sad and gloomy affairs, but every funeral he had attended since took him back to the miserable day he watched his parents get buried when he was only thirteen years old.

Mercifully, the service was brief. After the minister finished speaking, a line formed and those in attendance filed by Jack's sister offering their condolences. Jack and Sara held back until the procession of mourners neared its end and the crowd had thinned. Malone then led Sara forward to pay their respects. Just then, those sitting in the line of chairs stood up.

Jack's sister looked around until her eyes came to rest on Malone. She stepped toward him.

"Thank you for coming, Ben," she said. "Jack thought the world of you."

"Jack truly meant a great deal to me," Malone said. "He was the best friend I ever had. I'm so sorry for your loss, Karen."

"Thank you, Ben," she said. "I know that Jack's passing is as much a loss for you as for me."

"Karen, please meet my friend Sara Bernstein," Malone said. "Sara, this is Karen Milner, Jack's sister."

"I'm pleased to meet you, Karen," Sara said. "My heartfelt condolences on the loss of your brother."

"Thank you, Sara, and it's so nice to meet you as well," Karen said.

Turning back to Malone, Karen said, "There is something I wanted to say to you, but I'm a little tired, so I'll be brief. We can get into the details later, but I wanted to touch on this today. Honestly, Ben, Jack spoke of you more like a son than just a friend. Of all those he helped to train and was partners with during his years with the LAPD, you're the one he spoke of most often. He said many times that if you ever gave up police work, he was going to ask you to come to work with him. I think he hoped that would happen someday and that when he was ready to step away from it and retire that you would be there to take over Bright Investigations."

"That's quite a surprise," Malone said. "Jack mentioned none of that to me."

"No, he wouldn't have," Karen said. "He wouldn't have made you the offer as long as he believed you were happy with your police career."

"I'm sure I would have liked that, had things gone in that direction," Malone said. "I always enjoyed working with Jack when we were partners."

"Jack told me recently that you had been having some difficulties at the department," she said. "That's why I wanted to mention this. If you should have any interest in it, I'd like for you to take over Bright Investigations. Rhonda tells me she believes you could keep many of Jack's clients. Let me give you my telephone number. Call me at your convenience after I've returned home and you've had the chance to give it some thought. If you should decide you're interested, we can work out the details, then."

"Thank you, Karen," Malone said. "Candidly, I have been thinking about leaving the LAPD. I will give your offer some serious consideration."

"Then I'll expect to hear from you," she said. "Now I have to be going. Rhonda is going to take me back to the hotel so that I can rest a bit before my flight home this evening. Thank you, Ben and you too Sara for coming today. Again, it was lovely meeting you, Sara."

Rhonda Freeman stepped forward and gave Ben a hug. He introduced her to Sara, and they shook hands. Everyone said their goodbyes and Ben and Sara stood watching as Karen and Rhonda moved away towards the black limo provided by the funeral home.

"She seems very nice," Sara said.

"Yes, she reminds me quite a lot of Jack," Malone said.

"Are you really going to consider leaving the department to take over Jack's agency?" Sara said.

"A lot of things have happened the past month, that have made me think long and hard about my future career plans," Malone said. "I have been thinking seriously about leaving the LAPD after I finish the Anderson case."

"So I take it you are interested in Karen's offer," Sara said.

"It certainly took me by surprise," Malone said. "But yes. I am interested. It would certainly simplify the transition from the LAPD to a new career. And investigations have always been the part of police work that I've liked the most. I could continue doing that running Bright Investigations."

"I just want you to do whatever makes you happy, Ben," Sara said.

"One thing is for sure," Malone said.

"What's that?" Sara said.

"Being with you makes me happy," Malone said.

Sara smiled. Hand in hand, they walked back to the car.

Malone drove Sara back to her place. They passed a quiet afternoon together, and then Sara made them dinner. They spent the time discussing Malone's possible career change. He left for his apartment after eight o'clock. Sara had plans with friends on Sunday, and Malone needed some time alone to consider his options.

On Sunday Malone spent several hours on the internet learning what was required to become a licensed private investigator in the State of California. He discovered that his degree in criminal justice and his experience as a police detective met the eligibility requirements for taking the licensing examination. He simply needed to submit an application packet to the California Bureau of Security and Investigative Services to get scheduled for the exam. Also, he researched the requirements for obtaining a firearm permit, which he also found pretty straightforward. He just needed to attend a couple of classes and then qualify at a gun range.

By the time he went to bed Sunday night, Malone had decided.

31

Change of Plans

Malone felt tired when he arrived at work Monday morning. He hadn't slept well at all during the night. He had felt restless and had been impatient for Monday to arrive finally. That had kept him awake most of the night, unable to sleep. It had seemed as if he had awakened every hour or two throughout the night. Today was the day when they hopefully would get the DNA comparison report. The proof needed to arrest Vanessa Bachmann for murder.

Reyes was already at his desk when Malone walked in.

"Morning, bro," Reyes said.

"Good morning, partner," Malone said. "How was your weekend?"

Before Reyes could reply, the phone on Malone's desk rang. He picked up the receiver and answered.

"Malone," he said.

"Malone, my office, and bring Reyes with you." Lieutenant Turner said.

"Yes sir," Malone said.

Looking at Reyes Malone said, "That was Turner. He wants to see us right away."

Reyes got up and followed Malone to Turner's office.

When they arrived, the two detectives found the door to Turner's office open. After a perfunctory knock on the door frame, Malone and Reyes walked in. Turner was sitting at his desk. Two other men were sitting in the visitor's chairs. The men turned to look as Reyes and Malone entered the room. Turner acknowledged the seated men with a nod of his head.

Turner said, "Meet Detective Randy Griggs and Detective Joel Lozano, Homicide Special Section. I arranged with the captain to borrow them. They are going to help us with the Anderson case."

Malone looked puzzled.

"Help with what?" he said. "We're just waiting for the DNA report."

"I did a lot of thinking about the case over the weekend," Turner said. "When we get the results of the DNA comparison, if it's a match, I've decided to use some fresh faces to interrogate Bachmann instead of you guys."

"But, Lieutenant, it's our case," Reyes said.

"It is your case," Turner said. "That will not change. Just hear me out."

Malone and Reyes looked at each other, realizing they didn't have a choice. Warily, they both nodded their assent.

Turner said, "Here is what I was thinking over the weekend. First, I want Bachmann interviewed under non-custodial circumstances before we make an arrest. In other words, the interview must be voluntary and consensual. If you two pull her in for an interview, she will immediately become defensive. She already knows you both and is aware you've been working on the case. So, it's unlikely she will tell you anything. She will know she doesn't have to talk to you and she won't. But if someone else interviews her, it may catch her off guard. She just might tell them something we can use."

"I suppose that makes sense," Malone said. "So, how is it going to work?"

Turner said, "If we get the DNA match we're expecting, Griggs and Lozano will go see her. They will tell her they are working on a case that seems related to a case in her section. They will ask if she will help them by looking at it. If Bachmann agrees, they will invite her to sit in while they talk with their suspect. They will tell her they could use the benefit of her specialized expertise."

"Then instead they blindside her with questions about the Anderson case?" Malone said.

"Pretty much," Turner said.

"That could work," Reyes said. "By the time she figures out what they are really up to, she may be concerned enough to hang around to figure out exactly what it is they know and how damaging it might be for her."

"That's the idea," Turner said. "Plus, it solves the other problem that came to mind this weekend, a logistical one."

"Which is?" Malone said.

"Think about it," Turner said. "Bachmann is a cop. Assuming the DNA comparison implicates her, which we expect it will, she becomes a murder suspect. I'm not about to put whoever interviews her across the table from an armed murder suspect. Anything could happen. She could twist off and go postal. That's why we must disarm her first before the interview. But she needs to be disarmed in a way that seems routine so she doesn't get suspicious. That's where the invitation to sit in on the imaginary suspect interrogation comes in. It provides a plausible reason for Bachmann to accompany Griggs and Lozano to an interview room at the Metro Detention Center. It's routine policy for officers to secure their weapons in the lock boxes outside before going into the interview room."

"Good thinking," Malone said. "So what about Reyes and me? We're completely out of it?"

"No, you two just won't be doing the interview," Turner said. "But you can sit behind the one-way glass with the video camera and sound recorders and watch. You can listen in while Griggs and Lozano conduct the actual interrogation. Once they've finished, or she terminates the interview, whichever should occur first, you guys will be there waiting to make the actual arrest."

After hearing the plan and the rationale, it all made sense to both Reyes and Malone. It satisfied them they weren't being cut out of the case since they would make the arrest in the end.

Looking at Malone, Turner said, "From now until we get the word on the DNA comparison, I want you and Reyes to bring Griggs and Lozano up to speed on the case. Let them read the murder book for an overview of the original facts and timelines. Then fill them in on what you two have learned since you started investigating the case. They need to know as much as possible about the case before they talk with Bachmann. Time is of the essence since we don't know how much time we will have to prep them before the DNA results come through."

"Understood," Malone said.

"Another thing," Turner said. "I don't want the rumor mill taking off, and I especially don't want Bachmann seeing you four together. I've arranged for you to use the conference on the tenth floor to prep for the interview. Go up to the conference room separately and make certain you leave separately. Don't let anyone see you all together at any time, not inside this building or outside it until this is over. Questions?"

No one had any.

"Okay then," Turner said. Let me know the minute you hear anything from the lab about the DNA results. If it's the match we are expecting, I'll give Griggs and Lozano the go ahead. They will contact Bachmann and lure her over to the Metro Detention Center. That's all for now."

Turning to Griggs and Lozano, Malone said, "We will get the murder book and meet you upstairs in the conference room."

The two homicide detectives nodded. Malone and Reyes left Turner's office and went back to their desks. Malone retrieved the murder book from a desk drawer.

"We'll hang out here for a few minutes to give Griggs and Lozano time to get upstairs to the conference room before we head up there," Malone said.

"Okay," Reyes said. "You cool with this, bro?"

"Yes," Malone said. "After Turner explained the rationale, it made all the sense in the world. He's right about Bachmann not telling us anything. She would know what was going on right off the bat. We get to make the arrest, so it's still our case."

After the brief delay to allow Griggs and Lozano time to get to the conference room ahead of them, Malone and Reyes walked to the elevator and rode it up to the tenth floor.

Griggs and Lozano sat at the table when they arrived at the conference room. Malone placed the murder book on the table in front of them.

"You can read that first," Malone said. "Get a feel for the case and think of questions you need answers to. Once you've finished that, we'll walk you through what we've learned and how we learned it since we started working on the case."

"Sounds like a plan," Griggs said.

The two robbery-homicide detectives were thorough. They spent a couple of hours on the files. They read all the reports, looked at the crime scene photos, and pored over the coroner's reports. Halfway through it, Malone and Reyes tired of whispering at the other end of the table, so they left and went to the coffee shop down the block from the PAB. It was nearly eleven o'clock when they returned to the conference room. They still had heard nothing from the lab.

When Reyes and Malone walked into the conference room, Griggs was just closing the murder book.

"You get through it?" Malone said.

"Yes, we're up to speed on the original facts of the case," Griggs said. "I just don't get why Myers stubbornly kept his focus on the burglary gone sideways theory. If I'd walked into that crime scene, I'd definitely have had the impression that the murder had resulted from something a hell of a lot more personal."

"Tell me about it," Malone said. "That's what grabbed Reyes' attention and mine from the start. But guess we'll never know. Not unless they make him explain it at the trial. I called him and tried to talk to him, but he was completely uncooperative."

"The murder weapon was never recovered?" Lozano said.

Malone said, "No, it wasn't. But we found a police report where Bachmann reported someone broke into her car and stole a Model 36 Smith & Wesson .38 revolver. And she reported it just two weeks after Anderson's murder."

"We figure it was her backup weapon," Reyes said.

"Circumstantial," Griggs said. "But it looks suspicious, and in a case like this, every little bit helps."

"Myers had the two suspect burglary theory," Lozano said. "You think she had an accomplice?"

"Looking at the narratives and the crime scene photos, I think Anderson put up a protracted fight before they shot her to death," Malone said. "I don't think that would have been possible if there had been an accomplice. But I'll tell you. I have wondered how Bachmann got to the scene. If she had driven herself, she should have had a car nearby. She wouldn't have had any reason to take Robert Thames' Volvo from the garage. I think she did it because she wanted to get out fast and didn't want to hang around the area waiting for a ride."

"Okay," Griggs said. "I think we're ready to hear about the new information you guys have learned since you started your investigation. Like the DNA evidence. We know there was DNA evidence collected at the scene. But we need to know the details, how it came to light and eventually got processed by the lab."

Malone launched into the story, starting at the beginning when Reyes had first pressed him to read the file. He told Griggs and Lozano the entire story from beginning to end, not even leaving out the part about him continuing to work on the case while on suspension. Reyes interrupted now and again to add bits and pieces he felt were important, but Malone hadn't covered. At the end of the briefing, both Griggs and Lozano asked a few questions to clarify some of the finer points covered. Finally, they felt satisfied that they had all they needed.

"I think we have all the raw information we need," Griggs said. "Now we just have to script the interrogation."

"Yes," Lozano said. "I agree, and I think you've given us a lot of good ideas as far as points that we want to press her on so that she commits to a story. Then we'll go back to the points later and see if we can get her rattled enough that she contradicts herself and makes it obvious that she is being deceptive."

Griggs said, "I only know her by reputation, but her reputation is solid. Everyone regards her as a competent detective, and I'm not under any illusion that we are going to get a confession out of her. Once she figures out she is being played, I think she will deny and deflect as best she can."

"Here, I don't think a confession will be necessary to get a conviction," Malone said. "Obviously, the bite wound that provided us with the DNA evidence is going to be most damning, assuming it turns out to be her DNA. The rest of the case, unfortunately, is going to be circumstantial evidence, but there will be a lot of that, and I think that will be enough to convince a jury. We can now prove she wasn't on duty that day and the DNA evidence will put her at the scene. So we have the opportunity covered. And we have the contentious history between her and the victim and the jealousy angle of a former girlfriend scorned. So, I think we have a plausible and believable motive. Finally, while we don't have the murder weapon, she was already a cop at the time and familiar with using a firearm. That fact, combined with the firearm theft report from just two weeks after the murder, I think will be enough to raise the specter of means."

Both Griggs and Lozano nodded their agreement.

"Not a slam dunk by any means," Lozano said. "But I'm fairly confident we've got enough. Anything we get from the interrogation should only make the case stronger."

Malone's cell phone rang. He fished the phone out of his pocket and pressed the button to answer.

"Malone," he said.

"Detective Malone, this is Melanie Jackson, Forensic Science Division," the caller said. "We have the results of the DNA profiles you submitted for comparison."

"Give me the short version," Malone said.

"The profile from the reference sample was a match with the profile from the forensic sample," Jackson said. "Technically speaking, that means the chances that someone other than your suspect inflicted the bite wound are about one in over one hundred billion."

"Thank you, Melanie," Malone said. "That's great news, the news I was hoping for."

"Do you want me to fax the report over?" she said.

"No, this is a sensitive case, and I don't want it faxed," Malone said. "My partner and I will be over within the hour to pick it up in person."

"All right," Jackson said. "We will have it ready for you."

Malone disconnected and returned the phone to his pocket. He looked at the other three detectives.

"It was the lab, and we got a match on the DNA profiles," Malone said. "We've got Bachmann. I better tell Turner."

"Tell him we will go see Bachmann after lunch," Griggs said. "We need the time to go over our notes and to script the interview. You and Reyes can go pick up the report, get some lunch yourselves, and then head over to the Metro Detention Center. I'll call and tell them to keep an interview room open for us. When you get there, ask for the room they are keeping open for me. You guys can get the video and audio equipment set up. We will get Bachmann over there, and everything will be ready to go."

"Works for us," Malone said. "How will we know when it's time to get set up outside the interview room to make the arrest?"

Griggs said, "At the end of the interview, I'll thank her for her cooperation, make a little small talk, and tell her we're finished. I'll let her think she is being allowed to walk away. As soon as you see her stand up, hustle out to the entry door."

"Okay," Malone said. "We better get going. See you guys later at MDC."

Malone and Reyes left the conference room and took the elevator back down to the fifth floor. He and Reyes walked directly into Turner's office. Malone updated him on the briefing of Griggs and Lozano. He then told Turner that the DNA profiles were a match and that he and Reyes were going to the Forensic Science Division to pick up the report in person. Finally, he passed on Griggs' message that they would be ready to go after lunch. The arrangements satisfied Turner. He told Malone to call him after they made the arrest so that he could notify the chief. Then he wished them luck.

Reyes followed Malone out of Turner's office to the elevator. They rode it down to the ground floor and walked around to the police parking lot. Reyes signed out an unmarked pool car, and they headed over to Hertzberg-Davis.

Fifteen minutes after leaving the PAB, they walked into the Forensic Science Division. They signed for the report and went directly back to the car. Reyes jumped back on the 10 for the drive back downtown to the MDC on North Los Angeles Street. They had to make certain they arrived ahead of the two homicide dicks and Bachmann, so instead of stopping for lunch, they grabbed a couple of burgers from a drive through and continued downtown. They would eat once they arrived at MDC and had the video and audio equipment set up.

Reyes pulled the car into police parking at the MDC at a quarter to one. After parking the car, they went inside the center. Malone asked a sergeant at the desk about the interview room that was being kept available for Detective Griggs. The sergeant told them it was Interview Room 3 on the ground floor and gave them the directions. The door was closed with a sign taped to the window that said the room was in use. Reyes tried the doorknob and found the door unlocked.

They went inside, and Reyes hit the light switch. There was a narrow hallway that ran back from the interview room to a smaller room in the back that was behind a one-way window. The actual interview room was to the left. Reyes walked directly to the back. Malone paused long enough to hit the light switch in the interview room and then followed.

There was a tripod set up in front of the one-way window. A low counter below the window held a video and audio recorder. Both Malone and Reyes were familiar with the equipment, having used similar gear for recording interrogations many times in the past. Malone powered up the monitor and video camera. He then checked the focus and line of sight. He grabbed a blank video tape cassette from a shelf on the wall and put it into the camera. Satisfied, he dragged a stool to the counter in front of the window, retrieved his burger from the paper sack, and started eating. After powering up and testing the audio equipment, Reyes pulled another stool up to the counter and joined Malone with his lunch.

After about ten minutes, Malone's phone rang. He dug it out of his pocket and answered. It was Lozano, calling to see if they were ready. Malone told him they were good to go. Lozano told him they were on the way and that Bachmann was following in her own unmarked car. She had told them she had an appointment after they finished at MDC. He said they should be there in less than five minutes.

Malone and Reyes finished their burgers while they waited. They had just tossed their wadded paper bags into a metal trash can when they heard voices down the hallway. Moments later, Vanessa Bachmann came into view, followed by Griggs and Lozano. Griggs asked Bachmann to sit and pointed at the chair reserved for suspects. Bachmann's facial expression revealed a mixture of surprise and annoyance, but she sat down in the chair without comment.

Malone and Reyes cued up the video and audio recorders. The show was about to begin.

32

The Interrogation

Joel Lozano began the interrogation.

"Like we were telling you earlier, we caught this case," he said. "And there are some notes in the file that mention your name."

"Oh?" Bachmann said. "*Okay,*" she said skeptically.

Her facial expressions and tone suggested to Malone that she was already figuring out they had enticed her to the interview room under false pretenses.

"You're going to bring someone in, right?" she said.

Lozano ignored the question.

"Do you know Robert Thames?" Lozano said.

He intentionally mispronounced the name, pronouncing it phonetically.

After a pause, Bachmann corrected him.

"Do you mean Robert 'Tims'?" Bachman said.

"Yes," Lozano said.

Bachmann said, "Yes, I went to college with Robert. Let's see. I went to USC in nineteen eighty-four. I first met him in the dorms. We lived on the same floor."

"Were you two casual friends, close friends, or what?" Lozano said.

"Yes, we became close friends," Bachmann said. "I mean, what's this all about?"

She leaned forward in the chair, suggesting her mood was shifting towards confrontational.

"It's this case we've been assigned," Lozano said. "It involves Robert, and in some of the things we've reviewed, there is some stuff that involves you."

"I see," she said. "Well, that's how I know Robert. We met in college and lived in the same dorm. We became friends."

"Okay," Lozano. "Were you and Robert just friends or something else?"

"We were good friends, we were close," she said.

"Was there any kind of relationship that developed between you guys?" Lozano said. "Like, did you ever date each other?"

"Yeah," she said. "We dated casually. We went places together. We did things together. It wasn't exclusive or anything. I dated other guys, and I'm sure he dated other girls. That sort of thing. Why are you asking me these personal questions? I mean, what is this all about? Can you clue me in here, guys?"

"Well, it's related to his wife," Lozano said.

"*Okay*," she said. "So what does that have to do with me? This is starting to feel a little weird."

"Did you know Robert's wife?" Lozano said.

"No, not really," Bachmann said. "I mean, I knew of her, that he married her a long time ago."

"Did you ever meet her?" Lozano said.

"God, that was like a million years ago," Bachmann said. "I can't really recall if I ever actually met her. Maybe? I really don't remember us being formally introduced or anything."

"Did you know who she was at all?" Lozano said. "Like if you had met her on the street, would you have recognized her?"

"Well let me think," Bachmann said.

She leaned back in her chair and closed her eyes as if she was struggling to recall something from the ancient past. Then she opened her eyes and leaned forward slightly.

"God, that was so long ago," she said. "I may have met her at some point. I don't want to say categorically I never met her and then you guys say something like someone you talked with said they introduced us. You know?"

Bachmann was showing signs she was clearly annoyed and didn't at all appreciate the questions about her private life, but Lozano pressed on.

"You said you dated Robert," he said. "Let me ask you, how long did you guys date?"

"I mean, look, guys, what is this about?" Bachmann said. "Is this something?"

Griggs stepped in to calm her a little.

"Look, Vanessa, here's the situation," Griggs said. "Basically, we saw some things in the file that showed that maybe there was a relationship there between you and Robert. That's what the notes seem to suggest. That's why we're asking you these questions and why we asked you to talk to us here. We didn't want to ask you these kinds of personal questions in your work area. You know how people see things or overhear things. They start to speculate and talk, and rumors get started. We brought you here for the conversation to afford you the greatest confidentiality and privacy possible."

On the surface, Bachmann seemed to calm down and feel reassured. But to Malone, her body language and facial expressions were a dead giveaway that she had fully realized she was being played. He half expected that she would at any minute stand up, terminate the interview, and walk out. He suspected she didn't do that only because she was worried about how it would look, or maybe because now she was worried enough that she stayed because she really wanted to find out what was going on.

"It's just that all that was a million years ago, you know?" she said. "Robert and I dated in college. We hung out together with some mutual friends. I can't say that I ever considered him my boyfriend or whether he ever thought of me as his girlfriend. We just dated some. Then, after college, we sort of drifted apart. I can't even remember the last time I spoke with him."

"You met his wife, didn't you?" Griggs said.

"I may have," she said.

"Do you remember her name or anything?" Griggs said.

"Hmm…" she said, seemingly straining to remember some insignificant fact from long ago.

"Or what she did for a living, where she worked, or anything?" Griggs said.

"Well, I want to say she was in healthcare, maybe a dentist?" Bachmann said.

"Did you attend their wedding?" Griggs said.

"No, I definitely remember that I didn't go to their wedding," Bachmann said. "I can't even tell you when they got married. It was just such a long time ago."

"Do you know what happened to Robert's wife?" Griggs said.

"Yes, I know she got killed," Bachmann said.

"How did you hear about that?" Griggs said.

"Let's see… I seem to remember seeing a poster at work or something," she said.

The interrogation was like a choreographed dance. The two detectives were doing their best to get the most out of it by keeping the pressure on while not allowing it to turn into a confrontation for as long as possible. Bachmann had her own moves. She was determined to foster the appearance that any connection she may have ever had to Robert Thames' wife was so insignificant that any memories of the woman had been almost completely disappeared from her memory during the passage of time. She wanted the detectives to believe the relationship between her and Robert had been nothing serious, that he had been just one of a fairly large number of guys she had dated in college and afterward and that the relationship had ended a million years ago.

"How did you react when you heard that Robert's wife had been killed?" Lozano said.

"I'm sure it shocked me," Bachmann said. "I sort of remember calling his family, or maybe it was some friends of his to find out what happened."

"Do you know the circumstances of her death?" Lozano said.

"Hmm… Jeez, let me think," Bachmann said. "I want to say there was a burglary or something, and she was killed. It's been so many years. But the poster I mentioned earlier, I want to say that was what the poster was about. That she was killed during a burglary. I think that's right."

"Do you know her first name?" Griggs said.

Bachmann said, "Hmm… Terri… Sherry? Maybe Mary? Like I said, it was so many years ago."

"To the best of your knowledge, do you ever remember talking with her?" Griggs said.

"As I said earlier, I may have, you know… I may have spoken to her," Bachmann said.

"You mentioned she worked in healthcare, that she was a dentist," Griggs said. "Is it possible that you talked to her at work, at a clinic?"

"Yeah, I may have. Now that you guys are bringing up all these old memories. I may have spoken to her at a clinic where she worked. Jeez, it was just so long ago. But, yeah, maybe I spoke to her once or twice."

Malone and Reyes could see that Bachmann's story was starting to change. Not only was she now admitting that she knew Mary Beth Anderson, but that she had possibly talked with her at work and maybe on other occasions.

Bachmann said, "I'm thinking now because he would date other girls and I would date other guys. I think at one point, maybe he introduced us when he was dating her. But I don't know. Maybe they were already married when that happened. I really don't even remember. But I do recall saying to him, 'Like why are you still calling me if you're dating her, or married to her, or whatever?' I honestly don't remember the exact circumstances or the time frame. But I remember saying to him like, 'Come on. Knock it off. I'm not going to be involved with you when you're with someone else.' Now I'm thinking, I might have gone to her and said something like, 'Hey, you know what? If he's dating you, he needs to stop bothering me.' I vaguely remember that we had a conversation like that, once or twice, maybe. It could have been three times. I just don't want to say definitively that we had one conversation, or two conversations, or three, you know?"

"So these conversations, however many, they happened at her work or at their house?" Griggs said.

"No, I'm sure it was at her work," Bachmann said. "I'm sure he would have told me where she worked, some clinic in LA. What year was that? I'm trying to think. Where was I working then? What year did you say they got married?"

"I'm not sure," Griggs said. "Maybe 1990? Or 1991?"

Malone knew Griggs was being deceptive. He had read the file and knew exactly when Robert and Mary Beth had married.

"I would have been working at Hollenbeck then. I think that's right. If I was working there then, I want to say her clinic wasn't far away. I could have gone to her clinic and said, 'You know he is dating you, but he is still calling me. Why don't you tell him to knock it off?'"

"You would have told her that too instead of just telling Robert?" Griggs said.

"Oh, yeah, I would have," she said. "I'm just sort of remembering that I did tell him to stop calling, to knock it off, but it hadn't stopped. He kept calling me. So I'm thinking now I went to her and told her what was going on."

"When you talked to his wife and said, 'Hey, he keeps calling me—he needs to knock it off,' or whatever, was it civil or was it like confrontational?" Lozano said.

"Oh, I don't remember it being confrontational at all," Bachmann said. "I don't think any of the conversations lasted more than a few minutes. I can't even remember how long we talked, but it was very brief."

"So you're saying when you went to see her, as best you remember it, it was always at the place she worked, not at their house?" Lozano said.

"Yes, that's how I seem to recall it," Bachmann said. "I want to say her clinic was on the way to work at Hollenbeck. I may have just stopped by on the way to work."

Lozano said, "Oh, I see. If it was on the way to work for you, that would make it more likely that you would have gone to her work and had the discussions with her there?"

"That really sounds right," Bachmann said. "Now that you guys are bringing up all this ancient history, that sounds like it was the way it happened. But, again, I mean, you know, what do me dating him and her being killed have to do with your case? I didn't have anything to do with it."

Griggs said, "Like we said, we just literally got this the other day, and we're reviewing the notes, and your name popped out. We recognized the name, and we know you work next door to us, and so we are trying to get some background. We're trying to figure this out. I mean, this was a long time ago."

Lozano said, "Let me ask you this. Did the detectives on the case back then ever talk with you?"

"No. I'm sure no one ever talked to me about Robert or his wife getting killed," she said.

Malone noticed that her face immediately fell. Maybe she remembered a detective had talked to her, and that there was probably a record of it. She changed her story again, evidently trying to save herself from the slip-up.

"No, now I'm thinking maybe a detective did talk to me briefly about it," she said. "What division did you say investigated it?"

"Van Nuys," Lozano said.

"You know, very vaguely, I do seem to remember someone from Van Nuys speaking to me," Bachmann said.

"Were you ever at Robert and Mary Beth's home?" Griggs asked.

"I don't believe I ever went there," she said. "Honestly, I almost hate to say I've never been there because with these questions you guys have been asking, I'm almost afraid you will say someone said I was there at a party or something. But like I said, I don't recall ever going there."

"So it's safe to say that the only time you would have ever visited their home it would have been for something social?" Griggs said.

"Well, yes, something social if I'd ever gone there," Bachmann said. "Why else would I have gone there? But honestly, I don't think I even knew where they lived."

"And you never had any issues with her, right?" Griggs said. "Like you didn't have any ill will toward her over Robert dating her and or that they got engaged, and later they married?"

"No, absolutely not," she said. "That's ridiculous. I mean, if he were dating me and I found out he was also dating her, I probably would have said something like, 'Hey, you need to choose,' or something like that. I can't recall that there was ever any drama involved. Like I said, it was never anything serious between Robert and me. It was such a long time ago, but I'm really thinking that he and I had already stopped dating and that I was seeing someone else by the time things got serious with them."

Lozano said, "Back to the discussion you had with his wife at the clinic. You don't recall any drama there? It's just that someone told us that on at least one occasion there was a lot of yelling and screaming that occurred between you and Mary Beth and that at least as this person saw it, some threats were made. This person said they were about to call the police just before you left. You don't remember any of that?"

"Well, you know, and maybe that happened," Bachmann said. "But no, I don't recall that. It's been so long ago, but you know that is just not ringing a bell."

Lozano said, "Wouldn't you remember if she kind of snapped on you, and said something like, 'Hey, he is my man now, and you need to leave him alone,' that kind of stuff? You would remember an incident like that, wouldn't you?"

"Well, you would think so," Bachmann said. "Wouldn't you? But honestly, that just isn't ringing any bells. I'm not saying that didn't happen. It could have, but it was such a long time ago, and I honestly don't have any recollection of anything like that. People that know me can tell you I can get really angry and blow up, but then just as quickly, I'm over it and forget all about it."

Griggs said, "One concern we had while we were reviewing this, looking at some of the notes, was that some of Mary Beth's friends said that you and she were having a real problem because of Robert."

"You know what, I just can't say," Bachmann said.

"You can't say?" Griggs said.

"No, because I just don't recall anything like that," Bachmann said.

"To me at least, it seems like you actually would recall something like having a real problem with another woman over a guy, right?" Griggs said.

"I mean, I would think so," Bachmann said. "I would think I'd remember that, but I don't recall anything remotely like that. To me, that seems a pretty good indication it never happened. Maybe she was telling her friends stuff that wasn't true, stuff that wasn't really happening."

Griggs said, "Maybe there was a problem there, and she really thought it was serious, but you didn't think it was serious at all. You know just different perceptions of a situation."

"Yeah, you could be right about that," Bachmann said. "Maybe it wasn't an issue for me, but she thought I was trying to interfere with their relationship or something. That's certainly possible."

"But you never went to their house and had a dispute there like at the clinic?" Lozano said.

"I'm thinking that the clinic thing sounds familiar, that I talked to her there," Bachman said. "Maybe it got a little heated. The conversation I mean. But I just can't say that I was ever at their home. Again, was I ever there with other people? I don't think so. I have no recollection of ever going there. But I keep thinking you guys keep asking this question, so maybe you know I was there at some point. Like maybe someone saw me there and told you I was there. I honestly don't think I even knew where they lived. But if you guys know something, I don't want to say I absolutely, positively was never there because it would look like I'm lying or something."

"It would be safe to say that if you were ever at their home and there was a dispute, then you probably just went by there to drop something off?" Lozano said.

Bachmann said, "You know what, if somebody said I was there when they were there, then that's possible that I could have gone there to drop something off, but I just don't recall that. I mean, I don't think so. It does not sound familiar at all. But, yes, if I was there, then I have to say it would have been something like that, just dropping something off."

"Like I said, we're reviewing notes from the case. We've read notes from interviews with Mary Beth's friends saying you guys had words and it got heated," Lozano said. "That's why we asked you if there had been a dispute at her work that occurred. We also read notes where her friends said there was also a similar incident at her house."

"You know what?" Bachmann said. "That does not sound familiar at all. Again, if someone says I was at her house and I had an argument with her, that just doesn't sound familiar at all. Was it Robert who said this happened? Or other people that were there? I just don't recall anything like that."

"This was an incident where you showed up to drop off a surfboard," Lozano said. "You weren't supposed to show up, and things got heated."

"At their house?" Bachmann said. That just doesn't sound familiar. You know, it does not sound familiar at all."

"So you deny you ever went to their house to drop off a surfboard there for Robert to wax for you?" Lozano said.

Bachmann said, "You know what? I have to say I don't remember that happening. I really don't. It doesn't sound familiar at all."

"Did you ever have a fight with her?" Griggs said.

"Have we ever fought?" Bachmann said. "You mean a physical fight? Like did we ever duke it out?"

"Yes, a physical fight," Griggs said.

Bachmann said, "No! I don't think so. That's insane."

"You would remember it if you ever fought her, wouldn't you?" said Griggs. "It would be pretty hard to forget something like that, wouldn't it?"

"Yeah, I would think so," Bachmann said. "That honestly just doesn't sound familiar. I mean, what are they saying? I had a fight with her, so I must have killed her? I mean, come on. That's just ridiculous."

"Have you ever been in a fight?" Griggs said.

"Yes, you mean like at work, a use of force thing?" Bachmann said.

"No, not at work," Griggs said. "A personal deal, like when you were growing up or at school, like that?"

"Yes, a few," Bachmann said. "I grew up in a tough neighborhood in South Central. You couldn't always avoid it."

"So you remember those fights, right?" Griggs said.

"Well, yes, some of them I guess," Bachmann said.

"But you don't recall ever fighting with Robert's wife?" Griggs said.

"No," Bachmann said. "That just sounds crazy to me."

Lozano said, "Okay, this case, you know, this murder occurred in 1992, right? The scene was processed the best way they could do it back then. They processed it for fingerprints and all that stuff, the standard things. You know the drill. You've been on the job longer than I have. Anyway, the detectives looked at several people and different things in this case, but no one was ever arrested."

"You know what, if you guys are claiming that I'm a suspect, I've got a real problem with that, okay?" Bachmann said. "If you're doing an interrogation here and trying to pin something on me, I've got a real problem with it, you know? Are you accusing me of killing her? Is that what this is all about? Do I need a lawyer?"

"That's entirely up to you, Vanessa," Griggs said. "We're just trying to figure out what happened. You're here of your own free will."

Bachmann said, "I know, but I mean—"

"You're not under arrest, you can walk out," Lozano said.

"You're free to leave whenever you'd like," said Griggs.

Bachmann stayed silent, but she didn't get up to leave.

"One more thing," Griggs said. "When they processed the scene in

1992, they found some DNA evidence. There wasn't anything they could do with it then, but they knew it was coming, so they did the collection."

"Well, that's good then, right?" Bachmann said.

"If we asked you for a DNA swab, would you be willing to give us one?" Lozano said.

"Maybe," Bachmann said. "But you know I'm really feeling uncomfortable now. I'm thinking I'm probably going to need to talk to a lawyer. You're right. I have been doing this for a long time. I know how this stuff works. I'm starting to get the sense that you're trying to pin something on me."

"You know what our job is, as well as we do," Lozano said. "We identify and eliminate suspects. That's why we're asking you for a buccal swab. There was DNA evidence from the scene, and a DNA swab could eliminate you."

"I really can't believe this," Bachmann said. I'm in shock. I'm shocked that anyone would be saying that I did this. We had a fight, so I went and killed her? I mean, come on. That's just crazy."

Malone and Reyes sensed from her tone, demeanor, and body language that she was done with the interview. They got up quickly and hustled down the hallway towards to entrance to the interview room. The construction of the walls kept a suspect in the interview room from seeing anyone passing in the hallway, since it ended almost at the entrance door. Malone and Reyes couldn't see Bachmann either without turning the corner after leaving the hallway and backtracking a few steps to enter the interview room itself. They didn't see Bachmann stand up abruptly, but just as they got to the entry door, they overheard her thanking Griggs and Lozano for the courtesy of discussing the matter with her privately before she walked out of the interview room, obviously believing that she really was free to go. She got as far as the doorway,and then ran into Malone and Reyes.

"Vanessa Bachmann, you're under arrest for the murder of Mary Beth Anderson," Malone said.

Reyes walked behind her, pulled her arms back, and handcuffed her.

Malone said, "We're going to need you to go back inside for a couple of minutes."

"This is crazy," Bachmann said. "It's absolutely insane."

Reyes took her by the arm and escorted her back into the interview room. Griggs and Lozano stood to one side so that Reyes could sit her back down in the chair in view of the video camera.

"You have the right to remain silent," Reyes said. "Anything you say can and will be used against you in a court of law. Do you understand?"

"Yes," Bachmann said.

"You have the right to have an attorney present before answering any questions," Reyes said. "Do you understand?"

"Yes," Bachmann said.

"If you cannot afford an attorney, one will be provided for you at no cost," Reyes said. "Do you understand?"

"Yes," Bachmann said.

"Having these rights in mind, do you want to talk to us?" Reyes said.

"Of course not," Bachmann said.

Reyes assisted her to her feet and escorted her out of the interview room into the corridor. He and Malone took her to booking. Griggs and Lozano followed.

33

Outcome

On the day after they arrested Vanessa Bachmann, Malone was back at Central Arraignments Courts, but this time as a spectator.

They had transferred Bachmann to the Century Regional Detention Facility, the Los Angeles County women's jail the day before within hours of her arrest, so she appeared in court wearing orange coveralls with "Inmate" stenciled on the back.

While they knew they probably wouldn't be able to prove it, besides the first-degree murder charge in the death of Mary Beth Anderson, the district attorney's office had also charged Bachmann as a conspirator in the murder of Jack Bright and the attempted murder of Malone. The additional charges served a purpose. They supported the prosecutor's assertion to the court that Bachmann was a danger to society and the judge should order her confined in the county jail without bail until trial. Despite the strenuous objections of her attorney, the judge sided with the prosecutor. He denied bail and ordered Bachmann held in the county jail, pending trial.

Bachmann had pleaded not guilty to all charges. After the arraignment, the bailiffs escorted her out of the courtroom for transport back to the county jail.

Washington had called Malone earlier and told him they had arraigned Javier Alvarez on the charge of first-degree murder in connection with the death of Jack Bright and for the attempted murder of Malone. The presiding judge had also ordered Alvarez held without bail, which was a slam dunk in his case given his record. Both brother and sister faced twenty-five years to life on the first-degree murder charges alone. Malone figured that realistically, both would probably spend the rest of their lives in prison if juries convicted them.

By early afternoon the second day after they had arrested Bachmann, Malone checked into a hotel in San Francisco. He had called Jack Bright's sister Karen Milner, as she had asked him to do when they met at Jack's funeral. He had some time off coming and had offered to travel to San Francisco to meet with her in person to discuss her offer to take over Jack's private investigations agency rather than just having the conversation by phone. Delighted by the offer, she had quickly taken him up on it.

Malone and Karen had dinner together at Fisherman's Wharf. Karen told him that before the murder, Jack had recently signed a new two-year lease for the office and had already paid the first year of the lease in advance. She also told him that there was a little over twenty-five thousand dollars in Jack's business account. She said that she didn't need the money and if Malone would take over running the agency, he could keep the money to start with before he began getting his own clients.

Karen had only one condition. If Malone accepted her offer to take over Bright Investigations, he had to continue employing Rhonda Freeman until she was ready to retire. That wasn't a problem for Malone. He liked Rhonda, he could use a secretary, and he knew Rhonda would be a real help to him in getting established as a new private investigator.

With the deal done, Malone spent the night in San Francisco and flew back to LA the following morning.

One week to the day after they arrested Bachmann, Malone met with Lieutenant Turner. He gave Turner a signed affidavit, accepting all responsibility for working the Anderson case off the books. Malone hoped that the statement would spare Jaime Reyes disciplinary action from the chief for helping with the case. Malone then tendered to Turner his letter of resignation from the LAPD.

Turner told Malone that he hated to see the department lose such a talented investigator but didn't attempt to talk him out of resigning. Turner told him that despite how the Anderson case had turned out if he stayed with the department, chances were that after a lengthy suspension without pay, the chief would likely decide to put Malone back in uniform for at least a year. Only afterward could expect to get consideration for another detective position in a field bureau. Turner accepted Malone's resignation and said he would inform the chief. He shook Malone's hand and wished him good luck.

Just over three months after they arrested Bachmann, the Los Angeles County Superior Court held the trial for Vanessa Bachmann. As expected, Javier Alvarez refused to implicate his sister in the murder of Jack Bright or the attempted murder of Malone. So the prosecutor had dropped the additional charges before trial, and prosecuted her only on the first-degree murder charge.

Malone, by that time, a newly minted private investigator, testified at the trial.

It took only six hours for the jury to decide the case and to return a guilty verdict. The judge sentenced Vanessa Bachmann to prison for twenty-five years to life. She had to serve the full twenty-five years before getting any consideration for parole. It had taken over twenty-three years, but Mary Beth Anderson and her family finally received justice.

At his trial, the jury found Javier Alvarez guilty on all charges only a few weeks before his sister's trial. He was already serving his sentence in the custody of the California Department of Corrections at San Quentin.

Malone's decision to accept full and complete responsibility to work the Anderson cold case homicide without authorization had swayed the chief regarding taking disciplinary action against Jaime Reyes. That exonerated Reyes from any wrongdoing. He voluntarily remained with the cold case homicide section for several more months before the department transferred him to the RHD Special Homicide Section. Despite Malone's claims, that he'd worked the Anderson case alone, unofficially, the powers to be recognized Reyes had shown he was a skilled investigator. So,while the unauthorized investigation cost Malone his career, it propelled Reyes up the LAPD career ladder.

The relationship between Ben Malone and Sara Bernstein continued to blossom. Since neither was ready to discuss marriage, they talked about moving in together. It turned out that both of them felt they were already happy with the way things were. They mutually decided that they shouldn't change anything for the time being. After the discussion, Sara told Malone that she had been planning to take a couple of weeks off from her practice. She asked him what he thought about them taking a two-week vacation to Maui. Malone, needing little time to think it over, said, "We'd be fools not to."

About the Author

LARRY DARTER is an American writer of fiction, primarily of the mystery & detective and police procedural genres. He is best known for the nine novels written about the fictional Los Angeles private detective Malone. Darter has also written four novels based on the fictional character T. J. O'Sullivan, a female New Zealand expat, working as a private investigator in Honolulu, Hawaii, three recent police procedural novels featuring the fictional character LAPD homicide detective Howard Drew, and three novels based on the fictional Honolulu private eye, Rick Bishop.

You can connect with me on:

- http://www.larrydarter.com
- https://twitter.com/larrydarter

Subscribe to my newsletter:

- https://forms.aweber.com/form/65/1113224165.htm

Also by Larry Darter

Like this book? Then don't stop now. Enjoy binge reading the rest of the thrilling books in the Malone series, starting with the second novel in the series, Fair Is Foul and Foul Is Fair.

Fair Is Foul and Foul Is Fair

A gorgeous socialite. A maverick investigator. A deadly organized crime connection.

When a drop-dead gorgeous socialite with a wad of cash walks into Ben Malone's office with a sordid tale to tell, he does what any self-respecting private investigator with rent to pay would do – he takes the case. But when the bodies start piling up, he soon realizes he may have bitten off more than he can chew…

www.ingramcontent.com/pod-product-compliance
Lightning Source LLC
Chambersburg PA
CBHW021939120726

47992CB00001B/57